TRUE, BUT IRRELEVANT

Miles to Vietnam

Book 7

A Novel By

William Peter Grasso

ISBN: 9798300531836
Cover: ARVN soldiers move out from an LZ after helicopter insertion
Cover design by Alyson Aversa

TRUE, BUT IRRELEVANT is a work of historical fiction, not a history textbook. Events that are common historical knowledge may not occur at their actual point in time or may not occur at all. Apart from the well-known actual people, events, and locales that figure in the narrative, all names, characters, places, and incidents are products of the author's imagination and are used fictitiously. Any resemblance to current events or locales or to living persons is purely coincidental. The designation of military units may be actual or fictitious.

Sign Up For New Release Announcements at:
williampgrasso@gmail.com, with Mailing List as the Subject

Visit the Author's Website:
https://williampetergrasso.com

Connect with the Author on Facebook
https://www.facebook.com/AuthorWilliamPeterGrasso

Follow the Author on Amazon
https://amazon.com/author/williampetergrasso

Novels By William Peter Grasso

Miles To Vietnam

Butter Bar, *Book 1*

Reports Of Their Demise, *Book 2*

Forever And A Wake-Up, *Book 3*

Full Bloody Circle, *Book 4*

Vol-Indef, *Book 5*

No Bad Troops, *Book 6*

True, But Irrelevant, *Book 7*

Jock Miles-Moon Brothers Korean War Story

Combat Ineffective, *Book 1*

Combat Reckoning, *Book 2*

COMBAT: Parallel Lines, *Book 3*

COMBAT: Magic Bullet, *Book 4*

Moon Brothers WWII Adventure Series

Moon Above, Moon Below, *Book 1*

Fortress Falling, *Book 2*

Our Ally, Our Enemy, *Book 3*

This Fog of Peace, *Book 4*

Jock Miles WW2 Adventure Series

Long Walk to the Sun, *Book 1*

Operation Long Jump, *Book 2*

Operation Easy Street, *Book 3*

Operation Blind Spot, *Book 4*

Operation Fishwrapper, *Book 5*

Unpunished

East Wind Returns

Author's Note

To those of my generation, the Vietnam War was a transformational waypoint in our lives, whether one served in that conflict or not. To most who answered their country's call and made that trip to the other side of the world, it was a period of confusion, contradiction, and frustration. In no way does the fictional story presented here mean to denigrate the hardships and sacrifices of the individual American soldiers, marines, airmen, and sailors forced to fight a war they—and often their commanders—did not understand.

Dialogue occasionally uses terms deemed derogatory for people of various Asian ethnicities, African Americans, and other nationalities. The use of those terms by the author is not intended to denigrate any racial or ethnic group. Such language in this novel serves no other intent than to accurately represent the vocabulary of certain military personnel in the 1960s and 1970s.

It would take a host of maps to fully depict the locations and battles visited in this novel. Since it focuses on the exploits of fictional characters and doesn't intend to be a history textbook, I've chosen to include no maps. Those readers who wish to put the fictional action into a geographic context can visit a number of online sources. Here is a helpful link:

https://libguides.nps.edu/vietnamwar/maps

Dedication

To those who left too much of themselves on the battlefield, may you at last find peace

Chapter One

The Republic of Vietnam

Mid-January 1971

Saigon seemed different this time. Captain Jif Miles, US Army, had been there only fleetingly during his previous tour, but his earlier impressions were of a city trying to pretend it wasn't always on the edge of a disaster imposed by communist forces, be they local Vietcong or the North Vietnamese Army seeping across the border with Cambodia. Now—two years later—there seemed to be little concern about impending disaster anymore. Not that there was a jubilant sense of victory; it was more like finding out your cancer was in remission.

But remission didn't mean a cure was anything but temporary. Especially if that cure was the concept known as *Vietnamization*.

In the minds of the citizens of Saigon, the term didn't mean what its American creators preached: that the South Vietnamese military could now cope with the communist aggressors on their own. It only meant that the Americans were leaving, abandoning a commitment that began years before. Many GIs had gone already; roughly two hundred thousand remained, less than half the peak commitment of 1968. The simmering anger and fatalism that exodus caused among the South Vietnamese were present in every quarter of the city. There was no reason to expect that sentiment to be any different in the provinces.

Due to an unusual efficiency of military transport, Jif Miles had arrived in country two days earlier than his report date. Once he'd checked in with MACV headquarters at Tan Son Nhut Air Base, he'd had many hours to play at being a tourist armed with a .45-caliber sidearm on his hip, daring only to wander the main streets—the ones still regularly patrolled by American MPs—while waiting for Army paperwork to catch up with him. The unit patches he wore on both shoulders of his fatigues announced to civilians and military alike that he was a returning veteran of that war; the MACV crest on the left shoulder signified his current assignment, while the 1st Cavalry Division on the right represented with whom he'd served his previous combat tour. He could make out some of the Vietnamese invectives the locals hurled at him, things like: *The betraying fool is stupid enough to come back* and *Thanks for nothing, Number Ten.*

Number Ten: an insult derived from a Vietnamized American idiom. On a scale of one to ten, with one being the best, it meant the worst. When he'd explained that rating system to the woman he'd married six months ago—Marti Tanaka-Miles—she was so taken by it that she'd adopted it immediately to grade all aspects of life in general. He was surprised when she'd rated his return to Vietnam as *number eight.*

"Not *number ten*?" he'd asked.

"No, this tour's just six months. I lived without you once for six months and I can do it again. I don't like it, but as you and your family always like to say, I knew the deal when I signed up. And I could use that *alone time* to finish my thesis. So yeah, it still sucks, but it's an *eight*, not a *ten*." Then she'd added, "Just make sure you come back in one piece again, okay? This is going to be just staff work, right? No John Wayne hero stuff?"

"No hero stuff, honey. Just bloody boring paper shuffling and showing the flag."

The skeptical look she'd shot him was enough of a scolding in itself, but she'd cheerfully backed it up with, "You can be so full of shit sometimes, John Forbes Miles. You don't know how to stay out of trouble. It's not in your *bloody* nature. It must be that Australian half of you." The hug and kiss she'd administered before he could reply derailed anything he might've said in his defense.

"Hey, we're both half something—Aussie for me, Japanese for you. *Hyphenated-Americans*, right? I always reckoned it's why we're so good together. It broadens one's horizons, you know?"

Looking amused, she replied, "Yeah, that's us…East meets West."

*****

His third morning in Saigon marked the end of what he'd come to call his *ugly American vacation*. The day began early, joining Command Sergeant Major Sean Moon for an 0530 breakfast. The sergeant major was the top NCO on the MACV staff, a three-war veteran and right-hand man of General Abrams, the MACV commander. He was also a dear friend of the Miles family, having served under Jif's father, Major General (ret.) Jock Miles, during the Korean Conflict. "No need to rush, sir," Sean Moon said. "Your briefing with Colonel McKnight isn't until 0700, and it'll be right upstairs in this building. Do you have any inkling what your assignment is?"

"To be honest, Sergeant Major, not a bloody clue. I don't reckon I'm going to be an advisor to an ARVN battalion, though. I'm told we're now placing advisors only at the brigade level and up. Those are slots for field grades and generals, not captains."

"That's true, but you would've been right at home," Sean said. "After those last six months you spent at the Pentagon, you're used to swimming in deep water."

Jif laughed. "Give me a break, Sergeant Major. Two-stars are so far down the food chain at the Pentagon that they ride the subway to work. No staff car, no driver. Lowly captains are just batmen and secretaries. Not that I'm complaining about the experience, though. It was very enlightening."

"The word is you did real good there. That paper you wrote on defensive principles for the artillery battery caused a lot of buzz. I hear it's going into the curriculum at Fort Sill. Nothing like writing what you know, eh? But I can give you a quick rundown on what you're getting into here." His Brooklyn accent thickened as he continued, "Keep this little heads-up between you, me, and the lamppost, though, okay? Don't want anyone to think I'm talking out of school."

"Mum's the word, Sergeant Major."

"Roger that. Now, here's the deal…while you were playing instructor back at Sill after your first tour, we pulled off that Cambodia operation. It went pretty damn good from our standpoint. Actually, it went pretty damn great. We turned off the NVA supply operation on the southern section of the Ho Chi Minh Trail and captured shitloads of their stores…and I mean *shitloads*. Had to be a year's worth, at least. The ARVN actually kicked some serious ass, too, believe it or not. Really bolstered their confidence. But bear in mind that the NVA wasn't in a position to throw up too much opposition…and we did give the ARVN a whole lot of help. Regardless, it was a win-win for us."

"Wasn't much of a win-win back in the States, though," Jif replied. "That operation caused an absolute shitstorm, capped off with that Kent State fiasco. National Guard weekend warriors with live ammo…whose bright idea was that? A bloody disaster and a fucking shame all rolled into one."

"You're not telling me anything I don't know, Captain. But now you need to strap in, because we're going after the other end of the Ho Chi Minh Trail up in Laos. We're going to cut it off now, in the dry season, and keep it closed until the rains start back up and make big chunks of the trail impassible. After we capture all the NVA stores we can, that should shut their ops down in South Vietnam for a year or two. No supply trains, no offensives."

"Wait a minute…we can't go into Laos. Congress just saw to it—that Cooper-Church Amendment."

"Yeah, tell me about it," Sean said. "But get a load of this. We—as in *we Americans*—are not crossing the border. The ARVN, who can go wherever they want, are going to do all the heavy lifting. We'll give them engineer support here in country, cross-border artillery, and air support over Laos—which is still allowed, by the way—but no US boots on the ground. Not even advisors."

Jif asked, "So what will the advisors be up to instead?"

"They'll be doing their thing with the ARVN headquarters people at Khe Sanh and Dong Ha."

"Hold on," Jif said. "We're opening up Khe Sanh again? Hasn't that place been a ghost town the last few years?"

"Yeah, it has. But its time to be useful has come again."

Puzzled, Jif asked, "So if the advisors can't be in Laos with the ARVN, won't all the information they get be hearsay and probably bullshit? How the hell is that going to work?"

"That's where Colonel McKnight's team—the one you'll be on—comes in. General Abrams has picked the colonel to lead MACV's *Provisional Reconnaissance Team*. Quite frankly, we've been having issues with our advisors the past year or so. They've fallen largely into two groups. The first group is overly sympathetic to the ARVN commanders they advise. The other is pointedly hostile. The sympathetic guys keep obscuring our ally's problems with happy horseshit. That has a habit of blowing up on us when things get serious and ARVN suddenly can't cut it. Then there's the hostile crowd—they destroy any chance of us coordinating with the ARVN right off the bat. We have to relieve them before their time, causing premature turnover issues we don't have the personnel to support. General Abe wants an umpire—someone with clear eyes and no personal baggage—who'll tell it like it is so we can draw an accurate picture, smooth over the differences, and keep this operation on track."

"Umpire? Don't you mean spy?"

"Think of it as an *inspector general* for allied operations, Captain."

"But if we can't cross the border, how will we know what's really going on in Laos?"

"You can fly, right? Every man picked for this team has plenty of experience at aerial observation, you included. Your feet never touch the ground, so you're not violating the rules. But you'll still have a bird's-eye view of what's happening."

Jif answered his next question himself: *Why can't the advisors be the ones flying around in the scout birds, getting the big picture? Because they need to be keeping a watchful eye on the ARVN major unit commanders, who will not be in Laos. God knows what they'll do without adult supervision.*

Jif chuckled to himself as the reality of what this assignment would actually entail settled in. Then he said, "Oh, well, so much for the *no John Wayne hero stuff.*"

Now Sean looked puzzled. "John Wayne? What the hell are you talking about?"

"Just something I assured Marti would not be happening on this tour."

"And she knew you were full of shit, of course. Am I right?"

"I reckon so," Jif replied.

"I'm liking that lady even more, Captain. She'll keep you straight, that's for damn sure. You two had one beautiful wedding, by the way. I'm sure glad I was on leave and could make it."

Sean offered a few more specifics on the mission of the Provisional Reconnaissance Team. He concluded the *heads-up* with, "One more thing, and I'm sure Colonel McKnight will harp on this...don't tell the ARVN shit about what you see and what you know. Their headquarters still leak like sieves. Anything you say will probably be common knowledge in Hanoi by the next morning. Plus, some of the ARVN honchos still have a nasty habit of trying to twist plans to their advantage, usually to the detriment of the operation. And the politics between the various ARVN commanders is still vicious, too. You'll find it's the same old story...when an ARVN leader is bad, he's very bad. And when one looks like a star, there's still a real good chance he'll go bad when the chips are down."

"But their troops will still fight, right?"

Sean replied, "Oh yeah, they fight like tigers…when their leaders actually stick around to command them, that is."

"You don't paint a very rosy picture, Sergeant Major."

"We don't do rosy around here anymore, Captain. We just do *get it over with*."

"I suppose this operation has some fancy name?"

"You bet. It's Lam Son 719. Lam Son is the birthplace of some local hero who kicked out the Chinese invaders way back in the fifteenth century. Seven-one is for the year 1971, and nine is for Route Niner. You remember Route Niner, I'm sure."

Jif grimaced as if recalling a nightmare. "How could I bloody forget?"

“Hey, that was like three years ago,” Sean said. “Time heals all wounds, right?”

“Never completely, Sergeant Major. They’re not supposed to. If they did, you might forget what those wounds taught you.”

*****

Colonel McKnight’s Provisional Recon Team—PRT for short—was smaller than Jif had envisioned based on his discussion with CSM Moon. There were five officers—a major and two captains along with Jif and McKnight—crowded around the table in the small briefing room. Jif had never seen any of them before. After a quick round of introductions and thumbnail bios, the colonel laid out the concept of Lam Son 719 on a big wall map. A sizeable South Vietnamese force of four divisions—one marine, one airborne, and two infantry, with two armored brigades and two ranger battalions attached—would execute the penetration into Laos. Their objective: the village of Tchepone, a major hub on the Ho Chi Minh Trail snaking down out of North Vietnam. McKnight pounded the tip of his pointer against the map at Tchepone and said, “It’s a mere forty klicks from the border with the Republic of Vietnam, gentlemen, straight down Route Niner.”

If that was meant to be encouraging, it failed. Forty kilometers—twenty-five miles—sounded like an incredibly long distance to achieve and maintain a secure salient against a clever and tenacious foe. What McKnight said next crippled the team members’ enthusiasm even further: “And we’ll expect the ARVN to hold Tchepone until the rains crank back up the end of March."

With a kickoff date in early February—just three weeks away—the ARVN would have to hold the corridor into Laos for nearly two months. Nobody had to say it; the doubt hung in the air like a foul smell: *Never gonna happen.*

Picking up on that attitude, McKnight said, "I know what you're thinking, gentlemen. I've had those same thoughts. But I'm here to tell you that the mission of this unit—the PRT—is not simply to sharpshoot the operation. We're here to cut through the bullshit, improve coordination with our allies from a unique perspective, and find ways to help make Lam Son 719 work. You've been picked for this task because every one of you has experience working with the ARVN. You're well aware of how their national politics has a habit of interfering with effective command. When that happens, we need to identify the problem without delay so it can be rectified before turning into a disaster."

The major on the team—a middle-aged air defense artilleryman named Hutchinson—said in a slow, tedious drawl, "We're going to be stepping on the dicks of our advisors to the various ARVN commands, aren't we, sir? I can see a big ol' pissing contest brewing here."

McKnight replied, "If those advisors cannot effectively do their jobs for whatever reason, then let the pissing begin, Major. We don't report to them. We report to the MACV commander."

"But so do they, sir," Hutchinson rebutted. "General Abrams is going to end up with his own people at each other's throats. That can't be good for anybody…or anything."

"We'll let General Abrams be the judge of what's good for his command or not, Major. Do I make myself clear?"

"Crystal clear, sir," Hutchinson replied in that same languid monotone. It gave no clue if he was aware he'd just been reprimanded. If anything, it made him sound slow-witted.

McKnight's briefing continued with an outline of the American contribution to the operation. Within the borders of South Vietnam, two US infantry brigades would provide security for the several battalions of Army engineers who would rehabilitate the neglected Route 9 to the Cambodian border. The engineers would also rebuild the Khe Sanh Combat Base, which had been abandoned by the Americans over two years ago, for use by the ARVN. Several battalions of US Army heavy artillery would provide supporting fires into Laos from the South Vietnam side of the border.

On both sides of the border, tactical air support would come from squadrons of US Air Force, US Navy, and US Marine Corps aircraft. The Air Force contribution would also include the devastating, much-feared B-52 bombers from Guam and Thailand. Helicopter gunship and heli-lift capability would be the responsibility of the US Army, with an assist from USMC choppers for heavy-lift sorties. McKnight closed that part of the briefing with, "A pretty impressive display of firepower, wouldn't you agree, gentlemen?" The only man in the room who wore pilot's wings, the colonel was obviously impressed with the potential of airpower.

Jif was not alone as he thought, *Yeah, it is impressive...if the weather cooperates. Sure, it's still technically the dry season until the end of April, but Route Niner sits in a mountain valley all the way to Tchepone. The weather can get very fickle over terrain like that, despite the calendar. Seeing the ground from the air might get a little tough sometimes.*

One thing was apparent from McKnight's concept of his organization: it was considered a team for admin purposes only. Each man would, for the most part, be an independent operator, observing a specific ARVN unit or phase of operation. *Working alone might be a good thing, too*, Jif told himself, *because my first impressions tell me that two of these guys might be real pieces of work.*

For openers, there was Major Horace "Harry" Hutchinson. The first moment he'd heard Jif's Aussie accent, he'd looked at him with eyes dull like suede. During a break in the briefing, he'd asked, "Where y'all from, son?" in that same, languorous delivery that sought to impart far greater importance to trite words than they actually possessed. When Jif gave him the thumbnail sketch of his origins, he gave no reply other than that unwavering glare that seemed to look right through him. It was like being scanned by an X-ray machine in slow motion.

Jif figured he knew the major's type. Older than most in his grade—in his early forties, no doubt—Hutchinson was obviously a mustang, an officer who'd begun his military career as an enlisted man. The air crewman's wings on his fatigues, which signified he'd done something on board an aircraft other than pilot her, were the tell; they weren't authorized for wear by officers unless earned in the ranks.

Hell, if those wings were authorized for officers, I'd have earned a set as an aerial observer several times over.

Hutchinson was nearing the end of his career, Jif figured. He seemed to be just another *go-along-to-get-along* type of officer who lacked the people skills for higher command. There'd be no more promotions for him, and if you didn't move up, you moved out. For now, he was just filling a slot until Army regs forced his retirement.

And that pipe he smokes...I don't know what kind of tobacco that is, but it smells like burning animal dung.

Although he knew what Hutchinson had done in country—the major had been pulled from his slot as *the assistant something or other* on the staff of a field artillery group to join this team—Jif decided to pull his chain by asking, "Do you air defense types get much action here in the Nam? Not a whole lot of enemy planes to shoot down. None, in fact. That's why we've been using those dusters and quad fifties from ADA outfits for firebase defense. Got to put them to use somewhere."

Hutchinson snorted his reply. "That's not true, young captain. There have been incidents with North Vietnamese aircraft violating Eye Corps airspace." For all the gravitas he bestowed on that statement, he might as well have been reciting a few lines from the Gettysburg Address.

Jif fought the urge to smirk. *Sure...maybe they did it once or twice, probably straying into the DMZ by accident, with little effect on anything and no gunfire exchanged. Enemy aircraft don't even make the list of flying things that grunts worry about in the Nam.*

Moving on to the others on the team, he did a quick count of the West Pointers among them. There were three wearing the ring: Colonel McKnight, an armor officer and pilot, and two captains—one infantry, one armor.

The ring-bestowed infantry captain, Boyd Gray, was an outgoing young man just starting his second tour. When he heard Jif had already fought along Route 9 near Khe Sanh, he asked, "Are you psyched up about going back there?"

"Not really," Jif replied. "I was kind of hoping I'd seen the last of the place."

That didn't dampen Gray's bubbly reverence: "Man, you've been in the shit all over this country and lived to tell about it. That's pretty radical."

"Well, Boyd, I've never set foot in *Four Corps*, if you want to get technical about it."

The armor captain from the Point, Phil Jamerson, was anything but friendly. He asked Jif, "Hey, cannon-cocker…are you some reserve puke from ROTC?"

Like I thought, another real piece of work, Jif told himself.

"I was," he replied, "but I'm regular army now."

"How the hell did a foreigner like you manage that?"

"The usual way. I was appointed after my first tour. And by the way, according to my citizenship papers, I'm no foreigner, accent notwithstanding. But you already knew that, I reckon. Foreigners don't get commissions, right?"

"Where'd you go to school, war hero?"

When Jif replied *Berkeley*, the look of horror that came over Jamerson's face was cartoon comical despite being deadly serious.

"Don't get your panties in a bunch, dude," Jif told him. "I burned my Communist Party card when I graduated. And by the way, I can see by your ring that you're class of '68, right?" He could also see that the tanker didn't wear jump wings, an oddity among Academy grads, making him a *leg*—a non-paratrooper—in airborne jargon.

Jamerson replied, "Yeah, Class of '68. So what?"

"It means I outrank you by a year." Then, just to torque Jamerson up a bit more, he patted the jump wings on his chest and added, "So show some respect, *leg*."

Looking to wrap up this session, Colonel McKnight said, "At ease, gentlemen. As you can tell from the map, our base of operations will be Dong Ha, where the American and ARVN commands for this operation will be located. We'll depart for there in seventy-two hours. In the meantime, we'll be conducting continuous estimates of the situation to refine our own plan of operations. That situation will be evolving right up to kickoff time, since—as I've already mentioned—the ARVN were given the minimal time to put their operational plan together in the hope of preserving as much secrecy as possible. Less time equals less leakage of information. Any questions?"

Major Hutchinson had one. "Will we be provided with our own interpreters for dealing with the ARVN?"

"Negative," McKnight replied. "Considering your only face-to-face contact with the ARVN will be within the Republic of Vietnam, you'll be employing the translators already in place when and if necessary." He paused before adding, "I wouldn't worry about conversing with the ARVN, anyway. We'll believe what our eyes tell us, not the bullshit they might try to feed us."

Seeing there were no other questions, the colonel concluded with, "Our next session will be in the Bravo Five briefing room at 1000 hours. Be ready to brainstorm, gentlemen. Nothing will be off the table."

Chapter Two

Route 9, Quang Tri Province

8 February 1971

The ARVN's road march to the border with Laos had begun. Jif and Captain Mickey Spinoza—*Spinner* to his fellow pilots in an attack helicopter company—were sitting in a jeep parked on a hill near the intersection of Route 9 and the plantation road that provided access to the Khe Sanh Combat Base. An American interpreter—a spec-5—was behind the wheel. Spinoza's mission: coordinate gunship support for the ARVN column on this part of the route should the need arise. Jif's mission was to see how well that process was working.

Neither man was destined to accomplish his designated task that day. During the past week, there had been little NVA resistance to the large-scale American and ARVN reappearance in Quang Tri Province. US Army engineers, mainly unopposed, rehabilitated Route 9 along its entire forty-kilometer stretch from Vandegrift Combat Base, through a reborn Khe Sanh, and on to the Laotian border. There'd only been one call for gunship support by the ARVN that morning, and it had been a case of mistaken identity; a platoon of US tanks laagered near the Old French Fort outside Khe Sanh were thought to be intruding NVA armor. Spinoza had quickly sorted out the error and canceled the mission before Cobras converged on the alleged target.

As they watched the ARVN road march pass before them at a crawl, Spinoza asked Jif, "How would you classify this fiasco, man…a circle jerk or a clusterfuck? Their order of march gotta be screwed up! Look at that mix of unit markings on those trucks…different outfits are all clumped together. It must've taken some doing to get interspersed like that."

"Some doing, or just some people doing nothing, Spinner. I definitely rate it a clusterfuck. A circle jerk at least has an agenda. If this convoy has one, a lot of people didn't read it." Grabbing a mic from the jeep's bank of radios, he added, "There's some open terrain about five klicks down Route Niner where they can pull displaced vehicles out of the column and put them back in something like the right order. Maybe I can raise the Airborne Division's advisor and he can get the unit commanders to sort it out real quick."

Spinoza asked, "You sure the advisor is anywhere near this road? I heard they're all so pissed off that they're staying back at base camp. First off, they've got you guys looking over their shoulders, and they can't go into Laos with the units they advise, anyway, right? So why even bother showing up?"

"Regardless, they might want to get their asses out here," Jif replied. "Going into Indian country with disorganized units is begging for disaster. It's going to take some quick command action to fix that."

After Jif had made radio contact, Spinoza asked, "Any clue where that advisor actually is right now?"

"Sounds like he's on a chopper. Probably a real good place for him…at least he might be seeing the big picture. He didn't seem too thrilled with my suggestion about how to reorganize on the fly, though."

"Face it, Jif…I don't think they'd be thrilled with *anything* you suggest."

The rumble of truck engines was suddenly overpowered by the sickening *thud* and metal-on-metal groans of a vehicular crash. An ARVN deuce-and-a-half on the plantation road from Khe Sanh, the first in a line of ten such vehicles, had tried to bull its way into the Airborne Division's column trundling west on Route 9. After what must've been a split-second whirlwind of impatience, belligerence, bad judgment—and maybe even the driver losing control of his vehicle—the merging truck broadsided another deuce at good speed, tipping it halfway over on its left wheels, spilling men over the cargo bed rail. The vehicles were now locked together and motionless, blocking the two roads, both of which were narrow thoroughfares barely more than one lane wide.

Spinoza said, "Holy shit…if you didn't get the advisor's attention, that wreck sure will."

"Men are getting hurt down there, Spinner. The impact of that T-bone threw the guys on the beds of those trucks around like rag dolls. Call for medevac. We're going to need four lifts, maybe five. Can I borrow your interpreter?"

"Sure, take him. You're not really going down there, are you?"

"I'm not doing much bloody good lounging on this hill," Jif replied.

*****

It took only a minute to run down to the wreck. By Jif's quick estimate, there were at least twenty men badly injured. There were no ARVN officers and no medics on scene. A handful of sergeants—most from the Airborne Division, a few from the Ranger Division—were arguing. A few punches were thrown before cooler heads pulled the scrappers apart.

The interpreter told Jif, "That truck that smacked into the column is from the Ranger Division, Captain."

"I figured that."

"They're arguing about road march orders," the interpreter added. "Somebody's got their time slot wrong. Each side's claiming that the other guys are in error."

"Tell those sergeants to get their injured off the bloody road," Jif said. "We've got medevac coming."

"Where's it going to land, Captain? There's no room for an LZ here."

Jif pointed to a spot in the trees that lined the road. "There's a big clearing on the other side," he said. "We used it as an LZ in the past."

"Oh, yeah…I forgot," the interpreter said. "You've been here before."

"Yeah, and the bloody place hasn't changed a bit."

When they got back to the jeep, Spinoza said, "Good news. Once I told them we needed four or five lifts, they decided to send a Chinook. I guess she's between missions, sitting on the hot pad." He pointed down to the activity on the road, adding, "Good thing, too. Looks like a shitload of dudes are lining up for the dustoff."

"I hope the ARVN aren't still up to their old tricks," Jif replied. "Whenever they call for medevac, there are always some clowns who want to skip out on that ship whether they're wounded or not."

Two American armored personnel carriers were parked close by, part of an outfit protecting the convoy route. The crews of those tracks seemed relaxed and indifferent to the mayhem going on just down the hill.

Spinoza said, "I think those guys are stoned, Jif. They're a little too laid back to suit me. I've never seen dudes out in the bush actually smoking weed, though. Base camp, sure…but here? Always a first time, right?"

"Let's take a whiff and see what we've got," Jif replied.

As they approached the sergeant-in-charge of the APCs, Jif asked, "Can you use one of your tracks to pull those vehicles apart and get that road open again, Sergeant?"

"Is that an order, Captain?"

"No, it's just a question looking for an answer. How about it?"

"I'm not trying to blow you off or anything, sir, but my orders are to provide security for this road junction, not be a wrecker service. It's the gooks' problem, anyway, isn't it?"

"I'm afraid it's our problem, too, Sergeant," Jif replied. "We're taking care of this road for them all the way to the border."

They got a good look at the sergeant and his men. Spinoza made a big show of sniffing the air, trying to detect the odor of marijuana. But there was none.

Jif pulled him away, saying, "They're not stoned, Spinner, just exhausted. You would be, too, if you just had your brains beat in riding an APC all the way from Vandegrift. And the eyes of a pot smoker look a hell of a lot different than those of a man who's just tired."

"You know that for a fact, dude? Are you experienced?"

Jif laughed and replied, "Who the hell are you, Jimi Hendrix? Yeah, I'm experienced. I went to Berkeley."

"Holy shit…Berkeley! And I'm riding in the same jeep with you! Being a pinko better not be contagious." Even though it was said with a smile, Jif was sure there was some level of seriousness in that comment.

But his breezy reply wasn't meant as an insult, just repartee: "I wouldn't worry about it, dude. I'm pretty sure your small-town values have immunized you."

Something else occurred to Jif: *Spinner's never commanded anything bigger than the few men in a chopper crew. The care and feeding of the individual ground troop probably isn't in his skill set.*

He told Spinoza, "Let me handle this, okay?"

"Hey, knock yourself out, man."

As Jif returned to the APC, the sergeant explained, "Yeah, we can do it, sir, but it would take both my tracks to keep that leaning deuce from going all the way over on its side. If it does go over, it'll block the road even worse. If I commit both my vehicles to wrecker duty, though, I could get in deep shit for not doing the job I got sent out here to do."

Jif couldn't argue with that, but another solution manifested itself out of thin air. One of the men on the APC yelled, "Hey, Sarge, *Nugget Two-Four* is on the radio, saying the gooks got an M41 coming to clear this wreck. He's plowing his own road."

"Who's *Nugget Two-Four*?" Jif asked.

"Another track in our platoon," the sergeant replied. "He's watching the road half a klick east of here."

That tank will need to plow its own path through the underbrush, that's for sure, Jif told himself. *This roadway's bloody impassable.*

"Maybe we just wait for the gook tank then, Captain?" the sergeant asked. "By the time I got my guys set up, it'd probably be here, anyway."

"Sounds like a plan, Sergeant. But in the meantime, there's something else I need you to do." He explained his suspicion that some ARVN who weren't injured from the crash might try to force their way onto the medevac chopper. "I need one of your track crews to be on hand to provide security for the chopper and help out her crew, in case things start to get out of hand."

The sergeant thought it over for a moment before asking, "We can waste the gooks if they get nasty, right?"

"It shouldn't come to that," Jif replied. "If they're going to run for the bird, they'll throw down their weapons so you don't have an excuse to shoot them. Unarmed, they'll be real easy to handle. They're just little dudes, you know?"

*****

Less than ten minutes later, the medevac Chinook was overhead after the short hop from Khe Sanh. Once he tossed a smoke grenade to mark the LZ, Jif positioned himself as the signalman to guide in the big chopper. When she touched down, the APC and its crew moved into place near the tail of the ship.

Some two dozen injured ARVN were carried onto the bird, most on ponchos serving as makeshift stretchers. A handful more with broken arms and bleeding heads made their own way up the ramp. As the cabin filled to capacity, Jif noticed the entire process was being managed by ARVN sergeants, who'd handled the loading in an orderly manner. There still weren't any of their officers on scene.

And then it all fell apart. As if reacting to a starter's pistol, dozens of ARVN soldiers bolted for the helicopter's ramp. They'd dropped their weapons just as Jif had predicted, disarming themselves as if they were genuine casualties.

The APC sergeant had thought ahead. He'd had his crew tie down the vehicle's tall whip antennas so it would have the necessary clearance to drive beneath the Chinook's rear rotor, which it promptly did. The track and its dismounted squad were now effectively blocking access to the ship's ramp.

That didn't stop a handful of would-be ARVN runaways from doglegging around the APC and clambering onto the chopper's side-mounted sponsons. But it was difficult to maintain footing on the sloped surface of the sponsons. Most of them slipped off as quickly as they climbed on, to be dragged away while being punched and kicked by furious ARVN soldiers meting out punishment on those they saw as cowards.

Two of the fleeing troopers figured out a way to cling to the side of the Chinook. They'd reached up and grabbed the standoffs supporting the wire antenna running along the upper corner of the fuselage. But even that perch proved fleeting when Jif yanked both men down by their ankles. In seconds, they were dragged away to be beaten by ARVN troopers. The ship now clear of would-be external riders, Jif ran to the nose and signaled the pilots to lift off. They complied immediately; the resulting rotor wash was more than enough to prevent anyone else from snagging an illicit ride.

With the Chinook gone and order restored on the LZ, Jif sought out the senior NCO among the ARVN troopers. When he found him, the sergeant was still out of breath from the brawl and angry that some troopers had actually tried to flee. Turning to Jif, he said in thickly accented English, "Thank you for your help, Captain."

"No problem, Sergeant. But I'm very disappointed how many of your men tried to cut out."

"They weren't my men, Captain." Pointing to the patch on his sleeve, he added, "I'm from the Airborne. We don't run. The bastards who tried were Ranger support troops, like cooks and clerks. They didn't want to be here, so…"

Not wanting to say more, his voice had drifted off. It prompted Jif to ask, "Wait a minute…do you think they staged that crash intentionally, so they could catch a free ride out of here?"

"Perhaps, Captain. But whether that is true or not, they hurt my men. And that is unforgivable."

"I'm more than a little surprised to hear that, Sergeant. Aren't the Rangers—including their support troops—supposed to be right up there with the Airborne as one of the ARVN's best outfits?"

"There are many things that are supposed to be, Captain. Sometimes, they are not."

Jif asked, "Do you think that has anything to do with the fact that none of your officers are here?"

The sergeant gave a world-weary sigh and replied, "I wouldn't be surprised, sir."

*****

Jif rejoined Spinoza on the hilltop just as an ARVN M41 tank arrived, as promised, to clear the wrecks from the roadway. The APC sergeant's fear of poor vehicle recovery technique quickly became reality; the tank commander's clumsy attempt to push the deuces clear caused the listing truck to topple onto its side. Without missing a beat, the tank drove up against the vehicle's now-exposed underside and shoved it off the road, destroying the drive shaft to the rear wheels and puncturing the fuel tank. As the diesel spilled from the ruptured tank to the ground, Spinoza said, "Do you think the dude meant to do that? He just took a perfectly good truck…okay, maybe it was dented up a little…and turned it into scrap metal, not to mention a fire hazard. Do they think we're just going to give them another deuce in its place?"

"We just might," Jif replied.

*****

Later that afternoon, Jif was ordered back to Dong Ha. Grabbing a ride on one of the many choppers shuttling back and forth between there and Khe Sanh, he was in Colonel McKnight's office within ninety minutes. The colonel wasn't alone; a brigadier general named Parton was there, looking ready to bite someone's head off. McKnight shot Jif a look that he took to mean, *Tread carefully*.

Parton was senior US advisor to the ARVN Ranger Division. In a booming voice, he said, "I want to meet this young captain who thinks he can do my job better than me."

McKnight replied, "With all due respect, General, I don't think—"

"That sounds about right, Colonel," Parton interrupted. "It appears that neither you nor any of your team—it is officially a *team*, right?—does very much thinking. Rather than let the ARVN take care of their own goddamn business, your Captain Miles intervened and turned a simple traffic accident into a fiasco. When I first heard about your *team* last week, I was sure you'd be getting in the way and turning orderly operations into clusterfucks. But I didn't imagine it would happen so soon or that an entire company of my Rangers would be assaulted by a gang of Airborne thugs, all at your captain's direction."

Jif asked, "Permission to speak, General?"

McKnight gritted his teeth, hoping Jif was not about to dig himself an even deeper hole than the one he was already in.

Parton, sensing a chance to move in for the kill, replied, "Sure, Miles. Let's hear it."

"Very well, sir. To put it mildly, your Rangers fucked up. One of their vehicles caused the accident, which resulted in significant injuries."

The general scowled. "Deuce accidents always result in injuries, Captain. Nobody's strapped in. Can't be helped."

"But what happened in the wake of the accident, during the dustoff, *could* have been helped, sir." Jif went on to explain how dozens of uninjured Rangers tried to bull their way onto the medevac ship, even abandoning their weapons. Only the actions of Airborne troopers averted a hazardous situation that could've very easily become a catastrophe for an overcrowded Chinook, her crew, and the legitimately injured. Standing up to Parton's disbelieving glare, he concluded with, "There was a suspicion among those at the scene that the crash was staged as a ruse that would allow some Rangers to dodge the operation. In addition, there was not one ARVN officer present during the entire incident. That seems like a serious lack of command and control to me."

"I'm sure their officers were on the way, Miles," the general scoffed. "They were probably just stuck in that traffic jam."

"Sir, they ride in jeeps and choppers which can work around all kinds of traffic snarls. Unless there was something far more pressing going on—and I don't believe there was—it looks more like your ARVN officers chose to avoid the situation."

Parton, his face red with anger, turned to McKnight: "I've heard enough of this bullshit. I'd better not see a word of it in any of your reports, Colonel."

"With all due respect, sir, my unit's orders dictate otherwise." He didn't need to add that those orders came directly from General Abrams. *In other words, I don't work for you, so piss off.*

The general had the last word as he headed for the door: "You're fucking with the wrong cowboy here, McKnight."

As they listened to the stomp of Parton's boots reverberate on the hallway's plywood floor, the colonel said to Jif, "That, Captain Miles, is exactly why we're here. You did good. Keep it up."

Chapter Three

"Ain't gonna be no secret the ARVN are coming across the border," Chief Warrant 2 Jimmy Thigpen said to Jif as he piloted their OH-58 Kiowa scout helicopter over the Lang Vei camp, headed for the Vietnam-Laos border. Pointing down to Lang Vei, the aviator—barely twenty-one years old and halfway through his first tour—added, "They've been all bunched up around that place for two days now, watching the rain and the low ceilings. Ain't gonna get none of our close air support with weather like that, so they're sitting on their asses. How many of them are down there, anyway, Captain?"

"Something like four thousand from the ARVN Airborne and Ranger Divisions, Chief," Jif replied, "minus the ones already flown into Laos at first light to secure the firebase sites. There's at least a couple battalions of tanks there, too. And that's just for the opening push."

"It shouldn't be too hard for some sneaky NVA moseying around these hills to figure out what's coming," Thigpen said.

"I reckon they figured that out long before Route Niner became a parking lot," Jif replied. "The walls in South Vietnam all have ears."

"What do you mean by that, Captain?"

"It means the South Vietnamese are not real good at keeping operational secrets."

But there'd be no more delays. Today was the day that Lam Son 719 would kick off. Dawn had just broken to clear skies. A massive preparation by US heavy artillery and B-52 sorties had hit every known NVA strongpoint and anti-aircraft installation around the assault's initial objectives during those rainy days. They hadn't needed good weather to deliver their ordnance. The ARVN column—troopers in APCs and deuces interspersed with M41 light tanks—was finally on the move.

The Kiowa was flying higher than usual—almost too high—for scouting the activities of personnel at ground level. "We burned a hell of a lot of gas just getting up here," Thigpen said. "That'll cut into our loiter time a little. But we've gotta stay out of their way, right?" He was referring to a procession of Chinooks a thousand feet below that their ship was racing past. The Chinooks had sling-loaded 105-millimeter howitzers dangling below them as they brought a battery to Fire Support Base 30, a hilltop six kilometers inside Laos and four kilometers north of Route 9. Escorting the Chinooks were four Cobra gunships. They could hear a scout ship—a LOACH that was the target-spotting eye of the gunship team—on the frequency but couldn't see her. Darting at low level around the distant hilltop about to become an FSB, her tiny, egg-shaped fuselage and arc of her high-speed rotor blended invisibly into the terrain.

"Sounds like Charlie Floyd's driving that LOACH," Thigpen said. "That's his voice, all right."

There was no doubt the Kiowa had crossed into Laos; below them, Route 9 was now running parallel to the snaking, east-west run of the Sepon River. It would follow that river valley all the way to Tchepone, some forty klicks to the west. Thigpen said, "Technically, I can now cross Laos off the list of places I've never been."

Jif couldn't speak out loud what he was thinking. It was a secret he'd been sworn to keep indefinitely: *Can't say the same, Jimmy. I've actually been here before...and with boots on the ground, too. Nothing technical about it. It was a matter of life and death that couldn't be helped at the time.*

Staying high and to the north of FSB 30, they could see from their ship the dozen or so men of the battery's advance party preparing to receive the howitzers. Even when viewed from some distance, their actions seemed unhurried, almost casual.

"I think one of those gooks just waved to me," Thigpen said. "Friendly sort, ain't they?"

Or maybe they're just oblivious to what they're getting into, Jif thought.

They could see the LOACH now as she scouted the south side of the hill on which the battery would be inserted. That slope featured a shallower incline than the others and was shrouded in a thinner layer of forest. Jif observed, "That approach might even be shallow enough for armored vehicles."

Thigpen replied, "But howitzers on the hilltop could blow those tanks away with direct fire, right?"

"Sure, Chief, if they can depress the tubes low enough. The one-oh-five can only crank down to about niner-zero mils negative elevation."

"What's that in English, Captain?"

"Five degrees."

"Shit, that ain't much, is it?"

"It bloody well isn't."

They'd lost sight of the LOACH; she'd skimmed even farther down the slope. As the Chinooks began their single-file descent, a plume from a smoke grenade popped by the advance party rose from the hilltop, confirming location and wind direction for the approaching aircraft. "This looks textbook," Jif said.

But he'd spoken too soon. The terrified voice of the LOACH pilot—breathless and up an octave—wailed, "TAKING FIRE, TAKING FIRE. LZ IS HOT. REPEAT, LZ HOT. GOOKS WITH HEAVY WEAPONS ON SOUTH SLOPE."

"That's definitely Charlie Floyd," Thigpen said, his voice nearly as tense as the LOACH pilot's.

The parade of Chinooks aborted their approach, turning in a tight arc to orbit well east of the hilltop, closer to the border with Vietnam. The men of the battery's advance party, who'd seemed so calm just a few moments ago, were scurrying for cover. The gunship leader wanted to know how far down the slope the enemy was.

"NOT SURE," was Floyd's reply. "HALFWAY DOWN, MAYBE…COULD BE HIGHER." Then he added, "SHIT! FLAMED OUT! I'M GOING IN."

Jif told Thigpen, "Fly low around the east side of the hill. We've got to pick up that LOACH driver."

The tentative reply: "Oh, man! Well, roger that…I guess."

Jif added, "And while we're at it, we can spot for the gunships, too."

"You don't ask for much, do you, Captain?"

"He'd do the same for you, I reckon."

"Sure…but if he went into the trees on one of these steep slopes, we'll never get at him."

"Let's not get ahead of ourselves, Jimmy. Just fly. I'll look."

But Thigpen did have a point: the downed LOACH might be tough to find. As he banked the ship hard and put her into a stomach-lurching descent, he said, "If there are NVA on that hill, why aren't they shooting up the advance party?"

Jif replied, "They're not interested in taking out just a handful of dudes, Chief. They want to bring down choppers. More bang for the buck, you know?"

A minute later, they were barreling around the east side of the hill, searching desperately for the downed LOACH. They didn't see her on the first pass.

"Go farther east," Jif said.

"Might as well go east," Thigpen replied. "We go too far west, and we'll be in the Cobras' way. Maybe they'll see Charlie Floyd's ship even before we do."

The second pass was the charm. Jif spotted the LOACH's fuselage—minus her sheared-off rotor blades—nestled in the crown of a thick bamboo stand like an ornament in a Christmas tree. There was no level clearing where they could land anywhere in sight.

Thigpen asked, "You see Charlie?"

"Negative. Get directly over the LOACH. Put the skids right in the bloody treetop."

As the ship settled gingerly over the downed bird, Jif could see the pilot still inside. He was alive and moving; his hand signals were beseeching them to get closer.

The rotor wash of the Kiowa was beating the tree crowns like a gale, mixing with the mountain winds already rocking the ship. "I can't get any damn closer than this," Thigpen said. "I hit one fucking blade, and it's all she wrote."

"You're doing great," Jif replied. "Hold her right here as best you can. I'm going to try to get him onto the skid."

"That'll tip us down, Captain." He sounded frantic now. "We're gonna end up like—"

"Take a breath, Jimmy," Jif told him. "Nobody's shooting at us. Not yet, anyway. Just fly the bloody aircraft, okay?"

Chief Warrant 3 Charlie Floyd understood the pantomimed instructions Jif was giving him. He climbed outside his ship and, using the side armor on his seatback as a step, was able to grasp the rotor shaft fairing with his outstretched hand. He then pushed and pulled himself into a crouch atop the glazing of the forward fuselage.

"Come left about a foot," Jif told Thigpen.

"You gotta be shitting me, Captain. *A foot*? We're getting bounced around more than that in this fucking wind."

Jif needed more reach. He popped off his shoulder harnesses and loosened his seat belt as much as possible to still remain buckled in. Leaning out of the teetering Kiowa, he was finally able to grab Floyd's outstretched hand on the third try. That gave the man enough of a handhold to swing his foot onto the skid.

"GO," Jif told Thigpen. "WE'VE GOT HIM."

With Floyd still outside the ship, clinging with white knuckles to the structure between the frames of the two removed cabin doors, Thigpen lifted the chopper clear of the trees. Then he nosed her down the slope, building speed while she descended in a brisk, terrain-hugging escape. When he leveled the ship out near the bottom of the hill, their external passenger released his death grip on the door frames and climbed into the rear cabin. He was shaken but didn't appear injured.

Jif asked, "How's your day going, Chief?"

"Not worth a damn, sir. I'm sure glad you guys are here, though."

Thigpen: "What do we do now, Captain?"

Before offering an answer, Jif asked Floyd, "Any other hotspots around here?"

"Negative. Just that fucking south slope. How about hooking back to the west? We can still spot for the gunships." While Jif nodded in agreement, Floyd asked Thigpen, "You cool with that, Jimmy?"

"Sure, Charlie…but we've gotta stay low and out of their way."

"No shit, man," Floyd replied. "I mean, is the Pope Catholic?"

But after a quick radio discussion with the gunship leader, they were told his team didn't need help. "Just stay clear," he said. "We've got this covered."

Chief Floyd offered, "I was all over that goddamn hill. No problem until that south slope. I thought those NVA were ARVN Rangers at first. Boy, was I wrong." Then he added, "Funny thing, though…I was trying to reach the Rangers on the coord channel. Couldn't raise a living soul. They're supposed to be protecting the firebases along Route Niner, aren't they?"

"That's the story I heard," Jif replied as he pointed to one of the frequencies written in grease pencil on the windshield. "That's supposed to be their freq, right?"

"Yep, that's it."

"Sounds like somebody's not with the program," Jif said. "Tell you what…let's loiter near the north side of the hill. We'll be out of the Cobras' way…and we can be another set of eyes when the Chinooks are ready to do the drop." He asked Floyd, "You sure you don't need a doc, Chief?"

"I'm good to go, Captain," he replied. "I'll be more use up here with you guys than sitting back at Khe Sanh, anyway. And speaking of Khe Sanh, can I have the comm for a minute? I've got to report where my bird ended up. I don't think they'll try to recover her, dammit…probably just let some lucky Cobra driver or Air Force zoomie finish her off for good so the NVA can't strip her."

It took less than three minutes for the gunships to eliminate the threat on the south slope. One of the Cobras had been hit by ground fire on her second pass. She was already racing back toward the border, her front-seater wounded. Another ship from the team was covering her until she was safely out of Laos.

The other two gunships remained on station over FSB 30. Their leader told the Chinook flight, "Looks like this LZ is as cool as it's going to get. Y'all might as well stop wasting gas and bring those guns in."

*****

Twenty minutes later, the battery of 105-millimeter howitzers was in place on the hilltop known as FSB 30, firing its first mission in support of the ARVN thrust into Laos. The combined armored and infantry column had progressed four klicks past the border on Route 9 before encountering light NVA resistance. That opposition was quickly silenced by the firepower of artillery and tanks. The biggest hindrance to the column's advance was the road itself; rutted and washed out in countless places, it was proving practically impassable to wheeled vehicles larger than jeeps.

"Our engineers figured the road would be crap," Jif said as they viewed the stalled column from the Kiowa. "But it seems even worse than they thought. Too bad the ARVN have practically no engineering capabilities of their own, and our engineers can't go and help them. I reckon we'll be flying in tons of road-repair materials real soon. That's about all we can do for them."

More on his mind, though, was what Floyd had said about not being able to contact the ARVN Rangers on the radio. "I want to pay them a visit and see what their problem is," he said.

Thigpen asked, "Pay them a visit? Where'd you have in mind, Captain?"

"*Ranger Two*," he replied, referring to one of the two Ranger base camps just established in the mountains north of Route 9. "It's just three klicks due north of Fire Base Three-Zero."

"You mean you actually want to *land* there?" Thigpen asked. "Intentionally? Is that authorized? Ain't that *boots on the ground*?"

"Authorized? Who knows? But it's necessary if we're going to figure why they're not on the air." Then he asked Floyd, "Do you have a problem with going up there, Chief?"

"Negative, Captain. I'm cool with it."

*****

They were at Ranger 2 within minutes. An annoyed English-speaking lieutenant met them at the rough clearing that served as an LZ, saying, "You cannot stay here. Supply choppers should be arriving very soon. They have priority."

"I just want a minute of your time," Jif replied. "I need to know why we can't talk to you on the radio. We've been trying to raise you, but you don't appear to be on the coordination frequencies at all. Those supply choppers might not be able to contact you, either."

Glancing nervously at a sky still devoid of inbound helicopters, the lieutenant said, "Actually, we need to ask you Americans the same question. Follow me, please, Captain."

They walked a short distance to a CP tent surrounded by antennas, a battalion headquarters. A quick look at the sets found them still tuned to *yesterday's* frequencies. Shifting to French or rudimentary Vietnamese when his English failed to be understood by the officers in the CP, Jif's questions unraveled why the radios were tuned incorrectly: *The daily frequency changeover is posted in local time on their sigops, but I reckon they're reading it as GMT—Zulu time. The Greenwich meridian is seven time zones away. That means they'd be doing the changeover seven hours late. From what they're telling me, they're not planning to do it today for a couple of hours yet. That seems to prove the math.*

It's SOP to change frequencies at least once every twenty-four hours. It makes the enemy's attempts to intercept signal intel a little bit harder, since they've got to identify and locate units all over again. But everybody has to change freqs at the same time. Otherwise, commo falls apart...like it did this morning.

He suspected how this had come to pass: *In the past, American divisional staffs usually published the sigops that included frequency distributions to ARVN units. It was standard procedure that the changeover times on the American documents were expressed in Zulu. For this operation, though, the ARVN staff wrote the sigops on their own and, for some reason, decided to use local time. What's worse, they didn't even mark it as such on the sigops documents. The American headquarters reproducing the document didn't get fooled, but for the ARVN, old habits die hard. Their units in the field—or at least this battalion—are still reading the changeover time as if it's in Zulu. As a result, they can only talk amongst themselves during the window of that seven-hour error.*

To a man, the Ranger battalion staff went through a series of reactions to Jif's discovery. First, they shook their heads in disbelief and rejection. Then, as the validity of his conclusion set in, they became embarrassed. Finally, they turned on each other, looking for a scapegoat.

I'd hate to be the commo officer in this outfit, Jif told himself. *He's in a world of hurt right about now.*

The radios on the coordination channels came alive with American voices as the sets were retuned to the correct frequencies.

*****

By 1000 hours, Jif was back at Dong Ha, checking in with Colonel McKnight at the joint ARVN-US command center. On his arrival, he could see McKnight in a far corner of the room, deep in a heated but inaudible discussion with several American advisors. The only words he could make out were when the colonel said, *You keep sticking up for your ARVN…even when they're fucking up. That's going to bite this operation in the ass, gentlemen.*

Major Hutchinson was the only other PRT member in the center. He was seated by himself at a desk in a corner, shuffling papers. Jif asked him if he knew what the shouting match was specifically about.

"What do you think?" the major replied. "The advisors are telling our colonel that his captains—and that includes you, whizbang—are getting in the way and screwing up the works. It seems our boy Jamerson got all bent out of shape with some tankers from First Armored Brigade this morning. Started reading them the Riot Act about their lack of safety procedures during fueling."

"So? Something tells me he was probably giving them good advice."

"That's not the way the ARVN tankers and their advisor see it," Hutchinson replied. "According to them, Jamerson slowed them down so much that they were thirty minutes late over the start line. Apparently, it's better a few ARVN tankers set themselves on fire than a unit misses its departure slot."

"From what I've seen of the ARVN's progress so far," Jif replied, "thirty minutes shouldn't make much of a difference in anything right now. Once you're over the border, the road surface on Route Niner is worse than anyone thought. Their column is barely moving. It's walking pace only."

He recognized the forms Hutchinson was riffling through: supply requisitions. He asked, "What're you going to be doing with those, Major?"

Annoyed by the question, Hutchinson replied, "Not that it's any of your business, young captain, but I've been tasked with reviewing the supply procedures for this operation."

"Why? That's an all-American operation. We're handling every part of the logistics, from planning, to depot management, to transportation. I thought this team was supposed to be keeping an eye on ARVN units, not American ones."

"That's above your pay grade, Miles. If you've got a problem with that, take it up with the colonel." Adopting that unfocused stare of his—the one that seemed to be looking right through you—the major added, "If I were you, son, I'd skedaddle. Your name's mud with those advisors after you stepped on your dick yesterday and caused a gang fight during that medevac. If they see you in the flesh, they might want to shoot you all over again."

Jif wasn't sure if Hutchinson was busting his balls, playing Dutch uncle, or actually trying to give some straight-up friendly advice. His vacant expression yielded no clues. The next thing he said didn't make it any clearer.

"Do you really believe those gooks were clever enough to stage the hijacking of a medevac ship like you suggested, Miles?"

"I certainly do, Major. Saw it with my own bloody eyes. And even if I hadn't seen it, I would look at it this way…if some dumbass snuffy of ours is clever enough to shoot himself in the foot to get out of combat, our Vietnamese allies are more than clever enough to organize the hijacking of a chopper."

"That's a fool's game you're talking, Miles. Isn't it you who reported that an entire Ranger battalion doesn't know how to tell time? That doesn't sound *more than clever enough* to me."

Jif was going to reply that the sigops problem had nothing to do with telling time. It was the result of multiple staff errors—and more complicated than Hutchinson assumed—but he saved his breath. He doubted the major would believe him, anyway. *I think Colonel McKnight's got him pegged for a dim bulb, too. That's probably why he's got him doing busy work with those supply forms. Seems like a bloody waste of time, but like the major says, that's above my pay grade.*

Chapter Four

After only a day of clear weather, the skies turned unfriendly again. Constant low cloud cover and sporadic rain plagued the Sepon River valley, reducing visibility along Route 9 and making air support difficult, if not impossible. Those helicopters that ventured below the cloud deck still found themselves vulnerable to NVA anti-aircraft weapons situated on the hills north and south of the road, whose locations were often shrouded in mist and hard to pinpoint. Often, they were firing down on the low-flying choppers from the heights.

CW3 Charlie Floyd, piloting a replacement LOACH with Jif as the airborne observer, said, "If those NVA gunners didn't have to use tracers to get on target, we'd never figure out where they were. Of course, by the time we do figure it out, it could already be too damn late. I guess I'm living proof of that."

"Hey, at least you're *living* proof," Jif replied.

"Amen to that, Captain. What do you want to look at next?"

"Let's check out Route Niner as far west as A Luoi. There's an armored probe supposed to be rolling that way. Since *Ball Point Three-Seven* bailed out and went back to Khe Sanh, nobody has eyes on those tankers. I wonder why they pulled the plug with no explanation…you don't think they needed fuel, do you? We all took off with full tanks at pretty much the same time."

"Nah, they didn't need fuel," Floyd replied. "Either your buddy Captain Jamerson or his pilot had enough scud-running and bullet-dodging for one morning. Who knows…maybe both of them did. They might even invent some nit-picking mechanical discrepancy to write up as the reason they went back. It'll drive the mechanics nuts trying to figure out if there's actually something wrong with the ship or not. But sometimes, you can't blame a guy for pulling the plug. We all have our limits."

"I know what you mean, Chief. Did you ever have to do anything like that?"

"I'd prefer not to say, sir."

"I understand," Jif replied, wishing he'd never asked. "Completely."

As they flew toward A Luoi, Floyd had his hands full trying to stay just under the low cloud deck so the observation mission could continue. If engaged by ground fire, there was no place to go but straight up through the clouds until they broke out on top while flying dead ahead on the same course. To do any blind lateral maneuvering within the valley was inviting a crash-and-burn encounter with *hardcore cumulus*, the name pilots had given long ago to high ground shrouded in clouds.

They were still two kilometers from A Luoi when they spotted the armored probe trundling along Route 9. Jif counted eight of the ARVN's old M41 tanks in a staggered file. They appeared to be all by themselves.

"Where the bloody hell is their infantry support?" Jif asked, thinking out loud. "They've got no protection from sappers."

"I guess the ARVN grunts didn't want to come out and play today," Floyd replied.

"More than likely, Chief, the armor and infantry outfits didn't coordinate properly…or some infantry commander decided he just wasn't in the mood. They pull that shit a lot…and get away with it, too. Their political connections protect them."

"You mean it's a case of who you know and who you blow?"

"There it is," Jif replied.

"I guess those are things that you and your team are trying to straighten out, right?"

"That's exactly right," Jif said as he made notes on his map.

"How's that working out for you?"

"Let's just say that so far, it's barely working, Chief."

The tanks came to a halt as the LOACH passed overhead. Floyd offered, "Maybe they're going to wait for their infantry to catch up."

"I wouldn't hold my breath. Let's see what's going on in the ville."

"Sure, but I've got a question for you, Captain…according to the map, the name of this town is Ban Dong. But we call it A Luoi. Any idea why?"

"From what I gather, somebody up at Corps didn't like the word *Dong* appearing in ops orders—there are enough penis jokes about the Dong Ha Combat Base as it is—so for our purposes, they renamed the ville A Luoi. It might be a throwback—maybe even a tribute—to all our operations in the A Shau Valley. There's an A Luoi in the A Shau, right along the river on Route Five-Four-Eight. Do you know it?"

"Never been there, Captain."

"Well, that place was smack dab in the middle of our usual area of operations there. A lot of our effort in that valley centered around it. Ban Dong is just about in the middle of the road to Tchepone—in a river valley, too—so I reckon some high-ranking nostalgia buff thought it was fitting. I was in the A Shau on my first tour with the Cav during Operation Delaware in '68."

"I don't know, sir. That whole renaming thing sounds kinda like a bullshit story."

Jif laughed. "It may well be, Chief."

"So how'd Delaware work out, anyway?"

"Typical. We kicked the NVA out, disrupted the Ho Chi Minh Trail for a while, and then we left. Before you knew it, the NVA came back, so the One-Oh-First Airborne had to do it again in '69. And the ARVN's still trying to do it."

"Like we're going around in circles."

"Like full bloody circles, Chief."

*****

The village of A Luoi—aka Ban Dong—sat within a bend of the Sepon a kilometer south of Route 9. The only remarkable thing about it was the Huey helicopter sitting in tall weeds on the outskirts, her rotor motionless. Dropping the LOACH lower for a better look, they could tell it was a South Vietnamese Air Force ship.

"You got a tail number?" Floyd asked.

"Negative," Jif replied. "The boom's too far down in the weeds. The skids might be bent, too, like she came down real hard."

Floyd was getting nervous. "I don't want to stay down here forever, Captain. We're one hell of a low, slow target."

"Sure, Chief. Just give me a lap around the ville. Maybe we can see if this place is as much of a ghost town as it seems." He called in the location of the downed Huey to the operations center at Lang Vei.

As they turned south toward the river to begin the orbit of A Luoi, Jif said, "I can't even see the ARVN tanks anymore. The visibility must be getting worse."

"Maybe they split, Captain. They've got a reverse gear, too, don't they?"

They finished circling the village. Jif hadn't seen any sign of life, not even abandoned, starving animals rummaging for food. "So what do we do now?" Floyd asked.

There was a trail wide enough for vehicles running from A Luoi back to Route 9. They could see the trail clearly; there were the unmistakable impressions of tracked vehicles in its muddy surface. "The ARVN didn't make those tracks, that's for damn sure," Jif said. "They haven't been here yet."

Without enthusiasm, Floyd asked, "You want to follow the trail, then?"

"Yeah, Chief."

"I'm not liking this one bit, sir. I flew into one triple-A trap the other day. Don't plan to do that—"

His words were cut off by several streams of green tracers arcing in front of the LOACH. The rounds were coming from a thickly wooded patch half a klick from A Luoi.

But being low at this particular moment proved to be an advantage. Floyd forced the ship into a hard right turn, a rapid shift in the firing solution that was impossible for the gunners to track quickly enough as the chopper made good her escape.

"That would be a bad place for triple-A guns," Jif said. "Rotten fields of fire. I'm pretty sure the bursts came from tanks hidden in those woods. Two of them. That would jive with those tracks on the trail."

"It probably jives with why that Huey's sitting there, too," Floyd added. "Got her ass shot down. I'm surprised we didn't hear about that."

Flying over Route 9 once again, Jif spotted two more tanks on the north side of the road, nestled in woods near the base of a hill. They might've been difficult to see from ground level but were poorly concealed from above. They didn't fire on the LOACH; they had no machine guns on their turrets. Jif reported their locations to Lang Vei.

They could see the column of ARVN tanks again, stopped at that same point on the road two klicks from A Luoi. There was still no sign of supporting infantry with them. Floyd asked, "You suppose their infantry is on foot—maybe hunkered down alongside the road—and we just don't see them?"

"Not likely," Jif replied. "They'd ride in APCs and wouldn't dismount until there was contact. Nobody walks when they can ride."

Lang Vei was on the freq, saying the ARVN tankers wanted confirmation of the number and type of enemy tanks. Jif repeated that there were four—two on either side of the road—identified as PT-76 amphibious vehicles. They appeared fairly well concealed. When asked if they could mark the enemy tanks with smoke, Jif replied, "Negative. Unable."

Floyd's next comment was meant for Jif's ears only: "Make that fuck no. What do they think we are? A FAC ship?"

Lang Vei asked if enemy infantry was present.

Jif's reply: "Unknown at this time."

Floyd said, "There could be a thousand gooks on those hills for all we know, Captain."

"Yeah, tell me about it, Chief."

The net was silent for over a minute. Then Lang Vei asked, "Is the ceiling sufficient for air support?"

"Negative," Jif replied. "Ceiling eight hundred feet or less, visibility two to three klicks."

The ops center asked, "Can you adjust fire for artillery?"

"Affirmative. Two targets, engage separately."

The two fire missions were called in. The need to relay through the ops center would impose delays on their first rounds as well as on subsequent corrections. If for some reason the missions were given to the ARVN 105-millimeter batteries at FSB 30 and its sister, FSB 31, those delays would be even longer as target data to the batteries was translated into Vietnamese. Jif hoped the missions would go to the American medium or heavy artillery across the border. *That's the best chance we've got of doing any real damage to those tanks with indirect fire. The only way a one-oh-five round is going to damage a tank is with a direct hit...and the odds of that are pretty slim. We might be able to scare the crap out of those NVA tankers, though, so they'll pull out.*

Floyd was getting frustrated by the delays and nervous they were staying in the same area for so long. "Why can't those ARVN tanks just engage them, for fuck's sake? They've got them outnumbered two to one."

"Let's just say the ARVN tankers are not known for their aggressiveness against armed adversaries," Jif said. "Those M41s of theirs aren't exactly tank destroyers, either, but they're supposed to be slightly superior to the PT-76. Even so, the *Four-Ones* are old, cranky, and lightly armored. Those NVA tanks might be brand new."

A few minutes later, the first *shot* messages—indicating rounds had been fired—were relayed to the LOACH as it loitered well south of the target areas. The *splash* alerts that immediately followed were too late to fulfill their heads-up function. Delayed by the need for a relay, they arrived seconds after the first two adjustment rounds had already impacted. Fortunately, Jif saw them both. They hadn't missed by much.

He called in the adjustments and then told Floyd, "Shit, it's got to be one-oh-fives. Two different batteries, one target apiece. Real short times-of-flight, too, so the rounds have to be from FSB Three-Zero and Three-One. If the damn weather was clear and the tanks were in the open, those gunners on Three-One could probably see the vehicles on the north side of the road. The firebase is only like five klicks away and a couple hundred meters higher. They could call their own bloody shots."

It seemed an eternity until the second adjustment rounds landed. "Close enough for government work," Jif said to Floyd. He gave the ops center the fire-for-effect corrections.

The results were less than impressive. "No smoke, no fire, no pieces flying off, no crewmen bailing out," Jif said. He requested a repeat of both fire-for-effect volleys.

Those rounds didn't do any noticeable damage, either. But it did make the tanks move a few hundred yards. All four of them took up new positions astride the roadway, their bows pointed east, toward the stalled ARVN column still two kilometers away.

Jif reported his lack of success and the repositioning of the enemy tanks. He requested continuing the mission but only with the heavier American guns.

"Negative, negative," came the reply. "Not available at this time."

Neither Jif nor Floyd were surprised. They surmised the big guns were engaging targets to the north, near the outposts of Ranger North and Ranger South. They'd been warned to steer clear of that area due to *airspace conflict.* In these low ceilings that precluded tactical air support operations, that could only mean that artillery rounds were using that airspace.

The ARVN tanks had moved, too. They were retreating east down Route 9, back toward the border.

One of the NVA tanks with a large-caliber machine gun atop its turret started to spit rounds at the LOACH again. They didn't appear very well aimed and, fired from a distance of several klicks, were falling well short. The bursts seemed more of a warning than a shoot-down attempt.

Floyd asked, "You had enough of this bullshit, Captain? Until this scud lifts, we're just hanging our asses out and wasting gas for nothing."

He expected disagreement, even a countermand; *I'm cutting him a lot of slack since he saved my ass the other day, but the rumor mill's saying that Captain Miles can be a little reckless sometimes...a little too gung ho for some tastes. I'm beginning to see what they're talking about.*

But Jif's breezy reply surprised him: "Yeah, I reckon so. Let's go home."

*****

The clouds were forcing them still lower as they got to the border. Khe Sanh was reporting a four-hundred-foot ceiling. Floyd told Jif, "We might as well stay down on the deck. If we got on top of these clouds, we may never find Khe Sanh."

But being that low did help them spot something unusual. Just across the border, on the old abandoned airstrip at Lao Bao, an OH-58 Kiowa was parked beside a double line of APCs. The Kiowa was US Army, the APCs—twelve in number, roughly enough for an armored cavalry troop—were ARVN. There was some sort of confrontation going on between a big American and a group of much smaller soldiers.

They were close enough to the dust-up for Jif to recognize the American: Captain Phil Jamerson—*Ball Point 3-7*—of the PRT. He was fairly sure the Kiowa's pilot, still in his seat in the ship, was CW2 Thigpen. But he was quite sure the animated Jamerson was in a heated argument with one of the ARVN. His finger-pointing gestures were on the verge of poking the man in the chest.

"Land this bird," Jif told Floyd. "I've got to see what the bloody hell's going on down there."

"Not for nothing, Captain, but why is it any of our business?"

"Jamerson's already in deep shit for a clash with the ARVN. If he does it again, he's going to put himself—and our team—in a world of hurt. Just land the bloody ship, okay?"

Floyd's reluctant reply: "Roger that, sir."

Jif intervened just in time. He got between Jamerson and an ARVN captain named Thuong as the American captain was winding up to throw the first punch. The blow bounced off Jif's shoulder as he pushed his fellow team member away from the confrontation.

"Get the fuck off me, Miles," Jamerson said, his eyes wild and blood-thirsty, his spittle flying. "This is my deal."

"Your *deal* is going to bite us all in the ass, Phil. Get ahold of yourself. Turn it down a couple of notches. Why are you even here? I thought you were going back to Khe Sanh."

"I was…until I got a load of this clusterfuck. The assholes don't know how to take care of these very expensive machines we gave them." Pointing to an APC with smoke rising from the open personnel compartment, he added, "Look at that…some dumbass slopes are having a goddamn barbeque right inside the track. Open flame and everything. That's what got my attention. I thought they'd been blown up by the NVA while still on the Nam side of the border. But no…they're going to blow up all by themselves."

Jif said, "I take it you suggested they should stop cooking inside the vehicle?"

"Yeah, I did. But does it look like they gave a shit?"

"Then you've done all you can do, Phil. We're not in charge here. Hell, we're not even advisors."

"And look at the shape these tracks are in! Half of them will break down in the next couple of klicks. I don't think they even know how to check the tranny oil. Do you have any idea what one of these vehicles costs?"

"Write it up, Phil. That's all we can do."

Jamerson's eyes were still blazing with anger. "Look at those fucking useless gooks, Miles…they're laughing at us!"

No, they're laughing at you, Phil, Jif told himself.

Thuong, who spoke passable English, called to them, saying, "You American soldiers cut and run. You no help. Just send your airplanes with bombs. The rest of you go fuck off."

Still pointing an accusing finger, Jamerson replied, "You haven't heard the last of this, *dink*."

Thuong smirked and said, "Yes, we have. Go away now."

One of the other ARVN said something in Vietnamese that made his comrades laugh all over again. Jamerson didn't understand the words, but Jif thought he did. He'd heard the profane crux of what was said before, muttered by Vietnamese officers who'd been among his students at Fort Sill's artillery school. His loose translation: *The American sons of whores are already gone.*

Chapter Five

Jif was surprised to find Colonel McKnight waiting for him and Jamerson at Khe Sanh. "How'd you even get here, sir?" he asked. "Isn't the flying down from Dong Ha kind of dicey?"

"You made it, didn't you, Miles? My pilot followed Route Niner, just like yours did. Pretty hairy, though, I admit. We're not going to do it again until the weather breaks. So where the hell is Jamerson?"

"He landed right behind us, sir. He should be walking in here any second."

McKnight replied, "Outstanding. Get lost while I talk to him."

Jif knew what *talk* meant: *Jamerson's about to get his ass chewed. The colonel's extending him the courtesy of not doing it in front of spectators.*

*****

Phil Jamerson received more than an ass-chewing. He was being relieved from his duties on the PRT and shipped back to MACV-Saigon for reassignment.

Stunned by the sudden firing and the *aw, shit* on his record it would imply, he said to McKnight, "Begging your pardon, sir, but why am I getting singled out? What about Miles? Isn't the ARVN looking for his head, too?"

"None of that is any of your concern, Philip. Whatever Miles did—or the Ranger Division and their advisor want to think he did—it doesn't hold a candle to your fuckups. You've actually managed to interfere with ARVN tactical deployments *twice*. That's not a brilliant accomplishment, I'm afraid."

"With all due respect, sir, that's bullshit. Neither of those units I dealt with were in a hurry to go anywhere…not without our air support. That armored cav outfit this morning was parked at the border with their thumbs up their asses."

"Regardless, Captain, an ARVN armored advance to A Luoi got aborted this morning because their supporting infantry never showed up. And that infantry unit is reported to be the one you tangled with. Whether they planned to join the advance or not, everybody and his brother is now more than glad to make you—and by association, this entire team—the scapegoat for their failure. Sorry, Philip, but you've got to go."

"This must be Saigon's call, right, sir?"

"No, Captain. It's mine."

*****

By 1100 hours, the clouds had broken enough for the three members of the PRT at Khe Sanh—McKnight, Jif, and Captain Boyd Gray—to fly back to the joint command center at Dong Ha. They were met there by the team's remaining member, Major Hutchinson, who was still shuffling paperwork and had yet to leave the center. When the colonel announced the realignment of team responsibilities now that Jamerson had been dismissed, Hutchinson was horrified. He would now be flying over Laos on a regular basis, observing ARVN movements just like Jif and Gray.

"But who'll be handling the admin part of the investigation if I go out in the field, Colonel?" the major asked in protest. "I've already uncovered some glaring discrepancies in the logistics chain."

"Not that I don't appreciate your efforts, Hutch, but it's nothing some spec-five clerk couldn't handle. I need your abilities elsewhere now." McKnight didn't bother mentioning that everything Hutchinson had *uncovered* was already being corrected by the Army's logistics people even before he'd brought it to anyone's attention.

"I'm probably not the best person to be an aerial observer in this operation," Hutchinson persisted. "All my flight crew time was as a cargo chief on H-21s…you know, *flying bananas*. I have zero hours in a LOACH or a Kiowa."

"You don't have to fly the damn thing, Major," McKnight replied, "just strap in, look down, and take notes. I'm sure you can handle that."

Boyd Gray muttered to Jif, "And he's got the balls to cry about that while he's wearing aircrew wings. Ain't that some shit?"

*****

The return of clear skies reinvigorated the assault into Laos. Behind a massive curtain of airstrikes by both US tactical aircraft and B-52s, ARVN infantry and artillery were being heli-lifted into half a dozen LZs and firebases along Route 9. A Luoi was occupied two days after that first abortive probe. The ARVN force was halfway to its ultimate objective, the Ho Chi Minh Trail's waypoint of Tchepone.

But it wasn't a walkover. Strong pockets of NVA resistance were materializing all along the assault route. As the latest action reports streamed into the command center at Dong Ha, Colonel McKnight briefed the three observers that comprised his team. "The NVA seems to be focused on pushing the ARVN out of A Luoi. Disturbingly, NVA tanks have been reported on the heights to the north of the ville, particularly in the vicinity of FSB Three-One. If they can neutralize that firebase, they have a commanding position from which to execute a counterassault."

He then parceled out assignments to the team. "Miles, I want you to concentrate on the area I've just described, the hills north of A Luoi. Gray, cover Ranger One and Two." Finally, he told Hutchinson, "Hutch, keep an eye on Fire Bases Delta and Hotel south of Route Niner. You've inherited Captain Jamerson's call sign, *Ball Point Three-Seven*."

The major seemed relieved. The area he'd been assigned had experienced the least NVA activity since the incursion into Laos began.

In conclusion, McKnight said, "I'll be in the air monitoring ARVN armor operations in general. My call sign will be *Ball Point Three-Six*. I'll be with the commander of the ARVN's First Armored Brigade, Colonel Ng."

That was a startling piece of news. Jif said, "I'm surprised the advisors went along with that setup, sir. I mean, you riding with an ARVN commander…that's really stepping on their dicks, isn't it?"

McKnight smiled. "They didn't go along with anything, Miles. In fact, they blew a collective gasket, like I was pissing in their cornflakes. But I won't be there to give the good colonel advice, just observe what his command does without tying up another chopper to chauffeur me around. And by the way, I don't need the advisors' approval for anything, so fuck 'em if they can't take a joke."

*****

Half an hour later, as they walked across the ramp to their waiting choppers, Jif and Gray noticed Major Hutchison with some unusual baggage. Besides the map case aerial observers typically carried, he was lugging a flight bag that seemed as if it was laden with bricks. Gray called out, "What's in the sack, Major?"

Hutchison stopped, set the bag down, and beckoned the two captains to have a look inside. The contents: a bulky sixteen-millimeter movie camera, the kind a newsreel videographer might use.

Jif asked, "What're you going to do with that monstrosity, sir? Shoot some home movies?"

"You know what they say, Captain…a picture is worth a thousand words. And a movie is better than a bunch of still photos any day."

Gray asked, "Where'd you get it from?"

"The G2 shop at Corps. I've got a buddy there who loaned it to me."

"Loaned out of the goodness of his heart?" Jif asked. "Or made you sign for it?"

"None of your damn business, young captain."

As Hutchinson picked up the bag and walked off, Jif told Gray, "I hope *Cecil B. DeMille* over there doesn't expect his pilot to hold the ship still in midair so he can get his shot."

"You got that right, man. That sounds like the prelude to *mark the target with a burning LOACH*."

*****

They could see smoke rising from the scrub hills three kilometers northwest of A Luoi, on the north side of Route 9. CW3 Floyd, Jif's pilot, asked, "What do you make of that, Captain? That's not from artillery, is it?"

"Afraid not," Jif replied. "I think we're about to get our first look at tanks in action. That looks like a mix of smoke from vehicle exhausts, muzzle blasts, rounds impacting…"

"I don't see anything blowing up yet, though," Floyd said. "Where do you want to watch this show from?"

"How about we get up over the hills to the north? Shouldn't be much to block our view when we're looking downslope."

He could tell right away that his pilot didn't think much of that idea. Floyd confirmed it when he said, "There could be a shitload of triple-A up in those hills, sir. We'd be walking right up to them."

"All right," Jif replied, "stay down here near Route Niner. But get closer, okay? I need to see more than smoke signals."

Flying a kilometer from the action, it became clear what was happening. Four ARVN M41 tanks and eight M113 APCs—probably carrying two platoons of armored cavalry troopers—were engaging two NVA tanks at a distance of roughly eight hundred meters.

"This is something new," Jif said. "Those NVA tanks—they're not PT-76s. They're bloody T-54s. But I don't see any machine guns on their turrets, so there won't be any triple-A from them, at least."

"Maybe they can't shoot us," Floyd said, "but they're going to tear those ARVN tanks apart. T-54s are supposed to be the real deal, not like the little toy tanks we've seen so far. Any infantry with them?"

"Not that I can tell. But there are five or six trucks—like Russian deuces—a couple hundred meters behind them."

"Yeah, I see them, too. Hang on…I've got gunships on the air freq." After a pause, Floyd added, "They're going to be rolling in any second. We've got to get out of their way."

As the LOACH turned away, Jif lost sight of the tank standoff for a few moments as it passed behind the ship. When the maneuver was complete and he regained his view, he could see that an APC had just been turned inside out by a round from a T-54. Within seconds, the other APCs backed away, pivoted, and fled the fight. "So much for the ARVN's infantry-armor coordination," he said.

The Cobra gunships rolled in, launching salvos of 2.5-inch rockets aimed at the flanks of the T-54s. But they fell short, doing little more than spraying the vehicles with mud. Within seconds of the pass, both tanks fired their main guns. One of the ARVN tanks was struck and began to belch flames from its hatches and vents. The T-54s began a slow advance toward their adversaries.

Watching the M41 burn, Jif said, "I don't reckon any of that crew got out." He expected the other three ARVN tanks to turn and flee like the APCs had done, but they held their ground.

Floyd: "The Cobras are coming around to hit the T-54s in the ass this time."

That's when Jif saw the shapes of infantrymen—NVA, no doubt, in what seemed platoon strength or greater—streaming down the hill toward the ARVN tanks. "We've got sappers coming," he said. "I'll get the Cobras to work on them instead. Better than wasting their rockets on those tanks."

One of the T-54s had moved well ahead of the other. In an unusual but powerful example of fire coordination, all three M41s fired at it simultaneously. Two of the rounds were exactly on target. The NVA tank stopped dead in its tracks, its turret askew. The main gun, which a moment ago had been pointing like a menacing finger, was now sagging down in a gesture of defeat.

Following Jif's guidance, the Cobras rolled in once again, raking the swarming NVA infantry with their 7.62-millimeter miniguns. If there were survivors among them, they'd fled back up the hill before the mud and debris kicked up by the aerial attack had settled.

The sapper attack stymied, the Cobras had another try at the remaining T-54. This time, they barreled in from directly behind the vehicle, letting fly another salvo of rockets.

They didn't kill the NVA tank but somehow wounded her. The crew tried to pivot, but the tracks balked, refusing to provide the differential motion required for the maneuver. Then the crew tried to drive in reverse. That was more successful at first, but after about fifty meters the tank bucked and jerked to a halt. Hatches flew open as the crew abandoned the vehicle. They'd barely hit the ground running when smoke began to billow from those open hatches.

Glancing beyond the defeated tanks, Jif suspected the cabs of those Russian deuces were empty. As they flew closer, the unoccupied seats and doors left wide open confirmed it. He didn't know at what point in the fight the trucks had been abandoned, and he had no idea who or what was beneath the canvas roofs over their cargo beds.

The Cobra leader asked the LOACH if there was anything else to attack. Jif's reply: "The only other targets we can see are those trucks about three hundred meters west of the NVA tanks. Don't know what they're carrying."

Several hundred rounds from the gunships' miniguns quickly answered that question; the trucks were loaded with ammunition. The fiery explosions were spectacular, with rippling shock waves that rocked the LOACH and the Cobras while sending a column of dense gray smoke skyward.

"Whoa," Floyd said as he struggled to coax his ship through the turbulence. "Wasn't expecting that shit. Are we done here, Captain?"

Before Jif could answer, the Cobras reported that they, at least, were done. "Gotta gas up and reload," their leader said.

"But we're not finished yet," Jif told Floyd. "I reckon there's an NVA strongpoint on one of these hills, maybe even a supply cache. They were either about to receive that ammo or they were distributing it from there."

A reluctant Floyd replied, "Copy that, sir, but are we the only assholes doing recon today? Gotta be somebody else handling this."

He had a point. But other than their own communications, the net had been fairly quiet. He didn't figure Jif was about to change his mind, though, so he asked, "Where do you want to look?"

"Let's go north."

"North? I was pretty sure you'd say east or west. Why north?"

"Just a hunch, Chief."

"But that takes us up into the high ground. Like I said before, the higher we go, the better chance of running straight into triple-A."

Unfazed, Jif replied, "And where there's triple-A, I'm betting there's a strongpoint."

"Never a dull moment working with you, sir." Then Floyd added, "But I'm going to have to stay real low and fast. You might not see shit through the trees. Everything will go by in a flash."

"No problem, Chief. The tracers they might throw up will point right to them. They work both ways, right?"

Floyd said nothing in reply, but Jif was pretty sure he was rolling his eyes behind those aviator sunglasses.

*****

As they scoured the rising terrain, Jif said, "I wouldn't be surprised if they didn't shoot at us. No point giving your position away for one bloody LOACH when there's an outstanding chance it'll bring the world down on you."

Floyd didn't bother to hide the sarcasm in his voice as he replied, "Always looking for that silver lining, eh, Captain?"

But after several zigzag runs above muddy trails imprinted with tire tracks, they'd still seen nothing of the enemy. As the ship was being turned to explore another area of the hillside, Jif suddenly caught a momentary glimpse of what he'd been looking for: a crowded truck park in a thick stand of trees they'd already passed over twice and never noticed.

He felt vindicated; the NVA hadn't fired at them, at least not that they could tell in the absence of tracers. He hadn't needed to say a word of the sighting to Floyd. The pilot had sensed it in the sudden urgency of Jif's body language. In the cramped confines of the LOACH, it was impossible not to sense such things; the front-seaters practically rubbed shoulders in the tiny eggshell of the ship's cabin.

Floyd began to steer the ship over and behind the hilltop, seeking the cover of the peak. Surprisingly, it was a gentle maneuver, not an abrupt one born of panic. "How many?" he asked Jif.

"Lots. *Boo coo*," he replied. The bilingual repetition—especially the American-corrupted French of *beaucoup* so common in Nam—underscored his amazement that they'd flown through a hornet's nest unmolested.

"You think they know they've been spotted?"

"Not a bloody clue, Chief."

There was no time to rejoice over their good fortune. Jif was on the radio to Lang Vei, reporting the enemy position. But they didn't answer.

"We're too low," he said to Floyd. "Must be too many hills in the way. No line of sight for the signals."

"Climbing higher could give us big problems, Captain."

"Copy that. Is there a FAC on the air freq?"

"There sure is. He's high…you'll have good line of sight on him."

Jif was switching radios even before Floyd had finished speaking. After receiving the coordinates of the target, the FAC said, "Roger, be with you in three minutes. Stick around if you can. Might need your help."

The FAC ship—an O-2 mounting tandem engines on her fuselage, one forward, one aft—was on station in just over two minutes. With the LOACH standing off a kilometer to the south, the O-2 let fly two target-marking smoke rockets on the NVA location. Once they'd been launched, the ship executed a violent descending turn toward the lower terrain near Route 9. Knowing full well the danger the FAC was about to deliver, the NVA triple-A gunners tried to knock the ship down. But the tracers that rose to meet the O-2 failed to track her abrupt escape maneuver.

"I hope that smoke's close enough," the FAC pilot radioed. "Don't feel like doing it again, *over*."

Jif was tempted to reply *close enough for government work*, but this wasn't the time for lighthearted comments, and the FAC needed the frequency clear to guide his strike element to the rockets' smoke. Floyd asked Jif, "You got a visual on those zoomies?"

"Negative. Not yet."

Their discussion with the FAC had made it clear, though, that the still unseen fighter-bombers would be attacking out of the east. Floyd put his ship through a one-eighty, giving Jif a clearer view of the target area. It also repositioned them farther south, giving an even wider berth to the approaching jets.

And then they appeared, two glimmering dots growing exponentially bigger with each passing second, materializing into F-4 Phantoms as they performed a downhill run to bomb release through ribbons of triple-A tracers.

Undaunted, the Phantoms kept coming. Or maybe they just didn't see the triple-A. The spectacle of them running the gauntlet of tracers fired from several hillside locations reminded Jif of the water arches shot into the air by fire boats celebrating the arrival of some maritime vessel.

But there was nothing celebratory about this deadly display. The two jets were climbing away before their salvos of high-explosive bombs shattered a wide swath of the hillside. Then two more Phantoms suddenly arrived in their wake to dispense tumbling canisters that could only contain napalm. They turned the hillside into a pyre belching orange flames and a towering column of dense black smoke.

"Okay, I'm fucking impressed," Floyd said to Jif. Then he asked, "You got a plot on any of those triple-A sites that popped up against the F-4s?"

Jif nodded *yes*. He was already on the radio to Lang Vei, calling in artillery fire missions on the locations of those anti-aircraft guns. In a break between transmissions, he told Floyd, "Got to nail those bastards before they move again, Chief."

Chapter Six

"Trying to hit all these triple-A sites is getting to be a fool's game, Captain," CW3 Floyd said to Jif. "Knock one out, another pops up."

It was midafternoon, and they were flying their third mission of the day, still trying to observe what was going on in the hills north of A Luoi. Despite all the attention from artillery, helicopter gunships, and fighter-bombers, the NVA anti-aircraft fire was still murderous. At least half a dozen choppers of various types had been knocked down. It had also been reported that two USAF ground-attack aircraft had been damaged during their attack runs, each crashing after their pilots ejected once those jets were beyond saving.

As Jif handed off another ground target to a FAC for a strike by tac air, Floyd said, "I could've sworn you told me we'd be doing an observation mission, but we're right in the middle of the shit again. Face it, sir…we're not observers. We're active participants in this clusterfuck."

"Can't argue with that, Chief," Jif replied.

"Another day or two of this and I may need to drink myself into a serious stupor, Captain. That'll keep me on the ground, at least."

"C'mon, Chief, stay with the program. As good as you fly, I reckon we've still got a shot at beating those gloomy life expectancy statistics for aircrew."

"I love your confidence, sir," Floyd replied, not sounding as if he was loving much of anything at the moment.

There were plenty of frantic voices on the airwaves this day, but the one suddenly spilling from their headsets was going for the *most overwrought* prize. It was a familiar voice, too.

"*Ball Point Three-Four*," Jif said, "that's Boyd Gray's call sign. He's on the ground about a klick from Ranger South."

"He get shot down?"

"Negative. Sounds like some command and control ship did. That's got to be a Huey from the Republic of Vietnam Air Force. He's trying to rescue them…but he needs help."

Jif told Gray they'd be at his location in four minutes.

"Do better than that, if you can," was the reply.

*****

It wasn't difficult to find the crash site. The downed chopper had fallen into a thicket, and Gray's idling Kiowa was tucked into a tight clearing less than thirty meters away. The broken RVNAF Huey—her rotor shattered and tail boom bent—had been serving as an ARVN C&C ship, just as Jif surmised. As the LOACH orbited low overhead, he and Floyd could see there were five men standing on the Kiowa's skids, their hands clinging to any part of her they could grab. Her small aft cabin appeared stuffed with occupants, the feet of several prone men protruding from the open entryways.

"Let me guess," Jif radioed to Gray. "You can't lift her out of there with all those dudes on board, right?"

"Correct. We tried…but it's not going to work without a running start. Too hot, too many trees in the way. Counting me and my pilot, there are twelve guys on this bird. Any other rescue ship is still at least fifteen minutes out."

Jif asked, "You've got wounded on board, right?"

"Affirmative. Three injured bad. But this ARVN colonel and his staff keep forcing their way onto the ship. He even tried to kick the wounded off, but we told him he doesn't go if they don't go."

Jif asked, "Taking any fire since you've been on the ground?"

"Don't think so. Hard to believe, considering we've been sitting here over five minutes."

Floyd cut in: "You're blocking the whole damn clearing. There's no room for us to set down. Maybe if you slid a little to the right…like the length of a rotor blade…drag those hangers-on with you if necessary. You can handle that, can't you?"

"That extra baggage won't let go. It might take a couple of bounces."

"Bounce all you want," Floyd said. "If they fall off the skids, that's tough shit. They don't belong there, anyway. Give it a try."

Then he asked Jif, "You're thinking what I'm thinking, right? The minute we set down, those strap-hangers will come running to us."

"Yeah, exactly. Can we handle five more souls?"

"Probably. And if it's not working, I'll make sure a couple of them end up in the trees. It'll ruin their whole day…but sorry about that. Better than ruining mine."

The Kiowa began its attempt at a hover-taxi to the right. As her pilot predicted, it involved several bounces and some dangerous dragging of the skids laterally along the ground. But the ship didn't tip over into a rotor strike, nobody fell off, and there was just enough room now for the LOACH to land beside her.

Floyd told the Kiowa pilot, "Outstanding. Now, as soon as we touch down, those gooks on the outside should come running to me. The second they let go of you, pour the coals on and get the hell out of there…and pray one of those clowns doesn't run into either of our tail rotors."

He'd called it perfectly. The LOACH hadn't even touched the ground yet, but the five skid riders from Gray's ship were already racing toward her. Floyd told the Kiowa pilot, "Okay, man, GO!" The lightened ship struggled into the air, clearing the trees at the edge of the clearing by inches. Once she picked up some forward speed, she was able to turn toward Khe Sanh and fly away.

Three of the LOACH's new passengers wedged themselves into the minuscule aft cabin. One of them was a major, the other two were captains. Jif couldn't tell the ranks of the duo who were riding the skids. Every one of the five looked crazed with fear. The major still had a .45 pistol holstered on his belt; all the rest had no weapons. Jif figured he knew why: *They probably threw their rifles away in a panic trying to escape whatever imaginary threat they thought they were facing.*

He and Floyd exchanged a look that meant, *Pretty sorry bunch, these ARVN officers.*

Then the pilot asked, "No one's wounded, so bring them to Ranger South, right? Quickest way to get rid of them."

"Roger that, Chief. I'll call ahead." He laughed to himself as he thought, *Maybe I'll even get through to them if they've remembered to do today's frequency changeover.*

It took all of two minutes to reach Ranger South. Once on the LZ, the major refused to leave the helicopter, demanding in English, "You will take me to Khe Sanh!"

"Sorry, pal," Floyd replied, "but this isn't a fucking taxi. Get out of my aircraft." But the man wouldn't budge.

At least he hasn't drawn his pistol yet, Jif thought as he stealthily slid his own .45 from its holster and held it in his lap. *It'd be a bloody shame to have to shoot him after just saving his ass.*

A lieutenant ran out to the LOACH accompanied by two sergeants. It was the same lieutenant who'd worked with Jif on his last trip to Ranger South, when he'd sorted out the frequency changeover problem. The situation was explained to him very quickly, resulting in the lieutenant directing his sergeants to remove the major from the chopper. They accomplished those orders without a moment's hesitation, relieving the protesting man of his pistol in the process.

That prompt compliance surprised the two Americans, but they wouldn't have been if they'd understood what the lieutenant had told his sergeants in Vietnamese: *The major has a concussion that's making him irrational. Take his weapon, ignore anything he says, and get him to the aid station immediately.*

When Jif thanked the lieutenant for his help, he replied, "Just returning the favor you did for us the other day, Captain. Are we even now?"

*****

After leaving Ranger South, Jif and Floyd had been back in the air over A Luoi for just a few minutes when a FAC came on frequency. His message: an RVNAF helicopter with the call sign of an ARVN C&C ship had gone down ten klicks west of A Luoi and less than a klick north of Route 9. "I've spotted the triple-A site that knocked her down, *Ball Point*, but I won't have any of my heavy hitters on station for a little while. Sounds like a job for artillery, anyway. Can you handle that?"

"Roger," Jif replied. "I'll see what I can work up."

He called in the fire mission to Lang Vei, suspecting it would be assigned to an ARVN battery. He was right. FSB 31 got the job.

Floyd asked, "Isn't it a little strange to have *two* ARVN C and C ships in the air at the same time? Doesn't that jack up the odds that your Colonel McKnight just got knocked down? He was with the armored brigade commander, right?"

"Yeah, he was, and you're right…those are pretty good odds," Jif replied. "I'm wondering what that ship was doing so far west of A Luoi. We didn't hear anything about a push down Route Niner."

"Want to have a look after you wrap up this fire mission?"

"Sounds like a plan, Chief."

"But I've got to say it again, sir…are we the only assholes flying recon in this fucked-up operation?"

*****

The fire mission against the triple-A site was over in less than two minutes. Judging by the secondary explosions and flames from the target area, it had been a success. After he called for the mission's termination, Jif asked Lang Vei, "Is *Ball Point Three-Six* on the net? I can't raise him."

That was Colonel McKnight's call sign.

The reply from Lang Vei: "Negative. No comm with your *Three-Six*."

"That could be real good or real bad," Floyd said to Jif. "Which one do you figure?"

"I haven't the faintest bloody idea, Chief. Let's go find that crashed ship."

*****

Still several klicks short of the reported location of the shot-down C&C Huey, they were surprised to see a column of six ARVN M41s rumbling west along Route 9. Four APCs were following the tanks. Floyd said, "Well, as I live and breathe…are we witnessing the rebirth of ARVN combined arms operations?" He couldn't have sounded more sarcastic if he tried.

Jif's reply was equally snide: "Rebirth? I must've missed the original one."

A klick farther down Route 9, they could see the crashed Huey in a lightly wooded area a few hundred meters north of the road. Even from a distance, it seemed obvious her flying days were over. There was no one around her. If there were still people inside, the LOACH was still too far away to tell.

"She managed to fly pretty far from the site that shot her down," Jif said. "But why'd she fly west? That's where the bad guys are coming from."

"They might've not been able to do anything else, sir," Floyd replied. "Got their controls shot out, maybe."

They never reached the crash site. An NVA tank suddenly appeared from a hull-down hide in a gulley. Seconds later, two more popped up. One of them had a turret-mounted machine gun, which began to spray rounds at the LOACH.

The terrain to the chopper's north rose rapidly, eliminating any chance of escape in that direction. To turn south would present an even easier-to-track target to the NVA gunner than she was now. The only direction that offered half a chance at a getaway was to fly straight ahead as quickly as possible, right over the tanks. Once past them, Floyd could dive the ship into the same gulley that had shielded the enemy vehicles. That wrinkle in the earth would then change roles and become the LOACH's salvation.

"HOLY BLOODY SHIT," Jif blurted as they closed rapidly on the NVA tanks. He could swear their chopper wasn't going over trees, but through them. Involuntarily, his body twisted away from the open doorway, a reflexive reaction to the illusion of being flogged by tree branches. Tracers that seemed the size of basketballs were sketching their dotted green lines around the ship.

But it was all over in just a few racing heartbeats. The instant the LOACH was beyond the tanks, a vicious left turn dropped her into the gulley—barely wide enough for her conveniently short rotor blades—allowing her a safe passage to Route 9. They didn't realize the NVA tanks were the light, amphibious PT-76s until they'd passed over them.

There'd been barely a chance to catch a breath when *Ball Point Three-Six*—Colonel McKnight—came on the freq, saying, "Slick move, *Three-Five*. You guys okay?"

"Just barely," was Jif's unsettled reply.

"Outstanding. Get to the south of Niner. It's about to hit the fan around here."

"Copy that," Jif replied. "Glad to hear your voice. Thought you might've been in that shot-down Huey over there."

"Almost was," the colonel replied, "but that's a story for later."

They could see McKnight's ship now—a LOACH—as it stood off well behind the ARVN armored column. She was orbiting several hundred feet off the deck, high enough to have a good perspective on the battleground but low enough so as not to be too tempting a target for triple-A gunners on the heights.

At first, the ARVN tankers, who outnumbered the PT-76s two to one, had what seemed an opportunity to engage the enemy with a high chance of success. If several M41s moved quickly west on Route 9, positioning themselves past the NVA tanks, the entire ARVN force could, in effect, create a horseshoe-shaped trap that pinned the NVA vehicles against hills to the north too steep for them to climb. It looked like two M41s had started to exploit that opportunity, driving quickly west…

And then they stopped. Jif's first thought was that the halt was to provide stabilized gun platforms for long-range shots, possibly knocking out one or two of the PT-76s before continuing the advance. But they were a little too far away, and they never fired. The PT-76s rearranged themselves, spreading farther apart without getting any closer to the ARVN vehicles.

"I don't like this," Colonel McKnight transmitted. Then he told Jif, "Search south, all the way down to the river. There might be more NVA armor hidden down that way. Our boys here could be in a world of hurt if that's true."

"If the colonel's right," Jif said to Floyd, "it could be the ARVN tankers who are trapped, not the other way around."

The FAC was back on the freq, announcing, "I've got inbound fast jets from the south, three-zero seconds out. Make a hole, make it wide."

"That's us he's talking to," Floyd said as threw the LOACH into an abrupt turn to the east. "Can you see those zoomies?"

"Negative," Jif replied.

But he did see the enemy artillery rounds impacting among the ARVN APCs on Route 9. "Holy shit! Incoming on the road."

Everyone else in the area saw the incoming, too. The FAC told his attacking jets, "ABORT, ABORT. AIRSPACE CONFLICT."

The zoomies didn't need to be told twice. When Jif finally saw them, they'd become just rapidly moving specks high in the sky, heading east.

The APCs were trying to turn and head east, as well, but not quickly enough. Two of them were knocked out almost immediately. Watching the devastation, Jif said, "The NVA's got to have an FO in those hills. He's intentionally not wasting rounds on the tanks but tearing up those APCs. I reckon they've got this whole road dialed in."

Dialed in or not, the other two APCs were making good their escape from the kill zone. For good measure, the NVA FO tried to shift fire to the M41s. The rounds impacting around them caused no harm; the tanks were racing east as fast as they could, too. The fight was over. The NVA had won without suffering so much as a scratch.

Floyd asked, "You see *Three-Six* anywhere? Don't tell me he got knocked down in all that."

But McKnight answered Jif's call promptly. "I'm a ways behind you," he said. "I need you back at Dong Ha as quick as you can get there. There's a hell of a lot to talk about."

And I'll bet it won't be a very cheery discussion, either, Jif surmised.

*****

Thirty kilometers to the southeast and oblivious to the tank fight turned artillery ambush on Route 9, Major Horace Hutchinson was exploring the border area between South Vietnam and Laos in a Kiowa, looking for something interesting to capture with the movie camera. His pilot, CW2 Jimmy Thigpen, was confused as to why they were even in that area. Hutchinson had given him no briefing before their flight and once airborne, was directing the pilot where to go as if guiding a taxi driver street by street through an unfamiliar neighborhood.

As Thigpen understood the PRT's mission from his previous flights with Captain Miles, they were supposed to be monitoring the operations of the ARVN. They'd done that today, however briefly, as soon as they'd crossed the border into Laos. The major had kept tabs on an ARVN infantry unit patrolling the slopes of the mountain on which FSB Hotel was perched. For the few minutes their chopper had remained in the area, the patrol had encountered no enemy forces.

In fact, Thigpen reflected, *I think those ARVN were making rude gestures at us, like we were giving away their location.*

Now they were exploring desolate jagged hills, sparse forest, and destroyed villages ten klicks southwest of Hotel. As far as Chief Thigpen was concerned, they were entirely too far from a friendly base for comfort: *We might as well be on the freakin' moon. If we go down for whatever reason, we're shit out of luck. It'll be ages before anyone comes looking for us...and they might never find us, anyway. But something tells me there's a method to the major's madness. I think he's trying to stay as far from any action as he possibly can.*

When he finally came right out and asked the major what he was looking for, the annoyed reply was, "The Ho Chi Minh Trail. That should be obvious."

The only thing obvious to Thigpen was that it sounded like total bullshit. "Half the Air Force looks for that trail every day and night, Major. I didn't think that was part of our mission."

"Our mission is whatever I say it is, Mister Thigpen. You just fly this bird."

"Yeah, sure, sir. But Captain Miles told me—"

Hutchinson cut him off. "Captain Miles is not on board this goddamn flying machine, Thigpen. I am…and I'm calling the shots now."

In the strained silence between them that followed, the major began to fiddle with the movie camera, sighting in on random terrain features but shooting no film. Thigpen kept tapping the fuel quantity gauge, hoping that with enough abuse, the needle could be coaxed to drop erroneously from its true near-full reading, prompting an immediate return to base. But the mechanical gremlins weren't working with him; the gauge continued to insist the tank had plenty of fuel remaining.

He was about to invent another bogus mechanical reason to abort the mission when Hutchinson blurted, "Turn around! Give me a one-eighty to the left." He picked up the movie camera again and started filming.

But Thigpen couldn't see what had the major so excited. He asked, "What've you got, sir? Where?"

"Trucks, Thigpen, trucks. A whole slew of them hiding in those woods. They're hidden pretty well, but—"

He froze in mid-sentence. Heavy machine guns from several locations were bracketing the Kiowa, laying a trap from which there'd be little chance of escape. A few harrowing and indecisive seconds passed before Thigpen initiated an evasive maneuver—a hard turn to the right that caused Hutchinson to lose his grip on the movie camera. It struck the lower edge of the open door frame, hanging there for a moment as if offering one last chance to reclaim it before surrendering to centrifugal force and gravity. That chance passed quickly; it toppled out of the ship.

For an anxious moment, they thought they'd slipped free. But then they felt the hammer blows of big rounds punching through the thin skin of the chopper. There was a mechanical shriek as the engine was dismantled by the remorseless projectiles, quickly followed by a heart-stopping quiet that signaled the dismantling was complete. Thigpen could feel the controls in his hands and at his feet becoming more ineffective by the moment. The ship was going down hard and fast, and there was nothing he could do to stop her.

Hutchinson, suddenly calm, like a man resigned to his fate, transmitted the *mayday* call. Included were the approximate coordinates of where they were about to crash. He began to report the location of the trucks, too, but he could tell by the loss of sidetone in his headset that the radio had probably stopped working.

He had no idea if anybody had heard the distress call.

Chapter Seven

Only Hutchinson's mayday had gotten through; nothing about the NVA trucks ever made it to the airwaves. But what had gone out was enough to locate the crash site. Just before sundown, a USAF HH-3—a *Jolly Green Giant* search and rescue helicopter—found CW2 Jimmy Thigpen alive but badly injured near the wreck of his Kiowa. He'd broken a leg in the crash as well as taken a general battering. He was conscious, frightened, but not in shock. And he was alone. Harry Hutchinson was gone.

"The major saved my life," Thigpen babbled to the pararescue jumper who'd come down on the hovering chopper's hoist to retrieve him.

"Who's *the major*?" the PJ asked, "and where the hell is he?"

"The gooks took him, I guess."

"Gooks…you mean the NVA?"

"I think so. I could hear them, but I couldn't see them."

"How come you couldn't see them?"

"I couldn't really move, anyway, so the major told me to play dead," Thigpen replied. "That's how he saved me. I didn't think it was going to work…I heard one of the gooks standing over me…I figured I'd get a bullet in my head just to make sure. But he didn't do a damn thing. If he'd kicked my leg, I wouldn't have been able to stay quiet." He paused before adding, "I guess I should be thankful to that gook for being a pussy."

The Jolly Green was halfway to the hospital at Quang Tri when Thigpen, speaking through the morphine haze, asked, "All those trucks the major spotted…did he really find the Ho Chi Minh Trail?"

"Kind of doubt it, Chief," the PJ replied. "There's absolutely nothing going on in that area. Whoever shot you down is long gone. Why the hell were you fucking around in the middle of nowhere, anyway?"

*****

Word of Thigpen's rescue and Hutchinson's possible captivity reached the combined headquarters at Dong Ha while the meeting of commanders and advisors was in progress. The first reaction of Lieutenant General Sutherland, commander of American forces supporting Lam Son 719, was one of annoyance: "Shit. This operation is only a week old, and already we've got an American POW in Laos."

"We're not sure he's a prisoner, sir," Colonel McKnight said. "At this point, he's still being considered missing in action."

"Somehow, Colonel, I don't see much difference in those classifications. If the NVA's got him, he's a propaganda gift to the commies and maybe that useless Laotian prince, too. We swore that American forces would not be on the ground in Laos, remember?"

"Regardless, sir, Hutchinson may have been on to something, maybe some enemy movement we're unaware of. They didn't shoot themselves down."

"Unfortunately, McKnight, that doesn't jive with any of our intel. If the NVA is going to send reinforcements to stop this incursion, they'll be coming from the north, not the south."

The senior ARVN officers in the room—a handful of generals and colonels—were enjoying the diversion of the Americans' attention as they agonized over one of their field-grade officers becoming a POW. Until now, the Americans had done little in this meeting but heap criticism on the ARVN leaders' performance and that of their units. The Vietnamese had already adopted a glassy-eyed indifference to the analyses and suggestions of their US allies, a reaction the Americans were quite used to.

But one point of contention was promptly resurrected as soon as discussion of the Hutchinson fiasco was put aside. It was the continuation of the argument that had resulted in Colonel McKnight getting booted from Colonel Ng's C&C chopper. McKnight picked up where he'd left off by telling General Sutherland, "As I was saying, sir, I think I've developed insight into the ARVN's so-called *combined arms tactics*, and it's not what you or I believe those tactics should be. As I've told Colonel Ng, he—"

Ng jumped up from his seat, pounded a fist on the conference table, and said, "And as I told you, Colonel McKnight, I do not work for you. You are not even my advisor. As far as the Republic of Vietnam is concerned, your opinions are irrelevant. The opinions of *all* of you are irrelevant."

It was obvious the other ARVN officers in the room were totally on board with that position. The Americans considered it ludicrous coming from a military that had never consistently stood on its own feet.

Sutherland: “Take your seat, Colonel Ng. I’m very interested in what Colonel McKnight has to say, gentlemen. Let him speak without further interruptions.”

“Thank you, sir,” McKnight said. “To continue, the conventional definition of combined arms operations is the efficient integration of infantry, armor, artillery, and air support units. The ARVN definition, however, has deleted the infantry and artillery from the equation, for the most part. Their basic tactic has become to use a small force of Colonel Ng’s armor—no more than a platoon of vehicles—as bait. Once the NVA takes that bait, the ARVN units withdraw rather than engage and depend on American air support to deal with the enemy. We’ve seen it time and time again in the few days they’ve been over the border. This campaign isn’t the ARVN against the NVA. It’s American airpower against the NVA, with the ARVN only occasionally taking an active combat role. Now that they’ve finally reached A Luoi, they’ve made no attempt to seize and hold terrain beyond that point.”

Sutherland said, “Colonel Ng, what do you have to say?”

“That is simply not true,” the ARVN colonel replied. He pointed to Jif, who was sitting along the wall with the other junior officers, and said, “Your own captain witnessed my tanks brilliantly destroy two NVA T-54s, tanks that by all accounts are superior to the obsolete M41s you Americans gave us.” Like a prosecutor about to reveal the smoking gun, Ng demanded, “You will tell us exactly what you saw, Captain.”

Unruffled by the colonel's bombast—and with a nod of permission from General Sutherland—Jif launched into his testimony. "What I saw, sir, was three of your tanks—in a rare and momentary display of teamwork—work together to destroy only one of two T-54s, and that vehicle had already destroyed one of your tanks. Your APCs carrying the supporting infantry fled the fight as soon as rounds were in the air, however."

Waving his arms in disagreement, Ng insisted, "My people destroyed *both* T-54s. That is an outstanding achievement."

"I'm afraid not, sir, " Jif countered. "The second T-54 was knocked out by our Cobra gunships, not your tankers. By the way, all your tanks were in jeopardy of being knocked out by a swarm of NVA sappers once your infantry withdrew. Fortunately, the Cobras neutralized those sappers, too, before you lost all your tanks."

McKnight allowed himself a hint of a smile as Jif's commentary came to an end.

But it had the opposite effect on Ng, who became enraged and began to rant in Vietnamese. The Americans couldn't follow much of it, but they were fairly sure of one thing: somewhere in that jumble of angry words, the colonel had called Captain Miles a liar.

"At ease, Colonel Ng," General Sutherland ordered. "Multiple sources have confirmed that Captain Miles is telling it like it is. Your insinuations to the contrary are uncalled for and unappreciated."

Ng's only reply was the look on his face; it was that same smirk he'd worn when he'd stated earlier, *I do not work for you.*

An American lieutenant colonel named Lowe—who was the advisor to Ng's brigade and who, by US government mandate, was forbidden to set foot in Laos—was no fan of McKnight's PRT meddling in his business. He was, however, a big fan of Colonel Ng. He asked to speak, and Sutherland granted him the floor.

"With all due respect, sir," Lowe began, "isn't the practice that Colonel McKnight has been disparaging—the use of ARVN armor as bait—actually a pretty smart tactic? In fact, isn't it an excellent use of the air support resources we provide while protecting their vulnerable armor from grievous losses?"

Sutherland snapped, "With all due respect or not, Lowe, that's a pretty shoddy analysis. M41s are not vulnerable when properly employed. And the practice might be *pretty smart* if the ARVN was actually using it to seize its objective. Let me remind all of you that the mission of the ARVN in Lam Son 719 is capture and hold Tchepone. The only way to do that is to engage and defeat the enemy on the ground. Air support has never held one inch of terrain on its own. You are relieved, Colonel Lowe. Report to my office immediately and wait until I'm done here."

Boyd Gray leaned over to Jif and whispered, "Did he just get shitcanned?"

"I reckon so, dude."

If Colonel Ng had also gotten the impression that his advisor had just been fired, he didn't seem to care.

The ARVN generals in the room—two division commanders, one assistant division commander—had grown quietly livid at the continuous bashing being dealt them by the Americans. But the two division commanders—the ranking Vietnamese in the room—

preferred to continue their seething in insolent silence. They delegated the assistant division commander—a brigadier general, the ADC of the Airborne—to issue their rebuttal. The brigadier lashed out, saying, "Our forces have amassed very large body counts, General Sutherland. Every patrol finds scores—sometimes hundreds—of NVA dead."

Sutherland sneered at that assertion. "The only people inflicting mass casualties on the NVA are the B-52s and fighter-bombers of the United States Air Force. Mopping up after their bombing raids does not constitute *your* body count, General. It's theirs. But your mission is not to tally bodies or engage in penny-ante skirmishes and then gloat over the fucking handful of weapons and sacks of rice you captured. Your mission is to reach and hold Tchepone, disrupting that Ho Chi Minh Trail waypoint in order to starve the NVA of supplies. Then you're supposed to hold it until the rainy season begins again and does that job for us."

The Airborne ADC asked, "Are you implying our men are not fighting?"

"I'm not implying it, General," Sutherland replied. "I'm saying it straight up. But it's not the men's fault. It's the fault of commanders who'd rather be politicians than combat leaders."

"Now it is your comments that are uncalled for and unappreciated," the ADC replied. With a nod to the other ARVN officers in the room, he added, "You'd like us to ignore that our primary job is to protect our soldiers, I suppose?"

"If all you're interested in is protecting your soldiers," Sutherland replied, "you might as well ship them back to their barracks in Saigon. They'll be nice and safe there, and I won't be sacrificing any more of my aviation resources catering to your inaction."

As if obeying some silent signal, the ARVN generals rose from the table as one and headed for the door. The Airborne ADC said, "We believe you've insulted us enough for one evening, General."

Sutherland wasn't finished. "I have two questions before you go," he said. "First, we have yet to see the actual commander of the Airborne Division in the field. When can we expect him to drag himself off President Thieu's lap in Saigon and make an appearance at this headquarters?"

The Americans already knew the answer to that one: *never*. The Airborne Division commander—a favorite of President Thieu—outranked the ARVN supreme commander of Lam Son 719, another Thieu acolyte who left Saigon only occasionally. Flexing his seniority, the Airborne commander was refusing to take orders from a subordinate. Though this unorthodox situation was devastating to the unity of command needed for this operation, the president did nothing about it. *After all,* Sutherland told himself, *he's the one who created it. He picks the generals, and loyalty beats competence any day. As usual, warfighting is taking a back seat to political games. Welcome to another day in the Republic of Vietnam.*

Sutherland asked his second question: "Your battalions in A Luoi seem to be getting very comfortable there. But you're already days behind your own published schedule, and A Luoi isn't the objective of this operation. When can we expect the move from there to Tchepone to begin?"

"In good time, General Sutherland. "We are evaluating the situation. We will advance when we are ready."

*****

In good time stretched to one week, with no significant movement of ARVN forces toward Tchepone. The capture of Major Horace "Harry" Hutchinson was confirmed by Radio Hanoi and, as expected, was turned into anti-American propaganda aimed both at the Laotian officials who were half-heartedly cooperating with Lam Son 719 and the American public.

"The government of the United States continues to tell its lies to the world," the broadcaster from Hanoi announced. "They claim there are no American *boots on the ground*, but the capture of this officer—this American spy—as he violated the sovereignty of the Kingdom of Laos proves otherwise. The fact that he purports to be an unfortunate aviator is merely a ruse. He is an enemy agent and will be treated as such."

Listening to the broadcast at Dong Ha, Boyd Gray said, "What's this *purports to be an aviator* bullcrap? I guess the NVA doesn't know the difference between pilot's wings and the aircrew wings Hutchinson wears."

"Doesn't bloody matter, anyway," Jif replied. "He's just another bargaining chip for that peace conference charade going on in Paris."

Colonel McKnight joined them with some news: "No point in flying today, gentlemen. Once again, there are no offensive ops to observe, I'm afraid."

"Just like it's been the past week," Jif said. "Plenty of contact north of Route Niner but no forward movement. It's like the ARVN's just playing defense now."

Gray added, "I hear the advisors are pushing the rumor that since we've got nothing to do, the PRT's being disbanded. Any truth to that, sir?"

"Negative," McKnight replied. "MACV is still convinced the ARVN will be getting off their asses any day now, and our eyes will be more needed than ever once they do. Don't unpack your flight bags just yet." Then he added, "And by the way, those rumors are coming from none other than our dear friend, Brigadier General Parton. He's no fan of our operation, that's for damn sure."

"Yeah," Jif said, "but he sure thinks those Rangers he advises walk on water."

"And I'm not sure why," McKnight added. "The Rangers have been good fighters in the past, with decent leadership, but they're taking an awful beating at Ranger North right now. NVA artillery alone is pounding their asses every damn day. If this keeps up, they're going to lose that place. Parton's trying to sugarcoat it, but I don't think General Sutherland's buying it."

Gray asked, "You think he's going to get fired, too, just like Colonel Lowe?"

"I kind of doubt it, Boyd. Generals swim in a different pool than colonels, you know?"

Thumbing through a summary of the previous day's sitreps, Jif said, "This NVA artillery is a bloody nightmare. I'm surprised A Luoi hasn't been leveled already. I just can't believe how little success air recon has had locating and destroying the firing points."

"They're doing all they can, Jif," McKnight replied. "You know the scenario…they've got *Stinger* and *Spectre* gunships working in twos and threes all night long. You're a cannon-cocker…you know how easy it can be to hide artillery pieces, especially in the dark."

"Yeah…or in mountainous terrain loaded with caves," Jif added. "Even with top-notch target acquisition, it's hard to take out a piece that's tucked into the side of a mountain. That's the same problem we had when relieving Khe Sanh back in '68. Every night, we got plastered by artillery firing from Laos that nobody could ever find. But what gets me is they're firing 122-millimeter rockets all over the place, too. Hell, they even dropped some long-range shots on Vandegrift the other day. They were accurate enough to cause some KIA."

McKnight watched as Jif plotted arcs on a map, trying to deduce the locations of NVA artillery sites farther west in Laos, beyond Tchepone. He knew what was on his captain's mind: "You think this team could be looking for those artillery locations rather than sitting here with our thumbs up our asses, don't you, Miles?"

"Affirmative, sir."

"I hate to piss on a man's dream, Jif, but the answer is no. It's not our job…and you're not the only dude with crossed cannons on your collar. General Sutherland's G2 has a team computing the likely firing locations, just like you're doing."

"But we could be helping them, sir. More eyes on the prize."

"Look…I've already lost Captain Jamerson to bullshit politics, and only God knows why I lost Major

Hutchinson. I don't plan on losing any more of my team...especially over something that's outside our mission. So again, the answer is *no*, Captain Miles. Are you reading me?"

"Loud and clear, sir."

*****

During the following week, the ARVN moved not an inch closer to Tchepone. Instead, they were losing ground. After a week of brutal bombardments and intense ground assaults, Ranger North was abandoned, its personnel fleeing to Ranger South. Only half of its four-hundred-man complement survived the evacuation, and only half of those survivors were still fit for combat.

The demise of FSB 31 followed a few days later when it was overrun by NVA forces that had swelled to a two-to-one advantage over the ARVN.

"These NVA reinforcements didn't come from North Vietnam like we expected," General Sutherland told his assembled commanders and staff. "They've come from the south. We're seeing regiments in this area of operations that we know were in the A Shau a few weeks ago. It just took them a couple of weeks to get here...a couple of weeks the ARVN's sluggish performance gave them."

Colonel McKnight added, "According to the latest debrief of the pilot who was flying Major Hutchinson, they'd encountered an NVA truck convoy right before being shot down. The major apparently thought he'd found a branch of the Ho Chi Minh Trail, but it could've been reinforcements coming up from the A Shau. Too bad we didn't know about that at the time."

"Yeah, it's a fucking shame," Sutherland replied. "As you know, General Abrams arrived here at Dong Ha this morning. He's working with the ARVN high command to save this fiasco. It looks like we'll be shifting emphasis from north of Route Niner to the south. Forget the armored push to Tchepone—that's not going to happen. We'll get there by conducting a massive airmobile infantry operation instead."

McKnight asked, "Any plans to step up the search for the NVA artillery sites, sir?"

"In fact, there are. We're bringing in some unique assets to enhance our nighttime aerial recon capabilities. Until those assets are in place in a few days, I'm not able to discuss how they'll be used. In the meantime, we've got less than a week to organize a major air assault by the ARVN. We're going to need every helicopter we can get in the air to move them."

The members of the PRT knew what that meant: they'd be giving up their helicopters for the duration of the air assault.

Chapter Eight

With Colonel McKnight's permission, Jif was occupying his slack time at General Sutherland's headquarters, working with the artillery target acquisition team from the G2 shop. The team leader—a major named Mercer—introduced him to the problems they faced while trying to track down the NVA artillery sites: "To put it simply, Miles, the ARVN's target acquisition capabilities are for shit. Rarely do we get good data that allows us to pinpoint the firing location of a tube precisely. Most of their plot lines intersect well beyond the range of any weapon the NVA employs, and usually in terrain so rugged it would take big helicopters—the ones they don't have—to emplace the guns. The rockets launch sites are even harder to calculate without target acquisition radar or visuals on the launches, as I'm sure you're aware."

Jif: "Affirmative, sir. I know the drill."

"What's really pissing us off," the major continued, "is the Air Force's flareships and gunships, as well as the Navy's night-stalking Intruders, can't seem to catch a break. We all know the NVA guns, their ammo carriers, and the launcher trucks have to be moving around constantly, and they're probably doing it in the dark. But still, the flyboys are coming up with dog squat."

Jif asked, "What about caves, sir? Are there any in the possible areas?"

"Our information is really sketchy on that. Getting intel out of the Royal Lao Army is like pulling teeth…makes you wonder whose side they're really on. Supposedly, there are a handful of caves that could hold one gun. But concealing a platoon or battery…that's pretty unlikely. And of course, you can't fire a rocket from a cave unless you're a kamikaze. That's got to be done in the open."

"What about no-fire zones, sir? I don't see any marked on your charts."

"There are a few, Miles, mostly around villages southwest of Tchepone. But they're not being advertised to anyone besides our airstrike assets. I'm sure you know why."

"Sure," Jif replied. "There are ARVN staff officers all over this place, and if that intel gets into their hands—"

Mercer cut him off with a smile. "Like you said, you know the drill. If the ARVN knows something, there's a damn good chance the NVA knows it, too, and will exploit that information to their advantage. The leakage rate around this headquarters is un-fucking-believable. We've been pumping out bogus intel just to keep the bad guys off balance. And as far as those no-fire zones go, they're beyond ARVN artillery range at the moment, anyway, so they don't have the need to know."

A familiar voice boomed from the doorway. "I'll be damned. They let anybody in here."

As he and Sergeant Major Sean Moon shared an enthusiastic handshake, Jif said, "I figured you'd be around. Where General Abrams goes, so goes his sergeant major. But we're all in big trouble now."

That puzzled Major Mercer, who asked, "I can see you two know each other pretty well, but why are *we* in trouble?"

Jif replied, "Because every time the sergeant major and I get together, the shit hits the fan."

Sean added, "That's straight skinny, Major. It's like the gooks will get extra points for killing us together. And believe me, they've tried a few times."

But this wasn't a social visit. Sean presented himself to the G2, telling him, "Colonel, General Abrams is ready for you now. Follow me, if you will, sir."

As the G2 and a few of his people gathered their presentation material, Sean asked Jif, "You going to be working here all day, Captain?"

"Yeah. Don't have much else to do at the moment."

"Outstanding. Then I should be able to find you real easy. Save me some of that coffee, okay? It smells damn good."

*****

It was hours later when Sean was finally able to break free for a few minutes. He and Jif stepped outside the headquarters building to enjoy their coffee in the warm breeze of dusk. "Pull up a chair, Sergeant Major," Jif said as he offered Sean one of the five-gallon buckets the headquarters staff used for lawn chairs. A large cable spool, empty and turned on its side, served as a table.

"Seen my dad lately?" Jif asked.

"Nope. I hear he's been spending a lot of time in Vientiane, trying to keep the Laotians on board with this clusterfuck. They know plenty about what the North Vietnamese are doing within their borders, but they're keeping much too quiet about it."

"Like they're trying to play both sides of the fence, you mean?"

"Exactly, Captain, exactly." He smirked while adding, "You ever considered going into foreign service work?"

"You wouldn't be busting my balls, would you, Sergeant Major?"

"Wouldn't think of it, sir," he replied with a wink.

"Good to know. But level with me…is there any hope we'll be able to help the ARVN save this colossal fuckup?"

"If we could stick a sock in President Thieu's mouth for a couple weeks, then maybe there'd be a chance. But he's got an election coming up, and he's panicking that this operation's making him look bad…especially since those two hotshot reporters got killed when the chopper they were on got shot down. So he's been interfering with his generals' decisions way too much—he wants the appearance of victory without spilling too much ARVN blood—and those handpicked commanders of his ain't worth shit, anyway, with the rare exception or two."

"I don't know why he's worried about the election," Jif said. "In this country, all that hoopla just rubber stamps the person everyone already knows is going to win. Unless, of course, he's afraid of another coup."

Sean laughed as he said, "Again, Captain, have you ever considered going into foreign service? But seriously, Thieu's at the point where he just wants some of his forces to reach Tchepone so he can claim he disrupted the Ho Chi Minh Trail. Then he wants to pull the plug on the whole shebang."

"So they won't be holding Tchepone until the end of April, like the original plan says?"

"That's still what General Abe wants," Sean replied. "But Thieu's the puppet master here, I'm afraid."

"What about Washington? Aren't they worried about this operation failing?"

"I tell you, Captain…as long as American boys aren't dying in large numbers, Washington doesn't give a shit. This is what Vietnamization looks like to them, and they're fine with it. What bugs me, though, is that when Lam Son 719 falls on its ass, General Abe is going to take it in the shorts from those same politicians, even though the execution of this circle jerk is out of his hands."

Jif asked, "What ARVN unit will be tasked with the airmobile assault of Tchepone?"

"First Division. Compared to the Airborne and the Rangers, they're the least beat up right now."

"But are they the best unit for the job, Sergeant Major?"

"On paper, sure. But in actuality, nobody has a clue. Leadership's still a big variable. You know what really has General Abe worried? That old axiom that it's better for all your units to be average performers. No stars, no duds. You've heard the tale…the stars get thrown into the worst shit right off the bat and become combat ineffective before you know it. They collapse, and then all their sister units get enveloped and collapse, too. Same result with the duds. They get overrun in a heartbeat, and that breach causes everyone else to fall like dominoes. But if every unit is average, there's no weak outfit to exploit, and there tend to be no calamities."

Jif: "Okay, so as far as MACV's concerned, how do the ARVN outfits in this operation rank?"

"The Rangers are the stars…or at least they were until they got the shit beat out of them last week. The Airborne and the Marines are average. The other units are all duds."

"In other words, they're screwed?"

"That's the gospel truth, Captain."

Sean checked his watch, took a last gulp of coffee, and said, "I've gotta run. Supper break is just about over for the honchos. We'll be spending all night parceling out helicopter assets for this airmobile push coming up. Wait until those aviator types hear what they'll be expected to do. They'll be crying big tears real soon."

*****

Jif lingered outside after Sean left, watching the activity on the airfield adjacent to the headquarters. Darkness had nearly settled in when a strange aircraft rolled almost noiselessly onto the ramp. She'd made so little noise—just the highly muffled purr of her engine—that he hadn't been aware of her landing.

He'd never seen that type of ship before, but he'd heard of it: the YO-3A *Quiet Star*, a night surveillance aircraft so silent in flight that the sounds of her engine and propeller were virtually inaudible to those she flew over. With her wide-span, narrow-chord wings, she looked more like the sailplane from which she was derived than a conventional single-engine aircraft. Ground crewmen wasted no time pushing her into a revetment that concealed the unorthodox airframe.

So this is the "unique asset" for nighttime aerial recon General Sutherland was talking about, Jif thought. *I've got to have a look at this.*

When he reached the revetment, the plane had been shut down and her two-man crew had climbed from her tandem cockpit. But one of them, a warrant officer, seemed more in a rush than his partner; he jumped from the wing to the ground and immediately went to his knees, upchucking the contents of his stomach.

Jif recognized the other crewman: Jack Northcutt. He was the ship's pilot, and he'd attended artillery school with Jif back in '67, when they were both brand new second lieutenants. He'd earned his wings the following year. He, too, was now a captain.

"That you, Jif? What the fuck are you doing in this shithole?"

"Same as you, Jack, living the dream. What's the matter with your buddy?"

"My sensor operator appears to have a bad case of the punies. I think it's food poisoning. But I've got to say I'm proud of Mister Summers. He managed not to barf in the aircraft, even though he felt it coming on as soon as we left Phu Bai. Kinda puts the screws to the mission we were supposed to fly tonight, though. You know where the G2 shop is?"

"Yeah," Jif replied, "it's right through that door."

The medics they'd called for while still in the air drove up, and Summers was loaded into their vehicle.

Northcutt told Jif, "Okay, let's go give them the bad news…no flying for *Silent Sara* tonight."

"Wait a minute, Jack. What does the sensor operator do, anyway? I've done a shitload of aerial observer work…is it something I can learn real fast?"

"Man, you ain't too eager, are you? What are you trying to get out of?"

"Actually, nothing, because I'm underemployed at the moment. I'm trying to get *into* something…and if that something means finding some of that NVA artillery that's plastering the shit out of us, I'm all in."

Northcutt asked, "Well…did you ever use night vision gear?"

"Like a starlight scope?"

"Sort of…only this ship's equipment doesn't overload quite so easily when you stumble into something really bright. Climb in the front seat and have a look-see."

After a ten-minute familiarization, Jif felt confident he could use the night vision periscope. But he asked, "What's this thing next to it do?"

"That controls the infrared illuminator. It can bump the brightness of stuff you see in the scope way up. And being in the infrared spectrum, it's invisible to dudes on the ground."

"Cool. Now how about this panel? What does it do?"

"It's for the laser target designator. Forget about it. We don't use it."

"How come, Jack?"

"The strike aircraft have to have laser finders on board to see the marker, and almost none of them have it yet, so the system is just along for the ride."

"Copy that," Jif said. "How do we navigate? Finding things in the dark doesn't do much good if we don't know their coordinates."

"Radio beams, my man. TACAN, ADF…we shoot the bearings, plot them on the map. So…you think you can handle it?"

"Piece of cake, Jack. All I've got to do is point the scope and read the dials, right?"

"Pretty much. Let's see what the G2 has to say about it. He's my boss for this circus."

*****

When Jif told the G2 that he'd be glad to ride as the sensor operator on *Silent Sara*, the colonel seemed skeptical at first. But after thinking it over for a moment, he said, "I've got no problem with it, Miles, but you work for Colonel McKnight, not me. If he's good with you doing it, so am I. Personally, though, I think you're both out of your fucking minds. You're not exactly trained for the sensor operator's job, and things could get real hairy for you, Northcutt, having to run an OJT session over hostile territory."

"I'm willing to give him a chance, sir. Jif and I go back a ways, and he's a super-fast learner. The job's not exactly rocket science, anyway."

"If you say so, Captain," the G2 said. "Actually, I'm thrilled to have you. I really didn't think the honchos at the aviation brigade would agree to risking one of their precious YO-3s to help out the ARVN. How were you lucky enough to get picked for this mission?"

"Let's just say that I drew the short straw, sir," Northcutt replied.

When they tracked down Colonel McKnight in a meeting with MACV staff, his only question was, "Are you sure there's no one else on this base who can do it?"

"Affirmative, sir," Northcutt replied. "The *Quiet Star* fleet is a pretty small community. The ailing Mister Summers and yours truly are its only representatives here at Dong Ha."

"So be it, then," McKnight said. "Good luck to you both…and don't come back until you find that fucking artillery."

He didn't sound like he was kidding.

*****

There'd be a good hour of preflight planning and coordination before the YO-3A could take to the night sky. Working with Major Mercer's team, Jif and Northcutt plotted the most likely search areas. Then they shared this information with the Air Force liaison officer and his staff. "The most important thing," Northcutt told the air liaison, "is we need complete darkness to do our job right. Keep the damn flareships as far away as possible when we're on station. If they kick out just one of those *midnight suns* within eight klicks of us, or turn on a floodlight, that's the ballgame. Make all the noise you want but absolutely no artificial light. Once we spot a target, we'll report the coordinates and description to the control ship. Then we'll get out of your way so you can do your thing any way you see fit."

There was one other concern. Two of the search areas had terrain that rose rapidly to a thousand feet or more at their western boundaries. "When we're working those boxes," Northcutt explained, "we can't go below fifteen hundred feet. I don't need the report on my cause of death reading *controlled flight into terrain*. But don't worry...you'll still be able to see everything you need through the scope. At the other areas, though, we'll be able to go a lot lower."

Jif: "How low are we talking?"

"Two or three hundred feet, maybe."

"And the gooks won't see or hear us?"

"Nope," Northcutt replied.

*****

Silent Sara departed Dong Ha at 2200 hours. She followed Route 9 at the leisurely pace of one hundred miles per hour, cruising undetected over Quang Tri Province. That flight path provided Jif with several familiar locations to help him get used to the workings of the night vision periscope and infrared illuminator. Each place the ship passed over—Vandegrift Combat Base, Khe Sanh, Lang Vei—provided him another lesson in observing ground targets and coordinating with the pilot. By the time they reached the border thirty-five minutes after takeoff, Jif and Jack Northcutt felt ready for some serious hunting.

Once inside Laos, the ARVN firebase at A Luoi was the last friendly position they'd get to observe. "It's nothing but bad guys beyond here," Jif said. But they saw nothing of the enemy until reaching the village of Tchepone, identified by its road intersections and abandoned airfield. "The place looks kind of dead," Northcutt said. "Got anything moving down there?"

"Yeah…got a little bit of action. Couple of dudes walking around…a few trucks unloading cargo. But all in all, nothing worth calling in the world on them."

"Kind of surprising, Jif, considering it's supposed to be this big waypoint on the Ho Chi Minh. You'd expect a lot more activity, wouldn't you?"

"Roger that."

After confirming to the air control ship that they were approaching the first search area, Northcutt brought *Sara* down to five hundred feet. He told Jif, "Forty-five-degree turn to the left coming up in niner-zero seconds. That'll take us right across the box. Do you have a good grip on exactly where we are?"

Jif read off the coordinates of the grid square they were flying over. Northcutt replied, "Affirmative. We're thinking as one, amigo."

"I'm starting my scan, Jack."

But that search area had nothing to reveal. They moved on to the next one.

Northcutt: "You want me to go lower?"

"Not especially. I think I've got a damn good field of…HOLY SHIT!"

"What? Is it guns? Rockets?"

"Negative," Jif replied. "I've got a convoy…maybe more than one. There's a shitload of trucks moving south. I'm up to twenty-five vehicles and still counting."

Sounding skeptical, Northcutt said, "There's not even a road or trail showing on the map."

"Yeah, tell me about it, Jack. It looks like the gooks cut a trail of their own. They do that a lot, you know?"

"But are there any guns or rocket launchers?"

"Nope. Nothing but Russian deuces. They look like they're loaded to the rails, too. This infrared illuminator is hot shit. I can almost read the markings on the crates. I'm betting there are weapons and ammo inside."

Northcutt said, "Do we call this in right now and let Stinger and Spectre work them over, or keep looking for firing points?"

"Let's call it in now, before we lose them in the hills. After the gunships are done with them, we can come back and keep looking for artillery. You say we've got about three hours of fuel left?"

"Yeah, but cut that in half for mission purposes. We've got to figure in some hold time while the gunships have their fun…and we need an hour to get back to Dong Ha."

"Plenty of time," Jif replied.

"I'm not so sure about that, dude. But go ahead…call it in."

The voice from the air control ship copied the target information but had some news to pass on. "Be advised, *Night Eyes*, the metro forecast has changed. Pop-up T-storms rolling in from the southeast along the Route Niner corridor, ETA three-zero minutes."

"Dammit," Northcutt said. "That's all we fucking need…a storm between us and home. That shit was supposed to be well to the north of us, like all the way up in the DMZ."

Jif asked, "Can't we get around the weather?"

"Are you shitting me, man? Look…we've only got a handful of YO-3s in country, and in a year's operation, we've never lost one to ground fire. But we have lost two…one crashed due to a mechanical, and the other bought it trying to land in bad weather. See those big long glider wings out there? They're meant for fair weather ops only, amigo. Crosswinds and big gusts just might kill us."

"So what do we do about it, Jack?"

"We pray a lot, man."

Chapter Nine

Silent Sara and her crew were out of harm's way, at least for the moment. Northcutt had flown her to a holding pattern over the lowlands near the abandoned Tchepone airfield, bounded by landmarks that were easily identifiable even at night: Route 9 to the south and the Namkok River to the north.

Ten kilometers to the southwest, two USAF *Stinger* gunships were moving in to riddle the NVA convoy Jif had spotted. Any moment, they'd begin the first act of their unearthly light show by dispensing million-candlepower parachute flares.

The second act would be performed by their 7.62-millimeter miniguns and rapid-firing 20-millimeter cannons as they spewed red-orange cones of gunfire down to killing fields on the ground.

Well to the east, bolts of cloud-to-ground lightning flashed nonstop, turning the night sky between *Sara* and any friendly airfield into a different sort of killing field, a meteorological one.

"This feels like we're the meat in a death sandwich," Jif said to Northcutt.

"We'll be all right for the time being, amigo." The tension in the pilot's voice negated whatever comfort his reply had tried to offer.

The gunships were raining death and destruction on the NVA convoy. The fiery explosions, raging blazes, and pyrotechnic displays that resulted left no doubt the trucks had been carrying explosives. After completing two firing orbits over the target in ninety seconds, the gunship pilots declared the job done and left the area. *Silent Sara* was cleared to continue her recon.

"How are we doing on fuel?" Jif asked.

"We've got about five minutes less than the last time you asked. Ready to pick up where we left off?"

"Roger that."

Northcutt: "Okay, I've got a heading of one-six-five degrees to skirt that massif to our south. Check or hold?"

"Check. One-six-five looks good."

"Once we're past that rock in the sky, we follow the Banghiang River south to the next target box."

"Keep west of the river," Jif said. "No guns are going to be on the east bank. They'd have to fire high-angle to get over those hills, and we're just not seeing any high-angle impact craters from their incoming."

"I've never seen a high-angle crater," Northcutt said. "What do they look like?"

"Kind of round, not oval. And deep."

"How do you shoot a back azimuth off something like that when you're plotting counter-battery fire?"

"With great difficulty," Jif replied, "and very little precision."

*****

The storm to the east seemed to be intensifying. Jif said, "It looks like the bloody thing isn't even moving."

Northcutt asked the control ship for an updated forecast. The reply wasn't encouraging; the storm was, in fact, moving, but there was another line right behind it. From their perspective, having one storm behind the other gave the appearance of a stationary tempest. But beneath that illusion was the reality that the combined storms posed a lingering obstacle to their flight back to base.

The search of the next suspected area proved fruitless. There was only one more to go and barely enough fuel to do it. "I'd turn back right now," Northcutt said, "but maybe if we hang out just a little longer, that storm will be out of our way for the ride home. Then we won't get our brains beat in..."

He was about to add, *or worse*, but stopped himself.

Jif asked, "How long is *just a little longer*?"

"Two-zero mikes. That's bingo fuel..."

Again, he was about to add, *I'm pretty sure*, but didn't.

*****

Most of those twenty minutes went by without another sighting. With *Sara* flying at eight hundred feet, Jif was scanning the half-circle in front of the aircraft when the night vision scope lit up as if a flashbulb had just gone off. "Got something," he said.

"No shit, dude," Northcutt replied, almost shrieking. "Hang on!"

He was still talking as he abruptly threw the plane into a ninety-degree turn to the left. It wasn't enough warning to keep Jif's head from banging into the canopy.

Northcutt said, "I didn't need the scope to see that big-ass rocket that just crossed pretty damn close in front of us. Check your two o'clock, dude. The launch site's got to be right around there. Don't want to fly right through their trajectory."

Jif didn't hear much of that. His headset had been knocked off when it hit the canopy. He was struggling to get it back over his ears with one hand while still working the night vision gear with the other.

"You okay, Jif? Sorry about that."

Another rocket was fired, the flash of its ignition giving Jif all the light he needed to make out the launch site clearly in the scope.

"Don't be sorry, Jack. We just found ourselves another target."

"Call it in quick, dude. Our loiter time is just about up. How many launchers are there?"

"Four total. Two still have rockets on them."

"Good," Northcutt said. "They may not have time to move before the Air Force shows up."

The control ship reported a Spectre gunship was three minutes out. Jif asked, "We can wait, can't we? The gooks might start moving. Don't want the Air Force to lose them."

"I'll give it one more mike," Northcutt replied. "Then we've got to go, man."

They made another pass of the launch site, this one lower at four hundred feet. Illuminated by the infrared beam, Jif could plainly see men scurrying around the rockets yet to be launched. "They're real busy down there," he told Northcutt, "but I can't tell if they're preparing to fire or cutting a chogie."

"Keep watching, amigo. You've got two-five seconds left."

Jif found this casual orbiting above an enemy position terrifying and exhilarating all at once. He told Northcutt, "This is some bloody hot shit. They really don't know we're right above them, do they?"

"Nope. But the fun's over. Time to go. Confirm target position with the control ship and let's boogie."

Silent Sara was two kilometers away from the rocket site when Spectre rolled in, obliterating the enemy position with her cannons. Her crew hadn't bothered to light up the target area with flares or the searchlight.

"I guess they didn't need to," Northcutt said. "Spectre's got low-light TV to spot stuff in the dark…and you gave them an outstanding target placement to begin with."

In a matter of seconds, rapid-firing cannons blew up the site, including the rockets that hadn't been launched. The resulting flare-up from the incineration of explosive warheads and fuel lit the night, promising an inferno that would last awhile. The blaze lit up the cockpit of *Silent Sara*, causing Northcutt to swear: "Fucking shit! That fire's silhouetting us against the clouds. We were too goddamn close to the kill zone. We waited too long to get out of there."

It sounded like a death sentence. But as the moments passed without any enemy fire rising to meet their low-flying ship, their attention was refocused to the other perils they faced: the thunderstorm and their dwindling fuel supply.

"We're not going to climb," Northcutt said. "It'll waste too much fuel, and we'll never get over this storm, anyway."

Jif asked, "So I reckon we've got to stick to Route Niner all the way back?"

"Well, we need something as a guide so we don't blunder into the mountains. We can't climb over them, either. That brings up another problem. Where's the triple-A the worst? North or south of Niner?"

"It's worse on the north side," Jif replied.

"We won't be flying much higher than the five hundred feet we're at now. If I shade it a little to the south of Niner…like maybe follow the Sepon River instead of the road…you think that'll be okay?"

"Yeah, it'll be no different than flying in a Huey…same speed and everything…just nobody will hear us. But don't go south of the river. That high ground pops up awfully fast."

"Okay," Northcutt said. "I'm depending on you and that night scope to keep me honest."

*****

They were ten kilometers west of A Luoi when they met the full fury of the storm. Intense rain turned the canopy into a near-opaque bubble and rendered the night vision scope—even with infrared assist—useless. Northcutt had no choice but to hold heading and altitude blindly as the ship was tossed violently about by the gusty, turbulent winds. The sound alone of the deluge pounding against her thin aluminum skin was enough to scare a man half to death.

"This can't last long," Jif said, convincing neither of them. "It's not monsoon season yet."

But they both knew that even two or three minutes in conditions like this could bring on a crash-and-burn calamity. Jif asked, "Have you ever flown through anything like this before?"

"Yeah, but in a much sturdier airplane, not a souped-up glider like *Sara* here."

There was so much lightning. They were sure the plane was being illuminated to gunners on the ground in the strobe-like flashes. The only comforting thought: *Surely the NVA won't expect any idiots to be flying around in the dark in a storm like this. Maybe those gunners are taking the night off.*

Then a whole new sort of illumination plagued the ship. The air was so charged with static electricity that her entire airframe began to glow a bright purple. The electrical charge on the ship caused other problems, too. The crackle in their headsets was almost unbearable; the jittering magnetic compasses atop their instrument panels became useless ornaments.

"This directional gyro better not quit on me," Northcutt said. "With the mag compasses out of whack, it's the only thing keeping us pointed in the right direction. I'm worried this wind is making us drift north, though. You sure you've got no ground reference in the scope?"

"Not a bloody thing, Jack. We should be almost to A Luoi, though…"

If we didn't get blown off course went without saying.

"We're not as far along as you think, Jif. With this wind in our face, we've got great airspeed but diddly for ground speed."

And then, they thought they'd caught a break. The rain slackened; though they still couldn't see the ground with the naked eye, Jif thought he'd spotted the river in the scope. But it was much too far to the south, and that meant Route 9 should be south of them, as well, but closer. He couldn't see it, though, and the infrared illuminator was rendered useless as even this reduced amount of rain diffused its beam. He told Northcutt, "I reckon we're much farther north than we should be. Not sure *how* much, but—"

"You mean like we could be flying into the mountains?"

"Affirmative."

Northcutt started *Sara* into an abrupt right turn that changed her heading nearly forty-five degrees, losing about a hundred feet of altitude in the process. When she leveled out, Jif thought he could make out Route 9 in the scope. But it was much too far ahead of them than he'd hoped. They were still probably over rising terrain.

"We'd better climb right bloody now, Jack."

Northcutt asked no questions, just added power and brought the ship's nose up. Shuddering and lurching as she clawed her way up into the turbulent sky, *Sara* seemed to be winning for a few moments, holding a modest but steady rate of climb.

And then the bottom fell out. A downdraft began to push her toward the ground like a giant hand. The altimeters were going down in fits and starts as if someone was setting back a clock.

Northcutt instinctively hauled back on the stick, but that did nothing to slow the plummet. There was no training, no procedure, for being caught in a severe downdraft this close to the ground. Not knowing what else to do, he pushed the throttle to the stop and eased the stick forward.

He asked Jif, "We gonna hit trees?"

"Can't tell…"

They were so low that nothing but darkness showed in the scope. But when Jif looked up from the eyepiece, he saw the altimeter had stopped spinning down. The ship was in level flight, gaining speed. This time, easing back on the stick made her start to climb again.

Once she'd made it back to eight hundred feet, Jif could see A Luoi at their four o'clock and Route 9 dead ahead. The road looked like a tattered ribbon, shimmering in its wetness, pointing toward home.

"We're not going to make Dong Ha," Northcutt said. "We burned up gas like crazy back there."

Jif asked, "How about Vandegrift?"

"Negative. It's Khe Sanh or nothing. That's the closest runway."

*****

By the time *Sara* reached the border, the thunderstorm had diminished to moderate rain. There was still plenty of intense lightning to the north, off her left wingtip, but it was a spectacle rather than a hazard. The same couldn't be said for the weather at Khe Sanh, sixteen kilometers—ten miles—ahead. There was still a storm with plenty of lightning in that base's direction.

When Northcutt radioed the tower for field conditions, the reply was emphatic: "This base is closed. Ceiling four hundred with half a mile visibility and deteriorating. Dangerous crosswinds at one-two-zero exceeding three-zero knots. Two C-130s just waved off. They're diverting to Quang Tri."

"I'm on fumes now," Northcutt told the air traffic controller. "I don't have the fuel to divert to Quang Tri or anyplace else. You have runway lights?"

There was a long pause before the reply: "More or less. Vehicle lights only."

"That'll have to do. I'll be landing to the east."

"Negative. That is not—repeat *not*—authorized."

"Yeah? Copy that, but I'll argue with your C.O. later. Got no choice."

Then he asked Jif, "How fast can you stow that scope when it gets to be crunch time? We'll need whatever guidance it might give us on the approach, because we probably won't see much of anything out the canopy. But when it all goes south, I don't want you smashing your face against it."

"Understand," Jif replied. "If it comes down to that, I'll just pull it out of the mount and hang on to it."

"Just drop it to the floor, man. You may need your hands free. This could get really rough."

*****

Landing on the runway at Khe Sanh in a stiff crosswind wouldn't be the first problem they'd face; *finding* that runway was the more immediate issue. Northcutt asked Jif, "You've been around Khe Sanh a lot, right?"

"That's true, Jack."

"Looking at this map, we can't dogleg straight to the end of the runway…too much high ground in the way. We'd have to be so high, we'd probably overshoot the base, anyway…burn too much gas climbing over those mountains, too. Looks like we should follow Niner to the road that makes a beeline northwest to the base, right?"

"Yeah. That's called Plantation Road. Its intersection with Niner should be easy to spot—it forms a wishbone, and we'll be flying right up its handle."

"I hope you're right, man. But one thing's for damn sure…we're going to be on the ground at—or around—Khe Sanh one way or another real soon."

*****

Finding the wishbone sounded easy, but it wasn't.

I've missed the bloody thing, Jif thought. *It's been too long. We should've been there already.*

But he knew that beyond the wishbone, Route 9 took a hard right to the southeast. The road they were following was still meandering to the northeast…

So we can't have passed it. And there's no other road in these parts we could be mistakenly following…

But what if I'm wrong about that?

When he expressed those doubts out loud, Northcutt replied, "Just relax, amigo, and trust your instruments. Remember what I said about our low groundspeed from the headwind. Everything's going to seem like it's taking more time than it should."

It took another ninety seconds—an interval that seemed so much longer—until the wishbone finally came into view in the scope. When they turned left to follow Plantation Road, they picked up a tailwind component. "See?" Northcutt said. "Our airspeed's gone to hell now, but we've got to be really booking over the ground. Can you see Khe Sanh?"

"I can see some lights, but I can't tell exactly where the runway is."

"No sweat. Just let me know when we're coming up to that four-way intersection about three klicks ahead. We'll make a right turn there and start the base leg to the runway. Stay alert, dude…we're going to come up on it fast with this wind behind us."

Northcutt was right. They were at an intersection in little over a minute…

But is it the four-way? Jif wondered. *It doesn't look like what the map shows…but there's been so much renovation work to re-establish this base lately. Are the perimeter roads all different now? Or is the scope not giving me a real good picture?*

The deciding factor: *It might not look like the four-way that's on this map—and the one I remember—but it includes a right turn toward the runway, so it's got to be the one.*

"*Now*, Jack. Do it."

The turn put the ship abeam to the wind blowing from her right side. It felt stronger than Northcutt imagined. "Dammit," he said, "it's trying to push the nose away from the field."

They needed to make one more right turn to line up with the runway. Northcutt's fear: *Will this vicious wind allow it? She's more a kite than an airplane right now.*

And we still can't see the runway. Where are those fucking lights?

They figured the wind was blowing them away from the runway, so when it appeared, it would be off the right wingtip. But what Jif was seeing in the scope contradicted that assumption.

"Hey, Jack…I think we're already *over* the bloody runway, maybe a quarter of the way down it."

"You're shitting me. You sure?"

Jif replied, "Trust my instruments, right?"

But if that was the runway, they were still perpendicular to it. To align for landing would take a ninety-degree turn into a wind determined to prevent it. Trying to land anyplace else on the base would, no doubt, end in a collision with something or someone.

Northcutt aggressively applied ailerons, rudder, and throttle. *Silent Sara* pivoted abruptly in a stomach-wrenching skid. The wind, in a rare moment of benevolence, had allowed the maneuver…

But while she pivoted, *Sara* plummeted. The two men on board had the feeling of hurtling into a void from which there'd be no escape.

The descent stopped as abruptly as it had begun, and they could see the ground now, just fifty feet below.

She was aligned with the runway but displaced a hundred meters to its left, rapidly closing on a cluster of buildings. It took aggressive aileron and rudder inputs once again to slip toward the matting that comprised the runway's surface.

Northcutt: "I ain't believing this. I'm showing seventy knots on the dial, but we're barely moving."

And then *Sara* dropped heavily onto the near edge of the runway. The brutal crosswind promptly weathervaned her toward the far edge. Northcutt didn't dare fight it; he kept the power up, hoping to retain some control against the merciless wind. He didn't reduce the throttle until she careened onto a parking ramp, heading straight for several cargo aircraft. She came to a stop just feet from the nearest plane, a C-123 being rocked by the storm but, unlike *Sara*, heavy enough to be in no danger of taking flight on her own.

Ground crewmen raced toward the YO-3A, not sure how to deal with this strange aircraft that was at this moment more a victim of the wind than its conqueror. Northcutt gave them the hand signal to *install chocks*. They complied quickly.

He told Jif, "When I pop the canopy, you've got to hold onto it for dear life so the wind doesn't take it. She'll snap clean off if you don't. Once we're out, we'll close it behind us so the cockpit doesn't get too wet."

While talking, he was writing instructions on his clipboard in big letters with a grease pencil. Holding it against the still-closed canopy for the ground crew to read, it instructed them to put sandbags on top of the wings at the leading edges.

"There's no way to tie her down, but we've got to kill the lift," he told Jif. "Otherwise, she's gonna fly away all by herself and get wrecked."

The ground crew didn't have any sandbags handy. They used their bodies instead. The weight of the ten men—all of them soaking wet—lying on the wing was enough to stabilize the ship. Northcutt didn't have to manually shut down the engine; out of fuel, it sputtered and died. Once he and Jif exited the cockpit, they added their bodies to the hold-down weight. In a few moments, they were soaking wet, too.

A red-faced lieutenant colonel decked out in an olive drab rain suit—an authorized but extravagant and impractical accessory to the uniform in a combat zone—approached the ship, bellowing, "WHICH ONE OF YOU FUCKING IDIOTS IS THE PILOT-IN-COMMAND?"

"I am, sir," Northcutt replied, not impressed or intimidated in the least by the colonel's wrath.

"Well, then, Captain, you'd better have a goddamn good reason for landing without clearance."

When a man has just cheated death, the rage of administrators and petty tyrants matters not at all. That was obvious in Northcutt's nonchalant reply: "Actually, sir, I believe I do."

Chapter Ten

The storm finally moved on an hour after *Silent Sara's* arrival at Khe Sanh. A lengthy and tedious debrief ensued with headquarters at Dong Ha on a secure, voice-scrambled radio net. Once that was done, Jif and Northcutt somehow managed to catch a few hours' sleep amidst the noise and bustle of the operations shack. Shortly before dawn, they grabbed some chow, scrounged avgas for *Sara*, and prepared for the short final leg of their return flight.

At sunrise, the preflight walk-around of the ship found her none the worse for wear. The only squawk: the seat covers were still quite damp from the brief soaking they'd endured when the canopy had been opened to let her occupants out.

Northcutt said, "How about that shit, amigo? We finally get dried out, but now we're going to get our asses wet all over again."

"That should be the worst thing that happens to us," Jif replied.

"You got that right, dude. My hat's off to you, though…you worked that scope like you'd been doing it all your life. *Ol' Reticle Eyes* hasn't lost his touch, I see."

Reticle Eyes: that was a nickname Jif had earned at Fort Sill's artillery school during his early days of active duty. He'd forgotten all about it.

Northcutt continued, "I tell you, man…I still remember the look of shock on your face—and our instructor's, too—when the first round you ever called as a student was a direct hit. Blew that old car body to shit. None of this *inside of fifty meters, close enough for government work* bullshit. You went for *target* right off the bat."

"It was luck, Jack."

"Bullshit. It was those calibrated eyeballs of yours—*reticle eyes.* And you've still got them. Just like on the rifle range…you outshot everybody, even the old NCOs running the show. Boy, you used to piss them off. You could've made a lot of money if you were a betting man. Like Annie Oakley with a dick."

As they took the runway for takeoff, two large-caliber NVA rockets crashed down a few hundred yards away, just inside the base perimeter. Northcutt said, "I guess we didn't get them all."

"Too bad we can't go looking for them," Jif replied. "But I reckon it would be suicide taking this low, slow bird on a mission in broad daylight."

"You've got that right, amigo. Now let's get the hell out of here. I've had enough of this place."

*****

When Jif and Northcutt walked into the combined HQ at Dong Ha, they found an argument raging between the ARVN and US commanders. Colonel McKnight pulled them aside before they could enter the conference room, saying, "Captain Northcutt, have you ever been in a room full of pissed-off generals before?"

"Can't say that I have, sir."

"In that case, the G2 thinks it's better that you don't even go in. Let Miles do the talking. He knows the drill."

Northcutt had absolutely no problem with that.

McKnight turned to Jif, saying, "Make damn sure you've got your ducks in a row, because what you reported seeing last night at Tchepone and beyond is threatening to turn the concept of this entire operation on its head."

"I'm not sure I follow, sir."

"Then let me spell it out for you," the colonel said. "That convoy you found…it's raised serious suspicions that the NVA has actually moved the Ho Chi Minh Trail deeper into Laos, avoiding Tchepone entirely. The fact that you reported little activity in the town itself only adds to that suspicion. If it was still a waypoint along the trail, it should have been bustling. The Air Force has been ordered to shift their primary search patterns farther west."

"So what's the problem, sir?"

"The ARVN isn't buying it, Miles." Nodding toward the conference room door, McKnight added, "And their brass in that room want to hang you out to dry. The name of the game is shoot the messenger, because your observations are messing with their plans. You know how to handle it, though. Just be ready for the trick questions, okay?"

But nobody paid Jif a bit of attention as he entered the room. He wasn't really surprised: *I'm just another little captain in a sea of generals and colonels. My job is to keep my bloody mouth shut until someone asks me to open it.* He found a place along the wall with some other junior officers, taking a front-row seat for the verbal battle in progress. The main combatants: General Sutherland, the American commander, and General Lam, the supreme commander of the ARVN engaged in Lam Son 719.

Jif had never seen Lam at the headquarters before. *I reckon things have gotten serious enough that he needed to get out of Saigon and personally take command*, he surmised. *And by rights, he shouldn't even be the commander anymore. Disenchanted with his performance, Saigon tried to replace him, but that replacement got killed in a chopper crash on his way to Dong Ha a week ago.*

Knowing how crooked so many of these ARVN brass can be, it makes you wonder just how "accidental" that chopper crash was.

Sutherland, obviously frustrated, was cutting to the chase, telling Lam, "We've got two choices here, General. Either we revise our objective to a point beyond Tchepone, or we call this whole clusterfuck off."

Jif was fairly sure that despite his three stars, calling the whole thing off was above Sutherland's pay grade. Not by much, but being just one rung down the ladder—the rung that separated him from General Abrams—was all it took.

Is he trying to bluff Lam, I wonder?

If he was, it wasn't working. The ARVN general was adamant: "We will continue the airmobile assault to capture Tchepone…and only Tchepone. It will begin tomorrow, as planned."

Sutherland's reply was anything but conciliatory. "Do you have any goddamned idea the colossal waste of my aviation resources that will entail, all to accomplish absolutely nothing? And that's assuming we only lose a minimal amount of aircraft to enemy fire, which certainly hasn't been our experience to date."

That's putting it mildly, Jif thought. He'd glanced at the equipment status board when first entering the building; already, nearly two hundred helicopters either lay wrecked in Laos or sat damaged beyond repair on airfields and LZs across Quang Tri Province.

"Look," Sutherland continued, "the NVA figured out before this operation even started that you never intended to go beyond Tchepone. Of course they're going to pick up stakes and move the trail west."

"That is impossible," Lam rebutted. "They cannot reroute it so easily."

Sutherland wasn't the only American in the room who laughed out loud. "You've got to be shitting me, General Lam." Pointing to Jif, he continued, "I believe our Captain Miles can tell us a different story. He's the only man in the room who's seen it up close."

Lam looked at Jif as if he were dirt. "Your captain is mistaken," he told Sutherland. "What he thinks he saw during a brief flyover in the dark is not possible. And from what I'm told, he's not even a qualified crewman on the aircraft in question."

Sutherland replied, "All I can say, General, is this man you call unqualified is responsible for the destruction of a major enemy supply convoy and a rocket site, as well as seeing the NVA disposition—or lack of one—at Tchepone. Captain Miles, would you describe that town as an enemy stronghold?"

"Negative, sir."

"How *would* you describe it?"

"I'd describe it as abandoned for all practical purposes, General."

Sutherland smiled triumphantly at Lam, who was pointedly ignoring him.

"As far as it being impossible for the NVA to move the trail," Sutherland continued, "if there's one thing we should've learned about our worthy adversaries, there's very little they consider impossible. Carving out a road where there wasn't one yesterday is nothing to them. Hell, that's how most of the Ho Chi Minh Trail came to be in the first damn place. Large stretches of it don't even look like a goddamn road."

Lam tried to show on the big wall map just how impassable the terrain west of Tchepone was. But when Sutherland would have none of it, he tried a different tack. "You Americans are arguing a moot point. All plans are in place for the assault on Tchepone. To change those plans now would create confusion and disorder among my troops."

"How do you plan to handle that confusion and disorder, General Lam, when you waltz into Tchepone and the only greeting you get is from the artillery and rockets dropping on your head from NVA sanctuaries farther west?"

"If we are bombarded, General Sutherland, that will be the fault of your Air Force."

The comment caused an angry murmur among the American officers. Jif was sure the angry look Sutherland hurled at Lam meant *you ungrateful little son of a bitch.* But the words that came from the general's mouth were surprisingly matter of fact: "I believe you're talking about the air force that, so far, has made any success you've had in this campaign possible, General.

Without their help, you're getting your ass kicked. As dependent as you are on them, it would be in your interests to stay on their good side."

But Sutherland knew this game was being played with a stacked deck. Lam wouldn't change his mind because President Thieu had forbidden it; with the NVA continuing to overrun ARVN strongpoints, he needed a face-saving spectacle.

As the meeting broke up, McKnight put it this way: "This is all a show for Thieu's benefit so he'll look like a hero for the coming election. He'll be just as happy if his troops do find Tchepone abandoned. It'll just mean he's reached his stated objective with even less muss and fuss than expected. Of course, he'll make it sound like they just decisively defeated the North Vietnamese in the battle of the century."

Jif asked, "Since the PRT won't be doing much of anything while this big airlift is going on, can I continue flying the night recon flights with Captain Northcutt?"

"Is his regular observer still under the weather?"

"Affirmative, sir. The docs don't expect him to be airworthy for a few more days. And the aviation company at Phu Bai doesn't see any reason to ship another guy up here as long as I'm filling the seat."

"I'll have to clear it with the G2," McKnight said. "It's his show…but I don't imagine he'll have any problems with it, not after your mission last night. It gave him a bucketful of new intel to play with. I'm sure he'd love some more."

*****

Colonel McKnight was right—the G2 had no problem with Jif continuing as observer on Northcutt's aircraft. In fact, he was quite enthusiastic about it.

The Air Force, however, was not.

When Northcutt and Jif arrived for the afternoon briefing that would map out the air operations for the coming night, they were told their presence in the sky was no longer required. "All YO-3A flights in support of this operation have been cancelled," the Air Force liaison officer, a bird colonel, said.

Northcutt replied, "Begging your pardon, sir, but says who?"

"The commanding general, Captain. Is that good enough for you?" The liaison went on to say, "You're not needed. In fact, you're in my people's way. Now if you'll excuse me, I've got serious work to do. Have a nice flight back to Phu Bai."

His tone wasn't gracious in the least. It had the air of *don't let the door hit you in the ass on the way out.*

Jif and Northcutt went straight to the G2. He was apologetic for not getting the word to them sooner, but added, "It's out of my hands, gentlemen. It boils down to this…the Air Force is pissed that two guys in a powered glider are stealing the thunder from their big, bad gunships. They claim they would've found the shifted trail—and that rocket site—all by themselves, without your help. In fact, they say they would've found it sooner if they hadn't had to steer clear of your search areas."

"Pardon my French, sir, but that's bullshit," Jif replied. "They would've never found that stuff. They were looking in the wrong places. Those gunships search with broad strokes. They miss the details. We're much more surgical about it."

"Tell me something I don't know, Captain," the G2 said. "Might as well cool your roll, Miles…we've already lost this fight. The Air Force wants total control over the tac air scenario or they won't play. If we give them an excuse to scale back their operations, this whole campaign will go to hell in a handbasket even faster than it already is. General Sutherland has been pushing a string trying to get the ARVN to perform. He needs the Air Force's full cooperation in that effort. Let's not make it any harder on him."

*****

But it got harder anyway. While the ARVN prepared for the assault on Tchepone, the NVA threat to its existing firebases and LZs along the Route 9 corridor intensified.

Jif joined Colonel McKnight and Boyd Gray in the operations center as they listened to relayed broadcasts announcing the imminent demise of Fire Support Base 30. After days of mauling by NVA artillery, rockets, and infantry probes, its two howitzer batteries had been knocked out, and the firebase was being abandoned in a panic. Even with the air support of Spectre gunships and several sorties by B-52s that dropped their bombs *danger close* to the firebase's perimeter with incredible precision, FSB 30 could no longer be held.

"Listen to this," McKnight said, calling attention to a radio relaying one of the aviation frequencies. "The guys talking are medevac pilots."

Sounding distraught, one of those pilots was telling the base at Lang Vei, "Be advised…it looks like they've still got a shitload of dudes needing dustoff back there, but I've got about two dozen slopes on board, and none of these bastards seem to be wounded. One of them is a goddamn colonel. They're using us to cut and run like they're calling a taxi."

Another pilot, equally overwrought, added, "We're getting the shit shot out of us, too. Triple-A very heavy. Murphy and Crenshaw are down. Rescue's looking doubtful."

As the Americans watched the ARVN generals and colonels in the headquarters, they all came to the same conclusion: *They have totally lost control of their people. Their own battalion commanders won't even speak to them on the radio anymore. They're too busy running away.*

And tomorrow, these same generals—already in way over their heads—will be launching another assault directly into the teeth of strengthening NVA resistance. They're not ready for it. In fact, they're not ready for anything except parading around Saigon in their flashy uniforms while they suck up to their president.

A fish stinks from the head: whoever thought up that saying must've had the ARVN officer corps in mind.

This is shaping up to be an even bigger disaster than anyone imagined. People are dying for less than nothing.

The reports coming over the radio kept getting worse: more helicopters shot down, more ARVN officers and their soldiers fleeing in panic, forcing their way onto medevac choppers though not wounded. By late afternoon, the ARVN generals were still arguing among themselves whether their forces still controlled FSB 30 or not. General Sutherland pulled the plug on their dithering; to keep the abandoned equipment out of enemy hands, he ordered American airstrikes to level what was left of the firebase before sunset. He had something else to tell Lam, as well: “There’ll be no more evacuation by helicopter, General. Tell your remaining people to withdraw from the firebase on foot immediately…if anybody’s still listening, that is.”

An officer on Sutherland’s staff summed up the American reaction to the disaster: “It makes you want to puke, doesn’t it? Can you blame soldiers for not fighting when their commanders are fleeing the field of battle?”

*****

Colonel McKnight tossed the document he’d been reading onto the desk like it was so much garbage. “Isn’t that fascinating?” he said with a sneer. “Thieu wants to further cover his ass by requesting that a division of US combat troops cross into Laos.”

Captain Gray was confused by the colonel’s dismissal of the concept. Actually, he found it exciting and said so: “I’ve always felt that’s what this operation needs, sir. Just like Cambodia last year…let us do the heavy lifting while the ARVN mops up around the edges. Everybody wins.”

McKnight didn’t bother dignifying that with a verbal response. He just looked at Gray like he was nuts.

It was Jif who replied, “C’mon, Boyd…you know that’s not going to happen. Nixon’s already bet his ass on the promise there’d be no American ground troops in Laos. He can’t go back on that. After all the crap he’s said about how well Vietnamization is working, the whole world would be calling him a liar.” Holding up a fistful of documents he’d been reviewing, he added, “Thieu’s just trying to avoid committing even more of his troops across the border—in fact, he’d like to start pulling some of them out—but General Abe dug his heels in. That’s why a brigade of our 101st Airborne is going to the DMZ to relieve a couple of ARVN regiments so *they* can go jack up the numbers in Laos.”

Flipping to a page in one of the documents, he added, “But airlifting one of those ARVN regiments from the DMZ looks like it got planned by two staffs who didn’t bother talking to each other.”

McKnight: “Show me, Jif.”

“Right here, sir…the choppers taking the regiment from Vandegrift Combat Base into Laos are scheduled to depart *before* that regiment even gets to the base. That’s a lot of aircraft to have sitting on the VCB ramp, waiting. And it would blow the whole airlift schedule to hell.”

Giving the page a once-over, McKnight replied, “Yeah, I see what you mean. It’s the same old story—sloppy staff work with no follow-up. Go talk to our G3 shop…see if they can straighten out their ARVN counterparts.”

*****

At first—and as Jif expected—the ARVN operations staff insisted that *he* was mistaken; there was no scheduling error. But once forced to acknowledge the two-hour misalignment in the transportation scheme, they stated with much arrogance that the regiment could not arrive at VCB any sooner, so it was the American aviation command that would have to alter its schedule.

A major—a pilot from the G3 shop—rolled out a flow chart for aircraft movements and proceeded to explain just how disruptive to the operation it would be to alter the schedule. He went on to describe how the pickup point couldn't be changed, either, stating there was no suitable LZ at the DMZ for an airlift of that size and no refueling capabilities.

"Begging your pardon," Jif said to the ARVN staffers, "but isn't the regiment traveling to VCB on your own trucks?"

An ARVN colonel replied with a nod that meant, *Yes, but so what*?

Then Jif pointed to a spot on the DMZ buffer zone, the place the regiment was currently located, and asked, "The regiment is still here, right?"

Again, the colonel replied only with a nod.

"So we're talking a distance of just under two-zero klicks…about twelve and a half miles. Even at minimum convoy speed, that's less than an hour's drive, in vehicles that are already in position with the regiment. So why in bloody hell can't the convoy's departure time be bumped up a few hours?"

"Impossible," the ARVN colonel replied. "They would have to depart in darkness."

"That's really not a problem for vehicles with headlights traveling on established roads, sir. And those roads haven't seen much in the way of enemy activity in months. You run night supply convoys along that stretch of Route Niner all the time at normal driving speeds, and they haven't been hit in ages."

The colonel was raising his voice now: "No! The regiment will not travel before daybreak. That is final."

The major from G3 said, "Oh, for fuck's sake. Since when does the war stop at night? This is unacceptable."

Jif asked the major, "A word, sir?" They stepped into the hallway to talk privately.

"I think I know what's going on here," Jif said. "That regimental commander's made a deal to intentionally miss the airlift on day one. The initial air assaults for the Tchepone op look to be pretty dicey, so he fully intends to sit them out. He knows the chopper schedule is set in stone, and the odds of someone catching in advance a scheduling mismatch between two different documents is pretty slim. The only reason I found it is because I don't have anything better to do right now. If the regiment doesn't make their scheduled lift, it'll be a few days before it can be accommodated again. You know as well as I do that ARVN commanders revise, ignore, or outright disobey orders they don't like all the time."

"Sure, Miles. I'm fully aware of that. But aren't you kind of going out on a limb with this? They'd have to be really sneaky to dream up something like this."

"I don't think it's sneaky at all, sir. It looks like SOP for the ARVN to me. We'd better tell your boss what's going on right bloody now."

*****

The major's boss—the G3—was skeptical at first, too. But to ensure that his ass was covered, he immediately brought the matter to General Sutherland, who wasn't in the least skeptical or surprised.

"General Lam and that regimental commander are buddies," Sutherland said, "and they're both stooges for Thieu. Neither one of them is exactly a ball of fire. But I'm going to make Lam an offer…either his people are on that airlift at the scheduled date and time, or we're not transporting them at all. Let's see how crazy the president is about his First Division being short a regiment while he's so desperate to reach Tchepone."

Then he turned to Jif and said, "You're the one who figured this out, Captain?"

"Yes, sir."

"Excellent work. But I'm going to do you a favor…Lam and his people are already looking to hang you by the neck, so I'm going to keep your name out of this. Speaking of hanging by the neck, you PRT people have been digging up a little more truth than the ARVN wants to hear. I wouldn't be surprised if every one of you has a contract out on him. Do you keep a round chambered in that forty-five when you're on base?"

"Not usually, sir."

"I'd get in the habit of doing it, Miles. *Accidents* do happen, you know?"

Jif wasn't sure if the general was joking or not. But after giving it a moment's thought, he realized, *I've got nothing to lose by taking that advice.*

Then he asked, "Do you think your ultimatum to General Lam is going to make a difference, sir?"

"Fuck no, Miles. But I've got to look like I'm trying to do something, don't I?"

Chapter Eleven

The Tchepone operation's first wave—an airlift to establish a firebase named *Lolo*—was an unmitigated disaster from the outset. Within the first hour, eleven helicopters were shot down by murderous triple-A as they neared the location; another forty ships would be damaged before the assault was suspended, with only a small and vulnerable fraction of the assault force inserted. Colonel McKnight's team—himself, Jif, and Gray—could once again only listen to the calamity in progress over the radio at the Dong Ha headquarters.

"It's like the NVA knew in advance exactly where the landings would be," Gray said as he cast accusing glances at the ARVN staffers drifting about the HQ. "You don't suppose one of these assholes leaked the information, do you, sir?"

"Who knows, Boyd?" McKnight replied. "We already knew that all ARVN headquarters leaked like sieves. Why should this one be any different?"

"But they're sacrificing their own guys, sir."

The colonel said, "Look at them...do they seem upset about that? The only pissed-off people in the room are the Americans trying to put out this fire."

He was right; the ARVN staffers seemed indifferent to the catastrophe playing itself out across the border.

McKnight continued, "As long as it's not their asses in jeopardy, they don't give a shit."

Jif said, "I reckon a lot of ARVN officers are all playing the long game, one we westerners have a hard time understanding. It's like they're pretty sure the south will eventually fall, and they're going to keep playing both sides so they've got some chips to cash in when it actually happens. That way, they might have the credentials to switch sides. And if that doesn't look like it's going to work, maybe it'll give them time to escape this place before they end up prisoners in some re-education camp." After a pensive pause, he added, "You know, it's like everyone in this whole bloody country isn't focused on winning but just surviving."

Gray asked, "You really think there are going to be re-education camps?"

"It's something authoritarian regimes have always been fond of," Jif replied. "You've heard how it works...if you won't break and convert to their ideology, you just mysteriously vanish. My mom was in a Japanese prison camp for a year during World War Two, but she's so tough they couldn't manage to break or kill her. And my dad told me about the camps the North Koreans had back when he was in that war. The People's Army was real tough on their POWs. I don't reckon the North Vietnamese will be much different."

The devastation at Lolo was threatening to derail the entire Tchepone operation right at its start. The American solution: an aerial bombardment around the proposed firebase location that would last the better part of the day. "Tac air's already in the area," the G3 reported, "and B-52s will be on station in about two hours."

"Those buffs are sure getting a workout in this operation," Gray said. "My entire first tour, I think I felt the earth shake from exactly one B-52 strike. This time out, I'm feeling it several times a day."

But there were two other positions besides Lolo to be occupied within the next forty-eight hours; *Liz*, an LZ halfway between Lolo and Tchepone, and *FSB Sophia*, only five klicks from Tchepone. There was every reason to suspect that enemy triple-A would be waiting in force at those locations, too. The burden to suppress that menace was falling to tactical fighter-bombers, which, although much faster, were only slightly less vulnerable to enemy fire than the helicopters. Suppression of the triple-A would be an enormous job; there was little artillery in range to do it, and other than several USAF FACs, few observers in the air or on the ground to direct that artillery.

*****

For six hours, the enemy just beyond Lolo's perimeter was pounded by every fighter-bomber that could be scrambled from bases across South Vietnam, Thailand, and a US Navy carrier off the coast of Quang Tri Province. Three-ship packages of B-52s, cruising unseen and beyond reach high above the fray, dramatically punctuated the efforts of their littler siblings with cataclysmic bomb loads. Only a few of the fighter-bombers were damaged by enemy fire, and none were shot down. As the troop-carrying *slicks* and Chinooks prepared for another try at Lolo, helicopter gunships moved in to mop up the NVA who'd survived the aerial onslaught. There weren't many.

By late afternoon, FSB Lolo was, at last, operational. But soon, those air support elements that had made it possible would have to do it all over again at LZ Liz and FSB Sophia.

*****

The FAC pilots—the men who'd been doing the lion's share of artillery spotting—were getting frustrated. Almost all the terrain they had to cover searching for the triple-A sites was composed of steep ridges and jagged hills. It was dangerous and exhausting to navigate their mazes while dodging ground fire and, at the same time, looking for targets.

From their base at Quang Tri, the FAC squadron commander was on the landline to Dong Ha, telling General Sutherland's G3, "My people need help. They've got their hands full with their main job marking targets for the zoomies. I need to lighten their load a little…give me some aerial observers who can ride shotgun with them and call the artillery missions."

He'd hated using the term zoomies. It seemed to trivialize the elite status the Air Force conferred on its aviators who—like himself—had gone beyond mere mastery of ultra-high-performance machines, turning them into deadly weapons that were extensions of themselves.

But the ground-pounders like the expression—hell, they invented it—and I need a favor from them.

The G3 asked, "How many observers do you need?"

"Three, for starters."

"Let me see what I can work up," the G3 said. "Give me a few minutes. I'll get right back to you."

Colonel McKnight had overheard the conversation. He offered, "My team can do it, Hank. The three of us are just sitting on our asses here, shuffling paper. We could use the work."

"I'll take you up on that, Ted, but with one revision...*you're* not to go. General Sutherland's already taken a dim view of you flying as AO on scouting missions. In his book, that job is way below a bird colonel's realm. He knows you only did it because you were shorthanded, but that's not going to cut any ice this time."

"But you'll take my two captains, right? I'm sure they're raring to go."

"I'll take them, Ted, and I'll add a man from my shop. The Air Force wants three, I'll give them three."

*****

A quick pre-dawn jeep ride brought Jif, Gray, and the captain from the G3 shop—Davy Gonzalez—from Dong Ha to the Quang Tri airfield. As they walked into the FAC squadron's operations shack, the heads of a dozen Air Force pilots swiveled in their direction. Most had patronizing smirks on their faces, expressing the belief that a lesser breed of warriors—those shackled to ground combat—was suddenly in their exalted midst. But one of them was grinning from ear to ear as he blurted, "Well, kiss my ass! Jif Miles, as I live and breathe! How's the *Wonder from Down Under* holding up?" He turned to the other pilots and said, "Hands off this man, touchholes. He rides with me."

A stunned Boyd Gray whispered, "You know that major?"

"Yep. I flew with him in the A Shau on my first tour back in sixty-eight."

Jif walked over to Bill Jones—who was a captain the last time they'd worked together—and said as they shook hands, "Good to see you, sir. It'll be my great pleasure to warm your right seat again."

"You can ditch the *sir* stuff, dude. We've been through some shit together."

"Well, congratulations on your promotion, anyway," Jif said.

"Same to you, man. C'mon…grab some coffee. Let's find out what we're about to get into."

*****

They had a little time to catch up on each other's exploits during the truck ride to the flight line. Jones was incredulous that Jif had just come off a brief stint on the YO-3A.

"And you're still alive to tell about it," he said, shaking his head in wonder. "You won't catch me floating around just a few feet over the gooks' heads. I don't give a shit how quiet the bird is."

"Well, I won't pretend it wasn't scary at first," Jif replied, "but after a while, it got to be a real rush."

"Yeah…a rush to die. How low did you go, anyway?"

"We got down to a couple of hundred feet a few times."

"Fuck me! That's simply insane, man."

"Yeah, maybe," Jif replied, "but it got the job done. Just don't get stuck in a thunderstorm. That was the scariest part of the whole mission. Definitely brown drawers time."

*****

Their FAC ship—an O-2 *Skymaster* that wasn't graced with a nickname or nose art—was airborne just after sunrise. Twenty-five minutes later, she was above the ridge where LZ Liz was to be established. Per the recon plan Jif and Bill Jones had hastily put together, they'd stay high—3,000 feet or better—and to the south of the assault choppers' flight path.

"Man, the Spectres hit this place during the night like it was going out of style," Jones said. "I'm real glad I won the toss and didn't pull the midnight shift, trying to find targets for them."

As they picked up a search pattern, Jones added, "I doubt they're going to shoot at us now. That'd give their game away too easily. They don't want us, anyway…they want the slicks and shithooks. But even if they do shoot, we'll be hard to hit while we're up this high and jinking around. All we've got to do is find them…somehow. You still cool with the rules of engagement?"

"You mean use artillery against individual targets and tac air against large concentrations, especially ones on the move?"

"That's the ticket, Jif. Economy of force, right?"

"Well, I don't know how many fast jets you have on call, Bill…but the artillery's spread pretty thin at the moment. All we've got are the two batteries at A Luoi, one at Lolo, and a quartet of monster one-seven-fives over the border in the Nam that can actually throw stuff this far. It's going to be *economy of force*, for bloody sure."

The ships carrying Boyd Gray and Davy Gonzalez—the farm-out from the G3 shop—were on the frequency, reporting that they were in positions well to the north of Route 9. Jones asked Jif, "Are you guys expecting a lot of NVA movement from north to south across Niner? My briefing didn't say much about it."

"I reckon we are, Bill. There are no ARVN on the ground north of Niner anymore. The only people in position to catch the NVA moving south are recon guys like us. And if we don't find them and call the world down on their heads, there just might be a shitload of bad guys opposing today's assault."

"Just one problem…we recon drivers haven't actually found any NVA until they've opened fire on us," Jones said. "It's still going to be a bitch spotting them even with your extra eyeballs. They could be anywhere along that long ridge around LZ Liz…or the hills south of it."

"Not exactly anywhere, Bill. They can't hump anything bigger than thirty-seven millimeter guns up those hills, so to engage the incoming birds with any accuracy, they'll have to be within about three square kilometers of the LZ—and none of that area should be to the north. They'd be down too low in the valley, with shitty fields of fire. Let's stay where we are, to the south of the ridge. If those guns are here at all, they'll be up on that high ground."

"Sounds like a plan, Jif. I do like the way you think."

*****

The first sighting was by Boyd Gray, who'd been scouring the hills just north of A Luoi. It wasn't a triple-A site, but troops on the move toward that firebase in what seemed company strength or better, complete with some trucks and armored vehicles. Per the rules of engagement, Gray called for a strike by tac air on the moving target.

Jones told Jif, "If we come across more gooks on the move in the next few minutes, we're shit out of luck. My fast jets are going to be all tied up for a little while."

He checked the clock; it read 0800. The first wave of assault choppers headed to LZ Liz was due to arrive in one hour. Whatever was happening near A Luoi, eleven klicks to the east, wouldn't cause the assault to be delayed.

Jif, who'd been alternating between the naked eye and binoculars to perform his scan, said, "I need a one-eighty to the right, Bill. Think I've got something."

"Yeah? Where?"

"Right below us…heavy weapons…badly hidden." As the ship began her turn, Jif coached, "That's good…a little less bank angle, please. Keep the wing out of my field of vision." He wasn't using the binoculars at all now.

Jones was trying to look around Jif, through the window panels that covered most of the cabin door. "Can't see what you're looking at," he said.

As Jif began calling the artillery fire mission, he replied, "It's not that obvious until you look real close."

Lang Vei didn't assign the mission to A Luoi or the battery dropped into Lolo late yesterday. It went to the US Army's 175-millimeter guns near the border. Jif said, "Shit…that's going to slow the bloody mission down. The one-oh-fives at A Luoi or Lolo could pump out five or six volleys in the time it'll take to get one from those big guns."

Jones asked, "So how come they didn't get the mission?"

"Above my pay grade, Bill. But they might be too busy covering their own asses right now."

It would be almost three minutes before the first adjustment round arrived. That gave them time to orbit the target, which Jones still hadn't been able to see. As the ship banked, Jif used reference points on the right wing to help orient the pilot: "Look at that small patch of forest crown just forward of the rocket pod's nose. Does something look funny about it?"

"Funny? No…it looks like a forest to me, man."

"But that patch is a different color—more brown than green—and a different texture from the crowns hundreds of klicks in all directions. That's bad camouflage. The stuff they cut and hung over the gun is dying, and some of it's even facing the wrong way. You're looking at the bottoms of leaves when you should only see tops."

"Okay, I've got that now," Jones said. "But where do you see a gun?"

"The northern edge of the patch. You can see two muzzles and some of their barrels clearly. They're much too straight to be the work of Mother Nature."

"You sure that's what we're seeing from this distance, Jif?"

"What distance? At three thousand feet, we're a little more than half a mile away. That's nothing. We spot targets a few miles from OPs all the time, as long as we've got line of sight."

Now that they both knew where the target was, Jones flew the ship a bit farther away to stay well clear of the round's trajectory. "Yeah, we'll need a big safety margin," Jif said. "Those one-seven-fives are not known for their accuracy, especially at this range."

When the first adjustment round impacted several hundred meters from the target, Jif said, "See what I mean about accuracy? They're way off, but it shouldn't take much to dial them in. Just so the gooks don't run away while I'm doing it."

Over the next two and a half minutes, the second and third adjustment rounds did their job of bracketing the target. The fire-for-effect volley by the four guns would come next. Surprisingly, the NVA gunners didn't seem to have fled the position or fired at the O-2.

Jif said, "I'm worried there could be more triple-A sites we haven't seen yet…ones that might be camouflaged better."

Three rounds of the four-round volley crashed into the target in a tight group, the smoke and dust of their explosions followed in moments by what looked like a spectacular fireworks display: the secondary explosions of ammunition. But the fourth round landed hundreds of meters away from the group of three, farther west along the ridgeline. To Jif's surprise, it, too, caused stunning secondary explosions.

"Don't tell me…we hit another gun position by dumb luck," he said.

The *dumb luck* was actually the result of a gunnery error. One of the massive tubes had just undergone field maintenance and hadn't been boresighted after the repair, though it should've been. The misaligned tube had accounted for the incidental destruction of a second triple-A site.

But that still only accounted for three or four heavy weapons positioned near LZ Liz. "There's got to be more," Jif said. "They like to lay that stuff on thick."

"But we don't have a clue where they are, man."

"I'll bet there are more along that ridge. That's where the best fields of fire are."

He proceeded to walk fire-for-effect volleys along the ridge, shifting it in hundred-meter increments to either side of the targets already erased. After four shifts, the impacts had wiped out two more hidden triple-A sites, their destruction made obvious by the secondaries. "Now I'm going to shift it to the east," Jif said. "That should help clear the approach path of the assault ships."

He did the shift, but there were no further indications of guns being destroyed.

When the assault ships approached, several triple-A guns fired on them from a location well to the south of the ridge. But the guns were far enough away from the LZ, with degraded fields of fire, that they didn't seem to be doing much damage. Diving down to the treetops and slipping behind the site, Jones marked its location with smoke rockets. In less than a minute, a Cobra gunship with the assault wave followed the lead of the O-2, slipped behind the NVA guns, and destroyed them.

Once that was done, Jones began a steep climb, intent on returning to three thousand feet as quickly as possible. He'd made the move not a moment too soon; there were still more triple-A sites around the LZ that hadn't been discovered, and now they were firing at the O-2. For a few heart-stopping moments, the ship was bracketed by streams of green tracers.

"Hang onto your ass, man," Jones said. "I've got to get creative here." With a pained smile, he added, "Like old times, eh?"

It took what seemed an eternity of violent maneuvering to shake free. Jif had twisted around in his seat as much as the harness would allow to look out the back windows during the climbing gyrations, hoping to spot where the triple-A site was. But when the ship leveled off and the guns had stopped firing, he couldn't relocate them precisely.

Jones asked, "Got at least a rough idea?"

"Yeah. Very rough."

"Better than nothing, man. Give it a shot."

Jif called in the fire mission, and it was assigned to the guns at Lolo; they could fire the mission without the rounds crossing the assault's approach path. "That's a relief," he said. "I can shift those one-oh-fives around a hell of a lot faster than the one-seven-fives. I might get to hit something by dumb luck again."

But after shifting the volleys four times, there were no secondaries, no indications he'd scored a hit.

"Maybe they already moved," Jones said.

"Yeah…maybe, dammit."

*****

On the way back to Quang Tri to refuel and reload smoke rockets, Jif made direct radio contact with the American 175-millimeter battery that had shot his first mission of the morning. "Be advised," he told their fire direction center, "you've got a tube way out of boresight. It's not base piece. That narrows it down to three for you."

The reply was curt and lackadaisical: "Yeah, roger that. We'll look into it. *Out.*"

Jones said to Jif, "That was pretty fucking rude of them. Sounded more like *fuck off.*"

"Could be. Or maybe they were just too busy to appreciate some help."

But that might've been giving them too much benefit of the doubt. Jones was right; it did sound like *fuck off*…

And sometimes, even the clipped audio of a tactical radio couldn't hide the stink of an American unit with decaying morale.

That bothered Jif even worse than the ARVN debacle to which he'd been a witness.

*****

All in all, the assault on LZ Liz went much better than yesterday's first try at Lolo. Of the sixty-five helicopters taking part, eighteen were hit but only two destroyed. By late morning, Liz was fully established, with a battalion of ARVN on the ground and seeking out the NVA. They were in control of the area, at least for the moment.

Jif and Jones didn't get the full picture of the morning's success until they were back at Quang Tri. "Damn fine operation," the FAC commander said. "Nice work, y'all. Now let's get back out there and do some more."

But Jif still found the outcome bittersweet. He told Jones, "You and I did okay up there, I reckon…but I wish we'd done better."

"C'mon, Jif…I may've been born at night, but I wasn't born last night. If we hadn't knocked out those guns, it would've been another fucking disaster."

Chapter Twelve

With the new day came a new objective: establishing FSB Sophia. But the weather refused to cooperate. Low ceilings and driving rain postponed the ARVN's helicopter assault for hours.

It didn't stop the FAC ships from attempting to locate the NVA in the area, though, difficult and dangerous as that task would be in the restricted visibility. "I hate to say it, dude," Bill Jones told Jif, "but we're going to have to fly low if we expect to see anything on the ground. But the second we hit any soup, I'm going straight up. Can't risk hitting a fucking mountain."

"I hear that loud and clear, Bill."

Flying west at four thousand feet, following the Sepon River as it snaked its way toward Tchepone, their visibility of the ground was even worse than forecast. Jones asked, "You got a fix on anything down there?"

"Yeah…I think we just passed Liz. But this bloody river has too many fishhooks in it. If I missed one, we might be a couple of klicks off from where we think we are."

"I don't think we're off…being near Liz kinda jives with the radio nav. But if we get to the point where the Sepon T-bones the Banghiang, we'll know we went too damn far. That'll be the last chance to turn around before we go out of our box."

A blinding rain came out of nowhere, robbing whatever visibility they'd enjoyed to that point. Jones angrily pounded a fist against the glareshield and said, "If this stuff doesn't let up real quick, we'll be turning around a little sooner than we thought."

Jif was scanning radio frequencies, hoping to learn what, if any, contact the ARVN was having with the NVA. There was quite a bit of traffic on the airwaves, all in Vietnamese. But none of it was in the catchphrases and common expressions that made up an American warrior's very limited vocabulary. Judging by the frantic pitch of their voices, though, somebody was in a fight…

And one of the exchanges had the call-and-response cadence of an artillery fire mission request. But where the target was and who'd be firing the mission was lost in the enigma of an unfamiliar language, spoken in panic.

The rain wouldn't let up. "I'm turning around," Jones said. "Gonna try to climb out of this crap, too."

The radio fell strangely silent as the O-2 began her turn. Then she lurched violently with a *THUD*, followed by a sound like tin cans being crumpled. The ship began to vibrate severely, like some rotating machinery was terribly out of balance. Indicators for the aft engine all fell to the bottom of their scales as if they'd been unplugged. She nosed down like she'd lost interest in giving the gift of flight.

Jones shut down the aft engine as he struggled with the controls to stabilize the ship. Jif spun around in his seat to look into the aft cabin. Beyond the radio rack, he could see a ragged hole the size of a basketball in the fuselage below the engine compartment. With the engine shut down, the violent shaking, at least, had stopped.

"If I didn't know better," Jones said, "I'd swear we were just hit by flak. How the fuck could they even see us in these clouds without radar guidance? The intel was real specific that the NVA doesn't have that kind of capability anywhere near here."

They were still blind; the rain had gotten worse. "We can forget about climbing above it," Jones said. "Something's causing a shitload of drag. We've already lost a thousand feet, and on one engine, even our best rate of climb would be for shit, anyway. We've got to stay over that river somehow, or we're going to smack some fucking mountain, guaran-damn-teed."

When they called in their emergency to Lang Vei, the acknowledgment was overshadowed by an overdue warning: "Expedite north of grid line four-three. Fire mission in progress your vector."

Jones turned to Jif: "Son of a bitch! We didn't just get hit by our own artillery, did we?"

"Maybe not exactly *hit*, Bill…" Then he asked the controller, "Are they firing fuze VT?"

"Stand by one…"

A few seconds later, the controller was back: "Yeah, that's a roger. A Luoi is shooting VT."

"Tell them to knock it the hell off," Jif said. "Don't they know it's raining downrange? I think we just caught some chunks of a premature detonation. Have them change to mechanical time fuzes."

"Copy that," the controller replied, but he sounded skeptical, like Jif's story was too bizarre to be true.

Jones still had his hands full with the crippled ship, but he found time to say, "Goddamn Lang Vei should've warned us like a couple minutes ago."

"Yeah, they should've," Jif replied, "but they only know what the ARVN tells them, and the ARVN has never been real good about sharing information."

Jones replied, "From what I hear, they don't have much of a problem sharing info with the commies, though."

A few moments later, the controller at Lang Vei did share this: "You may be right about the VT in the rain. They just reported the round as *lost*."

"It's not bloody lost," Jif said. "We found it…or rather, it found us."

Jones managed to turn the ship north, heeding Lang Vei's warning. He told Jif, "When I get a free minute, you're going to explain what the fuck just happened, okay?"

Flying to a point *north of grid line four-three* would've been much easier if they could see the ground. Until they broke out of this storm, they'd be relying on the TACAN at Quang Tri for radio navigation; that would at least keep them pointed toward home. But it didn't guarantee they'd be higher than any rising terrain. Pointing to the chart on the center pedestal, Jones asked, "You see the course we're on, right?"

"Yeah, I've got it."

"Good. Give me the highest point along this route. I can't keep her straight and level and read those tiny elevation numbers on the map at the same time."

It only took Jif a few moments to have the answer. "We're good," he said. "On this course, we clear everything by at least a thousand feet."

"Yeah, as long as we hold this altitude," Jones replied. He didn't sound confident that was possible.

They popped free of the storm a few minutes later. Despite the broken clouds at their altitude, navigation by landmarks was now possible. Route 9 was clearly visible, only a kilometer to the south. Lang Vei confirmed they should now be clear of A Luoi's fire mission.

It took full power on the nose engine to hold altitude. "Doesn't look like we're losing any fuel," Jones said. "All we're missing is one engine…and whatever else got blown off the ship. With a little luck, we should make Quang Tri. So explain this fuze VT shit to me."

"Plain and simple, Bill, you're not supposed to fire VT in the rain. They're tiny radar sets…heavy rainfall can give enough of a return that it tricks them into thinking they're within forty meters of a solid object, so they blow up."

"You don't think *we* were that solid object, do you?"

"I don't think we'd still be here to talk about it if the round blew up forty meters from us. I reckon it was the rain that did it. We were just in the vicinity, picking up some fragments."

"I'll thank my lucky stars, then. Getting hit in the ass like we did, though…I just hope the tail stays on. Can you see anything banged up on your side? Like the tail boom?"

"Nope," Jif replied. "Everything looks like it's still there."

"Yeah, my side, too. Let's hope it stays that way."

*****

There was one more problem: as they approached the airfield at Quang Tri, the Skymaster's right main landing gear wouldn't extend. "I was afraid of that," Jones said. "Tucked up under the aft engine like the mains are, it wouldn't take much for some damage we can't see to jam them."

After some discussion with the tower, Jones told Jif, "I'm going to belly her in the weeds at the northwest corner of the field, parallel to the runway. It'll be wet and muddy. We may slide a long way…or we may not. Hopefully, she won't flip over." He reached down next to his seat, came up with a short-handled crash axe, and added, "You hang on to this like our lives depend on it…because they just might if we have to bust our way out of here…like if she's burning."

They circled the field twice, waiting for a three-ship flight of C-130s to land and clear the runway. Jif found that curious and asked, "Why do we have to wait for them? We're not landing on the runway."

"Can't guarantee we're not going to end up on that runway, man. Once you start sliding, all bets are off. That'd be all anyone needs…a ground collision blocking the runway. We'd be easy to push out of the way, but a wrecked Herc? Not so much."

Surprisingly, Jones was the calmest he'd been throughout this ordeal. His voice showed no stress when he said, "We're going to have to land a little fast, too. No, make that a lot fast. Every time I retard the throttle, the nose drops like a rock. Can't hold it up with the elevators, either, so I'm going to need power to the very last second. Make sure you're strapped in real tight…and pray that this works."

The final approach was surprisingly smooth but, as advertised, much too fast. When the ship got down to fifty feet, the ground was whizzing by as if they were on a strafing run, not a heartbeat from touchdown. She seemed only inches off the ground when Jones shut down the forward engine as required for a belly landing. At that instant, it was as if the aircraft simply gave up. His fingers hadn't even left the ignition switch yet when she fell hard onto the soft, wet ground.

There was no sense she was decelerating as she slid. To Jif, a hurtling sensation, coupled with the torrent of muddy water being flung to either side like a speedboat's bow wave, reminded him of an amusement park attraction—*The Log Flume Ride*—where you rode in a mock-up of a carved-out log that plunged down a watery chute at breakneck speed. But that ride eventually slowed and came to a stop. The O-2 didn't seem like she'd ever quit sliding. There was no controlling what direction she took, either. Those on board were at the mercy of physics and the elements.

Then she hit what must've been a shallow ditch that tossed her a few feet back into the air. The brief hop lasted but a second, but in that second she dropped her right wing and came down on her wingtip. It promptly dug into the muck. The ship spun around that wingtip like a tethered toy for nearly a full revolution, whipping her occupants against their harnesses like rag dolls until her energy was finally spent and she came to an abrupt stop.

It took some effort by Jif to push the cabin door open; a berm of mud had piled against its lower edge.

But with adrenaline flowing in abundance, they were out quickly enough, eager to finally see the extent of the damage the aircraft had sustained in flight.

What they found wasn't surprising. One of the aft engine's propeller blades was mangled and missing half its length. Most of the engine cowl panels were gone, fallen away over Laos, never to be seen again. But part of one panel, though displaced, was still with the airplane. It had knifed almost all the way through the horizontal stabilizer between the two tail booms. Looking closer, they could see the structure of the stabilizer was severely compromised. Only the aft spar—a thin aluminum extrusion just a few inches wide—was still keeping it from snapping in two.

Jones had squatted beneath the stabilizer for an up-close view of the damage. But once he saw it, he was instantly transformed from a man merely compiling data on a mishap to one suddenly aware of how close he'd just come to dying. Standing now on trembling legs, he repeated over and over again, "Holy fucking shit! Holy fucking shit! Holy—"

Not one for histrionics, Jif asked, "So what's the bloody problem, Bill? We made it, didn't we?"

"Do you know how close we came to *not* making it, dude? If that spar had snapped…

All at once, Jif understood the pilot's epiphany. He needed no further explanation; he, too, realized that had the spar failed, the ship would've entered a death dive from which there would've been no recovery. But he didn't see any point in making a scene about things that *didn't* happen, especially when there's enough bad stuff *actually* happening to get excited about.

As Jones took one last look at the near-fatal damage to his ship, he said, "No wonder that elevator was so fucking heavy."

"Yeah, but you handled it great. And didn't some pilot once say *any landing you can walk away from is a good landing*?"

Jones dismissed that with a shake of his head. "Whoever said that never had to sit through a post-crash debrief. Believe me, man…it's assumed from the get-go you screwed the pooch unless you can prove otherwise beyond a shadow of a doubt. Pilots eat their own, you know?"

*****

The weather cleared, and FSB Sophia became operational later that afternoon, with the loss of just a few helicopters. Temporarily without an airplane to fly, Jif and Jones had no further participation in the insertion. They were stuck cooling their heels at Quang Tri.

The following day, they were back in the air in a different O-2, covering the helicopter assault on *LZ Hope*, a point only four kilometers northeast of Tchepone and very near a reported NVA base area. It was a massive airlift that transported two battalions. The resistance was surprisingly light, with the loss of only one chopper. Several battalions soon moved into Tchepone, a ground assault that met no significant opposition.

With the town seemingly devoid of enemy—just as Jif had found it a few nights before in the YO-3A—the FAC ship received authorization to scout farther west of the village along the Banghiang River. It was terrain both of them were familiar with, Jones from his missions spotting for USAF tac air and gunships, Jif from his night sortie on board *Silent Sara.*

"There's been a lot of talk about NVA armor in these parts," Jones said. "You seen many tanks?"

"Some," Jif replied. "Saw quite a few get knocked out."

"I'm worried about those T-54s, man," Jones said. "They're supposed to be badass vehicles. We think we engaged some a few weeks ago. It was night…we could've been wrong…but a Spectre riddled a few of them for what seemed like forever. I'm talking thousands of rounds…some of them were even APIs—you know, armor-piercing incendiaries. Near as I could tell, they didn't do much damage to the tanks after all that. Probably gave those gook tankers some hellacious headaches, but…"

"I know. The Cobra pilots are saying the same thing…they don't have the weapon to knock out a serious tank like the fifty-four. Those little rockets they carry don't cut it, and like you said, bullets just bounce off."

"Something's supposed to be in the pipeline, though, Jif…a wire-guided standoff missile, perfect for use by attack choppers and mobile ground launchers. Can't get here soon enough…especially if the NVA's getting serious about armored warfare."

"I heard the rumor about those missiles, too, Bill. I await their arrival with bated breath."

For thirty minutes, their search pattern turned up nothing. The ground, still wet from rain, sent up no dust clouds to betray vehicle movements. Surprisingly, that same soft earth revealed no fresh imprints from tires or armored vehicle tracks along the countless trails.

Then, as they began a turn back toward Tchepone, Jones said, “Son of a bitch! Will you look at that!”

“Show me,” Jif said, leaning across the cockpit to get the pilot’s side window POV. But after a few seconds, he added, “I don’t see anything.”

“Just west of that bend in the river, about a klick away from us at the base of the massif. Wait for it…it’ll be back…”

And then it was visible again: a small patch of the forest crown that fluttered in a way not seen in nature. Jif said, “Bloody hell. It’s like they’re waving a giant flag. They must be wrestling with a camo net in the wind.” He took a better look through binoculars. “We’ve got ourselves a battery under that net. Looks like four tubes…big stuff, too, that can throw rounds past A Luoi. Probably one-five-two millimeter—can’t tell what type, though. We’re a little too far—”

“And we’re not getting any fucking closer, Jif. This isn’t like a chopper assault, where the triple-A is lying in wait for the troop-carrying ships and doesn’t want to give itself away. Out here in the middle of nowhere, they’ve got nothing to lose by lighting us up with whatever they’ve got. So what’s your preference—my jets or your artillery?”

“My artillery. It’s faster.”

“Roger that, dude. Just do those guns in quick, before they start shooting at our ARVN pals.”

*****

By the time the fire mission had neutralized the NVA battery, they'd expended their loiter fuel. As they were returning to Quang Tri, Jif said, "That was some find, Bill. Good eyes."

"Hey, I learned a lot about spotting anomalies in Mother Nature from you, man. Probably wouldn't have given that flapping net a second look before you schooled me."

"Glad to be of service," Jif replied. "But I've got a nasty suspicion there are a lot more artillery pieces that nobody's found yet. With the amount of NVA infantry that's around here, there's probably plenty of gun tubes and rockets backing them up. And it must all be damn well hidden."

A few minutes later, the NVA proved that assumption correct. Cruising past FSB Lolo at 5,000 feet on their way home, Jif and Jones witnessed the contrails of several large-caliber rockets streaking high overhead toward South Vietnam. A few minutes later, Khe Sanh was reporting damage and casualties from 122-millimeter rockets that had just struck the base.

*****

On arrival at Quang Tri, Jif got the word that he was to return to Dong Ha immediately. "Looks like we're getting broken up again, Bill," he told Jones. "It's been great working with you…even with that belly landing."

"The pleasure was all mine, dude. Until next time, eh?"

Thirty minutes later, Jif was back at Dong Ha's joint HQ after hitching a ride on a chopper shuttling mail to the various base camps. When he arrived at the entryway to the command center, Colonel McKnight intercepted him, saying, "We'd better stay out here for a few minutes. The shit's hitting the fan in there again."

Even from the hallway, they could hear what was going on. General Lam was giving an impromptu and boisterous speech in a jumble of English and Vietnamese, loudly boasting of *the great ARVN victory* at Tchepone. He was so full of himself—suddenly *the victor, the conqueror*—that Jif thought the general was going to start pounding his chest like King Kong any second.

Lam ordered one of his staff officers to detail the trappings of this *great victory*: the number of NVA bodies found—by the hundreds, supposedly—the number of weapons seized, and the many tons of rice that had been captured.

It didn't take long for General Sutherland's disgust with this ad hoc celebration to bring it to a stop. He told Lam, "Let's get one thing straight…you didn't kill any of those NVA. They're not *your* body count. They belong to the American air support."

His tone imperious, Lam insisted, "Irrelevant! My forces have eradicated the NVA in Tchepone itself."

"I don't mean to piss in your mess kit, General, but by all accounts—from *your* own people, too—there wasn't more than a platoon of NVA in Tchepone, which you entered with *three battalions*. That's not exactly something to brag about."

But Lam's spirits would not be dampened. He replied, "I have achieved President Thieu's objective. I claim victory for the Republic of Vietnam!"

"Oh, bullshit," Sutherland said. "You can't claim a damn thing yet. If you want to really impress me, show me your plan to start engaging the NVA west of Tchepone, where the NVA—and the Ho Chi Minh Trail—have relocated."

Lam glowered at the American, as if convinced he didn't have to show him anything.

"And while you're at it," Sutherland continued, "let's review your plan for holding the Tchepone region until the start of the rainy season seven weeks from now. That was the whole point of Lam Son 719, wasn't it?" Everyone knew the comment was meant strictly as sarcasm, for it was no secret the South Vietnamese president had abandoned that goal weeks ago.

Without so much as a word in reply, Lam stormed from the room, his lackeys in tow.

Chapter Thirteen

The ARVN remained in Tchepone for a grand total of two days. Their presence was uncontested. Then they began a *voluntary withdrawal*, which was declared appropriate since their objective of taking the town had been met. In conjunction with this withdrawal, they announced two new objectives: neutralizing two NVA base areas, one a few kilometers northeast of Tchepone at a village called Ta Louang, the other in the A Shau Valley of South Vietnam, some forty kilometers to the south. Neither of these new objectives would have any impact on the current status of the Ho Chi Minh Trail, now rerouted roughly ten kilometers west of Tchepone. They were nothing more than face-saving gestures.

Furious with the ARVN's lack of resolve, General Abrams flew to the Dong Ha headquarters with key members of his staff. He found General Sutherland and his staffers equally enraged. Sutherland expressed his apprehensions this way: "Withdrawal, my ass, sir. This is a retreat, plain and simple…and it's about to turn into a fighting retreat or worse. They're going to lose just as many men, if not more, on the way out as they did on the way in. And all to accomplish nothing. The trail has not been cut off. Not even close."

The resigned look on Abrams' face reflected the accuracy of Sutherland's assessment. He had this to add: "I'm very concerned about the continued loss of helicopters, General. I'm afraid this withdrawal might jack up an already unacceptable loss rate even higher. What's your plan to mitigate those losses?"

"Well, sir, I thought at first the best plan was to tell them that if they wanted to pull out prematurely like this, they could do it walking, but—"

Abrams interrupted: "But you had the good sense to realize that was an unsatisfactory idea, right?"

"Of course, sir," he replied, a little embarrassed for sounding less than serious in a critical situation. "But here's what I actually intend to do…there will be *no* helicopter extractions of units in contact with the enemy. They'll have to either defeat that enemy or break contact and withdraw on foot to a cold LZ."

"And you'll provide all the air and artillery support you have available to help that unit accomplish either of those options, correct?"

"Absolutely, sir."

"Outstanding," Abrams said. "Make damn certain that General Lam advises every one of his commanders of this policy. I'll handle the powers that be in Saigon and Washington. One thing I need you all to be cognizant of…we can expect the NVA pursuers to be a heavily armored force, equipped with enough T-54s to give the ARVN a real problem." He pointed to a one-star general and said, "Parton, you're the advisor to their armored division. Tell us how the ARVN has prepared itself to deal with an onslaught of tanks possessing superior firepower."

"Extensive training has been accomplished on the strengths and weaknesses of the T-54, sir," Parton explained. "Rearguard units are being amply supplied with M72 LAW, as well."

Abrams tried not to laugh out loud. “I’m hoping there are at least a few ARVN troopers with the balls to get close up behind a tank with their LAWs. Otherwise, they’ve wasted the weapon…and probably their own lives, too. But I’m sure they—and you, General Parton—realize the strengths of the T-54 far outweigh its weaknesses. In the same vein, I have no doubt that properly utilized M41 tanks of the ARVN can defeat T-54s. Hell, our outgunned Shermans tore up German Panthers and Tigers back in Europe not with superior firepower but with sound tactics and skillful maneuver. There’s no reason the ARVN tankers can’t do the same. What troubles me most, though, is the tendency of ARVN crews to abandon their tanks when faced with a serious threat. I don’t suppose you’ve found a way to discourage such behavior?”

“I can counsel their commanders until I’m blue in the face, sir, but—”

Abrams finished the sentence for him: “But the answer is no. I understand that, believe me.” He turned to the Air Force liaison and said, “The burden of tank killing will probably fall to your tac air, Colonel. I want double the number of sorties loaded with napalm. If we can’t pierce their armor, the best we can hope for is to roast their crews.”

“Copy that, sir,” the colonel replied. “We’ll make it happen.”

“Very fine,” Abrams said. “Now, I don’t need to remind any of you that if the ARVN disintegrates during this *withdrawal*, as they call it, there’ll be no one except our American forces to keep the NVA from flooding into Quang Tri Province. Such an incursion absolutely cannot happen. We'll all be looking for new jobs by the next sunrise."

He let that sink in for a moment before adding, "Bear in mind, gentlemen, the ARVN forces that undertook this misadventure constitute a significant portion of the Republic of Vietnam's troops. If those forces are rendered combat ineffective, President Nixon won't be able to proclaim the success of his Vietnamization plan. Even as things stand right now, it might be a stretch to make that proclamation…but I'm confident he'll find a way. That's what we politicians do, isn't it?"

Every man in the room with one star or more on his collar smiled inwardly, feeling certain that he was a member of that elite, collective *we*. Everyone of lesser rank thought the general's use of *we* was just a Freudian slip.

Sutherland asked, "What about the press, sir? How much access do we give them now?"

"Even less than before, General," Abrams replied. "Restrict them to the headquarters here at Dong Ha and feed them a daily briefing. Do everything you can to limit their access to aircrews. I don't want to see another orgy of inaccurate reporting on how the ARVN are fleeing the battlefield en masse, clinging to the skids of helicopters. Those incidents were limited to just four battalions—each one poorly led, I'm afraid—out of the eighteen deployed. It was not—and is not—indicative of the entire South Vietnamese Army. But the press would love to keep tarring and feathering President Nixon—and me—for any and all ARVN failures. We don't want to give them the opportunity to do that. We're busy enough as it is without having to rebut horseshit masquerading as journalism."

He scanned the assembled faces until he picked out Colonel McKnight, saying, "That's why I'm going to need your PRT just as much—if not more—as I have in the past to provide me with the truth of what the ARVN is actually doing versus what they claim to be doing, Colonel. In fact, I'm looking to pump several more qualified officers your way, but this fiasco may be over before we can get them to you, so we'll play that by ear. On the plus side, with the mass airlifts over now, General Sutherland has assured me you'll once again have the helicopters you need to fulfill your mission."

*****

The PRT would be back in the air over Laos at first light tomorrow. As Jif studied maps, aerial photos, and situation reports for his upcoming mission, the familiar voice of Sergeant Major Sean Moon boomed from the doorway: "I'll bet you're glad to be getting back into action, Captain Miles."

"I thought you might be here with General Abe, Sergeant Major. But I've got news for you…I never left the action. Been flying with a FAC the last couple of days."

His face a disapproving scowl, Sean replied, "Don't tell me you volunteered for that duty."

"Nope. I was ordered."

Sean lost the scowl. "All right, then…you had no choice. I trust you had an interesting time with the blue-suiters?"

"Sure did. Only crashed once…a belly landing, actually."

"And lived to tell the tale once again, I see. How many of those nine lives have you used up so far?"

"Lost bloody count, Sergeant Major. But while I've got you—a bona fide armor expert—tell me all about the T-54. Give me the down and dirty."

"Okay, here's the deal," Sean began. "It's got good armor and a real good gun—better than an M41, that's for damn sure—but it's got a few serious weaknesses, too. The sighting system is kinda primitive, so they can't hit shit at long range. Inside of five hundred yards, though, it'll turn you inside out every time. And it's useless in a hull-down position on a backslope, because the tube can't be lowered past the horizontal."

Jif asked, "That's it?"

"Nope. There's one more weak point, and it's a biggie. There's no crew basket that rotates with the turret when it traverses, just a fixed deck. They gotta do a dance every time it spins to keep up with the moving machinery, so it takes them extra seconds—precious seconds—to point and shoot."

"Good to know, Sergeant Major. Thanks."

After glancing at the items Jif was working with, Sean asked, "Looks like you're going to be scouting that ARVN picnic up at Ta Louang."

"Why do you call it a picnic?"

"The NVA base area around that ville has been plastered a couple of times recently by B-52s, Captain. They're not going to find anything there except bomb craters, dead bodies, ruined weapons, and fried rice. They'll count it all up and claim another *great ARVN victory*. In other words, another bullshit dick-wagging exercise for Thieu and his generals. But they won't be hanging around there too long. Intel already says the NVA is fixing to make the ARVN retreat down Route Niner a living hell. It's just a question of who can move faster. But I guess they already told you that, right?"

"Affirmative," Jif replied. "I've got a hunch this withdrawal is going to be like watching a movie in rewind."

"Roger that. Just do me, your wife, and your family a favor, will you? Try not to be the goddamn hero, okay? I mean it, Captain. We're getting down to the last chapters of this circle jerk."

"Do you mean the last chapters of this operation? Or the war?"

"Both. It'd be a fucking shame to buy it now."

*****

Sean Moon had been right about the *picnic*. Looking down from the LOACH, Jif could see a battalion or so of ARVN infantry strolling around Ta Louang, casually picking through the debris of demolished heavy weapons and ammunition stores, even gleefully taking pictures of each other with the trophies of their make-believe victory.

Jif had been reunited with CW3 Charlie Floyd, his pilot for much of Lam Son 719. Venturing a look at the activities a few hundred feet below, Floyd recoiled in disgust. A handful of ARVN troopers were posing for pictures with the corpses of NVA soldiers whose bodies, shattered by the unspeakable concussive force of a B-52 strike, resembled rag dolls. "Shit like that makes me want to puke," the pilot said. "All gooks are just fucking animals. Doesn't matter what side of the DMZ they're from."

"We're not exactly lily white when it comes to atrocities, Chief."

It was as if Jif had spoken blasphemy. Even with his face largely concealed by the flight helmet and aviator sunglasses, there was enough of Floyd's face visible for Jif to read his expression; it was one of adamant rejection, like a locked door to which no amount of truth held the key. There'd be no point mentioning how it had necessitated action at the division level to stop the collection and proud display by American soldiers of ears and fingers severed from their dead adversaries.

Some dude even tried to sell me a necklace of ears back at the start of my first tour. He seemed like such a normal kid, too...a real Midwestern farm boy. A year before, he'd been home, sharing milkshakes and sweet nothings with Suzy Creamcheese. But a few months in the Nam taught him it was okay to mutilate dead bodies.

And there'd be no point in bringing up My Lai, an atrocity born of abysmal leadership at the company level and then amplified by generals at Division and Corps as they covered it up for over a year, until the public clamor for truth and accountability became too great to withstand.

And those are just the headlines, Jif told himself. *There are so many acts of cruelty and depravity by both sides every day. Just ask any Vietnamese peasant who's had his ville burned to the ground because "it had to be destroyed to save it."*

All of us have a war criminal lurking inside. Even if you manage to keep him at bay, he'll taint your soul forever.

We're all fucking animals, Chief.

But the morality play would have to wait. Their heads on swivels, scanning the terrain in all directions, they were still trying to decide if this was a sightseeing mission or a combat patrol. Floyd asked, "Where the hell is the actual village of Ta Louang, anyway? There's not a damn thing standing at these map coordinates. Did it get flattened by *Arc Light*, too?"

"I reckon so, Chief. I'm not surprised the NVA used it as a base area, though. The terrain is tailor-made…not too hilly, a shitload of trails beneath the concealment of the forest, and only about four klicks north of Route Niner. Even a couple of streams for fresh water."

"Yeah, sounds like fucking heaven, sir. Right out of the tourist brochure."

Then Floyd said, "We've got some business coming up from Niner. Looks like ARVN tanks." He climbed the ship while putting her into a wide orbit for a better look.

Jif counted six M41s in column, moving toward the troopers at Ta Louang.

"What the hell are they going up there for?" Floyd wondered aloud. "Maybe they want to get their pictures taken with some stiffs, too?"

"I'm not so sure," Jif replied. "There's a lot of radio chatter on the ARVN command freq. I can't understand any of it, but they're sure worked up about something. Let's go north, over the gap between those two hilltops. Maybe we can figure out what's going on."

They didn't have to go very far north to see the NVA tanks coming the other way. There were four of them, still a kilometer north of Ta Louang.

Floyd asked, "Are those tanks what I think they are?"

"Yep. They're T-54s."

"Never saw one before," Floyd said. "I'm gonna get a little wider on them, just in case they've got triple-A on the roof."

"Yeah," Jif replied as he scanned the column with binoculars. "Looks like there's some infantry in trucks behind them. Don't see any really big triple-A weapons…but they could still be packing some twelve point seven millimeter."

"I don't think those ARVN walking around Ta Louang realize they're about to be in a world of hurt, Captain. They're still diddy-bopping around like they're on some school field trip. Can you raise them on the radio?"

"I'd have to go through the translators at Lang Vei. The fight's going to be on before I ever get the message across."

The ARVN tanks were within a few hundred meters of their fellow troopers at Ta Louang. Jif told Floyd, "Put me on the deck next to the M41s."

Floyd's reply: "Begging your pardon, sir, but are you out of your fucking mind?"

"Yeah, I might be, Chief. Just do what I say. You don't have to stay on the ground. In fact, you can keep an eye on the NVA armor for me from up top. I'll call you when I need a pickup."

"With all due respect, Captain, what are you trying to prove?"

"I'm trying to prove that the ARVN can take advantage of a golden opportunity."

Floyd did as he was told. Armed with his M16, a hand-held radio, and two smoke grenades, Jif jumped from the LOACH. Then she was airborne again. The pilot's shout—*Good luck, Captain. You're going to fucking need it*—was lost in the whine and buzz of the little chopper making her exit.

An ARVN captain ran over to meet him. His name was Phang, and his English was rudimentary, at best. As near as Jif could tell, Phang was more concerned that the helicopter had flown away. Jif assumed the man considered the chopper a vehicle for his escape when he asked, "He come back, yes?"

The urge to reply, *Sure, but not for you*, was strong. But it wouldn't be helpful. Instead, he launched straight into his suggestion on how to fight the NVA tanks.

The very idea terrified Phang, who began searching the skies for Floyd's LOACH and its promise of escape. Thinking it odd that a mere captain was the senior officer of what seemed a battalion of troops, Jif asked in English, "Who is in command here?"

Phang didn't grasp the question. Jif tried again in his rudimentary Vietnamese.

There was still no glimmer of comprehension.

Finally, Jif tried it in French: "*Qui commande?*"

Phang understood that version perfectly, even though he was surprised that an American—and one with an incongruous Australian accent, to boot—seemed to be multi-lingual. His reply: *"C'est moi."*

It is me.

Now that they had a common language in which to converse, Phang explained that the actual battalion commander—a lieutenant colonel—had already been flown to FSB A Luoi.

That's a new one, Jif thought. *A colonel abandons his troops even BEFORE the shit hits the fan.*

When Jif began to explain how the ARVN tanks could engage—and maybe even destroy—the approaching NVA T-54s, Phang shook his head, explaining he'd already been directed to call for an airstrike against the armor threat. He'd been preparing to do so when Jif's sudden arrival interrupted him. Then, in Vietnamese that Jif had trouble following, he told a subordinate to move his troopers south to Route 9, out of harm's way.

Still working in French, Jif explained that there was no time; air support wouldn't arrive for at least twenty minutes and the T-54s would be on top of them long before that. Phang then began to shout for his forward observer; he was going to request an artillery barrage on the T-54s.

Jif told him that would be a good idea, but they'd have to stop the enemy tanks from moving first. Hitting targets in motion with indirect artillery fire was more a matter of guesswork than certainty, one with a fairly low chance of success. It would change the calculus of this brewing battle very little, if at all.

He'd already identified a choice ambush site while still airborne. He showed his marked-up map to Phang, saying, "The best thing to do is bottle up the NVA tanks with your tanks. At that curve in the trail a few hundred meters to the west of here, your M41s could engage them from both flanks at a safe range. T-

54s can't shoot accurately at long range, and they'll have trouble taking on targets in two different directions simultaneously."

Phang didn't look like he wanted any part of the plan. But the sergeant leading the tanks—older and wiser, perhaps, than the captain—had joined the two officers, and he seemed willing. To make things even easier, he was far more facile with the English language than Phang.

"We can try," Sergeant Ky told Jif as his fingertip pinpointed a spot on the map, "but we must stop them no closer than here. Once we do stop them, we must have artillery support to help finish them."

"That's your call," Jif replied. "You've got a bloody good chance to destroy them all. Just remember…they have supporting infantry, and that infantry might cause you more problems than the T-54s unless your own infantry keeps them off you. I'm not sure your captain understands that."

If Captain Phang did understand, he still wasn't interested. He and his men were in full, disorganized retreat, intent on running all the way to Route 9 some four klicks to the south. In doing so, they were streaming right through the column of their own tanks, with no intention of joining forces with the vehicles.

Ky wasn't surprised by their exodus. He told Jif, "My tanks will do the ambush alone, but as I just said, we must have the artillery support. I'm sure the forward observer is fleeing with the rest of them, however, and I can't call artillery from a buttoned-up tank. I can't talk to the guns directly, anyway."

"I know," Jif replied. "Your radios don't tune the same frequencies. But I can be your aerial observer, and

I can talk to everybody from the helicopter. Just give me the freqs you're on."

Ky wrote those two frequencies on Jif's map. Then he sketched the ambush site location onto his own so he could explain the scheme to his crews.

"We have a plan, Captain Miles," Ky said. "I will divide my tanks between the two areas you marked."

"Roger that, Sergeant. I'll be your guardian angel overhead."

"I very much hope so, Captain," Ky replied.

The LOACH returned within ninety seconds of Jif's radio call. Floyd asked, "What happened, Captain? You look like you're waiting for a bus all by your lonesome. They all leave you flat?"

"Not all of them, Chief. Head north and get up high. About two thousand feet ought to do it. We're going to play aerial observer for the tankers."

"Ah, for fuck's sake, not again. I thought we were just going to watch this war, but you keep wanting to participate."

"This may be our last chance to play army, Chief."

"I sure don't like the sound of that, sir. Not one bit."

Chapter Fourteen

Sergeant Ky's six tanks moved slowly through the thin woods, three vehicles on either side of a trail that rose gradually toward high ground. Viewed from the LOACH, their progress seemed ponderous, almost reluctant. Jif wished they were moving faster; it would give the tankers more time to establish optimal firing positions for engaging the NVA tanks.

Floyd asked, "Aren't those trees going to be a problem, Captain? You know…restrict their fields of fire and all?"

"Sergeant Ky doesn't seem to think so," Jif replied. "Scrawny trees don't pose much of an obstacle to tanks. But they sure are taking their sweet bloody time."

Floyd: "Do you think those T-54s even see the ARVN tanks?"

"Sure they do. I reckon they haven't shot yet because they're trying to get into better firing positions, ones that are farther downhill so they don't have to worry about tube elevations bottoming out on them."

Aware of his tanks' sluggish progress into the ambush positions, Ky told Jif he was now worried that NVA sappers on board the trucks might dismount, sneak through the woods, and get behind his vehicles even before he could take on the enemy tanks.

"I can help with that," Jif told him. "Those trucks are vulnerable to artillery whether they're moving or not."

"Please hurry," Ky replied. Even over the radio, the tension in his voice expressed the fear that things might already be going wrong.

There was still time to make sure they went right. Jif picked a point two hundred meters ahead of the slow-moving trucks and targeted it with an adjustment round.

Floyd asked, "You think that's enough of a lead, sir?"

"Doesn't matter, Chief. It just gets us in the ballpark."

"You want me to get higher to see the gun-target line better?"

"Nah, don't bother," Jif replied. "A Luoi's going to shoot it. I've got the line visualized close enough for government work. I can adjust off it, no sweat."

The adjustment round came crashing down, arriving in just over a minute from the call for fire, much faster than expected considering the translation and relay necessary at Lang Vei. It impacted just off the trail, about fifty meters in front of the lead truck, which came to a dead stop. The three trucks behind didn't stop until they were bunched up bumper-to-bumper off the leader's tailgate.

"That's an unexpected gift," Jif said to Floyd. "They just made themselves a compact target for me." Then he told Lang Vei, "Right four-zero, drop five-zero, fuze VT, fire for effect."

He expected it would take a little longer for that six-round volley to arrive. There'd be the extra computation for the airbursts, VT fuzes to set, and five additional tubes on which to pick up sight pictures and level the bubbles. But to his surprise, the report of *Shot, over* was in his headset in just under a minute.

Fourteen seconds later, a tight cluster of six airbursts exploded over the trucks. Viewed from the LOACH as she stood off well to the west, the vehicles seemed strangely unaffected, as if they'd been hit by just a brief blast of wind that ruffled their canvas tops and kicked up dirt all around them. When the chopper made a pass behind the trucks, dead or dying troops were plainly visible on the beds; only a few survivors were seen running into the woods. On closer inspection with binoculars, the vehicles' canvas tops were holed like Swiss cheese from the shower of deadly steel fragments.

Floyd asked, "Well, it doesn't look like they'll be shooting at us now. You ready to shift fire to the tanks?"

"Not yet," Jif replied. "Not until they stop. We'd just be wasting rounds. Ky's people need to do their thing first."

But it was still taking too long for them to *do their thing*. The three M41s of the eastern element had taken up what seemed to be commanding positions. Jif knew that Ky's vehicle was among that group.

But the three ARVN tanks making up the western element were still not where they should've been. They'd used the bend in the trail to mask their crossing of it—a smart tactical move—but then seemed to lose the plot, taking too long to swing their bows toward the enemy tanks, leaving their far more vulnerable flanks exposed. Jif thought, *It's like they're being a little dainty with the trees, as if this sparse forest is going to actually provide concealment for their twenty-ton monsters.* All the while, the four T-54s were bearing down on them. Within seconds, they'd be less than five hundred meters from the closest ARVN tanks and capable of delivering accurate, devastating rounds from their 100-millimeter main guns.

Floyd said, "What the fuck, over! Are the ARVN going to shoot or not?"

"We'd better give them some help," Jif replied, "for whatever bloody good it will do." He called in a continuation of the fire mission that had devastated the trucks, shifting a volley to the T-54s. But he had to guess where they'd be in a minute's time.

In the moments before that volley arrived, the fight began. From one of the tanks on the east side of the trail—Ky's element—a well-aimed shot was fired that struck the lead T-54 in its turret ring. It shuddered to a stop as if a dead man's switch had been tripped. It didn't burn, but no one clambered from its hull; it was now a tomb that would be nothing but a barricade for the rest of this fight.

The second T-54 in the column took quick advantage of that barricade, driving into position on its far side, using it as a shield from Ky's element. Then it stopped and fired a round that penetrated the exposed flank of an M41 in the western element on the opposite side of the trail.

Everything fell still, as if some supernatural finger had pressed the pause button on reality. But that lasted only a few rapid heartbeats, until the struck M41 exploded with a force that rocked the airborne LOACH despite her being hundreds of meters away. When the smoke and dust settled, the tank's turret was lying upside down alongside its hull, which had become a cauldron of flames spewing thick black smoke, punctuated by the flashes and shock waves of ammunition cooking off.

Another M41 in the western element was in the process of traversing its gun onto T-54 number two but never got the chance to fire. Struck in the flank by a round from that same enemy vehicle, it exploded just like its sister, but without the time delay.

There was one tank still alive in that element. Watching its movements, Jif said, “That crew doesn’t know whether to shit or go blind.”

From above, that tank’s actions looked like a comedy of errors as it started to back up and then stopped to pivot left, exposing its soft stern to the T-54s. It was given a brief reprieve when the artillery volley fell among the NVA tanks, though no round actually hit any of them. But the shock of the impacts dazed the enemy tankers, giving the crew of that last serviceable M41 of the western element the opportunity to abandon their still untouched vehicle and run away.

The NVA tankers were incapacitated for only a few moments, however. Not knowing the ARVN vehicle was now unmanned, T-54 number two dispatched the M41 with a single shot to its engine compartment. Within seconds, the tank was burning like the other two in the western element, its ammunition cooking off like lethal popcorn.

What had so briefly been a six versus three numerical advantage for the ARVN vehicles was now an even fight: three versus three. Jif had a far better view of the action than Ky, and when he told the sergeant that his western element no longer existed, the reply was, “Continue the artillery. You must cover my withdrawal.”

The three surviving T-54s turned their attention to Ky's eastern element. With numbers two and three now masked behind their destroyed leader, the number four vehicle pivoted rapidly to be head-to-head with Ky's three M41s, which were backing away from their ambush positions. Before the NVA tank could get off a shot, another volley of artillery crashed down. Again, there were no direct hits, but the punishing percussion bought Ky's element precious seconds. It gave two of them time to sight on T-54 number four. They fired a split-second apart…

And watched as one round sailed past the hull while the other struck it squarely on the bow. But the direct hit didn't stop number four for long. After a few seconds, the crew shook off the pounding in their heads and their bleeding ears and continued moving toward the ARVN tanks. After pushing forward about fifty yards, number four stopped to get off a shot…

Which scored a direct and devastating hit on an M41 at the driver's compartment. Every hatch blew off the vehicle as the interior became a blast furnace.

Floyd said, "I'm not believing this shit. The ARVN had them! They fucking had them! But half the team dragged their ass and got burned. And because of that, now the whole team's getting burned." He paused before telling Jif, "I guess that answers your question, Captain."

"What question is that, Chief?"

"You know…the one about seeing if the ARVN could take advantage of a golden opportunity."

Jif couldn't disagree. At least in this encounter, the answer was a definite no.

T-54 number two decided to come out from behind the cover of its dead leader. It was a fatal mistake. An M41—Jif figured it was Ky's tank—killed it with a shot to the flank as it drove around the inert hull. Number two's interior was ablaze instantly. Only one man got out, and he was on fire. He collapsed after just a few steps and was consumed by his own flames.

With both sides further reduced by one vehicle apiece, the fight was still at even numbers: two versus two.

"The NVA is trying to close the distance," Jif said. "The old grab 'em by the belt buckle and don't let go trick. That way, our artillery and air support won't be able to do a bloody thing to help."

Floyd: "Will it matter, sir? The Air Force hasn't even shown up yet, and the artillery isn't helping a whole lot right now, anyway."

Ky was talking on the radio, so one of those two M41s still alive was his. He was begging for any fire support he could get. As he pleaded, yet another artillery volley fell around the NVA tanks with little effect.

Floyd asked, "The T-54 that's still hiding behind its buddy…is it dead? It hasn't done anything in—"

But before he could finish his thought, the NVA tankers in number three answered the question. Their hull still masked behind the corpse of the lead T-54, they'd swung the turret toward Ky's element and fired a series of shots. Number four—in the open and on its own—was on the move again and firing, too.

Both the remaining tanks in Ky's element were struck at least once. One blew up spectacularly, like all the others killed before.

But Ky's vehicle was still alive and on the radio. It kept driving in reverse until its left track, damaged by NVA rounds, finally fell off. Unable to maneuver anymore, it fired off a round at each of the advancing T-54s. They were both hits…

But neither was a killing shot. Or even a wounding one. The T-54s stopped for a moment but then continued their advance.

Jif told Ky, "There's a clearing about two hundred meters off your stern. Get out and run to it right now. We'll pick you up when you get there."

Floyd hated that idea. "Are you kidding me, Captain? You want to become another sitting duck for those NVA tanks?"

"Relax. This'll be quick. Can't just bloody leave them."

"This is starting to sound like *mark the target with a burning LOACH*, sir."

"Shut the fuck up and fly the bird, Chief."

A FAC was on the radio now, asking, "I see a whole lot of smoke down there, but I can't tell who's who. You still need me?"

"Hang loose a minute," Jif replied. "Can you see the LOACH?"

"Affirmative."

"That's great. We're going to make a quick pick-up. After that, you're going to have three to four tanks in a knot just to the west of our present position. Roast them all."

The FAC asked, "Aren't some of them friendlies?"

"Affirmative, but they're dead friendlies. Write them off for good, before they end up in the wrong hands."

"Copy that," the FAC replied, "but isn't there an artillery mission still in progress?"

"Negative. I just shut it off."

"Outstanding. Fast movers three minutes out."

Floyd said, "This ain't gonna work, Captain. We're gonna be shit out of luck, just like those tankers."

"Keep your drawers on, Chief. Look…Ky and his crew are halfway to the clearing. Put the ship down."

Floyd did what he was told and eased the LOACH into the tight clearing. As she entered a hover a foot or so off the ground, Jif yelled, "SWING THE NOSE RIGHT!" Then he was hanging out the doorway as far as his seat harness would allow, spraying the tree line with short bursts from his M16.

Startled by the gunfire, Floyd was slow on the pedals; the pivot Jif wanted wasn't happening.

"NOW, CHIEF! NOSE RIGHT."

The incoming bullet that smacked off the side armor of Floyd's seat convinced him to make the maneuver, and make it immediately: *Yeah, why not? Then this batshit-crazy captain will be in the line of fire and not me.*

Slewing the ship's nose gave Jif the wider field of fire he needed. Ejecting the expended magazine from his rifle and slamming in a full one, he told himself, *I hate that I can't really aim, but I've got to keep their heads down any way I can, or we're going to get our asses riddled.*

Hanging out the door like he was, the best he could do was use the dust and debris of his bullet strikes to move the bursts around, like aiming with tracers. It seemed to be working, at least so far.

"I don't see them," Floyd said. "How many?"

"No idea," Jif replied, still firing with one hand, reaching for a third magazine with the other.

They both knew that the time they could remain there was down to seconds. Ky and his men still hadn't broken out of the woods.

Hovering just inches off the ground in this tight clearing was like trying to fly in a closet. It was hard work for the pilot but better than landing. They could make a quicker getaway from a hover.

But Floyd was getting too antsy; it seemed like the clearing was closing in around them and the whirling rotor blades. He appeared ready to jerk up on the collective and rocket them into the air as he said, "Where the fuck are those tankers? We can't be here anymore. It's goddamn suicide!"

"Give them a couple more seconds," Jif said, the calmness in his voice surprising even him. "Wait for it…"

"Are you even hitting anything, Captain?"

"Can't tell. But they're not shooting at us anymore, right?"

The hovering ship rocked as two of Ky's men broke from the tree line on the dead run and hurled themselves into the aft cabin. It shuddered again as Ky and his last crewman jumped onto the skids and clung to the frame of the open doorway. All the ARVN were screaming, "GO! GO!"

The quickest way out for the LOACH was to buzz directly over whoever was trying to shoot at them. That path involved no turning, no exposing the sides of the ship to their fire. Jif kept up his fusillade during the escape, firing his M16 straight down until the magazine was empty. Once they'd flown a few hundred meters at treetop height, Floyd dared to gain altitude and turn south toward Route 9.

Jif spun around in his seat, asking the ARVN tankers, "Everyone okay back there?"

Surprisingly, they were. Ky and the other skid-rider were now wedged into seated positions on the floor of the cramped aft cabin, their legs still dangling outside.

Looking down at what had been the scene of the battle, they watched as the fifty-ton T-54s plowed forward, leaving a swath of flattened trees that were like arrows pointing right to them. Those arrows were of great help to the FAC, who planted his smoke rockets practically right on top of the tanks.

Floyd asked, "Where do we drop these guys, Captain?"

Jif shouted the same question to Ky, who replied, "Take us to Captain Phang."

As they adjusted course to where Phang and his people had withdrawn, two F-100 fighter-bombers streaked low over the site of the tank brawl, cleansing it with multiple canisters of napalm. The inferno that resulted—and the continued ammunition cook-offs it caused—would burn for another twenty minutes.

Both sides had lost all of their tanks: the NVA four, the ARVN six. Floyd said, "How much you want to bet the ARVN brass write that action up as a draw?"

Jif replied, "Maybe…but I wouldn't be surprised if they claimed it as another *great victory*."

*****

It wasn't hard to find Acting Commander Phang's battalion. They were a klick south on the trail leading to Route 9, a few hundred men milling aimlessly. Viewed from the air, they looked more like a mob queuing for a train than a unit in a combat zone. Considerations like flank security and tactical dispersion seemed the furthest things from their minds. They became very attentive to the helicopter passing low overhead, preparing to touch down in an open spot along the trail.

Jif told Floyd, "Forget it. Don't land here. We'll take these dudes to A Luoi instead."

"Why, Captain? I really need to get rid of this extra weight."

"Bear with it a little longer, Chief. Those troopers down there…they see these guys already catching a ride…it's like the *big green taxi* has arrived. I reckon they'll storm the ship the moment we touch down. We'll never take off again without having to kill a bunch of them."

"Okay, I can dig that. But can't we just dump our load off down the road apiece?"

"Cut them some slack, Chief. They're having a real bad day. Bring them to A Luoi."

"They don't deserve that kind of courtesy, Captain."

"That's not your call, Chief."

Chapter Fifteen

General Sutherland's prediction about the ARVN withdrawal was proving prophetic: *They're going to lose just as many men, if not more, on the way out as they did on the way in.*

"And it's a fucking shame," Boyd Gray said. "So many of the ARVN are fighting like tigers. But their leaders…they're not worth a damn, even if they bother to stick around when the shit hits the fan."

"Tell us something we don't already know, Boyd," the colonel replied as he tossed aside the latest revision to the ops order from General Lam's HQ. "There's not much point even reading that pile of bullshit. All the coordination, the timetables, the fire support, and the orderly movement that's being spelled out on those pages aren't worth the ink they're printed with, because none of it's going to happen. The moment an ARVN unit smells the NVA anywhere near them, they'll high-tail it toward the border, ops plan be damned. We've been watching them do it over and over again for a week now. Those people really know how to put the *us* in clusterfuck."

Jif entered the room, the last one back from the morning's observation flights. It was obvious from the look on his face that it had been another frustrating experience. The colonel asked, "I take it you don't have any good news to lift our spirits, Captain Miles?"

"Negative on the good news, sir. That ad hoc convoy from A Luoi—you know, the one using tanks and APCs to pull the artillery pieces out of there—got as far as LZ Bravo before the NVA started plastering it with their own artillery."

"And they got stopped there? They were practically to the border, for cryin' out loud."

"Roger that, Colonel…but it gets worse. As soon as the artillery shut off, NVA infantry moved in. The vehicles that could still drive tried to drop their tows and flee down Route Niner, but they came under fire from rockets and recoilless rifles. Most of them were abandoned where they sat. It looked like the bulk of them could probably still fight, too. Before you knew it, Niner looked like a motor park full of ARVN vehicles and howitzers. We had to call in the Air Force to destroy them all before they fell into NVA hands."

McKnight pounded a fist against the wall map. "Those assholes were in easy range of all that American artillery at Lao Bao, just sitting there waiting to help them. If the ARVN brass could only get their heads out of their asses long enough to coordinate…"

His voice dropped off. He knew he was preaching to the choir.

*****

Three days later, there was still one more regiment of ARVN soldiers some twelve kilometers inside Laos. They were trapped at LZ Brick by an NVA force blocking their escape route east to the border. The only reason they were still alive was the massive air support being provided by the USAF, two B-52 strikes in the last twenty-four hours alone. Those missions, plus countless sorties by Stinger and Spectre gunships, fighter-bombers, and attack helicopters—along with American artillery support from across the border—were taking a devastating toll on the NVA siege of the trapped regiment. But the enemy kept coming, as if they enjoyed a limitless pool of replacements. Worse, resupply helicopters were falling victim at alarming rates to the abundant triple-A around Brick. The volume of anti-aircraft fire made any suggestion of a helicopter evacuation for the trapped battalions out of the question. They'd have to walk out of Laos.

"We've got to eliminate this constant influx of NVA fighters," General Sutherland told his staff. "Otherwise, *we'll* be fighting them right here in Quang Tri Province in a day or so. Where the hell are they all coming from?"

His G2 replied, "We still believe they're coming mostly from the A Shau, sir. There's little evidence of any movement out of North Vietnam."

"Goddammit," the general said, "how many fucking divisions does the NVA have in that valley, anyway? We thought we put the screws to that infiltration weeks ago. Lacking visual confirmation, is there at least infrared or radar intel to back up your claim, Colonel?"

"We believe so, sir."

"Believe? Or know, Colonel?"

"Let's just say it's not one hundred percent conclusive, sir."

Turning to his Air Force liaison, Sutherland asked, "I suppose that explains why your night birds have had little contact with the enemy along that route?"

"To a point, sir. The other problem is that we're spread very thin providing round-the-clock fire support to the withdrawing ARVN units. Right now, the siege at LZ Brick is tying up almost all my air assets. At least we can be sure we're actually killing the enemy when we're supporting a unit under attack."

Sutherland couldn't argue with that reality. But it was still difficult to hear and impossible to change. Shaking his head sadly, he replied, "Thank goodness for small favors, eh? At least we're killing the bad guys *after* they break into the house. But it sure would be nice to keep them out of the house completely."

The general asked his G3, "What's the status of Lam's plan to rescue his regiment at Brick?"

"Two battalions of South Vietnamese Marines are still moving into position to envelop the NVA, sir," the G3 replied. "The battalion comprising the southern element of the pincer had a great deal of trouble getting all their forces to the jump-off point. The terrain caused more problems than envisioned getting their heavy weapons in place. As a result, the kickoff time for the counterassault has been moved to fourteen hundred hours."

An acetate overlay on the situation map diagrammed the rescue plan in detail. Sutherland gave it a long look and said, "Well, gentlemen, this appears to be the last chance for one of General Lam's major commands to actually do what they say they're going to do." Looking to Colonel McKnight, he added, "I'll need a detailed critique of their execution from your team immediately after this rescue is concluded. Maybe we can still put some sort of happy ending on this pointless fiasco."

*****

General Sutherland's HQ had placed one restriction on the PRT's scout helicopters: they were not to enter the battle area around LZ Brick until the assault by the Marines was well under way. "That comes directly from General Lam," the G3 told Colonel McKnight. "He doesn't want any of our snooping birds giving away the locations of his assault troops."

"No argument there," McKnight replied, "but to ensure the general's wishes are met, we're going to need a clear—and I mean *clear*—signal that the attack is, in fact, underway. Not the ARVN's usual equivocating bullshit."

"Copy that," the G3 replied. "I'll see to it that Lang Vei keeps you in the loop."

*****

To no one's surprise, the counterassault did not kick off at 1400 hours. It was nearly 1500 when Lang Vei announced in a coded message that it was finally underway. "Damn good thing we cooled our heels here on the ground at Lao Bao," Colonel McKnight told Jif and Gray. "Otherwise, we would've wasted tankfuls of gas flying around for nothing. Probably would've had to go refuel and miss the whole damn thing. At long last, gentlemen, let's get airborne and see what's going on."

Jif, once again in the LOACH piloted by CW3 Floyd, covered the double envelopment's northern pincer. Right away, they could tell there was no question the Vietnamese Marines were doing an efficient job routing the NVA. "Call me crazy," Jif observed, "but I think they even achieved the element of surprise."

"Yeah," Floyd replied. "Looks like they walked right up on those NVA from behind, and those commie gooks had no idea they were coming. How the fuck did the ARVN, of all people, ever pull that off?"

"Even a blind pig finds a truffle once in a while, Chief. Or maybe they caught the NVA sleeping. And they should be bloody tired, considering how much ground they've covered on foot lately."

"I hear you, Captain. Sounds like the Air Force has been having a field day blowing NVA trucks to shit. Walking is safer."

*****

The battle was decided in less than twenty minutes. The Vietnamese Marines overwhelmed the NVA, whose survivors were fleeing south, seeking to melt into the high, heavily forested terrain that rose in that direction. From his LOACH, Boyd Gray had a bird's-eye-view of their exodus.

"There's a lot of them getting away," he radioed to Colonel McKnight, "and the Marines aren't pursuing. Some artillery could put an instant world of hurt on those NVA right about now. Quicker than requesting an airstrike, for sure."

"That's Lang Vei's decision," McKnight replied. "Call it in."

Gray did just that. The American controllers at Lang Vei presented the idea to their ARVN counterparts, who approved it immediately and without reservation. The fire mission would go to an American battery at Lao

Bao. Within two minutes, that battery was laying devastating fire on the withdrawing NVA.

The fire mission had another effect no one had envisioned: the trapped ARVN battalions, thinking the American rounds were NVA artillery now free to zero in on them without killing their own, began to flee into the dense jungle to the north, the opposite direction of the NVA's withdrawal.

"Why are they going north?" Jif asked Lang Vei. "They've got a clear shot east to the border now. I'm losing them under the jungle canopy. Can't help them if I can't see them."

For a very brief moment, he'd considered landing at Brick, racing after the ARVN on foot, and telling them they were fucking up. But he knew what would happen if the LOACH did land: *They'll storm the helicopter, clinging to her any way they can, and we'll never get off the ground again.*

The senior officers will probably be the first to climb on board, too.

What none of the Americans realized—not McKnight's team, not the staff at Lang Vei—was that the Marines never informed the ARVN battalions at Brick that their escape route east was now open or the artillery fire falling to their south was friendly and no threat to them.

Sensing that something was seriously amiss, Colonel McKnight flew to Lang Vei, arriving there in minutes. When he reiterated what Jif had reported about the ARVN fleeing north for no reason—which the controllers had already heard and done nothing about—he was told by the colonel in charge, "Sorry, Ted, but it's not our job to tell the ARVN what to do. We just relay and coordinate."

"But how can they know what to do if they don't have accurate information?"

"You know the old saying, Ted? You can lead a horse to water…"

"Sure," McKnight replied, "but you'll step in a pile of his shit whether he drinks or not."

*****

Captain Gray and his pilot, CW2 Wadley—a twenty-year-old ex-high school sports star who thought combat helicopter flying was an absolute *gas*—were becoming a little too adventurous as they flew close to the fleeing NVA while adjusting fire on them. The adventure came to a sudden and frightening end when some triple-A rounds tore through the LOACH's engine compartment at the rear of the fuselage. The only thing keeping the little ship flying was the energy still in her whirling rotor, and that was dissipating fast. "Prepare for an outstanding autorotation," Wadley announced, his voice cracking like that of a terrified child. There was nowhere for the ship to go but down…and quickly.

They had no time to seek out a good place to land. The terrain below was completely covered with trees. Even if they could spot a clearing, it would have to be almost directly below the low-flying bird. The blades lacked the energy to get them any farther.

And wherever they ended up, it would be in close proximity to the NVA they'd been plastering with artillery. There was barely time for a mayday call before the LOACH fell into treetops and tumbled through splintering limbs to the ground.

When they heard Gray's mayday call, Jif and Floyd knew they could beat any other rescue ship to the crash site by a large margin. "Just so we can actually find them," Floyd fretted. "You know how the jungle can swallow up a LOACH." As they got closer to the reported location, he added, "Damn…I was almost wishing there was some smoke. This could be needle in a haystack time." Their first pass was at low level; they saw nothing but the airbursts of Gray's fire mission almost a kilometer away.

"Get higher so I can see better," Jif said. "We're going to have to take over adjusting these rounds while we look for the chopper."

Floyd looked at him like he was crazy. "Higher? Are you fucking kidding, Captain? They already knocked down Wadley's ship. You want to give them another easy target?"

"Yeah, you're right, Chief. Never mind." He still hadn't caught sight of the NVA, so he called for continuous repeats of the last volley. It was better than nothing until he could actually see where the enemy was.

Then, by sheer luck, they passed directly over the donut hole in the forest crown made by the falling LOACH. The ring of snapped-off limbs around the opening made it obvious something big and heavy had gone through. On the second pass, they could just make out the downed LOACH despite the veil of shadows at ground level.

"It'd be swell if we had a hoist to lift them out," Floyd said, "but we're shit out of luck on that score. What the hell are we gonna do?"

Jif noticed a small stream about a hundred meters to the west of the crash site. There was a tight spot along its winding course that wasn't overhung with jungle canopy; its banks featured narrow ribbons clear of trees, too. Pointing it out, he asked, "You think we can squeeze in there, Chief? Might get the skids a little wet, but—"

"Sure, we'll fit. But I'm not going to sit there and wait."

"Nobody asked you to," Jif replied. "Besides, I'm going to need you in the air to relay shifts in this artillery mission."

"Who's gonna call those shifts? You?"

"Roger that."

"Won't you be a little busy, Captain?"

"If I get bogged down, you'll pick up the slack adjusting the artillery."

Floyd seemed a little surprised. "You're really going to trust me to do that? This could get *danger close* real fast."

"I know bloody well that all chopper pilots can adjust artillery." With a devilish smile, he added, "Not as good as me, of course, but yeah, I trust you to cover my ass. Just remember where the gun-target line is. The battery firing is at Lao Bao."

Floyd eased the LOACH down over the stream. "No way I'm putting the skids under the water," he balked. "Don't want to risk getting snagged on something."

"No problem," Jif replied. "I'm Airborne…I don't mind a little jump." He tested the handheld radio, gathered a few smoke grenades, and grabbed his M16. As Floyd held the skids just off the surface, he jumped from the ship into the stream. It turned out to be only shin deep, with the bed rocky and uneven; *The chief's right…probably not the best place to land the bird*, he told himself as the chopper shot back into the air.

The jungle was thicker than he thought, but hardly impassable; it took him about two minutes to reach the crash site. The crashed LOACH lay on its right side, shorn of its rotor, windshields completely crazed, and looking much like a cracked egg. The ship seemed so much smaller than it did when right-side up. Wadley, badly injured, was still in his seat, which was now pressed against the ground at the bottom of the overturned cabin. Gray, though not seriously injured, hadn't been able to lift him up and out of the ship. He'd just found the ship's crash axe, which he'd use to break out the damaged windshield and drag the pilot out that way, no lifting involved.

"He's got a broken leg," Gray said. "How far away did you land?"

"About a hundred meters over yonder," Jif replied, pointing in the direction of the stream.

"That's a long way to carry a man, especially one with broken bones."

"We'll take turns, Boyd. We've got no bloody choice at the moment. How bad are you hurt?"

"I'm okay, Jif. Just generally beat up, like I lost a boxing match."

Another volley of American artillery landed to their east. It sounded farther away than Jif expected.

"I'm going to shift it closer," he said as he scanned the jungle, looking for signs of approaching NVA. "I reckon we'll need the protection. Keep working on that windshield."

Using the handheld radio, he told Floyd, "I want to walk the rounds closer. Tell them to add one hundred."

"I don't think that's going to be enough. You've got gooks closer than that. I can see them now and then."

That came as a surprise to Jif, considering he couldn't see any enemy activity at all. Floyd added, "How about I make it add two hundred?"

"Do I need to dig a hole and start praying first?"

"Let's hope not. You said you trusted me, right?"

"Yeah, I do," Jif replied. To himself, he added, *Like I have another option right now.*

Gray had succeeded in pulling the wailing pilot from the wreckage. "You're not done yet," Jif told him. "Get him behind the LOACH."

"Why? What's the…oh shit, are you shooting *danger close*?"

"Bloody right."

They'd barely hunkered down behind the remains of the ship when the airbursts seemed to explode right over their heads, the *cracks* of their detonations like claps of very close thunder. But they weren't as near as they sounded. No shell fragments buzzed past them like angry insects, no trees in their vicinity were torn apart.

"Let's get moving," Jif said. "Give me your weapons. You carry the chief first."

Gray handed over the two M16s, scooped up Wadley into a fireman's carry, and started toward the stream. As he brought up the rear, Jif told Floyd over the handheld to head for the stream, too.

It was slow going carrying a wounded man, but adrenaline was working wonders. Jif figured they were about halfway to the stream when Gray and Wadley went down in a heap. The pilot was screaming in pain, but Gray was yelling in alarm: "IN FRONT! THEY'RE IN FRONT!"

Then came the chatter of AK-47s.

Now Gray, too, was screaming in pain: "SHIT, I'M HIT!"

Jif had expected to have to deal with NVA trailing them, if they encountered any at all…

But we walked right into them. How the bloody hell did they get over there?

He could see where they were from his prone firing position: three NVA pith-style helmets with the wrong vegetation for this forest attached as camouflage, standing out like sore thumbs just above the undergrowth. They were forty yards away, at most, yelling at each other while firing short, wild bursts that were now striking nothing but trees. It seemed like one man—the leader, no doubt—wanted them to keep moving forward. The other two wanted no part of that.

The leader…he's the one in the middle, I reckon.

A three-shot burst from Jif's M16 took him out.

The man to the left stood up and tried to run away, firing blindly to his rear. It only took one shot to drop him.

The last man—still just a helmet above the undergrowth—seemed frozen in place, protected partially by a tree trunk. He and his AK-47 presented such a small yet lethal target. But he was so close…

Too bloody close to miss.

The pith helmet was no protection against a 5.56-millimeter bullet. In a mist of red and pink, it went flying along with the top of the man's head.

The firefight had taken only seconds.

Gray was shot in the shoulder; a painful wound, but he could still walk. And he still had a good arm to one-hand an M16. Using his web belt, Jif fashioned a sling to immobilize the damaged shoulder.

Then he slung Wadley over his shoulder. "My turn," he told Gray. "Let's *di di*. You cover our six."

Stepping past the three dead NVA as they made their way to the stream, Gray—his awe managing to show itself through the pain—said, "Where'd you learn to shoot like that, man?"

"No big deal," Jif replied. "My mother…she taught me."

Chapter Sixteen

As March 1971 wound to a close, so did Lam Son 719. Both North and South Vietnam were claiming a magnificent victory, with each army reporting that the casualties they'd inflicted on their adversary were an unlikely ten times what that adversary had publicly announced. The ARVN's original mission—the interdiction of the Ho Chi Minh Trail—had not been accomplished. If anything, the opposite had been achieved: traffic on the trail would increase several times over in the weeks and months that followed. "It's like we did them a favor pushing the trail farther west," General Sutherland said. "It's carrying more traffic than it ever did."

There were two other consequences that couldn't be denied. First, both sides were exhausted and had suffered crippling losses of equipment. "Nobody will be in a position to launch a major campaign for months, maybe longer," Sutherland added.

Second, the ARVN had proven once again that their command structure lacked the ability to plan large operations, coordinate the actions of major units, and lead their troops effectively once in contact with the enemy.

MACV's Provisional Recon Team—the PRT—was out of business. There was no further need for airborne observers to keep tabs on ARVN operations beyond the borders of South Vietnam. From a practical standpoint, they now lacked the manpower to be effective in such a mission, anyway. With the wounded Boyd Gray at a hospital in Japan, the team could only list Colonel McKnight and Jif Miles as combat evaluators, and there'd be no point providing fresh blood now. The day after the last ARVN unit crossed back over the Laotian border, both men were on a plane to Saigon, headed to new assignments at MACV.

Once at General Abrams' HQ, though, they were given one more PRT-related task before moving on to new jobs: write a comprehensive after-action report on the ARVN's performance during Lam Son 719 from their first-hand perspective. The report took three days to complete…

And less than three hours to have it bounced back with the following directive: *Minimize the use of terms like incompetent, ineffective, grossly negligent, and dereliction of duty when referring to the ARVN command structure. Emphasize their dedication, determination, and commitment to continuous improvement.*

"Are they bloody kidding?" Jif said. "They're asking us to talk up qualities the ARVN leadership doesn't have…and maybe never will."

McKnight just smiled and said, "There you go, telling it like it is again, Jif. But this is a political exercise, Captain, plain and simple. Just do what the honchos ask—write whatever fantasy they want to hear—and don't stick a fork in your own career. Let the ARVN brass screw themselves into the ground."

If Jif needed another lesson in politics, it was delivered the following morning when the MACV staffers gathered to listen to a live speech by President

Nixon over Armed Forces Radio. The president declared that Lam Son 719 was a shining example of the success of Vietnamization and announced the drawdown of another one hundred thousand US troops over the next twelve months.

Command Sergeant Major Sean Moon was seated next to Jif. He let out a frustrated sigh and said softly, "Well, Captain, I guess our commander-in-chief didn't hear about the two-hundred-plus choppers we had to write off…or the two hundred casualties we took."

When Nixon's speech was over, the staffers filed out of the room without a word, disgusted at the nonsense they'd just heard. Sean asked Jif, "You had breakfast yet?"

"Negative, Sergeant Major."

"Me either. C'mon…my treat."

The eggs seemed especially tasteless that morning. Maybe it was just a reflection of the gloom that had settled over MACV. It was one thing to have a combat operation fail. A soldier was expected to pick himself up, correct what went wrong, and, with an eye still firmly on his mission, push on. But it was another thing entirely to have it fail due to the actions—or inactions—of others, with little you could do in the way of correction.

"We lost the ball game when the ARVN sat on their asses for two weeks at A Luoi," Sean said. "It gave the NVA all the time they needed to readjust, reinforce, and kick ass. If it wasn't for our flyboys—especially those B-52 crews—a huge chunk of the Army of the Republic of Vietnam would've been annihilated."

"Can't argue with that," Jif said. "Are there going to be any repercussions in the US command? You'd know if there were, right?"

"Yeah, I'd know. And I'm here to tell you that nobody on our side's getting relieved. A few of the ARVN honchos at battalion and brigade levels are getting the sack, but that's about it."

"Are you serious? No ARVN generals are getting shitcanned?"

"You heard me right, Captain." Sean looked around, ensuring no one could hear their conversation. "Now, you didn't hear this from me, but I talked to your dad last week—"

"He was in country? Really?"

"No, it was on the secure link from DC. He told me there was a shitload of pressure in Washington to send General Abe packing. The reasons were that he didn't supervise the ARVN effectively and didn't react quickly enough when things were going to shit."

Jif replied, "That sounds like something coming from the press, right? They're obsessed with that image of ARVN troopers hanging off the skids of choppers. Sells a lot of papers, I reckon."

"Yeah, and it lit the fuze for a whole new round of anti-war demonstrations stateside, too. But it's more than just badmouthing from the press. You've still got ol' Westy at the JCS trying to cut Abe's legs out from under him every chance he gets. And there's that one-star politician Haig, Kissinger's puppy dog, who's happy to do the same. He keeps showing up at MACV with all these suggestions that sound like orders, like he's actually in the chain of command. So yeah…all those people are glad to scream that Lam Son symbolizes the failure of Vietnamization. But Nixon can't have that. He got elected on the promise that it would be the greatest thing since sliced bread, for fuck's sake. Relieving the commanding general would mean that Lam Son was a failure and Vietnamization isn't working, so the commander-in-chief has decreed that General Abe's not going anywhere. And that's just as well, because there's still no better man for the job, even if..."

His voice dropped off, as if realizing that maybe he'd said too much.

"What do you mean, *even if*, Sergeant Major?" When Sean hesitated, Jif added, "Is the general slipping? Maybe he's frustrated just like the rest of us?"

"Hell yeah, he's frustrated," Sean replied. "And sure, it gets a man down. But not too many people know him like I do. He's a bulldog. He'll never give up. If he was a quitter, I probably would've been dead about thirty years ago, buried somewhere in France or Germany. What I'm worried about is his health. He's no kid, you know? And all this bullshit pressure takes a toll on a man."

"So you think he might be having medical problems?"

"I'm not a doctor, Captain. I've got no fucking idea."

Jif let it drop.

*****

Something Jif couldn't let drop: he needed sharper uniforms right away if he was going to be working in the halls of power. He was down to one good set of fatigues; all the others looked like they'd been through hell. His Class B uniform, the khaki shirt and trousers that were the tropical go-to uniform for office work, had spent the last three months stuffed into a duffel and wasn't fit to wear, either. Getting new uniforms was no problem, but having them altered and the appropriate patches sewn on the fatigues was another story.

Sean Moon gave him a solution: a tailor shop near the US Embassy in Saigon catered to American servicemen and did fast, first-class work at reasonable prices. He'd gone for a fitting the next day. The khakis just needed the trousers hemmed; for a lavish gratuity, the tailor took care of that on the spot and promised the fatigues in two days' time.

When the deal was done and he exited the shop, his vehicle and its driver, Spec-4 Santilli, were gone. Looking up and down Rue Pasteur, the jeep was nowhere in sight.

But then it roared around the corner, coming to a screeching halt in front of him. "We gotta get the hell out of here, Captain," Santilli said. "Some deep shit brewing."

"What kind of deep shit? And how the bloody hell do you even know about it? The vehicle doesn't have a radio."

"Some MPs drove by and put out the word. Told me to get the hell outta here. Gooks are on the warpath."

Jif laughed at the thought. "Gooks on the warpath? That sounds like a welcome change."

"Seriously, sir…there's a mob doing some kind of anti-American protest, bitching about the pullout. They're headed toward the embassy. All GIs are supposed to get off the streets."

"Toward the embassy, eh? Let's go check this protest out."

"You're pulling my leg, right, sir?"

"I'm dead serious, Specialist. Make a left at the next intersection."

"But we'll be going in the opposite direction from Tan Son Nhut, Captain."

"I know. I can read a bloody map. Just do it. This might be educational."

When they got to within a block of the embassy, they could see the crowd surging ahead. As the jeep slowed to a crawl, Santilli asked, "Okay, *now* can we turn around?"

But there'd be no chance to do that. More young Vietnamese men—all in civilian clothes, all military service age—were filling the street behind them, pressing in on the jeep. As Santilli pulled his .45 from its holster, his next question was more a cry of panic: "What the hell do we do now, Captain?"

"Start by putting that pistol back in its holster," Jif replied. "They're not armed with anything but signs."

"But those fucking signs are on sticks that look like spears!"

"You've been watching too many horror movies, Santilli. None of those dudes look big enough to drive a stake through our hearts. Stop the jeep."

"Stop? Why? What're you gonna do?"

"I'm going to talk to them, see what's on their minds." As he climbed from the jeep, he added, "Stick around this time, okay?"

"But what if there's VC in the crowd? We're fucked, big time!"

"I don't think the VC will be protesting the US pulling out of the Nam. Cheering, maybe, but not protesting."

Then he was standing on the hood of the jeep, turning back to face the mob.

The signs they carried were in a mixture of Vietnamese and English. The ones Jif could read all carried the same message: *America does not keep its word.* The crowd's angry chants said much the same thing, only with profanity added.

A protester stepped forward from the throng, screamed something in garbled English that sounded like *another failed imperialist runs away*, and hurled a piece of fruit—a mango—at Jif. He caught it with one hand and held it up as if thanking the protester for the gift.

Unable to compose what he wanted to say in Vietnamese—he just didn't possess the vocabulary—he tried addressing the crowd in French, asking, "How many of you are ARVN veterans?"

But few, if any, understood him. The mob was starting to encircle the jeep while still maintaining a wary distance. They were chanting their angry denunciations of America louder than ever.

Then one young man stepped into the gap between the protesters and the vehicle. There was something different about him; he wasn't full-blooded Vietnamese, but a genetic blend of the West and Southeast Asia. More than likely, he was the offspring of a French father and Vietnamese mother.

In excellent English, he asked Jif, "You speak good French, but you sound Australian. Are you really an American?"

"Yes, I'm an American officer," he replied, pointing to the MACV patch on his left shoulder.

"Then you might as well speak English. I don't believe this is much of a French-speaking crowd. For the most part, they're too young. The French were leaving while they were still at their mother's breast."

"Good to know," Jif said. "My name's Jif Miles."

"Like the peanut butter?"

"Yeah, but I had the name first. How do you know about brands of American peanut butter, anyway?"

"I've been to the United States. I've been all around the world, actually. I am Marcel Van." Pointing to the elevated stage of the jeep's hood, he asked, "Were you planning to give a speech, Jif?"

"I was just hoping for a little dialogue…and if that fails, a chance to get out of here without having to run anybody over."

"I can interpret for you, if you'd like."

"All right, then, Marcel. I noticed a few of them are wearing army-issue articles of clothing, like shoes and belt, mixed with their civvies. I think some of these people are ARVN, maybe active, maybe deserters. I've worked quite a bit with the ARVN, and I wouldn't be surprised in the least if some of them have taken to openly protesting the American drawdown."

"There are a few ARVN here, but none are deserters, who are hunted men and would be fools to show their faces at something like this."

Jif shook his head. "It's probably the safest place for a deserter. Neither your National Police or the QC are going to lock up any anti-American demonstrators.

More likely, all the police—civil or military—will run the other way when there's trouble, like they usually do. But okay…you say just a few of them are ARVN. That means the rest are probably from politically connected families who've been exempt from serving…until now, that is. Am I right?"

He was looking straight into Marcel Van's eyes as he said it. Those eyes promptly betrayed the fact that Jif was, in fact, right, and he was one of those whose connections might no longer shield him from military service.

The helpful attitude disappeared. Anger took its place. "You're calling us cowards, aren't you? How dare you!"

"No, I haven't called anyone a coward. I'm just saying that maybe it's finally time for you to fight for your country, like the tens of thousands of Americans who've died in your bloody place."

Van replied, "Irrelevant! A drop in the fucking bucket! You forget that a million of our men and women have died, too." He turned to the crowd and, in Vietnamese, began whipping them into a screaming frenzy.

It was then Jif noticed a news team had arrived to film the encounter. The reporter was a white man; the cameraman and soundman were Vietnamese. They wouldn't need translators to provide a subjective, after-the-fact translation of what Van was saying.

Jif climbed down into the jeep, telling Santilli, "Just drive straight ahead. Don't let the noise scare you. It's just hot air. Believe me, they'll get out of the way. They're not fighters, and they're not looking to be martyrs."

"What if they start throwing shit again?"

Looking at the mango he still held in his hand, Jif replied, "Then we'll have more snacks for later."

*****

It took two days for the article about the demonstration to hit the wire services. The headline: *Allied Officer Calls Vietnamese Demonstrators Cowards, Draft Dodgers.* The article featured a grainy picture of Jif standing on the jeep. He looked like he was a politician making a speech.

Summoned that same day to the embassy's Public Relations Office, Jif, who'd caught wind of the article but hadn't seen it yet, could only suspect his ordered presence might have something to do with him being at the demonstration. He also suspected that if the article's political fallout cast Vietnamization in a poor light on the world stage, there'd be hell to pay…

And I just might be the one presented with the bill.

When he saw the array of diplomatic and MACV talent in the embassy conference room, his worst fears were confirmed: *I'm in deep shit.* But one of those heavy hitters was Command Sergeant Major Sean Moon. Seeing the anxiety on Jif's face, he gave him a wink and a reassuring nod.

The public information officer from USAID—the United States Agency for International Development—was waving a transmitted facsimile of the article as it appeared in the New York Times. He cut to the chase, asking Jif, "Did you refer to those people as cowards and draft dodgers, Captain?"

"No, sir. If that was actually said by anyone, it was the multilingual spokesman for the group. He could've easily twisted my words. By the way, as near as I could tell, that crowd was composed mainly of men who've long escaped military duty and were now facing induction."

"*Spokesman*, you say. Could he have been the leader?"

"Couldn't tell you that, sir. He just appeared to be the only one in the group with a command of English."

The article was handed to Jif. As he started to skim it, the term *Allied Officer* immediately got his attention. "Who is this allied officer they're talking about?"

"It's you, Captain Miles," the PIO replied. "Read on. They identified you as Australian military. From a distance, all fatigues look alike, apparently. The sound of your voice, though…" There was no need for further explanation.

A bit confused, Jif replied, "But there aren't any Aussie troops in country anymore."

"Not so, sir," CSM Moon said. "There's still a small, non-combat contingent here in Saigon, embassy guards and such. And like the gentleman said, *From a distance, all fatigues look alike.*"

Jif was about to ask *Okay, so why am I here?* when a CIA man in the room said, "These demonstrations are a new thing, but we don't feel they pose a significant threat. However, we're not sure who's behind them. You had the misfortune of being in the middle of one such demonstration. Can you give us any insight into the organization responsible?"

"Afraid not, sir. But like I said, the crowd seemed to be composed of privileged men who were about to lose that privilege."

"This multilingual spokesman…does he have a name?"

Jif told them. The CIA man registered no recognition, but sent an underling out of the room to run a check. "Could be a pseudonym," he said. "Would you recognize him from photos?"

"Probably," Jif replied, "but he's not in this news shot. If I may ask, though, what's the reaction in Washington to the article?"

"Actually, Captain, Washington doesn't give a damn about it. It wasn't an American running his mouth…it was an Aussie."

Jif wasn't sure whether the comment was meant as an insult or the celebration of a lucky break. But still curious about the article's blowback, he asked, "What about Canberra, sir? Aren't they bent out of shape over the misrepresentation?"

"They couldn't give a shit less, Captain. They lost all interest in this war last year, when their only combat regiment went home. You might say they were well ahead of the US when it came to Vietnamization."

After a few more minutes of speculative banter among the diplomats about subjects on which Jif could offer no insights, the CIA underling burst back into the room, brimming with excitement as if he'd just discovered the cure for cancer.

"We know this Marcel Van," the man said as he handed some papers to his boss. "He's the nephew of Colonel Van, a member of President Thieu's staff."

Holding up a photo, the CIA man asked Jif, "Is this the young man?"

"Yes, sir. That's him."

"Well, looks like you had him and that whole mob pegged, Captain. This Van kid is very well-connected. His mother is Colonel Van's sister. She shacked up with some French diplomat back in the day, and *voila...*"

A very concerned MACV officer asked, "Any chance of this guy being PLF?"

The CIA man laughed, replying, "PLF? Fuck no, Major. He's not a commie. Quite the opposite. He's just like those student protesters back home, all those rich college chickenshits making a lot of noise to duck the draft."

"Begging your pardon, sir," Jif said, "but the makeup of the protesters isn't exactly the same thing. The ones back home aren't rich. They're just average kids who are afraid of the very real possibility they'll get drafted. American rich kids don't get drafted and never will…their medical deferments are ironclad, the best money can buy. If they're involved in any protests, they're just there to get laid."

"What on earth makes you say that, Captain?"

"I went to Berkeley, sir. I've been to a few demonstrations."

As they left the conference room, Sean couldn't hide his smirk as he asked Jif, "You didn't go to that demonstration thinking you might get laid, did you?" He'd meant it as a joke, but it didn't land that way.

Clearly annoyed, Jif replied, "Don't be fucking ridiculous, Sergeant Major. I was just curious what was going on…and I'm a married man now, remember?"

The sergeant major wished he could reel that snide remark back in; *His dad is the definition of a straight arrow, and I've got no reason to suspect the apple didn't fall far from the tree.*

"No offense meant, sir," Sean said. "But once again, you took a chance you didn't need to. Demonstrations can get ugly real easy. You could've got your ass killed. Your driver's ass, too."

"There are a lot of ways to get killed in this country," Jif replied. "That wasn't one of them."

"One more time, I'm gonna ask you to do me a favor, okay? What've you got…three months left in this tour?"

"Yep."

"Good. Spend it boring yourself to death in that cushy little staff job you fell into."

Chapter Seventeen

As they strolled to the restaurant on a balmy August evening in Georgetown, Marti Tanaka-Miles—Jif's wife—asked him, "Did you hear what your sister said to me?"

"This ought to be good. Lay it on me."

"Her exact words—'Now that Jif of the Jungle is back, you two need to go make a baby right away.'"

"That's pretty funny," Jif replied, "especially coming from Jane, who couldn't care less about marriage and children. What'd you tell her?"

"I told her to mind her own damn business. With all due respect, of course."

He kissed her on the forehead. "That's my girl. You've really learned how to hold your own in the Miles family."

Then he added, "I'm a little surprised Jane took that job with a lobbyist here in D.C. I always figured her more of a New York City career woman. By the way, what accent did she say it in? She stunned me when she actually spoke like an Australian yesterday. I hadn't heard her talk like anything but an American the last few years."

"Your sister is a uniquely adaptable person, Jif...and she's an absolute riot, too. Listening to her and your mother go at it is like being in the middle of a Pinter play."

He smiled, not so much for what she'd just said, but the fact that a few short days ago, he was in Saigon, with its dangerous streets, the clashing odors of exotic foods and sewage, and the air of a rotten government propped up only by dwindling supplies of American dollars and resolve. He'd never been a fan of Washington, D.C., but suddenly, with his wife at his side as they walked picturesque streets without the need for a sidearm, he felt blissfully happy, like being in paradise.

Marti broke his reverie by asking, "Are you sure you really want me to come down to Georgia with you and your parents? I mean, I don't even know this Patchett fellow, and he certainly doesn't know me. Won't I just be in the way?"

"There's no chance of you being in the way, baby girl. I want you there. You're family. So is Patch. I'm afraid we may not get another chance."

They walked hand-in-hand in silence for half a block before she said, "I read a theory by some guy—I think he was a medical doctor, but I'm not sure—that claimed cancer was actually desperation expressed at the cellular level. I don't buy it. Do you?"

"I reckon if that was true, everybody would eventually have bloody cancer. Patch is just old now—he's in his seventies, for cryin' out loud—and he's had a tough life. But no bullet ever found him in three wars, so cancer's taking its turn. If it wasn't for Miss Ginny, he probably would've packed it in a long time ago. But knowing that tough old buzzard, I wouldn't be surprised if he beats it."

"If what your mom says is true, Jif, he's past that point now."

The restaurant, a small Italian *trattoria* a friend at Georgetown U had recommended to Marti, was doing great business. Jif asked, "Should we eat on the patio? We'll probably get a table faster."

"Sure. Why not?"

They sipped wine at the bar as they waited to be seated. Jif raised his glass in a toast: "To Martine Marie Tanaka-Miles, now a Master of Arts in International Relations, and her new job on the staff of Senator Inouye, from the great state of Hawaii."

Marti laughed and said, "Another *hāfu* girl makes good. I was kind of a ringer for the job, though. The senator and my dad are in the same Nisei vets club back in Honolulu."

"The academic credentials didn't hurt, though."

"Yeah, I suppose," she said. "But now it's my turn…I propose a toast to Captain John Forbes Miles, who has just returned from his second and *final* tour in the Republic of Vietnam and will *never* venture down that rabbit hole again."

He raised his glass, ignoring for a moment that words like *final* and *never* could be dangerously deceptive.

"I have one more toast," Marti said. "Additional congratulations go to Captain Miles for his new posting at the Pentagon, which will allow him to enjoy the comforts of home and hearth with his wife for at least a year while he shares his considerable expertise with the powers that be."

"Baby, I still can't believe how lucky we are that a Pentagon assignment fell into our laps again. You should've heard the *whoop!* that came out of me when I read those orders. But you do realize that captains at the

Pentagon are little more than bellhops and busboys, don't you? I expect my desk will be in a closet somewhere in the basement. And as far as sharing my *considerable expertise* goes, I'm quite sure the place is still chock-full of highly experienced officers, all of whom will outrank me and couldn't care less what I might have to say. I'm planning to chalk the whole thing up to a learning experience."

"You don't suppose your dad used some pull to get you that assignment, do you?"

"I sincerely hope not, Marti."

"Well, if he did, I'm going to give him the biggest kiss..."

A waiter appeared; their table was ready. As they walked away from the bar, they didn't notice a man hunched over his third whiskey giving them the side-eye.

*****

Once they'd ordered, Marti asked, "You said Sergeant Patchett was in three wars. Wasn't your pal Sergeant Major Moon in three wars, too? Isn't he only in his early fifties?"

"All true, but we're not talking about the same three wars. Believe it or not, Patch served as a teenage doughboy in World War One as well as being my dad's top sergeant all through World War Two and Korea. Sean Moon's service started with World War Two in Europe, serving with General Abrams, who was then a light colonel and tank battalion commander. Then he was with Dad and Patch in Korea and the Nam with General Abe again."

"I can't imagine anyone going through all that," Marti said. "I'm still a bit intimidated being in the midst of your family and all their warrior friends."

By the time they'd finished their salads, the man who'd given them the dirty look at the bar had consumed enough whisky to jack up his guts beyond the point of good sense. He approached their table and, at great volume, said, "So you brought your gook whore back with you, eh?"

As Jif rose to face him, Marti tried but failed to grab his arm, saying, "Jif…don't."

"*Jif*?" the drunk said. "What kind of stupid ass name is that?"

"Listen here, friend…this lady is my wife. She's an American—"

"An American? Just like you? Where the fuck are you from, anyway, talking like that?"

The reaction of the other diners on the patio went from being curious to annoyed in a split second. A voice called out, "Hey, asshole…get lost and leave them alone."

Jif held up a hand as if to say, *I've got this. It's my problem.*

Even though they were outdoors in a bustling city, it became so still you could hear heartbeats. But not a breath.

"As I was saying," Jif continued, "this lady is my wife, and you owe her an apology." The righteous force in his tone—a command voice if there ever was one, impossible to ignore or deny—made the offender take a step back. But it didn't shut his mouth.

"I was there, man, the fucking Nam," the drunk said, his chemical courage slurring his words. "I was a goddamn E-5. I knew a bunch of dudes like you…fell in love with the first slope they fucked and were actually stupid enough to jump through all the hoops and bring the slut back to the world. You make me—"

It was over so quickly. Almost nobody saw Jif's fist lash out with a perfect jab to the chin. The inebriated vet lay prone and stunned on the tiled ground, hidden from most eyes between two tables and their startled occupants. Only after the man was down a few seconds did those people sense a threat and skitter away.

But the drunk would be a threat no longer. Pulled to his feet by two waiters, he was unceremoniously ushered off the patio and into the alley adjacent to the restaurant, where he was given the choice of leaving quietly or awaiting the police. The maitre d' fluttered over Jif and Marti's table, gushing with apologies and insisting he'd comp their meal.

"That's a very kind offer," Jif said, "and we greatly appreciate it. But I think we've provided enough entertainment for one evening." He dropped a twenty onto the table, took Marti's hand, and headed for the sidewalk to the sympathetic cheers of patrons and staff.

Back on the street, Marti said, "That was some shot, Superman. My bloody hero! But for a minute, I was afraid you'd killed him."

When Jif didn't reply, she asked, "You okay, honey?"

"I'm pissed off. I didn't spend two years in the Nam to come home to ignorant shit like that."

She didn't know how to express how worried she was: *I've never seen Jif like this. Sure, he's always been dynamic and forceful when necessary, but he's never been so quick to lash out. He seemed spring-loaded to fight, and it was scary just how calm he was about it, too, as if there was no reason to consider any other course of action…like just walking away from that shit-faced idiot.*

I've heard the stories about guys coming back from that stupid war with all kinds of psychological baggage. How much of that baggage is Jif carrying? Look at his face…it's showing so much pain all of a sudden.

And then she understood why: "My hand is bloody killing me, Marti. Let's pop into the next place we come to. I'm going to ask for a bucket of ice and soak it while we eat."

As a relief she wasn't quite sure was warranted swept over her, she told herself, *I pray that a sore hand is all that's bothering him right now.*

*****

Two mornings later, Jif and Marti joined his father and mother, Jock Miles and Jillian Forbes-Miles, on a flight to Atlanta, connecting to Columbus, Georgia. Arriving at their destination midday, they rented a car and drove north for half an hour into the rolling hills and pine forests of the West Georgia Piedmont. On a winding two-lane, they came to a roadside rural mailbox with *Patchett* painted on its side. Jif, who was at the wheel, turned the car into the long, steep upslope of the driveway. In jest, he said, "It's only another bloody hour from here, folks. Should an oxygen mask drop from the compartment above your seat…"

His dad added, "You could always depend on Ol' Top to pick the most favorable high ground."

Jif marveled that the dirt of the driveway had been recently graded with meticulous care, just as it had been every other time he'd visited. He wondered, *With Patch sick, who's driving the tractor that pulls the grader? Ginny? Or is he still able to do it himself?*

Marti had a deeper concern. That old fear of having Asian blood while among those who'd fought wars against Asian foes welled up inside her once again. The fact that she was born an American and only half Japanese made no difference to a stranger; *Those Asian eyes are all they see. The drunk asshole in the restaurant the other night thought I was Vietnamese, for Pete's sake.*

That fear had long been banished as a member of the Miles family, who accepted and loved her as a daughter without reservation. *But the Patchetts*, she thought, *they're a whole new ballgame. Will Patchett and his wife be as welcoming to me as my in-laws are? When I heard that Ginny Patchett had been an Australian guerrilla fighter against the Japanese just like Jif's mom, I nearly had a heart attack. I'm afraid of being right back at square one, offering myself up for rejection all over again.*

Jif says I'm being ridiculous...

But does he really understand how deep hate can run in people sometimes? He may be Aussie-American, but he's still all white.

The cabin sat atop the hill like a watchtower over the forest below. Patch and Ginny rose from their porch chairs as the car pulled up. Jock took one look at his old senior NCO and muttered, "Oh, shit...look at him!"

True, Patchett's body had wasted; cancer and the fight against it were taking its degenerative toll. But his spirit wasn't diminished in the least. Standing ramrod straight, hands on hips like a drill instructor, he called out in a booming voice that still possessed the power to command, even when joking: "Did you come to bury Caesar or to praise him?"

Jock's response: "Praise him, of course."

Turning to Ginny, Top said, "Then I reckon we oughta let 'em in, right?"

Marti whispered to Jif, "Does he reference Shakespeare a lot?"

"From time to time. But I'm not sure he knows he's doing it."

When Jock and Patch bear-hugged in greeting, the senior Miles tried to be gentle, a concession to the man's weakened condition. But Patchett would have none of it. "I ain't going to break, sir. Gimme a good one. Show me how much you missed me."

Jif and Jillian were next. Top told them, "Don't you good folks go sissy on me, neither."

A big, friendly dog—a Black Lab—was prancing happily around them, wanting to get in on the action. As he knelt to pet her, Jif said, "You finally got a dog! What's her name?"

"That's Sheila," Patch replied. "Good Aussie name, eh? Better show her some love, too, before she gets all tuckered from the excitement."

Then he fixed his gaze on Marti, saying, "And this pretty young thing gotta be Marti. C'mere, darling…give Ol' Top and Aunt Ginny some sugar. Welcome to our humble home."

The hugs and kisses administered, Patch continued, "I hear your dad was Nisei. Let me tell you, sweetheart, I've got the utmost respect for those men, fighting for a country that spit on them. And fighting damn well, I might add. I'd love to meet the man someday. You should be real proud of him."

"I am, Top, believe me."

She couldn't say why she was so comfortable calling him that. But she was glad she did; there was no doubt it delighted him.

And just like that, her fear evaporated.

*****

At dinner, the conversation was mostly a long and detailed stroll down memory lane. Little was said about the current war, and any discussion of mortal illness was scrupulously avoided. Sheila was curled beside Patch's chair the whole time. Ginny whispered to Jillian, "You know how dogs are. They protect the sick ones."

Once they retired to the porch for pie and coffee, the discussion of Vietnam was thrown wide open. Patchett launched into a monologue about the futility of the war and the devastating effect it was having on the Army. He wrapped it up with, "Miss Jillian over there had it right from the beginning—the US of A has been doing all the wrong things for all the wrong reasons from the get-go. That article you wrote, ma'am, was probably the best damn thing I ever read." Raising his cup in a toast to Jif, he added, "I'm just glad our boy here finished those two tours intact. I've gotta say that we were worried about you every damn day you were over there. I'm glad that things are finally winding down. You've done your bit…more than your bit, in fact. Can I get an amen to that?"

"You certainly can, Top," Jillian said as she gave Marti's hand a motherly squeeze.

Then he added, "I wouldn't want Creighton Abrams' job for all the tea in China. No way he walks away from this a winner. No one ever gets credit for being the last man out, the one who turns off the lights."

When Patch went for a second slice of pie—Ginny had seen to it that his first piece had been just a sliver—she blocked his move. "You know you can't have that, Melvin," she scolded.

"All right, woman. You win." Turning to the guests, he added, with a hint of embarrassment, "That's what you gotta put up with when those VA docs cut out a big piece of your gut."

A fraught silence hung in the air for a moment. Jock broke it by asking, "Tell me, Top, what do you see as the biggest challenge to the Army coming out of this war?"

"That's a simple one, sir…junior leadership retention. Too many of the outstanding young officers and NCOs got frustrated with a war that made no sense. How could they tell their soldiers to fight—and maybe die—for something even their own commanders didn't understand?" He gave a nod to Jif and continued, "Present company excepted, of course, but the Army's left with too many mediocre officers and sergeants in its company-grade positions. You know the type—the hangers-on who can't wipe their asses unless a superior tells them to. I don't envy the task of the fine young officers like you, Jif, who are choosing to stay. You've got a shitload of rebuilding to do, but I know you're up to the job."

Jock plied Patchett with more questions, provoking discussion on subjects like improving NCO career development, novel training ideas, and the tactical lessons of Vietnam. The discussion went on for another half hour before Patch said, "Okay, I guess we've solved all the Army's problems and some of the world's, too. Now tell me and Miss Ginny what all y'all have been up to." It seemed like a dodge, a continuing effort to keep the conversation away from his sickness.

But they played along, reciting the list of new jobs for Jif, Marti, and Jane. The topic of potential Miles grandchildren wouldn't come up; it had already been covered. A few hours earlier, Marti had already fielded Ginny's question in private: *Are you up the duff*?

Two days ago, Marti hadn't known that *up the duff* meant pregnant. Jane had used it then and promptly had to explain it.

"Give us a break, Ginny. He's only been home four days."

When she added that both of them weren't ready for children, Ginny had smiled and said, "That's all right, girl. Do it at your own pace. You two are going to make the most beautiful little ones."

Patchett sought one more update: "When's ol' Bubba Moon ever gonna get his ass the hell out of Vietnam?" With a big grin, he added, "Taught that boy everything he knows, me and the general here."

Jif replied, "I reckon General Abrams might've had a hand in it, too, Top. I fully expect that Sean Moon won't leave the Nam until his boss does."

Patchett nodded in agreement. "Gotta admire that loyalty. Bubba's a good boy…he learned to put up with political bullshit a hell of a lot better than I ever did."

But it was inevitable; the conversation finally came around to Patch's illness, and he was the one who brought it up. "Sure, I'm in remission now, but any damn fool knows that's temporary. It's a crapshoot, and everything might get turned on its head tomorrow. But hey…I'm an old man now, ain't I? Nobody's supposed to live forever, right?"

Then he looked at Jock Miles and said, "General, you remember that old Army saying? One of my favorites…it sums up perfectly how I feel right now, having all y'all here with me. It goes like this…*I've had better assignments, but I've never been with better people.*"

*****

The summer sun was dropping to the western horizon, casting long shadows that draped the Georgia woods in evening darkness well ahead of what the clock demanded. It was time for the visitors to go. They'd catch the last flight to Atlanta, overnight there, and return to D.C. in the morning.

It was so difficult to say goodbye. The fear of it being the final one clawed at every member of the Miles family. But they were all too brave, too proud, or too afraid to cry. When the parting round of hugs, handshakes, and kisses was done, Melvin Patchett said, "Don't be worrying about me, because Miss Ginny ain't gonna let me die quite yet. There's just too much work to be done around here. Y'all come back, ya hear?"

*****

There was a gloomy silence in the car the first few miles of the drive back to Columbus. Jock was about to break it with a comment like, *That was pretty tough, wasn't it*? But realizing that their parting had, no doubt, been far tougher on Top Patchett, he said nothing.

Later that night in their Atlanta hotel bed, Marti said to Jif, "You know what really blew my mind? The way your dad—a general and a statesman—sincerely wanted to know what Top thought on so many topics. I could tell he took every answer to heart, too. I didn't think it worked like that. Do all generals really care about what their sergeants think?"

Jif replied, "Only the great ones, baby girl."

Chapter Eighteen

Marti glanced out the window of the coffee shop, catching a glimpse of the gray sky over D.C. on that February afternoon as it began to unload another wave of snow. She'd been inside the warm and cozy establishment for ten minutes waiting for Jif's sister, Jane, but she'd yet to remove her coat and scarf. The occasional shivering wouldn't allow it. She'd only taken off her gloves once she had a hot mug of cocoa to wrap her hands around.

Jane breezed in a minute later, stomping her feet in the doorway to knock the snow from her glistening high-heeled boots. Heading for the table, she cued up her Australian accent, calling to the counter girl for a coffee and bagel.

As Jane peeled off her coat, Marti asked, "You're Australian today?"

Shifting on a dime to her New York accent, she replied, "Gets better service, dear sis. You cold or something, all bundled up like that?"

"Janie, I don't think I'm ever going to get used to winter."

"Well, I guess growing up in the tropical paradise of Hawaii does that to a girl."

"For sure," Marti replied. "But you're eating? Isn't it a little close to supper?"

"Honey, this *is* supper. Got meetings all bloody night. My group is running a full-court press on some southern congressmen for the AFL-CIO…maybe convince them to be a little less anti-union." She sighed and added, "Of course, I don't have to tell you that 1972 is an election year. It's going to be like this until November…I'll eat and sleep when I can. You've got it easy…your boss doesn't have to run this cycle." Watching the snowfall build, she added, "I'll bet you're looking forward to your trip back home next week."

"Can you believe Jif and I haven't been there together since our wedding? That's two years!"

"I know! And this summer…your first trip to Oz! I wish I could be there with all of you, but like I said—busy year. You're going to have such a great time in Brizzy! You guys planning to ride the winter surf?"

"Hope to. Never had to wear a wet suit before, but there's a first time for everything."

As she prepared to devour her bagel, Jane said, "Make the most of your time together, sis, because you're in the Army now. You know what Mom says about being at the mercy of the Green Machine, right?"

"Yep. Never expect anything…"

The two of them recited the last part in unison: "And then you'll never be disappointed."

*****

Jif would be late getting home. He'd left a message to that effect on their apartment's answering machine. Even though he didn't specify what was keeping him, Marti knew something was wrong the moment she'd heard his voice.

During the two hours until he finally walked through the door, a parade of unpleasant scenarios had run through her mind. But she could only think of one that would stop him from putting it on the tape.

*****

It was exactly the scenario she'd thought. "How long this time?" Marti asked.

"Six months…maybe a little more, depending…"

She turned and walked to the couch without a word. Her only gesture was to kick a throw pillow sitting on the floor into the next room.

"Depending on *what*, Jif? Aren't we done with this fucking war yet?"

"Not quite, I'm afraid."

"You said your presence was *requested* by MACV. Does that mean you can decline?"

He had to stop himself from laughing. "You know bloody well it doesn't work like that, Marti."

"But the assignment at the Pentagon was supposed to last a year! It's only been six months…"

She was about to add *that's not fair*! But she knew the workings of the military were rarely fair. There was nothing she could do or say—no protest, no bargaining—that could prevent his going. And this probably wouldn't be the last time in Jif's Army career a sudden change of plans dropped on them like a bomb, either. All she could do was try to come to grips with it…and save her tears for a different day.

She asked, "Is it staff or field work?"

"Not really sure. Probably a mix of both."

She thought back to his last tour, the one that was supposed to have been only boring staff work in Saigon. But he'd managed to come home with a stack of commendations that didn't sound like the sort a man would earn riding a desk.

"But *why*, Jif? What's going on there that you have to go running back?"

"It looks like things may turn to shit again, baby, and real soon. They're rounding up experienced hands to help prevent another calamity."

"So it's like your mom says—the US is determined to drag out the inevitable South Vietnamese collapse as long as it can, magically achieving that with none of its own troops in country. Except you. You're required, apparently."

He pulled her into his arms. It took a few moments for her to return the intensity of his embrace. He began to whisper, "I'm sorry, baby. I'd give—"

But she stopped him with a kiss. "Jif, I'm a Miles now. I know what I signed up for. Nobody held a gun to my head."

Then she added, "But seeing you go back to Nam again is definitely *Number Ten*."

*****

Six days later, Jif stepped off a C-141 at Tan Son Nhut. It felt like he'd never left. The heat and humidity that enveloped a person like a stinking shroud certainly hadn't changed. Even the ground equipment on the airfield seemed not to have moved since his departure six months before. As he caught the shuttle van for the short drive to MACV headquarters, he thought, *It's still yesterday back on the East Coast. Marti's already gotten on a plane for the first leg of her trip to Hawaii…on her own. It kills me to have to disappoint her and her family by not being able to make that trip, too.*

But war is hell, right? Or at least it sucks, big time.

It gets worse...this tour's going to ruin the trip we planned to Australia in August...and after all the deals I had to make to wangle that leave! I told her she should go with my parents, anyway, but she refused. I still don't understand that...she was dying to go, right?

But she won't do it. In her words, "Yeah, I've been dying to go...WITH YOU. I love your mom and dad dearly, Jif, but I won't be a third wheel. I know they'll understand."

She was right. My parents understood completely.

But I still feel that I've let her down twice...even if she is a Miles now and understands what it means to be an Army wife. Mom certainly gave her a good grounding on that subject.

After checking in at HQ, he was directed to a conference room where a meeting for just-arrived advisory personnel was already in progress. As he stepped through the doorway, the colonel leading the meeting called out, "If your name isn't Miles, Captain, you're in the wrong damn room."

There was a burble of laughter from the meeting's other participants, a dozen officers all in the grade of lieutenant colonel or major. Apparently, he'd be the junior member of this group, the only captain.

"Sorry, sir," Jif explained, "but the flight was delayed. Mechanical problems."

The colonel wasn't interested in excuses. He plowed ahead, saying, "Now that Miles has deigned to grace us with his presence, we can cut the bullshit and get down to the business at hand."

And a gloomy business it was. The colonel described how MACV had *stepped on its dick* in the eyes of Washington by crying wolf about another Tet Offensive. Tet had now come and gone without any assault by the communists. "Intel strongly suggests, however, that the NVA is planning something very big and very soon," the colonel said. The pointer in his hand circled four areas in turn on a big wall map of Southeast Asia: the DMZ; the tri-country border area west of Kontum in the Central Highlands; the Mekong River in Cambodia; and finally, the Tay Ninh corridor leading to Saigon. "We see their buildups in these four areas, and it appears certain they're massing for conventional attacks with a heavy armor and artillery presence. There are grave doubts here at MACV, gentlemen, that the ARVN can repel a four-pronged attack without serious intervention by American airpower."

Jif thought, *What else is new*?

Then came a litany of statistics on ARVN troop deployments and strengths, airpower capabilities now and in the foreseeable future, and the availability of naval gunfire support for the coastal regions.

"Now, here's the thing," the colonel said. "We don't expect the North Vietnamese to violate the Geneva Accords and cross the DMZ into *Eye Corps*. They seem to hold that arrangement sacrosanct, probably because they don't want to sabotage their bargaining position at the peace talks."

Jif was surprised at the lack of reaction among the others at the meeting to that last statement. *Maybe I don't understand the politics of the peace talks very well, if at all, but I reckon the North wouldn't hesitate to cross the DMZ if they had a good chance to seize territory and rout the ARVN division facing them.* He wanted to suggest that such a result would put the North Vietnamese in an even better bargaining position, but decided to keep his mouth shut.

He hadn't imagined he'd be staying in Saigon very long, and he was right. The colonel announced, "Across all corps zones, we're terribly short of advisors at the regimental and battalion level. That's where you come in, gentlemen. Over the next few days, we'll be matching your qualifications—who you've served with, where you've served—with the available slots. Then you'll be on your way to join an ARVN command in the field as its advisor."

One of the group—a major—had a question. "Sir, I was told that some of us would be remaining here at MACV headquarters. Can you tell us how many?"

"Sure I can," the colonel replied. "That number is zero. Whoever told you otherwise was talking out his ass. We're not dispensing cushy desk jobs this time around, Major. Sorry about that."

He didn't sound sorry at all.

*****

Jif had a premonition his experience in country would land him in I Corps, probably with the ARVN Airborne Division. *But then again,* he thought, *I know the territory in every zone except Four Corps.* Experienced enough to know that the Army's administrative processes often defied logic, however, he wouldn't be surprised if IV Corps—the swampy, low-lying southern tip of Vietnam he'd never set foot in—was where he'd end up.

He'd been cooling his heels for two days, waiting for orders, when Command Sergeant Major Sean Moon tracked him down at his temporary quarters on the MACV compound. Jif asked, "What've you been up to, Sergeant Major? Nobody would tell me where you were. Big secret?"

"General Abe would like it to be a big secret, but the word's going to get out. Hell, it's probably already gotten out. Those fucking news hacks can smell shit better than rats." He seemed hesitant to say another word about it, but he did, anyway: "Ah, shit…it's nothing you don't already know, probably. You didn't hear it from me, though, copy?"

"Yeah, I copy," Jif replied. "More problems with incompetent ARVN brass?"

"Negative. This time, the problem's in our house. We've only got a handful of combat troops left in country, some armored cav squadrons doing recon and security. They're all getting ready to leave in a few months, too. But in the meantime, this outfit up at Da Nang—F Troop, if you can believe the fucking irony—really screwed the pooch."

"*F Troop*? Really? Like that comedy on TV?"

"Yep," Sean replied. "Those whipdicks got assigned a base security patrol. But they didn't go where they were supposed to…opened up a hole in the perimeter you could march a brigade through. Turns out the whole damn unit was stoned out of their fucking minds, from the CO right down to the last snuffy. The flyboy base commander at Da Nang had a shit fit. Wanted the Army to toss the whole bunch into the stockade and throw away the key. Says we were damn lucky the gooks didn't waltz right in and blow up half the base. And he's right…we were damn lucky."

"*Everybody* was stoned? What about the first shirt?"

"Ah, that's a whole different ball of wax, Captain. That troop's first sergeant hasn't gone on an operation since Grant took Richmond. He conned his CO into appointing a *field first sergeant*—some shake-and-bake E6—to fill his shoes outside the wire while he leisurely shuffled paperwork at the NCO club. Never mind that MACV strongly discouraged the practice of field first sergeants years ago. But there's more. CID is on his case now, and it looks like he and the club manager are into some serious black market shit. Nothing to do with drugs, though. The wheels are already turning to bust them both down as far as we can and retire them."

"And the troop commander?"

"Already replaced," Sean replied, "with a career-killing commentary being written into his OER."

"And it was just marijuana? No heroin?"

"Just weed, no smack. Thank God for small favors, right?"

"So what about the potheads? How do you discipline an entire company-sized outfit and still function? It's not like there are people to replace them with."

"Actually, me and the squadron commander came up with a pretty good solution—peer pressure. The other three troops in the squadron have begun policing their fellow cavalrymen in *Fuckup Troop*, making sure they won't be high en masse if the shit hits the fan.

They're all going home soon, so they're gonna make sure that one bunch of dumbasses doesn't get their whole squadron decimated at the closing bell. It also tends to hold down on the fragging incidents when the guys busting your balls are your equals, not your superiors."

"C'mon, Sergeant Major…is that actually going to work? You don't really think the men in the other troops are all straight arrows, do you? None of them ever get stoned?"

"I didn't fall off the turnip truck yesterday, sir. Of course they get stoned…but not when they're on the wire…and definitely not when they're outside it. Those other troops have *real* leaders keeping them in line."

Still skeptical, Jif asked, "General Abe's cool with all this?"

"In a manner of speaking. Let's just say he understands the young soldier of today a lot better than your typical old warhorse…like me, for example. And he knows this current batch was into drugs *before* they ever put on the green. It's not the first time something like this has happened, either. It's been going on in varying degrees the last couple of years. You know that, right?"

"Yeah, sure. But I have to admit I've never heard of an *entire* company-sized unit under the influence until this moment."

"Well, live and learn, Captain. All General Abe wants now is to get his rear guard out of here in one piece. He'll take care of rebuilding the Army once we're back on our home turf. But while we're talking about *real leaders*, I hear the Miles family got to visit Top Patchett not too long ago."

"We sure did. I'm glad we got the chance."

"He writes me a lot lately. Really wants me to come visit."

"You'd better hurry," Jif replied.

"He's that bad, eh?"

"I reckon he's going to fight it to the end, but…"

They let a somber silence fill in the rest. It was broken when Sean asked, "Got orders yet?"

"Negatory."

"Well, let me spoil the mystery. I've seen them," Sean said. "You got a field jacket handy? It's going to be cold at night where you're going."

"So it'll be Kontum, then?"

"Bingo. It's the Central Highlands for you, Captain Miles. Right back where your Vietnam adventure began…how long ago was it?"

"Four and a half years."

"Time sure does fly, don't it?"

"Level with me, Sergeant Major…I'm getting the Highlands because I'm the junior guy and it's considered a crap assignment, right?"

Sean laughed out loud. "Captain, they're *all* crap assignments. You're working with the ARVN, for fuck's sake. But there's a silver lining…the chief of the Second Regional Assistant Group—your new boss—happens to be something of a legend in this part of the world. And he's a *civilian*. Used to be a light colonel in this man's army, but he hung up his uniform to become a full-time political operative. He's good people—a real mover and shaker—and a master at making the impossible happen. Understands the Asian mind better than any white man on God's green earth. Your dad knows him well, by the way."

"What's this wizard's name?"

"Vann. John Paul Vann. You're gonna learn a shitload from him, Captain. I guaran-damn-tee it."

Chapter Nineteen

The first words John Paul Vann spoke to Jif Miles: "Are you a praying man, Captain?"

"Can't say that I am, sir."

"Well, the Central Highlands have made a praying man out of me," Vann said, "and it just might do the same for you. And when it does, start praying for better weather like the rest of us are doing. This damn rain is killing our close air support, and when this fight finally comes to Two Corps, we're going to need that support if we're going to survive."

As if to punctuate—or perhaps emphasize—Vann's concerns, the floor of the building they were standing in at Kontum began to tremble ever so slightly; yet another B-52 strike was falling on suspected NVA positions to the west near the Cambodian border. The rainstorms and the low ceilings were little impediment to the big, high-flying bombers, who used radar guidance to pinpoint the location of their targets. But they were among the very few aircraft with that capability.

When this fight finally comes to Two Corps: it was late March, and the only zone in which the predicted battle raged was I Corps. Contrary to the presumption that the NVA would never cross the DMZ, they had done just that, their armor-heavy assault forcing the stunned ARVN defenders into a chaotic retreat. Dong Ha had fallen quickly; Quang Tri was under siege. The enemy's sights were clearly on taking the old provincial capital of Hue. "And when that happens," Vann said, "President Thieu is going to go out of his ever-loving mind. We could lose all of *Eye Corps* before we knew it."

But sympathetic as he might've been to the plight of those fighting there, I Corps wasn't Vann's problem at the moment; II Corps was, and the NVA still hadn't moved from the Cambodia-Laos border area to the west. The cities of Kontum and Pleiku, where Vann maintained his headquarters, seemed ripe targets. If they fell, the Central Highlands would be out of the ARVN's control, and South Vietnam could easily be cut in half from its western border to the Gulf of Tonkin. But so far, those cities had only been the victims of sporadic artillery and rocket attacks. Only a few of those attacks had caused serious damage, mostly to aircraft on the ground at Pleiku.

"For the life of me," Vann wondered aloud, "I don't know what the NVA is waiting for. This rotten weather might not be our friend, but it's certainly theirs. Once it clears, we'll get back the full might of our tactical air support, and they'll pay a massive price. Hopefully, that break won't come too late. You know what my nightmare is, Miles? A battalion of Russian and Chinese-made tanks rolling at us along Route Fourteen from both directions, north and south."

He still needed to figure out what to do with Jif. In the three days since he'd arrived in the Kontum-Pleiku area, the captain's only assignment had been to coordinate radio frequencies between the US helicopter units and the headquarters of the ARVN 22nd Division, the unit tasked with protecting the Central Highlands. Both he and Vann knew he was being wasted in that job.

"Your file says you were with the One-Seventy-Third around Dak To and Ben Het a few years back, Miles. And though you're only a captain, you're the most well-rounded one I've ever run into, combat experience-wise." He flipped through some paperwork as if looking for the answer to some mystery. Or perhaps divine guidance. "But you're still just a captain, and this job calls for majors and colonels. Don't get me wrong…I'm glad to have you, but ordinarily, I'd only use you as an *assistant something or other*."

Jif could see Vann's dilemma; it was clearly diagrammed on a manning chart affixed to the wall. There were several ARVN battalion-sized units that had just a blank space where the name of its American advisor should be…

And units that size get majors, not captains, as advisors, he knew all too well.

Vann called out to an ARVN colonel in amazingly good Vietnamese. Jif couldn't follow much of what was being said, but he could tell it was about him. At first, the ARVN officer shook his head vehemently, a firm refusal of what the American chief advisor was offering. But Vann didn't back down. His tone became firmer, that of a teacher—or perhaps a preacher—schooling a recalcitrant child. What happened next left Jif amazed:

Usually, when you browbeat a Vietnamese like that, they get that faraway look that means they're not in the least bit interested in anything you have to say. But this colonel actually looks remorseful—almost terrified—and he's suddenly compliant. I wish I knew what the boss was saying to him. Sergeant Major Moon is right…Vann understands the Asian mind better than any other white man. He certainly seems to know how to get them with the program…or at least scare the shit out of them.

Dismissing the colonel, Vann turned to Jif and said, "Okay, that's settled. You're going up to Ben Het as the new advisor to Second Squadron, Fourteenth Armored Cavalry Regiment. Division will arrange a vehicle to drive you up there. With this weather, you might have to wait days for a chopper. Better you get on site and down to business right away. Beats playing with yourself around here, am I right?"

"I reckon so, sir."

'One more thing, Miles. That Montagnard bracelet you're wearing…lose it. You won't be working with any Yards, and it'll only piss off the ARVN. I don't have to tell you that there's no love lost between those two groups, do I?"

*****

Two hours later, Jif was in an open-top gun jeep with two ARVN soldiers, a private at the wheel and a junior sergeant manning the .30-caliber air-cooled machine gun mounted on a pedestal behind the front seats. Jif had winced when he first saw the weapon, a pre-WW2 relic the US Army hadn't had much use for the past ten years. Called an M1919, it was a model from a bygone era when the Army still fancied naming weapons by the year of their inception. In well-trained hands, however, it could still get the job done.

Supposedly, the sergeant spoke some English. But Jif doubted that claim right off the bat when, as the jeep tried to make its way out of the base onto Route 14, the driver stopped, intending to let a six-truck convoy take the road first. "No," Jif said, "get ahead of them. I'm not about to get stuck behind some slow-moving deuces for fifty bloody kilometers."

But the sergeant misunderstood the order. He told the driver to merge the jeep into the middle of the trucks' column. It took more than a few intense hand gestures—and a few choice words—to get his ARVN companions to understand what he wanted. Several minutes of playing chicken with opposing traffic commenced as they leapfrogged one vehicle in the rolling convoy after another, but the jeep finally got around and ahead of the deuces. Leaving those trucks in the dust, they could now make good time north to Ben Het. Barring further obstacles, the trip on the fairly well-paved road would take little more than an hour, despite its surface being slick with rain.

*****

They had about thirty minutes to go in the journey when, out of nowhere, an RPG streaked across the road just a few meters in front of the jeep. The driver panicked and jammed on the brakes. That action toppled the sergeant on the machine gun, who fell forward against the private's head and shoulders, pushing the man's face hard against the steering wheel. The stunning blow caused his feet to slip off the pedals.

The jeep hadn't fully stopped. It began to veer toward the ditch at the far shoulder. From the right seat, Jif pushed the driver off the wheel and took control of it with his left hand. With his right, he pulled the hand throttle control on the dashboard fully out, rather than trying to straddle the gear shift like a contortionist to get a foot on the gas pedal. The wide-open throttle propelled the jeep forward, accelerating it briskly as small arms fire ripped across the road through the space it had occupied just a split-second ago. The sudden burst of speed had saved them from the rounds, but it nearly threw the gunner out of the vehicle. He was hanging on to the back seat with one hand, his legs dangling over the tail end of the jeep. The driver had recovered enough to take the wheel of the speeding vehicle again, but he couldn't understand at first why the gas pedal seemed stuck to the floorboard. It took a second for him to realize the hand throttle control had been pulled all the way out; he pushed it in and restored the operation of the gas pedal to normal. But he no longer had any intention of slowing down.

Several of the ambushers had run onto the road and were firing again. The jeep couldn't outrun their bullets, and it was still far from being out of range of rifles and machine guns. A bullet had already pinged off the machine gun mount. Jif had been climbing over his seat to the rear of the jeep when it happened. The ricochet missed him, but it couldn't have been by more than an inch. The shower of sparks from the metal-to-metal contact was his only clue of the close call.

Grabbing the dangling sergeant by the web gear, he hauled him into the rear footwell. In all the exertion, Jif didn't realize that a bullet had just struck the man in the thigh.

Figuring that the belt-fed machine gun would pump out more sustained suppressive fire than his M16, Jif grabbed the .30-cal's spade grips and swung the weapon aft. He pressed the trigger.

Nothing happened.

"FUCK! ISN'T THIS BLOODY THING EVEN CHARGED?"

Neither ARVN answered. Even if they could've understood Jif's English, they didn't hear him over the howling engine and wind stream of the speeding jeep. It wasn't really a question, anyway.

He yanked back on the bolt handle and let it slam forward.

She'd better shoot now.

The weapon did fire, but mounted on the careening, bouncing jeep, it was impossible to aim down the sights. He remembered what helicopter door gunners always said: *Don't bother aiming, just point the gun. Put the rounds somewhere in the ballpark and then walk them onto the target.*

That shouldn't be too hard...there's no deflection involved.

No deflection: there was no lateral movement of the target to compensate for, only the ever-growing distance from it. But within seconds, Jif couldn't really tell if he was firing into the enemy soldiers on the road or well over them. All he knew was that they weren't hitting the jeep anymore.

They may not be firing at all. And I think there are less of them than a few moments ago.

Did I actually hit some? Or are they missing by so much now that they're just wasting rounds?

But in the preceding seconds, the ambushers had certainly hit the jeep a number of times. The spare tire bolted to the aft end was shredded. The rear seat's backrest was, too. The windshield in front of the right seat, where Jif normally would've been sitting, was a spider web of cracks radiating from a jagged bullet hole. Miraculously, the jerry can with five gallons of gasoline strapped to the tail wasn't burning or even leaking.

But a dark fluid was puddling in the jeep's aft footwell. Jif had thought the sergeant had stayed on the floorboard to take cover; he couldn't see the wound on the back of his leg. But now he could, and it looked serious. The man's life was being pumped out in a pulsing flow of arterial blood.

Pulling the belt from the sergeant's trousers, Jif fashioned a tourniquet right below the groin and, ignoring the man's screams of pain, yanked it tight. The bleeding slowed to a trickle, but it needed to be cut off completely. Jif took his own belt and applied a second binding below the first. That stopped the blood loss.

If they could maintain this breakneck speed without sliding off the wet pavement, it was still a good ten minutes to Tan Canh, the nearest ARVN camp. In those precious minutes, there was nothing more Jif could do: *This jeep has no bloody radio, so I can't call ahead to have the medics ready or report on the ambush location. The convoy that left Kontum right behind us…they're going to be sitting ducks.*

I'm so fucking glad we didn't get stuck following them.

*****

They made it to Tan Canh in just over nine minutes. The sergeant wailed in agony the whole time. Jif had to constantly prevent him from loosening the belts around his upper thigh in a delirious attempt to relieve the intense pain. He was beyond the point of understanding that doing so meant quickly bleeding to death.

As they screeched to a stop at the aid station, Jif and an ARVN medic communicated in hand signals: *The tourniquet has been on for ten minutes*. Then the sergeant was whisked into the tent, hopefully to have his life—and his leg—saved.

Jif found the senior US advisor at Tan Canh, a bird colonel named Hardesty. Spreading his map on the jeep's hood, Jif pointed out the ambush location and his fear that it might already be too late for the convoy that was some distance behind.

Hardesty asked, "The ambush…was it VC, Miles?"

"Couldn't really tell, sir. Once they came into view, they were pretty far away."

The colonel stroked his chin, looking very worried. "They'd better be VC," he said. "If the NVA have already infiltrated this far, we're in much deeper shit than we figured. Could you tell how many there were?"

"I only saw the handful who came out onto the road, sir. There could've been more in the woods. Has traffic on Route Fourteen been hit before?"

"Negative, Captain. You get the honor of being first." Then he added, "Hang loose for a little bit. I'll get you another ride to Ben Het. That vehicle's in no shape, and you're short a gunner. But first, I've got to see what we can do to help that convoy."

*****

It took nearly an hour to scrounge up a ride down Route 512 to Ben Het. Once on that rugged road, Jif covered the twenty kilometers—roughly twelve miles—in just over half an hour. The journey was uneventful, made under a ceiling of clouds so low he felt he could reach up and touch them.

But his arrival was hardly uneventful. Artillery shells were falling on and around the base at sporadic intervals, driving the men of the two ARVN armored cavalry squadrons stationed there into bunkers and trenches, none of which had been well prepared. From what Jif could see, the bunkers were open-ended and had only plywood or culvert sections for roofs covered with a layer or two of sandbags. They'd afford little protection from a shell landing forty meters away, let alone one closer. But none of the incoming appeared to have done any serious damage yet. Jif released his ARVN jeep crew at the gate to the camp; they wasted no time turning the vehicle around and speeding back toward Tan Canh without so much as a farewell.

He walked to the command bunker without ever having to dive for cover. That structure, at least, looked as if it had been built with some effort and attention to detail. *It won't withstand a direct hit*, Jif thought, *but then again, what will*?

Inside the bunker, he found an American major named Parker, the advisor to one of the two armored cav squadrons. The other squadron—2nd Squadron—was Jif's assignment. There were at least a dozen ARVN crammed into the bunker, as well. It took a moment to figure out who among them were the two squadron commanders. Aside from the few enlisted men manning radios, the others were officers and NCOs probably looking for a safe place to ride out the bombardment.

"Welcome to Ben Het, Miles," Major Parker said, offering a perfunctory handshake. "You sure picked a hell of a time to show up. The NVA seems pretty thrilled to see you, too."

"That would be the second welcome I've gotten from our communist friends today," Jif replied. He related how his jeep had been ambushed on Route 14.

Hearing the details, Parker looked as disturbed as Colonel Hardesty had been when he'd heard them. "That's not real good," he said.

No shit, Sherlock, Jif told himself. *That's got to be the bloody understatement of the day.*

The commander of the squadron Jif would be advising, Lieutenant Colonel Phong, seemed disturbed by the crossed cannons of the artillery on his collar. He spoke English well enough to express his distress succinctly: "You are not armor branch like Major Parker. How do you advise armored cavalry if you are not even a tanker?"

Surprisingly, Parker came to Jif's rescue before he could offer anything in his own defense. "Not to worry, sir," he told Phong. "Miles here has bucketloads of experience across every type of unit, to include working with the armored cav." Then he delivered the punchline: "He's *Dau Dang Vann's* personal choice to assist your squadron."

Just the mention of Vann's name turned Phong's attitude on its head. Suddenly, he was Jif's best buddy, eager to get his opinions on everything from counter-battery fire to perimeter defense.

When Phong turned back to more immediate matters, Jif asked Parker, "Do all these ARVN bow down to Vann like this? I've only been here a couple days, but I've seen it happen twice already."

"Get used to it, Miles. Vann is big medicine to these people, all the way up to President Thieu."

"Roger that, sir," Jif replied. "But you referred to him as *dau dang*. I've never heard that before. What does it mean?"

"Chief, leader, boss…take your pick."

"Okay, but how are we supposed to address him ourselves? I know he doesn't want to be called colonel, and *mister* or *chief* sounds like you're talking to a warrant officer. So far, I've just been calling him *sir*."

"Sir works fine, Miles. He likes boss pretty well, too."

A round crashed down less than a hundred meters from the CP, very close to a cluster of bunkers. Within a minute, casualty reports were being called in and then loudly repeated to the commanders by the RTOs.

"Somebody just got his whole day ruined," Parker said.

The major must be the master of understatements, Jif decided.

A sudden *THUMP* silenced the yelling in the CP. It wasn't an explosion, just some sort of impact, mysterious and very close, like the slamming shut of a vault…or a tomb. Parker said to Jif, "You thinking what I'm thinking?"

"I reckon so. A dud, right?"

"Bingo, Captain Miles."

*****

The incoming stopped a few minutes later. It was time to find the dud—if there was, in fact, a dud—and neutralize its latent threat. Phong told Jif, "I will get the engineers to deal with it."

"Where are these engineers, Colonel?"

"Pleiku."

They might as well have been on the moon. Pleiku was an even farther journey up Route 14 than Jif had taken, and with this low overcast, the odds of them flying in on a chopper were almost nil. But when Phong took to the radio to request their help, he was advised that traffic on Route 14 had been suspended. The reason: a convoy on that road had been wiped out a few hours before. Traffic wouldn't resume until armored escorts were arranged. In all likelihood, that wouldn't happen before tomorrow.

Can't say that I'm bloody surprised that convoy got hit, Jif thought. *I just wish there was something I could've done to prevent it.*

He said to Phong, "Since we're not getting engineers anytime soon, sir, we'll have to find this dud and take care of it ourselves. Can't have it sitting there waiting to kill us when it gets good and ready. I'll take the lead, if you'd like."

The colonel gave him a look that said: *Better you than me*.

When Jif walked out of the CP bunker, a few of the more adventurous ARVN troopers were already looking for the dud's crater. They seemed intent on merely cordoning it off so it could be avoided. But they hadn't found it yet. They were expecting the typical fan-shaped gouge carved by a round's explosion on impact.

Then one of the ARVN stumbled over a small hole, nearly twisting his ankle in the process. When Jif went to help him, he realized this small hole in the moist ground, barely larger in diameter than a softball, was the impact point. The round would be down the tunnel it burrowed into the soft earth, perhaps several feet below the surface.

"We dig it out," an English-speaking ARVN sergeant said.

"No, we won't," Jif replied. "We're going to blow it up where it sits. What do you have on hand—C-4? Thermite?"

They had both.

"Let's go with the C-4," Jif said. "Roll a block of it into a cylinder a little smaller than that hole. Stick the detonator in the tail end and run the wire to the CP bunker."

Standing over the approximate place he figured the round was below the ground, he added, "Stack as many layers of sandbags as you can in a ten-foot radius around this spot."

The sergeant balked at that, saying, "We need all the sandbags for the bunkers."

"This comes first," Jif replied. "We'll get more sandbags."

The C-4 and sandbags were ready in about twenty minutes. But nobody was willing to stick his hand down the hole to plant the explosive. Some were even grumbling that this was a waste of time; that couldn't be the impact point, anyway.

"Bloody hell, I'll do it," Jif said, taking the cylinder of plastic explosive and pushing the detonator into one end. "Anybody without a pair of balls better get lost."

He pushed the explosive down the hole as far as his arm would reach, but it didn't feel like he'd reached the dud. He called for a trooper to toss him the survey pole the man was holding, something they'd intended to use as a marker for the crater. Using the pole, Jif carefully pushed the C-4 until it wouldn't go any farther. He looked up to realize he was all alone. Nobody was within fifty meters of him. He slid a few of the sandbags over the hole.

He was halfway back to the CP bunker, only twenty meters from the dud, when he had the sudden but brief sensation of flying…

And then his world went pitch black.

Chapter Twenty

Seconds later, Jif began to come to. He found himself lying face down in the soft, wet dirt. Still dazed and disoriented, it felt like he might be at the bottom of a grave, with shovel-loads of dirt to fill the hole raining down on him. The shock wave of the dud's subterranean auto-detonation had hurled him practically to the doorway of the CP bunker.

He opened his eyes to see a pair of boots standing before him. A voice—Major Parker's—was saying, "At this rate, Miles, you're not going to be with us very long."

Jif guessed that if the major could crack wise, he mustn't look in too bad a shape.

Parker added, "Must've been some blast. Aside from triggering that sand storm from all those bags, it looks like it blew your belt off, too."

Jif's strained laugh was more of a groan. Up on his knees now, he realized his fatigue jacket was bunched around his chest, looking like someone or something had tried to yank it over his head. Pulling the jacket down to cover his waist, he told Parker, "Didn't have a belt to start with, sir. It got donated as a tourniquet earlier today. That ambush, remember?"

He looked back to where he'd first found the dud. What had been soft, flat ground was now a two-foot-tall mound, still venting smoke and dirt from a number of fissures. It was a scene that resembled pictures he'd seen of First World War battlegrounds in France, where level pastures had been transformed into fields of hillocks, with each earthen lump the result of an artillery shell's impact and detonation.

Looking around anxiously, Jif asked, "Anybody hurt?"

Parker replied, "Just your pride, it looks like."

The ARVN troopers who'd helped prepare the dud for demolition were slowly emerging from their places of cover. The sergeant-in-charge, perhaps intent on pre-empting any finger-pointing at him or his men, insisted, "We did nothing! Son of bitch blew up by itself!"

That wasn't hard to confirm. He was pointing to the detonator wire—or what was left of it—which was still coiled at the entrance to the CP, with no triggering device attached.

"You brave man, Captain," the sergeant added. "Lucky, too. Very lucky."

The subtext: *You may be stupid, crazy, or both. But you've got guts. Lots of guts.*

Colonel Phong thought so, as well. He told Jif, "You did very fine, Captain. I am in your debt."

Be he still had that *better you than me* look on his face.

*****

With all the rounds that had landed within the perimeter at Ben Het, they had more than enough evidence to perform some serious target acquisition analysis. The NVA had been shooting 122-millimeter field guns at them from the north; the shell fragments and lay of the impact craters left no doubt of that. Based on a map analysis of the terrain in that direction, those guns had already crossed the Laotian border into South Vietnam. How far away they were from Ben Het, though, was still a guess. Jif sketched his theory on a map: "They've got to be along this line, somewhere between ten to fifteen klicks from here as the bullet flies. Anywhere farther, they'd have to be firing high-angle over mountains, and those guns can't shoot high-angle."

"You really think they're that close?" Parker asked.

"The numbers don't lie, sir. They're down in that valley somewhere, concealed by cloud cover. And they'll stay hidden from aerial observation, beating our brains in on a regular basis, until the rainy season's over if we don't do something."

Beating our brains in was a euphemism for the harsh reality that Ben Het had already taken seventeen casualties from the incoming artillery.

But Phong seemed unconvinced. "What do you suggest we do, Captain?"

"I suggest we go find them, sir," Jif replied, "so we can hit them back with our own guns." He wanted to add, *You should've run a patrol days ago*, but he was supposed to be building a working relationship, and comments like that wouldn't help. What he did add: "Your squadron has a scout platoon, right? Sounds like a job made to order for them."

"No," Phong replied. "My mission is to prevent an NVA assault from the west, out of Laos. I need every one of my men here to accomplish that mission. The same goes for the other squadron at this base."

"The NVA can come at Ben Het from any direction, Colonel," Jif said. "But the northern approach, where the guns hitting us are located, looks like the easiest path for an armored threat trying to get here. It's a flat river valley with a road running through it. Every other direction—including west—is nothing but mountains and jungle. Not impossible terrain from which to launch an attack, but very challenging."

"Those are not my orders, Captain Miles," Phong replied. "I will not waste my men running long-range recon patrols in any direction."

Jif was ready to debate the point further. He considered Phong's argument an excuse to avoid the problem, not solve it. But before he could say another word, Parker pulled him aside, saying, "Last time I checked, Miles, you and I are *advisors*, not commanders or operations officers. You said your piece. If you're not happy with the reply, take it up with Vann. He'll be here tomorrow, weather be damned."

"I intend to, sir," Jif replied.

*****

Jif still needed to get clean after the dud's dirt shower. A helmet bath outside his bunker was the best he could manage. As he was toweling off, Phong approached, saying, "Come with me, Captain. There are things you need to see."

First among those things were the four 106-millimeter recoilless rifles scattered in fixed positions along the perimeter. The colonel sounded triumphant as he said, "These weapons are excellent tank killers. Can you get me more of them?"

Jif replied, "In all honesty, sir, if I could get you a dozen more, they wouldn't be much use against an attack by massed armor. Sitting in fixed positions like they are, they'll get off one shot—and maybe get one kill—before the next tank in line blows them away. They've got to be able to shoot and move—and move quickly—to have any lasting worth. You'd be better off if I got you four jeeps on which to mount the weapons you've already got."

Phong didn't buy it. "Have you ever used a one-oh-six in actual combat, Captain?"

"Personally? No, sir. But I've seen them used, and their power is exceeded only by their vulnerability. If they can't move, one shot is all they'll get. And by the way, we're at a place that bears witness to that fact. I'm sure you're aware that a few years back, when Ben Het was a US Special Forces camp, a handful of NVA PT-76s overran the place. The *ruff-puffs* working with Special Forces used a couple of one-oh-sixes exactly the way you're doing now. One actually killed a tank…and then they were all promptly destroyed by another tank."

Phong seemed insulted. "My men are not *ruff-puffs*, as you call our regional militia, Captain. They are highly trained and experienced armored cavalrymen."

"I don't doubt that, sir, but unless they can load and accurately fire eight or ten rounds a minute with those one-oh-sixes, they're going to get blown away quickly. And I'm willing to bet they can't shoot that fast."

"Your opinion is noted, Captain," Phong said while dismissing that opinion with a disgusted wave of his hand. Jif decided it was the time to say something complimentary, and there was one facet of the base's defensive scheme he considered excellent and worthy of praise. "I do admire the way you've deployed your tanks and APCs, sir," he said. "They're well dispersed, protected by berms without their mobility being compromised, and their fields of fire look to be very well thought out."

"I'm so glad you approve, Miles," Phong replied acidly.

But there was something Jif didn't approve of, and he couldn't help but say so. It concerned the six 105-millimeter howitzers on the camp. Three of them were emplaced in Phong's half of the perimeter, primarily as direct-fire defensive weapons. The other three were similarly employed by the squadron Major Parker advised.

"Sir, your howitzers are not being utilized to their full potential," Jif said. "Rather than functioning as a battery, they're set up as two independent platoons strictly for perimeter defense with direct fire, with no coordination between the two platoons. There is no FDC here, so they have no organic capability to shoot indirect fire missions in support of this base or any other—"

"That is not a problem," Phong interrupted. "The FDC at Dak To controls all indirect fire missions for our guns as well as their own."

"How, sir? The gun platoons have no radios, so fire commands have to be relayed by landline from your CP once they arrive from Dak To. That's much too slow, and the data passes through too many hands not to be accidentally altered. It's the *telephone game* dressed up in Army green. To make matters worse, your howitzers are boxed in so they only have good fields of fire to the west, even though those M102s can easily traverse through three hundred sixty degrees. We're already taking punishment from a live threat to the north. And like I said before, the NVA might come from *any* direction."

"Well, Miles...you're the artilleryman. How would you correct these problems?"

"First off, sir, I'd unify the command of the two gun platoons, designating one of the platoon sergeants as acting battery commander, and give him a bloody radio that can monitor Dak To. Second, we need to provide the acting battery commander with basic fire direction capabilities."

"As we've already covered, Miles, we do not have an FDC here."

"Don't need one, sir. All we need to get down and dirty is a map, a flat surface like a field table or the hood of a jeep, a compass, and a straightedge. And I'll bet your gun sergeants already know how to compute firing data in their heads."

"But will that data be accurate enough, Captain?"

"Maybe not the first round, but it'll get you in the ballpark...and quickly. You know how it works, sir...when the shit hits the fan, some off-target fire support *right now* is worth ten times more than an accurate round that's minutes too late."

No sooner had he said that, incoming artillery rounds began to fall around Ben Het again. As they sprinted to take cover at the CP bunker, Jif told Phong, "It sure would be great if we could put some counter-battery on them, sir. It'd just take one patrol to find the bastards. I'm telling you...they're not that far away."

*****

The next morning brought a surprise: a slight break in the weather. For a few hours, the solid, low overcast gave way to a broken cloud deck that produced no rain. While it didn't provide much of an opportunity for aerial recon ships, it did allow resupply choppers to deposit their much-needed loads. Among the deliveries was a pallet of sandbags, making Jif look good on the impulsive promise he'd made under pressure. Their arrival surprised even him; after assuring the ARVN sergeant who'd balked at using their available sandbags on the dud that they'd get more, he'd only gotten around to requesting them—informally, at that—late last night. The rapid delivery made him a hero among the ARVN troopers, who were praising him as a man of his word.

Maybe the ARVN logistics system works a little bit better than I thought, he told himself, *although I hope they don't get it into their heads that I can work magic.*

One of the helicopters taking advantage of the slightly improved flying conditions was John Paul Vann's LOACH. As promised, he arrived at Ben Het midmorning. To the ARVN, it was as if the messiah himself had alighted from the sky. After giving a pep talk to the two squadron commanders, Vann gathered Parker and Jif for a private meeting. He seemed to know every conversation that had occurred at the base camp since Jif arrived. Regarding the 106-millimeter recoilless rifle situation, he told Jif, "I like what you told Phong, Miles, but I'm afraid he's not getting any more of the weapons, and he's not getting any jeeps to mount them on, either. My most pressing priority is getting these squadrons some M48 tanks to replace their old M41s. They need the updated armor capabilities badly. The trouble is, with the fight going on in Eye Corps, the available M48s are going there."

Parker said, "But Eye Corps already has more M48s than anyone else, sir. MACV needs to share the wealth."

"It's not MACV's wealth to share at the moment, Major," Vann replied. "It's President Thieu's, and he'll do anything to prevent Hue from falling to the NVA. If that city is lost, it's a catastrophic blow to his regime. We'll work with what we've got here in Two Corps for the time being if it helps keep the Saigon government alive."

"Copy that, sir," Parker replied, more a pro forma response than a heartfelt agreement.

Vann continued, "It looks like we've got a problem brewing to the north of here. I'm very concerned the NVA will try to sweep down on Dak To from that direction, cutting the division in two and then trying to destroy the halves piecemeal. I agree with your position, Miles, that since air recon is on hold until there's a serious break in the weather, we need ground recon to find and neutralize that NVA artillery without delay."

It seemed amazing that Vann, without having spoken to Jif, seemed to know all the details of his discussion with Phong on that topic.

Is the man clairvoyant? Jif wondered. *Or does he have the greatest backchannel communications network in history?*

"I've convinced Colonel Phong to conduct the recon patrol you suggested," Vann said, "and I want you to lead it, Miles."

That was the last thing Jif or Parker had expected to hear. But the reactions of the two were quite different. Parker looked like he'd just been told his dog had died. Jif, on the other hand, said, "I've got no problem with leading a patrol, sir. But I've got to ask… why do they need me?"

"Because Phong's people have a habit of half-assed patrolling, Miles. He won't admit it, but he's well aware of it. You know the drill…they go out a nice, safe kilometer or two and then hunker down while they report back that they've gone much farther. If you're with them—and they know that I'm the one who sent you with them—they won't do that. They'll fulfill the mission as ordered with no bullshit. I guarantee it."

Parker didn't like the sound of this one bit. He asked, "Are you sure about this, sir? I mean, we shouldn't be taking charge of ARVN units, should we? That's not our—"

"Not your job, Major? Is that what you were about to say? Well, I'm here to tell you that your job is to do whatever it takes to get the ARVN to succeed. If you have to lead them by the hand—or just plain lead them as a commander—then that's what I expect you to do."

It took a few moments for Parker to muster a halfhearted reply: "As you wish, sir."

Vann turned to Jif and said, "Leave the major and me alone for a minute."

That *minute* took nearly five. When it was done, though, Parker seemed a different man. He'd either been read the riot act or had just found religion. *Maybe both,* Jif thought. *Either way, I don't reckon the major will be challenging the boss again.*

Vann turned to Jif and said, "You still here, Miles? I thought you had a patrol to run."

"Affirmative, sir. On my way."

*****

Jif's first concern—that an ARVN lieutenant was the leader of the squadron's recon platoon—turned out to be baseless. There was no lieutenant; a senior sergeant named Vung was in charge. But Sergeant Vung spoke very little English or French. A junior NCO named Tham from the squadron's headquarters section, who spoke English and French with a fair degree of fluency, would join the team as Jif's interpreter. The patrol would be squad-sized: eight men, not counting the drivers and gunners of the two APCs that would transport them to the start point of the foot patrol, six klicks north of Ben Het.

"Why so many men for a recon patrol, Captain?" Colonel Phong asked.

"We need to hump a lot of stuff, sir," Jif replied, "and we need men to do that. It's already midafternoon, so we'll probably be out there all night and into tomorrow. The additional food, water, and radio batteries alone require about four extra men right there."

Phong asked, "How far will you take the APCs?"

Jif showed him on the map. The colonel had no problem with that location, but he had another question: "What happens to the APCs once your patrol sets out on foot?"

"They'll move to the top of the ridge two kilometers west of the drop-off point," Jif replied. "There'll be good line-of-sight transmission from that high ground for their radios. Since we don't have any C and C aircraft overhead, those APCs will have to be the relay for our Prick-25s."

"But why do you need *both* vehicles, Captain? One can carry all of you."

"Sure it could, sir…but I'd appreciate the safety that an extra set of powerful, vehicle-mounted radios provides. And I'm sure the APC crews will appreciate the added security of mutually supporting fire they can provide each other…"

He paused, watching the dismissive expression on Phong's face change to a more introspective one. No doubt, he was weighing his objections against the possibility of suddenly being on Vann's shit list. After all, this was Jif Miles' patrol; Vann had made it so. To defy the *dau dang's* wishes could spell the end of his career.

Relenting, Phong said, "Very well, Captain. But I must ask you this—how sure are you that the APCs will not return on their own to Ben Het at the slightest excuse?"

"Because that would put the lives of their fellow troopers—and my life, too—in extreme jeopardy, sir. And I know you'll make sure that doesn't happen."

*****

Sergeant Vung seemed fully up to the task of organizing the patrol. He selected the men who'd be going with the easy, confident skill of an experienced leader. Even though he couldn't clearly express it in a language other than Vietnamese, he exhibited great respect for Jif Miles, proudly calling him *dai uy*, pronounced *die-you*, meaning captain.

A little goodwill from that shipment of sandbags seems to be going a long way, Jif surmised.

But Vung was apprehensive on one point: his men were not accustomed to night patrolling. In fact, most were totally inexperienced at it, but *they are the best the squadron has*, he insisted. When Jif conducted the final equipment inspection, he found two glaring problems relating to night operations. The first: most of the men's flashlights had no red or green lens to muffle the beam's glare at night. The second: none of their headgear—helmets or soft caps—had a stripe of reflective tape on the back side that allowed a trooper to keep track of the man in front of him while moving through the darkness.

Sergeant Vung quickly came up with solutions to both issues. When Tham, the interpreter, suggested they attempt to appropriate the lenses from other men in the squadron, Vung said, "No time for that. They won't give them up easily, anyway." Instead, he produced a roll of GI tape, had the men install strips of it over the flashlights' clear lenses, and then cut slits in those strips with a razor blade to let just a little bit of light through. "Like the blackout headlights on our vehicles," he explained.

They had no reflective tape for the headgear, but Vung improvised a solution for that, too. Cutting a rectangular stencil the size of a finger in a piece of cardboard, he had his men paint that rectangle on the rear of their helmets and soft caps with the orange reflective paint they used for safety markings. The rain even cooperated with the stenciling process; it gave the paint a full thirty minutes to dry before coming down again.

Just after 1630 hours, the patrol's two APCs drove out the gate at Ben Het. They headed west along Route 512 before picking up a trail that ran north toward the enemy guns' suspected location.

*****

They followed that trail north until reaching an abandoned settlement alongside the river called Dak Poko and Route 14, the muddy road that paralleled it. Though the river valley provided relatively level terrain, the road was suitable only for tracked vehicles; wheeled vehicles could easily become mired. After one last crosscheck of their map information and a final test of the radios, the eight-man patrol was ready to set out on its trek north to find the NVA guns. The APCs would then move to their elevated holding position on the wooded ridge two klicks to the west. They'd reach the ridge just as darkness fell. Once in position, their radios had no trouble working both Ben Het and Dak To.

For Jif and the men on foot, it would be a bone-chilling walk in the rain through a bamboo forest. The closest he figured the guns would be was four kilometers north of where they'd dismounted from the APCs. It would take almost an hour to get there. Before they'd arrive, the storm clouds and bamboo canopy would render the night moonless and pitch black.

Vung asked, "Why have we not heard the enemy guns?"

Jif's answer: "Maybe they're out of ammunition…or they've moved."

After plodding through the eerie darkness of the forest for another half an hour, Vung's question suddenly became moot; the NVA guns were firing again. Judging by the almost simultaneous sounds of the muzzle blasts—their *booms* delayed slightly by distance—and the rounds whistling directly overhead, Jif figured they couldn't be more than a kilometer away.

Stopping the patrol, he told Tham, "I believe we've hit the jackpot. Tell Sergeant Vung to get the radioman up here."

But neither Vung nor the RTO appeared right away. When the sergeant finally approached out of the darkness a few minutes later, he had bad news: the primary radio had stopped working…

And the two men with the backup radio had vanished into the night.

Chapter Twenty-One

The NVA rounds flying over their heads might as well have been aimed right at them. The tension they created among the men of the patrol—seeming so close but yet coming from a kilometer away—was enough to drive a soldier not superbly disciplined to flee for his life. Two of them did flee, running south into the darkness toward the APCs and Ben Het.

That left four still with Jif. Two of them were the patrol's sergeants, Vung and Tham.

Vung was hovering over the RTO, who was fumbling in the dark with his inoperative radio. Tham was practically sitting on the last man, forcing the anxious cavalryman to hold his place covering *the six*—the rear quadrant—of the contracting perimeter. With four men gone, it had shrunk to the diameter of the tight circle in which they now crouched, which measured just a few meters.

"What the bloody hell's wrong with the radio?" Jif asked.

Vung didn't need much of a translation. He pointed to two defects: first, the long-range whip antenna had been snapped off near the base of its ten-foot length; the second was the spare audio connector, which the RTO was trying to clean and dry with a rag.

The RTO was blathering excuses as Tham provided a running commentary. The gist: apparently, he'd stumbled a few minutes ago, and hadn't realized the whip had struck a tree trunk and broken as he nearly went sprawling with the unit strapped to his back. He also hadn't realized the protective cap for the spare audio connector—the item that would keep it clean and dry when not in use—had fallen off somewhere after the time they'd set out on foot, when it had been confirmed in place. The connector—facing upward into the rainfall—had become slick with water that glistened in the muted glow of Vung's flashlight.

If that wet plug shorted out the whole bloody set, we're screwed, Jif thought as he watched them work.

Miraculously, the cleaning and drying got at least the receiver working, but they couldn't hear anything but the hiss of white noise from the handset when the squelch was turned off.

That's a start...but the transmitter's a whole different story. We don't dare test it without a good antenna, and Vung seems to understand the damage that could do. He's got a firm grip on the handset, guarding that push-to-talk switch. And he's got the RTO reaching into the accessory bag for the jungle antenna.

There was no need to speculate; they all knew the short, flexible jungle antenna probably wouldn't provide the range they needed to talk to the APCs. To make matters worse, they were deep in a rain-soaked forest that possessed enough overhead canopy to shorten the radio's range even more. But with their backup unit missing, they had nothing else to try.

The jungle antenna now installed, Tham called the APC that served as the relay.

There was no reply.

Jif was about to check the radio's control panel, but Vung beat him to it. After one glance, the sergeant slapped the RTO on the head. It wasn't a playful blow; it almost knocked the man over. Then he adjusted the tuning knob and told Tham to try again. Apparently, in the hectic effort to repair the radio, the set's frequency had been accidentally changed.

This time, the APC replied. Tham told Jif, "We're weak but readable. Surprising, but we'll take it, right?"

Within seconds, they sent the fire mission request. The last words of that request were *fire for effect*.

In English, Vung asked, "No adjustment rounds?"

"Negative," Jif replied. He made Tham translate his next sentence, so there'd be no misunderstanding: *Too dangerous. It'll give us away.*

*****

They wouldn't hear the relay to FDC at Dak To; it was being done on a different frequency. Jif and his team could only hope it had gone through. But after waiting three minutes for *Shot, over*—the announcement that rounds were just fired—Jif told Tham to ask the APC for confirmation the fire mission had actually been acknowledged by FDC.

The relayed reply: "Affirmative."

But still they waited. Jif thought, *If the guns at Ben Het are shooting this mission, it might take quite a while. Colonel Phong hadn't put any of the changes I suggested into play by the time we left on this patrol. I don't reckon they've done much about it since then, either.*

The NVA battery kept right on firing, a volley every twenty seconds or so.

A shout that sounded like a panicky challenge came out of the darkness, followed immediately by frenzied voices in Vietnamese, trying not to speak loudly but still sounding as if scared half to death. The stir of a brief scuffle came next; Vung had snatched the rifle from Nguyen, the man covering the team's rear. Jif couldn't see it well in the darkness, but Vung appeared to follow up the rifle grab with a blow to the man's head, even harder this time than the formidable one he'd dealt the RTO.

The cause of the commotion: the two men who'd fled the patrol at the sound of the NVA guns were back, locked in a whispered dispute with Vung that sounded like vipers hissing. Tham explained, "They're blaming you, Dai Uy, for their leaving. They claim you ordered us to withdraw. When they realized nobody was with them, they got scared and backtracked. Nguyen would've shot them as they approached if Sergeant Vung hadn't stopped him."

"What the bloody hell did I say that gave them that impression? And since when do they understand English?"

Tham replied, "It doesn't matter what you say, Dai Uy. Frightened men only understand what they want to hear."

Jif's reply, spoken only to himself: *Tell me something I don't know.*

As Vung shoved the returnees back into defensive positions, he said something to them that Jif didn't understand but certainly sounded like a threat.

Tham's translation: *If you run away again, I'll shoot you myself.*

In the distance to the north was a *thud*—the impact of just one round—and it was nowhere near where Jif had wanted it. He couldn't see the impact, just approximate its location by sound…

Like we do blindly in the jungle all the time.

The relay of *shot, over* didn't arrive until seconds after the round hit.

We'd better not depend on those alerts, Jif told himself. *They're changing hands too often to arrive on time. Rounds in flight aren't going to wait for them.*

It didn't bother him that the round was well off-target, short and far to the left; he could be to blame for that inaccuracy just as easily as the gunners. *I'm probably not exactly where I think I am. But why just one round? I called fire for effect. Shooting adjustment rounds one at a time is a dead giveaway that there's an FO in the area.*

Shit. That's all we need…now they know we're out here somewhere. The question is, what will they do about it?

He gave Tham a whopping correction to call in, emphasizing they wanted *fire for effect*—a volley from the entire battery.

Then there was another voice on the air, claiming to be the RTO of the backup radio that had vanished from the patrol with its two-man team. The voice said they were lost and needed guidance to rejoin the patrol. Jif told Tham, "Tell them to be quiet and stay put. We'll deal with them in a minute."

In the midst of that chatter, Jif's next round impacted, again heard but not seen. It was more where he'd wanted it, though still short. But it was still only one round, not the six-round volley he'd requested. He mumbled, "What the bloody fuck, over?"

He told Tham to demand a reason for the ARVN guns not shooting fire for effect.

The answer came back surprisingly fast: *restrictions in effect.*

And then it dawned on Jif what might be going on: *Because of the weather, they haven't gotten their ammo resupplied regularly by choppers—they've been depending on the infrequent trucks—so the artillery commander has imposed rationing rules. I'll bet they're considering a first round and any subsequent corrections of one hundred meters or greater as part of the adjustment phase, deserving of only a single round. But if I give them "add five-zero"—a shift of just fifty meters—I bet they'll honor the fire for effect.*

And if I still need to move the rounds even more, I can call it a moving target and shift fire fifty meters at a time.

It's worth a shot. We're getting nowhere fast this way...and we're becoming more vulnerable by the minute. And it would've been nice if they'd told us about restrictions before we set out on this little adventure.

He'd been up against ammunition restrictions before, and he knew its ramifications could get worse. *If they're also limiting how many rounds can be fired on any one mission, that might shut us down completely.*

He gave Tham the next correction: "Add five-zero, fire for effect."

Vung was agitated about something. His nonstop diatribe—which Jif couldn't follow—was a serious distraction from the mission at hand. Using the little

Vietnamese he knew, Jif told him, "*Im!*" Spoken angrily, it meant *shut up*.

Dutifully, the sergeant complied.

Without shifting his eyes from downrange, Jif asked Tham, "What's on Vung's mind?"

"The voices on the backup radio, Dai Uy…he says they're imposters."

"Imposters…like maybe the radio's been captured?"

"That's correct."

"Tell him not to jump to conclusions. But if NVA troops really do have a radio on this freq, they'll use it to sabotage this fire mission with erroneous corrections, even try to shift the fire onto us…but they probably don't know where we are."

When he heard the translation, Vung nodded in agreement.

There was no mistaking that a volley had just landed in the target area. "I actually got to see some of those flashes," Jif said. Then he told Tham to declare the target as moving and issued the correction: "Left five-zero, add five-zero, repeat fire for effect."

A fire ignited within the impact zone. Contained in a small area, the flames were vivid orange, with no secondary explosions, probably spewing black smoke that was invisible in the night.

"Looks like fuel burning," Jif said. "We're getting in the ballpark now."

But the ballpark began to fight back. Several streams of tracers from near the target area were raking the bamboo forest. The glowing, supersonic balls of green fire flew silently at first until, after a few seconds, the reports of the distant heavy machine guns, traveling only at the speed of sound, finally covered the distance and became audible. The rounds were shredding trees and plowing the ground a few hundred meters east of the patrol's location and well short of it. But they were steadily sweeping west.

"Looks like triple-A guns," Jif said, "probably thirty-seven millimeter. With this weather, they haven't had any aircraft to shoot at, so they've got nothing better to do than ruin our whole day." He told Tham, "We're pulling back. Get everyone moving…and I mean an *orderly* withdrawal, with everybody staying together."

"Is the fire mission over, Dai Uy?"

"Negative. We'll keep shifting the fire while we're on the move."

Vung had the men organized into a column in just over a minute. They were just about to start walking when the next volley crashed down. Within seconds, the sky above the target area lit up like a Fourth of July celebration. What had been a small fire suddenly spread a hundred meters or more. Secondary explosions—ammunition, no doubt—were expanding the blaze even further.

But it didn't stop the heavy machine guns from firing into the forest. Their rounds were moving closer to the patrol.

Vung made himself point man at the head of the single-file column. Jif was *Tail End Charlie*, hanging on to Tham, who was hanging on to the RTO. With the interpreter pulling him along, Jif could continuously look back over his shoulder, watching both the target area—brilliantly lit up as if an illum round had fallen into its midst—and the machine gun rounds. In the light of the flames he could see the movement of many vehicles—tanks and trucks—scrambling to leave the burning area. It looked like much more than an artillery battery position; it was an assembly area for a major unit. He told Tham, "Next correction—Add five-zero, repeat fire for effect."

There was another plea from the voice on the backup radio, begging to know where the patrol was. Tham told Jif, "I asked him to identify himself. He didn't."

When he told Vung the same thing in Vietnamese, the senior sergeant laughed and replied, "You're not surprised, are you?"

They were all worried that whoever was using the backup radio would try to jam their transmissions by talking at the same time. But the APC read back the requested corrections clearly. Jif told Tham, "Tell our relay to shift to Channel Bravo. See if that gets rid of the suspect backup radio."

Tham replied, "The channels are written right on the control panel, Dai Uy. If the NVA has the radio, all they've got to do is read them and change frequency with us."

"You're right, but let's try, anyway," Jif said.

The machine guns were now firing directly toward the patrol. The rounds were falling short, but a few of the tracers were bouncing dangerously close. Some of the ball rounds between the tracers would be doing the same, no doubt, just invisibly. Jif ordered, "Everybody down. Let the sweep pass us by."

Tham was getting a call from the APCs. With the RTO and his radio now flat on the ground, the tip of its antenna practically stuck in the sodden earth, the message was weak. But it couldn't be misunderstood: *Mission terminated by Dak To.*

"Shit," Jif mumbled into the mud an inch from his face. "I knew it. They're restricting ammo expenditure."

He told Tham, "Ask if another base can pick up the mission. Ben Het's in range. Tan Canh is, too."

But the backup radio was on the air again, despite the frequency change. The voice sounded like it was crying in terror. Tham asked Jif, "Should I tell them to fuck off?"

"Roger that…and then make Dak To answer my bloody question."

Nobody noticed that the NVA artillery had stopped firing.

A few moments later, the machine guns lacing the forest stopped, too.

"Get us moving," Jif told Vung.

It took almost ten minutes for Dak To's reply to come through the APC relay. In that time, the patrol had increased its distance from the NVA assembly area by hundreds of meters. The news was good: the long-range 175-millimeter guns at Tan Canh were picking up the fire mission from the ammo-restricted 155s at Dak To. Two minutes after that came, *Shot, over.*

As before, the warning only told Jif what he already knew; he'd seen the flashes from the impacts of the 175 battery's four-round volley seconds before the relayed message reached the patrol. Even from this increased viewing distance, he could tell the rounds were on target, or at least fairly close. Giving Tham his next correction—*add five-zero, repeat fire for effect*—Jif would keep trying for maximum coverage of an area that possessed dimensions at which he could only guess.

Knowing the slow rate of fire of the big 175-millimeter guns—roughly a round every two minutes—he was hesitant to move much farther away from the NVA assembly area; he might end up too far away to see the impacts of the next volley…

But if I tell this patrol to hold up, or even slow down, some of them—maybe all of them—will keep right on moving as fast as they can. We'll get strung out, separated….and we may never find each other again in this dark, wet forest.

We've already got two guys missing for no bloody good reason…

And I've got to keep my eyes on the target. The "shot, over" cue won't arrive in time. If I as much as blink, I'll miss the impacts…and at this distance, I need to see them rather than hear them. It'll be five seconds or more before the sound of those impacts reaches us…and that's much too long to get a good fix with just your ears.

Vung, walking point, had come to a swift-running stream that was swollen with rain. They'd crossed it hours ago on their way north, but it had been just ankle-high then. Still, its banks would provide good cover while walking along its sunken bed in the knee-deep flow, and this stretch of the stream ran generally in the direction they wanted to walk. The added protection its banks provided—a natural trench—would be most welcome, and they were already soaked to the bone and shivering from the cold, wet night, anyway. One by one, the men of the column followed Vung down into the stream.

That process worked well until it was Tham's turn to drop down the bank. Jif was still holding on to him while walking backward to keep the target area in view. As Tham took that big step, he didn't warn Jif quickly enough it was coming, and the patrol's lone American toppled over backward down the three-foot-tall embankment. The splash he made while pancaking into the water seemed loud enough to be heard kilometers away.

Cursing while scrambling to his feet, Jif climbed back up the bank just in time to hear the explosions of the volley. He'd missed the visual of their impacts while floundering in the stream. He was staring frustrated and helpless into the distance as Tham reported, "Shot, over." While the late arrival of the warning had been expected, it only added insult to injury.

Tham offered one more piece of information: *The fire mission has been terminated again due to ammo restrictions*. But Jif could hear nothing but the pounding of his own heart, with good reason: the silhouettes of men—maybe two, maybe a hundred—were standing not ten meters away between him and the target area. He jumped down the embankment for cover, praying that his M16, still wet from its dunking in the stream, would actually fire.

As if the world had not turned terrifying enough, the NVA heavy machine guns were hurling their bright green balls again, this time at such a low trajectory that the tracers didn't appear to be getting closer for seconds that felt like eternities. They just seemed to hang in space, oscillating silently, until suddenly they arrived, buzzing low through the trees all around them, filling the air with mud, wood splinters, and the promise of certain death.

Down in the stream, Jif and his men—though scared stiff—were safe from the machine gun fire. The silhouettes on the bank above were not. The large and powerful bullets, designed to dismantle airplanes with their mass and velocity, made incredibly short work of human flesh and bone.

But the machine guns' aim was not fixed. Their fusillade shifted away, chewing up a different swath of the forest before finally ceasing. The last tracers were burning out as the distant *thud-thud-thud* of their firing finally caught up to them.

The familiar uneasiness that followed a life-and-death encounter settled over the patrol, each man hoping it was over yet fearing it was not. Jif had much he needed to say, but the necessity to translate everything made the process futile and frustrating. Reassurances and postmortems could wait. He told himself, *Remember KISS—keep it simple, stupid. Just say what absolutely needs to be said to get us out of here alive. Worry about everything else later.*

Vung, like everyone else in the column except Jif, had no idea that men had been following them…until now. He and the dai uy entertained the same tragic possibility: *that was our two-man backup radio team who just got cut to ribbons.*

But it wasn't. A quick count of the carnage revealed five severed arms and three torsos, one of them headless. There had to be more body parts scattered in the darkness—maybe even some intact bodies, still alive—but they wouldn't search for them. The uniforms and equipment on those torsos were NVA, not ARVN.

There was, however, a shot-up American radio set lying on the ground, a Prick-25. The frequency reminders written in grease pencil on the control panel left no doubt it was the patrol's backup radio. There was no sign of the two ARVN troopers who'd carried that unit.

They bought it, I'm sure, Jif told himself. *The poor bastards should've stayed with the patrol.*

Jif began to give Tham a new correction for the fire mission, but the sergeant interrupted, saying, "I guess you didn't hear what I said just before the shit hit the fan, Dai Uy...the mission was terminated. Ammunition restrictions again."

Jif's reply: "Isn't that just fucking great?" Then he added, "All right…tell Vung he's my hero for leading us into this stream. Now, let's get the hell out of here."

It was only then that he began to appreciate how cold and miserable he was. It seemed ages ago when Sergeant Major Moon had spilled the beans on where his assignment would be by asking, *You got a field jacket handy*? But it had only been a matter of days.

Tropical paradise, my ass, Jif thought. *It gets cold as a witch's tit at night in the Central Highlands...and this bloody rain is only making it worse.*

Chapter Twenty-Two

Dawn was breaking on another rainy and overcast morning as the APCs carrying Jif's patrol rolled through the gate at Ben Het. They pulled up to the CP where Colonel Phong was waiting to meet the wet, bedraggled, and exhausted men. He wanted to shake every man's hand as they stumbled from the vehicles, as if they'd just won the war all by themselves.

After lavishing praise on Sergeant Vung in Vietnamese, he turned to Jif to do the same in English. But it was falling on deaf ears. "What's the matter, Miles? You destroyed the assembly area of an NVA regiment. That's cause for celebration."

"I'm not so sure that's what we did," Jif replied. "We might've caused them some damage, but they're hardly destroyed. And begging your pardon, sir, but why the bloody hell wasn't I informed that ammunition restrictions were in effect?"

Either Phong was one of the world's greatest actors, or he was genuinely surprised to hear about restrictions he'd known nothing about. "I had no idea, Miles! We'll get to the bottom of this immediately."

Jif fought back a smirk; *If he really didn't know, it sounds like typical ARVN staff work. One hand never bothers to tell the other what it's doing.* Then he replied, "Getting to the bottom of it would be a good idea, sir. I might've conducted the patrol a lot differently had I known I was fighting with one hand tied behind my back. And I don't consider an operation that resulted in two men missing and probably KIA as a great success. You have Sergeant Vung to thank for the whole patrol not being KIA."

"He said the same about you, Miles. Dau Dang Vann will be here shortly. He wants to hear all about your mission. You'd best freshen up and look sharp."

*****

The only freshening up Jif got to do was shave and don dry fatigues. But the pallor of a sleepless, terrifying night couldn't simply be washed away. An energetic Vann, who looked clean and pressed as if his tropics-friendly civvies had just come from the laundry, offered this for a greeting: "You look like shit, Captain Miles. Tough night, I gather?"

"I've had better, sir."

"Let's get into the CP and out of this rain," Vann said. "Then you can tell me all about it."

Once inside, Jif gave his boss a blow-by-blow retelling of the night's effort. He had no trouble convincing Vann that his artillery bombardment had probably not been a killing blow to the NVA assembly area. He expressed his anger again at not being told of the ammo restrictions.

Vann was fuming about it, too. "I found out about the restrictions too late to help you out, Miles. And believe me, I ripped a few new assholes over it, too. But you do understand why they're in effect, right?"

"Of course, sir. The division is low on rounds, so they're saving the bulk of them for base defense. From where I was sitting, though, it seemed like we could've done a lot more for base defense by neutralizing that NVA assembly area with as much fire as we could muster. Dead soldiers and destroyed vehicles can't attack you. And when they shot single adjustment rounds instead of the fire-for-effect volleys I asked for…that put me and my men in a world of hurt."

"So true, Miles, so true. I've ordered the division commander to raise the restriction limits for observed fire missions. He's agreed to triple that limit. Our advisors at Dak To will be monitoring those limitations closely. They'll also ensure that missions are not modified by the receiving unit but fired as requested, as well. And tomorrow, we should get a break in the weather. It won't last long, but I've already got our aviation battalions ready to take advantage of it with a massive airlift of ammunition, fuel, the whole works."

"That should be a great help, sir," Jif replied, "but that alone isn't going to make the assembly area go away. What are the odds of getting a B-52 strike on it…before they can sweep down on us?"

"You really believe that's called for, Captain?"

"Yes, sir, I do."

"Well, then, let's dial one up," Vann replied. "I'll beg, borrow, and steal to make it happen. Can't do it from here, though…radio link isn't secure enough. I'll do it from Dak To as soon as I get back there in a little while."

"That's great, sir…but I'm still concerned the NVA might pick up stakes in the meantime."

"If they do, Miles, they won't go very far. One thing about the Vietnamese mind, whether NVA or ARVN…once it makes a plan, it's incapable of changing that plan until it's completely in ashes. Rest assured that twelve hours from now, the assembly area will still be in the same location for the buffs to plaster."

Shifting gears, Vann said, "You know, Miles, I've heard that those ARVN you led would go to hell and back with you. You made quite an impression on them."

Jif thought, *How the hell did he hear that? He just got here.*

Vann continued, "What did you think of the ARVN personnel you worked with? Is the feeling mutual?"

"I had two NCOs with me, sir, and they were both outstanding leaders. The men themselves were just like any other army…they performed well when led effectively. But I've got a question, sir…like most ARVN outfits I've observed, these NCOs had no qualms about getting physical with their men. Two of the troopers got punched by the senior sergeant when they screwed up. It makes me wonder if behavior like that leads to fragging. I'm not aware of any incidents, but some would call my experience as an advisor limited. So from your perspective, do you see fragging incidents by ARVN troops against their leaders?"

"No, Miles, I don't. The typical behavior of a *Marvin the ARVN* who's got problems with his superior is to go AWOL. It's a lot easier for an ARVN to do that in this country than a GI. He blends into the populace better, and he doesn't have an assault or a murder charge hanging over his head when he gets caught."

"I can understand that, sir. But what about the firefights from time to time between Catholic and Buddhist units? How's that any different from fragging? They're still trying to kill their own people."

"Ah, Miles…there's a world of difference. Those religious conflicts are deeply engrained in Vietnamese society. They're not aimed against an individual sergeant or officer someone's got a gripe with but an entire sect that was hated in the first place. I'm sure you've noticed the pains we go through to keep Catholic and Buddhist battalions nowhere near each other when they're not actively fighting the communists."

Vann checked his watch. Though impatient to deal with other issues at the base, he had another question for Jif: "Do you have any recommendations for ARVN patrols led by Americans, Captain?"

"I have one, sir. If an American is going to be in charge—and like me, he's not fluent in Vietnamese—his ARVN second-in-command *must* be a fluent English speaker. Having to constantly go through an interpreter just doesn't get things done quickly enough. It also wouldn't hurt if we had airborne relay ships with Vietnamese speakers on board for longer-range communications. That would save us even more time. The weather wouldn't be a problem for them since they work above it."

"Let me ask this, Captain…suppose there isn't a fluent English speaker as second-in-command?"

"Then he becomes the commander, and the American stays home, sir."

Vann didn't need to verbally shoot down Jif's suggestion; his scowl had already done that. But he replied, anyway: "I don't know if we can guarantee that, Miles. Let's see how it goes. Concerning the airborne relay ships, we have only a handful to work with in country, and guess where they all are…"

Jif: "Eye Corps, right?"

"You got it, Captain. When the fight up there finally dies down, things will get very different as far as resource allocation goes. Until then, we'll stay flexible and creative." Vann seemed rushed as he asked, "Anything else on your mind?"

There was. Jif explained how the artillery situation at Ben Het hadn't improved at all since he'd pointed the problems out to Colonel Phong yesterday.

"That's disappointing, Miles…but very important," Vann replied. "I'm going to call Phong over here. I want you to tell him in no uncertain terms that what needs to be done with the artillery will be accomplished immediately."

"Is it appropriate that *I* chew him out, sir?"

"Under the circumstances, it's totally appropriate, Miles. You do the talking, I'll be right behind you. But I won't say a word. I won't have to."

Jif still seemed uncertain about the propriety of it all, so Vann added, "I need these people to know that when one of my advisors speaks, it's the same as if I'm speaking. Let's get it done, Captain."

At first, Phong was startled—and quite indignant—that he was being ordered around by a mere captain. With body language alone, he beseeched Vann, who was standing just a few feet away, to intervene. But it wouldn't happen; it was obvious that this was the way the dau dang wanted it. That was all Phong needed to know. When Jif finished reiterating the changes and improvements that would be made before end of day, the colonel said, "Affirmative, Miles. I will see to it personally."

It was lost on no one that addressing Jif merely as *Miles* was his attempt to salvage some small modicum of superiority.

Then Phong nodded respectfully to a satisfied Vann, who returned the gesture in kind.

They were joined by Major Parker and the armored cav squadron commander he advised, LTC Diep. Drawing their attention to the situation map, Vann announced that the two squadrons at Ben Het would now be responsible for providing road security along the twenty-five-kilometer stretch—roughly fifteen miles—along the two highways that doglegged south to the town of Dien Binh, located roughly halfway to Kontum.

Diep protested immediately. "That is Kontum's job. We do not have enough people or armored vehicles to patrol so much road."

Vann replied, "Nobody, Colonel, and I mean nobody, ever has enough of anything they think they need to get the job done. It's the ones who find a way to make it work with what they have that survive and win. And as far as whose job it is, I'll be the one who decides that."

Diep bowed his head in submission; Vann's dictum, delivered like the word of God, was as effective as a slap in the face. The colonel felt foolish, as if he wished he'd never challenged a man who embraced the art of command so effortlessly.

Jif glanced at Parker, wondering what expression would be on the major's face. He was surprised by what he saw. *I thought he'd be wearing one of his usual seen-it-all smirks, as if thinking: Listen to this rah-rah, gung-ho bullshit. But he looks ready to whip out a little American flag and start waving it.*

I reckon the dau dang definitely worked his magic on him, too.

Vann then laid out his plan on the map; roving patrols would synchronize themselves into the convoy schedule, providing the firepower to keep the roadways as secure as possible. Both ARVN colonels were relieved that the vehicles involved were only their upgunned APCs and jeeps—vehicles only their squadrons had in any quantity—and none of their precious, fuel-thirsty tanks. Then he got to the question of fire support. "Per Captain Miles' guidance, the one-oh-five-millimeter howitzers at Ben Het—now being organized into one autonomous unit which we'll call *Mike Battery*—will provide primary fire support for the patrols along the road between here and Dak To, which is the limit of their range. I agree with the captain…those guns have been sorely underutilized since arriving here. Now they'll be able to provide rapid fire support. With the lack of tac air and gunships due to weather, you're going to need that artillery support."

Phong had to concede the point. But he raised another issue: "Who commands this *autonomous* Mike Battery?"

Vann passed the question to Jif, who replied, "Senior Sergeant Cao will be the acting commander."

"Unacceptable," Phong said. "I will designate one of my officers to—"

"No need, Colonel," Vann interrupted. "Sergeant Cao will report directly to my advisors."

If any of the ARVN officers in the CP had, to this point, failed to understand that Dau Dang Vann was their de facto commander, they were now enlightened.

Colonel Diep asked, "With all due respect, sir, is General Du in agreement with all this?"

"Your corps commander is completely on board, Colonel," Vann replied. "Now, you've all seen the convoy timetable. Security patrols will be on the road as of thirteen hundred hours today. My senior advisor at Dak To will oversee the patrolling operation."

Jif shot another glance at Parker. He still looked like he was waving that little flag.

Vann said, "If there are no other questions, gentlemen, I'll be on my way back to Dak To." To Jif and Parker, he added, "Walk me to my vehicle, gentlemen. I've got some odds and ends to discuss with you."

A few minutes later, Vann's jeep drove through the gate at Ben Het. Parker told Jif, "You'd better catch yourself a nap. These ARVN can work without you up their ass for a few hours, at least."

"Not yet," Jif replied. "I've got to make sure these guns transform themselves into a functioning battery on the spot. I don't want them wasting a lot of time and effort on bullshit. Anyway, what's that old saying—I'll sleep when I'm dead?"

"Don't make that happen sooner than it has to, Miles."

Parker turned and walked away. He didn't bother saying he was headed to the latrine.

When the NVA artillery barrage began to fall on Ben Het a few minutes later, Parker was caught with his pants down. He'd never get to pull them up again; a direct hit blew up the wooden-roofed revetment housing the latrine along with the three men inside.

*****

"The incoming, Dai Uy…I'm sure it's from the same direction as before," said Sergeant Tham as he crowded into the CP bunker with Jif. "Probably the same NVA assembly area is doing the shooting."

Colonel Phong didn't want to hear that. He snapped at Jif and Tham, saying, "It can't be. You destroyed those guns last night."

Shaking his head, Jif replied, "Like I said, sir, there's no proof of that. We need to put counter-battery on that same spot again…lots of it…and we've got to do it blind this time."

Phong pondered the Hobson's choice for just a moment before deciding to call Dak To, requesting counter-battery fire on last night's target.

The fire direction officer refused the request. The reason: *unobserved fires are forbidden due to the ammo restrictions.*

Jif couldn't believe what he was hearing. He exploded, "How many bloody rules does this restriction have?" What made the refusal more ludicrous: Dak To was coming under fire, too, but wasn't trying to strike back and silence the NVA guns.

"Let's shoot the counter-battery ourselves," Jif said. He was already turning a map table in the CP into an emergency FDC.

"But our guns are not ready," Phong replied.

"They're ready enough," Jif said. "Two of them can't shoot north yet…too much junk still blocking their fields of fire. But four tubes are better than nothing right now...unless you want to lose more than just the shithouse."

The one improvement that was in place and functioning was a landline net linking all the howitzers with the CP. Jif sent the fire commands he'd just calculated down the wire; as expected in these circumstances, the data was more approximate than precise. Sergeant Cao, the acting battery commander, prodded his disbelieving and reluctant gunners through the large shift in deflection, something they'd been told would never happen. There was a problem in one gun section; the gunner couldn't get a usable sight picture on his sloppily positioned aiming equipment after the big shift. Visual obstructions prevented gun-to-gun laying, too, so Jif provided an azimuth of fire to supplement the given deflection. Cao then used that azimuth and his compass to align the tube *close enough for government work.*

It was a slow process; rounds that should've been in the air within twenty seconds took well over a minute. But within the next two minutes, they'd put four more volleys totaling twenty rounds on the assumed target location while receiving only three rounds inbound, two of which fell well outside the perimeter.

But the incoming wouldn't stop. Single rounds continued to fall intermittently on Ben Het. One was a direct hit on an APC that killed the two men inside, wounded four nearby, and destroyed the vehicle.

Jif asked himself, *This is a crapshoot. Which way do I shift our bloody rounds to actually hit these bastards?*

He came up with a scheme to move the volleys in an ever-widening circle. When he told Phong, the colonel said, "No! You're wasting too much ammunition."

Another incoming round crashed down very close to the bunker, causing damage only to an antenna mast. But it shook the structure like an earthquake, coating everyone inside with a dusting of dirt liberated from the roof. Jif said to Phong, "Sir, I'm afraid we're going to need to waste some more rounds if we want this to stop. Our inventory's good. We've still got seventy-two boxes of HE…that's one hundred forty-four rounds. And if you're worried about close-in perimeter defense, there's also twenty boxes of beehive containing forty rounds."

"Are you sure about that, Miles?"

Jif pointed to the battery status board he'd put on the wall, one of his mandated improvements; an ARVN artilleryman designated as battery recorder was maintaining the running count. It confirmed the numbers he'd just given. "Yeah, I'm sure, sir."

Phong replied, "Very well, but do not reduce inventory below one hundred rounds HE without my approval."

Jif was too busy to argue. He considered the colonel's mandate just another administrative restriction, divorced from their current reality, to be ignored if necessary. He kept up the pattern he'd established of shifting the volleys of counter-battery fire.

By pure chance, a momentary lull occurred in the concussive noises of battle; there'd been no incoming for almost a minute, and Ben Het's howitzers were still loading their next volley. That incongruous tranquility made the sudden firing of an APC's .50-caliber machine guns all the more alarming. As the phones in the CP came alive and officers began to shout a confusing cacophony of orders and counter-orders, Colonel Diep raced in with a disturbing confirmation: "We're being hit—southwest quadrant! Prepare to fire beehive!"

Just as he said that, an NVA round crashed down just beyond the perimeter in the southwest quadrant, the area supposedly under attack.

"Are we sure about getting hit, sir?" Jif asked. "Kind of odd the NVA would still be shooting a prep while they have infantry in the target area."

"That means nothing, Captain," Diep replied. "You should know that the NVA can never effectively communicate during combined arms operations."

Gee, the ARVN's got that problem, too, Jif told himself.

From the CP, they could clearly see the area in question as .50-caliber rounds and small arms fire ripped through it, all from the ARVN defenders. If there actually were NVA attackers there, they'd gone to ground.

Jif reminded Diep, "Beehive's only going to work if we can see the people we're shooting at, sir. If they're down in holes or behind trees, forget it. If the NVA is out there about four hundred meters or more, though, we can shoot killer junior instead."

But they couldn't see anyone out that far, either. Though the terrain around the base was relatively flat and the forest sparse, it could still hide a group of men intent on staying concealed.

The colonel was seething, as if Jif had just told him to go fuck himself. Whether this mere captain was Vann's man or not, he didn't appreciate being second-guessed by him; *It's bad enough that I have that lazy dullard Parker in my business all the time.*

Trying to accommodate Diep, Jif said, "Guns Two and Four can provide beehive if necessary, sir. They can't shoot the counter-battery mission, anyway."

One of Diep's tanks had now rolled up to the perimeter wire, adding a few rounds from its main gun to the defensive effort.

Jif wanted a closer look at the southwest quadrant. He quickly calculated the firing data to shift the volleys three times more, telling Sergeant Cao to use that data to continue the counter-battery fire. Then he climbed on top of the CP bunker with binoculars in hand. Diep and his RTO were right behind him.

After scanning the quadrant, Jif said, "I don't see a bloody soul out there, Colonel."

Diep had had enough of this *too big for his britches* captain. He demanded, "Where is Major Parker?"

Jif was inclined to reply, *It's not my turn to watch him*. But his actual reply was, "I don't know, sir. I thought he'd be with you."

An ARVN lieutenant ran up to the bunker, calling to Colonel Diep. In the lieutenant's hand was the blood-soaked soft cap of an American major, identified by the subdued brown oak leaf insignia of rank pinned to the peak. In Vietnamese, he told Diep that Parker had been killed in the direct hit on the latrine.

Jif didn't need a translation. One look at the cap was enough.

Chapter Twenty-Three

Everything stopped. The incoming, the defensive fire along the perimeter, the counter-battery mission. Even the rain. That incongruous tranquility returned once again, this time for much more than just a few moments. It was almost as unnerving as the sounds of gunfire.

Jif's call to Vann, reporting the death of Major Parker, was met with a different silence—equally unnerving—from the radio's speaker. He was beginning to think one of their radios might have gone inoperative until Vann finally transmitted a one-word reply: "Goddammit."

After a few more moments of dead air, he told Jif, "You are in complete charge of Ben Het for the time being."

Colonel Phong, who'd been eavesdropping on the conversation, had this acidic comment: "Congratulations on your promotion, Miles. I sincerely hope you're up to the broadened responsibilities." He didn't need to supplement with words what his sour expression was already expressing: *But I have my doubts*.

Colonel Diep had gone to the perimeter wire of the southwest quadrant, intent on assessing the enemy assault his men had just repelled. To the colonel's displeasure, Jif joined him there. They could see nothing to suggest that enemy troops had gotten anywhere near the perimeter.

"We should send a patrol to investigate, sir," Jif said. He was already beginning to suspect that the *attack* might have been a phantom, a case of jittery nerves amongst the ARVN troopers on the perimeter. But he wouldn't say that out loud. Not yet, anyway.

"I don't need you to tell me that, Miles," Diep replied. He gave an irritated sigh and added, "I'm sorry your Major Parker has been killed...and in such an undignified way. It's no secret I didn't think much of him, either...but at least he didn't speak when it wasn't necessary."

Jif knew the use of the word *either* meant that Diep also didn't think much of him. He wondered if the colonel had meant to use some other word than *undignified* to describe Parker's death. To his mind, there was no such thing as a *dignified* death in war. Demise didn't come in a variety of flavors. His death would've been no different had the major been killed by a direct hit while hunkered down in a bunker. He just happened to be on the shitter. It was all just a matter of circumstance.

Jif asked, "Did the perimeter receive any fire from attackers? Everything I saw was going the other way. Doesn't look like you took any casualties, either."

Diep's reply: "There was no incoming fire because my men suppressed it. They heard the enemy approaching."

"I'm surprised they could hear much of anything with all the artillery coming in and going out," Jif said. That earned him an angry look from the colonel.

Diep then summoned one of his captains, telling him to send a squad beyond the wire to find the evidence of an enemy assault. The captain turned around and delegated the assignment to a lieutenant. Within moments, the lieutenant had assigned a squad to the patrol, led by a young sergeant. It was obvious the lieutenant had no intention of going with them. None of that process—a textbook example of shit rolling downhill—surprised Jif until Diep told him, "You'll be in charge, Miles. The dau dang seems to want every patrol led by an American, and that, I'm afraid, leaves only you."

Still exhausted from the adventures of the previous night, Jif had no intention of leading another foot patrol. If Diep wanted an officer in charge, he had plenty of his own to send. But he asked, "Does that squad leader speak good English, sir?"

"No, Miles, he does not."

"How about French? Or is he too young to speak that language fluently?"

"He speaks no French," Diep replied. "You will have to take a translator."

"Then I'm not going."

"I'll be reporting your refusal to the dau dang immediately, Captain."

"That's your prerogative, sir. Just let me know what the patrol finds, okay?"

On the way to his bunker, Jif checked on the progress Mike Battery was making with his mandated improvements. The biggest issue: relocating tents, sheds, and armored vehicle revetments to remove the obstructions they presented, allowing all the howitzers to fire in any direction. Colonel Phong was pitching a fit to

Sergeant Cao over some of the relocations, but when he saw Jif coming, he desisted, threw his hands up in surrender, and walked away.

Satisfied with how things were coming with the battery, Jif left word at the CP that he'd be in his bunker. He knew Vann would arrive in a few hours. At their last meeting, he'd *looked like shit*, in the dau dang's words…

What's worse, I'm so tired that I'm probably thinking like shit, too. I need a bloody nap.

He was determined to take one.

*****

Around 1400, the whine and buzz of a LOACH awoke him. At first glance, Jif thought his wristwatch had to be wrong, but then realized it wasn't. He couldn't believe he'd actually slept four solid hours; *That's got to be some kind of in-country record.* But his next thought was, *What the hell did I miss while I was conked out*?

The helicopter, as he suspected, was Vann's. And the only thing he'd missed while asleep was the arrival of a tiger's bullet-ridden carcass at the CP, dragged there by an APC. As Jif hurried to the LZ, Sergeant Tham explained how the big cat came to be there: "The *enemy activity* they heard on the perimeter was that tiger prowling near the wire."

Jif found that hard to swallow. "You mean they couldn't see it was a bloody tiger? That thing must weigh three or four hundred pounds. There's no scrub out there that would hide him completely. If he tried to get into the camp, they'd have to kill him, anyway. Why make up a story about an NVA attack?"

"I don't know what to tell you, Dai Uy. They must've wounded it, and then it dragged itself away, leaving a big blood trail that got the patrol all excited when they went outside the wire, as if it might've come from wounded enemy soldiers. The tiger was down but still alive when they found it, so they put it out of its misery. Colonel Diep wants to have it stuffed and mounted at the gate like a trophy."

Jif's sarcastic reply: "Great. That'll scare the NVA away, for sure."

Stepping from the chopper, John Paul Vann was his usual high-intensity self, managing somehow to look cool and crisp in the stifling humidity while wearing office civvies, complete with necktie. His first words: "What's your situation with the incoming, Miles?"

"Haven't had any for almost five hours, sir. How about Dak To and Tan Canh?"

"They haven't been so lucky. Target acquisition shows the rounds hitting them are coming from that same area you identified." Glancing up at the solid overcast, he added, "I took a big chance using the chopper, but with the ceiling up over five hundred feet, the time saved was worth the risk. Just have to stay low and follow the roads. That keeps us away from the mountains. What's with the fucking tiger?"

Jif related the story, including his refusal to go on the patrol. Relieved to learn there'd been no infantry or armored assault against Ben Het, Vann said, "Wasn't much point in you going on a tiger hunt, was there?" Then he asked, "Are Major Parker's remains ready to go?"

"Affirmative, sir. On their way to the LZ."

"It's a damn shame, Miles...but it doesn't matter how you died, does it? And I've got to write something that consoles his family and honors his sacrifice. How about this...*A valiant American fighting man has selflessly given his life assisting Republic of Vietnam forces in their struggle to stave off the communist yoke*?"

"Sounds about right, sir," Jif replied.

"I'll take his body down to Pleiku with me. I've got a meeting of crucial importance there with President Thieu in an hour. He wants the B-52s hitting nothing but Eye Corps targets, like he's gambling everything so as not to lose Hue. That would mean no buffs for us, Miles."

Jif asked, "You mean he won't give us even *one* strike package?"

"Not if he has his way. But I'm going to do a *come-to-Jesus* session with the man and change all that, hopefully. He needs to understand that if the Highlands collapse, there will be nothing to stop the NVA from driving to the coast, cutting the Republic of Vietnam in two. Once that happens, Eye Corps and Hue become irrelevant, and his regime is as good as finished. Doesn't sound like it should be too difficult to sell, does it?"

"No, sir, it doesn't."

"Well, Miles, be thankful you don't have to deal with the man. He's a shining example of how the thirst for power has a way of distorting logic. And by the way, I'll be pushing for *three* strike packages, not just one. As you pointed out, our target could be anywhere in a fairly large area, so we need the extra coverage."

"I just wish there was some way we could get an accurate bomb damage assessment after the strikes," Jif said.

"You're preaching to the choir, Captain. But I don't have to tell you the days of American tech wizardry in this country are over. We just don't have the ready access to hardware we once had. That includes ground surveillance radar and electronic surveillance aircraft. And the weather, of course, is screwing us over big time lately. We can't even do basic photo recon. We're flying by the seat of our pants, so to speak."

They could see the body bag containing what was left of Major Parker being loaded into the LOACH's aft cabin. Vann said, "One more thing…I'll be filling the open slot here at Ben Het with Major Swanson from Pleiku. Do you know him?"

"No, sir."

"Well, you're going to get to know him real soon. He's a tanker, with lengthy armored cav experience. He'll be a good fit here. If the weather allows it, he should be able to fly in later today. But if the damn overcast closes in on us again, he'll have to come over the road. It'll be another day before he arrives."

And then Vann was gone, his LOACH lifting off and vanishing into the low cloud deck. Sergeant Tham asked, "Is flying blind like that such a good idea, Dai Uy? Wasn't he just talking about following roads and not crashing into mountains?"

"I guess Pleiku's reporting better visibility than we have here," Jif replied. "But you're right…it doesn't seem like such a hot idea with the weather like it is. Conditions could change really fast. The man's in a hurry, though, and the war doesn't wait for you. The cloud deck only goes up to about fifteen hundred feet, according to the latest report. Once you're above it, it's a beautiful day. You can see the mountain peaks real easy."

"I still think it's foolish, Dai Uy. Is it worth the minutes saved?"

*****

There was no incoming at Ben Het that afternoon. Tan Canh wasn't so lucky; it got hammered by a steady stream of NVA artillery that lasted over thirty minutes. The only saving grace: half the rounds fell outside the base, keeping the casualties and destruction to a minimum.

Jif told Colonel Phong, "It's a good thing the NVA are shooting as blindly as we are. They obviously don't have any FOs adjusting their fire missions."

"Are you complaining, Miles?"

"Negative, sir. I'm just not sure why they don't have OPs a klick or two away from our bases. They could set up a radio relay halfway to their gun batteries, just like we did, and paste the crap out of us with accurate fire."

Phong replied, "Maybe they're afraid we'd locate their radios with direction finders and wipe them out."

Jif had to laugh. "What direction finders, sir? The only tracking station I've heard of is at Tan Canh, and it's not even operational. *Waiting on parts*, as usual."

"But the enemy doesn't know that, Miles."

Wonderful, thought Jif, *we're fighting a war of guesswork and wishful thinking.*

*****

Just before 1630 hours, the radios came alive; a convoy headed to Tan Canh had been hit on Route 14, just north of Dien Binh. The nearest security patrol was a kilometer away from the ambush site. At Ben Het, they could only hear Tan Canh's end of the radio exchanges; the patrol vehicles' transmitters were too far away.

But those at the Ben Het CP could hear the occasional American voice—with a steady, high-pitched whine in the background typical of transmitting from a helicopter—sounding as if the man was adjusting artillery fire in a mix of English and Vietnamese. Using Tham's translations of the broken transmissions, Jif tried to construct a map plot of what was going on.

"This ambush is in the same area where I got hit when I drove up here," he said. "There's got to be some NVA getting very comfortable in those hills. They sweep down to hit traffic on the highway whenever they feel like it. It'd be nice if we could get rid of them."

Phong shrugged, his disinterest obvious. "That's not our problem, Miles," he said.

"Not ours specifically, maybe," Jif replied, "but isn't it the entire division's problem?"

Again, Phong shrugged, as if the sharing of intelligence wasn't part of his job.

That's just so bloody typical of the ARVN command structure, Jif fumed to himself. *Nobody cares about anything outside their own little bubble. Everybody else can go to hell.*

But the American voice, working with the artillery at Dak To, seemed to have put an end to the ambush. When the security patrol arrived, they reported the situation under control, with one deuce burning and abandoned but no serious casualties.

Then they asked if they should pursue the NVA who were retreating into the hills west of Route 14. The reply from Tan Canh: "Negative. Do not pursue. Resume patrol."

Jif blurted, to no one in particular, "Sure, don't bother pursuing. By all means, let's give them another chance to hit a convoy."

Diep said, "You seem very eager to get my men killed, Miles." Phong nodded; he thought so, too.

There were a number of caustic responses rattling around in Jif's head. Any one of them would have permanently destroyed whatever working relationship he had with the ARVN commanders. And that would displease John Paul Vann.

So he said nothing.

*****

Ten minutes later, a LOACH approached Ben Het along Route 512, scud-running beneath the lowering overcast. That solid cloud deck, coupled with the lateness of the day, had made it dark at ground level. The pilot called for ground flares to mark the LZ.

Once those flares were burning, the ship wasted not a second offloading her passenger and his baggage. Then she was gone, whipping back down the roadway to Dak To at treetop height, quickly vanishing into the gloom.

The passenger, Major Larry Swanson, looked genuinely glad to be there. Shouldering a duffle, with a canvas satchel and M16 in his free hand, he walked with purpose toward the CP, carrying his heavy load as if it were weightless. When he saw Jif, he called out in a booming voice, "You've gotta be Miles, right?"

The voice sounded vaguely familiar. As they shook hands, Jif said, "Glad to have you with us, sir. That wasn't you, by any chance, adjusting artillery on that ambush, was it?"

"In the flesh, Miles. We just happened to be blundering down Route Fourteen when the shit hit the fan. You know…right place, right time. But you're the artilleryman, so tell me…how'd I do?"

"Sounds like you took care of business, sir. Done much aerial observer work before?"

"Nope. First time ever. Sat through a lecture about it once, though. What that instructor said was right...just use the gun-target line to adjust the rounds. The only trouble was, I couldn't see the guns. Too much overcast. But I could guesstimate where they were pretty easy…and my pilot was a big help. He knew the drill by the numbers."

"That's for sure," Jif replied. "Pilots can't help but become good AOs. They get a lot of practice."

"I'll need you to give me the lowdown on this place and its people," Swanson said. "I want to hit the ground running. But first, I've got some big news from J.P. Vann."

It was good news, too. Vann had convinced Thieu to give Two Corps the three B-52 strike packages he'd asked for. "Didn't take much arm twisting, either," Swanson added. "It's gonna happen tonight, around twenty hundred hours. We'll definitely know when it does. Should be quite a show."

*****

Around 1930 hours, Ben Het received another dose of incoming artillery. Even in the darkness, there was little doubt the rounds were launched from the same direction as all those that had come before. But this bombardment seemed more accurate than its predecessors. Falling at the rate of two to three rounds a minute, they damaged several trucks, destroyed a water buffalo, and tore to shreds a tent city—mostly unoccupied—where troopers slept. By 2000 hours, the ARVN had taken six casualties, one of them KIA. Pending the promised B-52 strike, Jif had reluctantly agreed to Phong's and Diep's demand that the cannoneers be allowed to take shelter rather than being exposed while shooting counter-battery.

A few minutes past 2000 hours, men in the watchtowers of Ben Het could see what looked like flashes of lightning being reflected in rapid sequence within the cloud deck to the north. Less than a minute later, the sporadic explosions of the incoming were replaced by a distant but awesome rumble. They were seeing and hearing the first B-52 strike package delivering its massive load of ordnance on what they hoped was the NVA assembly area. The rumbling lasted twenty seconds.

But the incoming at Ben Het didn't stop. Two more men died when their perimeter bunker was struck.

Fifteen minutes and twenty inbound rounds later, the second B-52 package dropped its bombs. The explosions sounded closer this time.

When the echoes of that strike package faded, an anxious quiet fell over Ben Het. It lasted until the third strike package unloaded its wares. These explosions were less audible and their flashes had been unseen, as if the bombs of that final run landed much farther north than the first two.

After those echoes faded, a quiet descended over Ben Het like a blessing. It had a feeling of permanence about it that was unexplainable but welcome.

Chapter Twenty-Four

For the next three weeks, the only thing falling on the ARVN base camps at Ben Het, Dak To, and Tan Canh was rain. Once the B-52s had struck that fateful night in March, the incoming rounds of NVA artillery ceased. Though the absence of incoming was a relief, no one in II Corps was deluded enough to believe it would last forever. The same could be said for the ARVN defenders of III and IV Corps. To date, they'd withstood only sporadic, mostly ineffective artillery and rocket attacks and skirmished with small NVA probes infiltrating from Cambodia. But they were well aware the enemy was massing just over that border.

I Corps remained a very different story. The conflict still raged there, but the battered ARVN defenders, bolstered by the American heavy bombers, had managed to stop the NVA advance short of Hue. The outcome of that battle, however, was still a long way from being decided; the enemy's continuing ability to resupply and reinforce itself across the DMZ ensured the fight could go on for months.

But the only conflict engulfing Ben Het at the moment was between the ARVN commanders and their American advisors. Jif was locking horns with Phong on an almost daily basis over one simple issue: the colonel was not inclined to compel elements of his cavalry squadron to patrol in search of intruding NVA forces, attempting to locate them before they got too close to the base camp. Major Swanson was encountering the same reluctance from Diep.

The two squadron commanders had manipulated to their advantage Jif's insistence that an American would only accompany a patrol if that patrol's Vietnamese leader spoke English. They claimed that condition couldn't be met with any regularity, so Vann decided to support his junior advisor and rescinded his directive that Americans would lead the patrols. Once that policy change was in place, the ARVN returned to their practice of lying about the conduct of those operations, never going very far beyond the wire despite claiming they'd covered much more territory. It didn't take long for them to merely pretend they'd gone beyond the wire without actually leaving base camp.

After he'd been at Ben Het a few days, Swanson said to Jif, "These squadron commanders simply aren't interested in aggressive action. They just want to sit on their asses and let American airpower do all the work for them. Didn't anybody tell them that once the bad guys get close enough for you to see their faces, airpower can't do you a whole lot of good anymore? Unless they're interested in losing a lot of their troopers in friendly fire incidents, that is."

Another point of contention that shouldn't have been one at all: both colonels were angry at how well Jif had molded Mike Battery into a fully functioning fire support element, even training several men to staff a basic but effective FDC. "All that has done," Phong raged, "is allow the battery to shoulder missions that should be shot by other firebases. As a result, our guns constantly expend all their ammunition, forcing their basic loads to be resupplied at the expense of replenishing the other large-caliber weapons."

"That's an interesting argument, sir," Jif countered, "but considering the other weapons haven't shot a bloody round other than the occasional test firing, their resupply isn't an issue at the moment."

The practice of test firing weapons brought to light another problem, which Swanson pounced on. He told Diep and Phong, "The main guns on your tanks are out of boresight. Not one practice round your vehicles have fired has hit what it was aimed at."

"Not likely," Diep replied, making himself the spokesman for both squadrons. "Our tanks haven't fired enough rounds yet to need boresighting."

"Did they drive over the road to get here, Colonel?"

"Of course."

"And did you boresight them once they got here?"

"Negative."

"Then they've been jostled more than enough to need boresighting," Swanson insisted. "You've got the equipment. Just do it. You won't be sorry."

That was a week ago. The ARVN tankers still hadn't performed the task. And that meant the odds of their tanks scoring long-range, first-round hits on attacking NVA tanks were just about zero.

And if you didn't kill an adversary's tank with your first round, he'd kill you with his.

*****

During one of Vann's frequent visits to Ben Het, a new issue came to light: the ARVN troopers were agitating for their families to be relocated from their compounds at Kontum and Pleiku to take up residence at the base camp. It had been standard practice for ARVN troopers to live with their families when a major unit was in a static position. "But that's not the case here," Vann told Phong, who was acting as advocate for the troops. "Ben Het isn't some long-established base camp where the cav squadrons have been stationed for years. It's a blocking position—at the forward edge of the battle area—and an NVA attack in force could happen at any time. This is no place for dependents to be wandering around, getting in the way. And you'll have to feed them, making the already difficult logistics of this place many times worse."

Phong was unbending. "My troops have heard that Division HQ personnel at Tan Canh already have family members living with them," he said.

"That's simply false, Colonel," Vann replied. "But if it was actually true, I'd put a stop to it. It's true there are civilians on the base at Tan Canh, but they're being employed by Division for housekeeping and maintenance duties. They're not family members, so any rumors your men have heard are bullshit."

Phong adopted that glassy-eyed stare that seemed to look right through you at some truth—or some fantasy—far in the distance. He said, "We'll see what General Du has to say about it."

Vann found the empty threat amusing, thinking, *Du hasn't been able to find his ass with both hands since this operation began. The last thing in the world he's going to do is challenge me over an issue as trivial—and as problematic—as this one. Du might think he knows what side his political bread is buttered on, but he doesn't fully grasp that I'm the one holding the knife.*

*****

Despite the persistent rain, the raised ceiling that allowed Vann to arrive by LOACH also permitted supply choppers to arrive at Ben Het. As they watched Chinooks deposit their sling loads of ammunition and then touch down to offload their cabin cargo, Jif commented, "Too bad that cloud deck hasn't gone up even more. I was hoping it might get high enough for aerial recon and gunship support."

Swanson added, "Man, wouldn't that be sweet?"

But Vann's attention was fixated on a Chinook approaching the base camp's main gate, slowing as it prepared to deliver its sling-loaded crate. The crate seemed destined for a wooden pedestal that had been constructed over the last few days. "What's going on?" Vann asked. "Isn't that collection of sticks going to be another watchtower?"

"That's what they told us, sir," Swanson replied.

"So what the hell's in the box, Major?"

He was about to plead ignorance—Jif was, too—when it dawned on Swanson what was inside. "Ah, shit…it's that fucking tiger you told me about, isn't it?"

The crate, now hovering just inches over the pedestal, was being manhandled into position by ARVN troopers. Once it was lowered into place atop the structure, the men pulled the crate apart with crowbars, revealing a taxidermy mount of the tiger killed outside the wire three weeks ago. The Americans, preoccupied with more pressing needs during that time, had forgotten all about it. But Diep had somehow made good on his plan to turn the animal carcass into a statue. The finished product was being returned now to serve as Ben Het's gate guard.

Turning the dead beast into a monument didn't bother Vann at all. He liked the idea of it as a morale-building symbol. But what infuriated him was the fact that a valuable Chinook helicopter was being wasted on a vanity project. The ship, having nothing else in its cabin to unload, had flown away once the crate was released. He bellowed, "WHO THE FUCK OWNS THAT GODDAMN ANIMAL?"

Like an insolent schoolboy, Diep replied, "I do. Isn't he beautiful?"

"Yeah, he's fucking gorgeous, Colonel. But who authorized using—no, make that *wasting*—a multi-million dollar aircraft for your personal gratification? A truck would've done the job just fine."

Diep sounded insulted as he said, "It is not for me, sir. It is for the men. Besides, you have so many helicopters. Who's to say what is wasted?"

"*I'm* the one to say, Colonel. And I'll say this, too…pull another stunt like this, and I can predict a transfer to Eye Corps in your immediate future. Same goes for whoever pulled the strings for you down in Pleiku. That's a criminal misappropriation of government property. Somebody must've told my aviation people one hell of a whopping lie so *Operation Tiger Lift* could happen. It better not have been you."

*****

Two days later, Vann and his advisors were at Pleiku, meeting with General Du, the II Corps commander, his staff, and representatives from MACV HQ. The tone was urgent; enemy forces in the II Corps coastal province of Binh Dinh, 190 kilometers to the east, were raiding ARVN firebases, intent on harassing—and perhaps severing—the north-south national lifeline that was Route 1. Two colonels from MACV G2, along with Sergeant Major Sean Moon, provided an analysis of the raids.

"We think it's a diversion, without the capability to become a sustained attack," one of the colonels from intel said. "The forces involved are regular VC, not NVA, and they have no armor and no direct fire support other than their own mortars and RPGs. General Du, your local forces have been holding them off well, so far. There have been no penetrations of ARVN or US facilities in the province."

The other intel colonel took over from there, adding, "But diversion or not, sir, the VC have been persistent, inflicting casualties slowly but steadily on your outposts and firebases, as we're sure you're aware. We've come to suspect there are many more VC in the mountains to the west of Route One than previously believed."

General Du looked like his world was threatening to crumble around him. He asked, "How many more?"

"Difficult to say, sir. But no more than a battalion or two."

Du had considered the defense of the coastal region in II Corps an area of little concern. But the mention of entire enemy battalions in the area struck fear into his heart. The briefer from MACV might as well have said the VC were at division strength.

"I must have massive airstrikes to destroy the VC," Du said, his voice as jittery as his body language.

"We'd love to do that for you, sir," the colonel replied, "but we need precise locations of their base camps, and we don't have that. Your people have provided little, if any, useful intel in that regard."

Nobody needed an explanation as to why that was so; Du's units weren't doing any meaningful patrolling in Binh Dinh province. Or anyplace else in II Corps, for that matter.

It was Sergeant Major Moon's turn to speak. "If your people could get out in the boonies and give us some idea where the VC camps actually are, sir, we could give you airstrikes within hours. And if the weather's too lousy for the flyboys, we could provide naval gunfire from ships sitting offshore. General Abrams would like nothing better than to make this annoying distraction in Binh Dinh go away."

Du paced nervously at the map for a few moments, occasionally stopping to measure distances point-to-point along its surface with outstretched fingers. Then, as if having a eureka moment, he exclaimed, "I am pulling the Airborne Brigade from Kontum immediately and sending them to Binh Dinh Province."

That sounded like a really stupid idea to every American in the room, especially since the solution proposed by Sean Moon was far more practical, much less of a logistical undertaking, and wouldn't leave the heart of the Central Highlands vulnerable to an NVA walkover. The Airborne Brigade, spread thin along a twenty-kilometer stretch of high ground known as Rocket Ridge, was the only unit protecting the border northwest of Kontum.

Jif, who'd been sitting quietly against the wall with the other advisors—taking it all in, not speaking unless spoken to—was sure he wasn't the only one who heard Sean Moon's mumbled response to Du's pronouncement: "You gotta be shitting me."

But Du didn't seem to have heard it. Unaware of the retort, he kept blabbering about how many helicopters he needed to move the Airborne Brigade. And he needed them immediately, if not sooner.

The only man with the horsepower to tell Du it wasn't going to happen was John Paul Vann. He told the meeting's other attendees, "Give the general and me the room, please." They filed out without a word, each man disappointed not to be witnessing the spectacle of a three-star ARVN general getting his ass chewed by an American. They huddled near the door, hoping to at least hear snatches of what was said.

Vann, however, was going for the soft sell, another of his *come-to-Jesus* moments. But it was being delivered slightly above a whisper. The crux of what he told Du: *These are just feints, trying to get you to fuck up and take the bait. I guaran-damn-tee that if you pull the Airborne from the Kontum area, that city will fall to the NVA within days. Pleiku will fall right behind it, and your units at Tan Canh, Dak To, and Ben Het will then be isolated and destroyed. Don't be a fool in front of the whole world...just do what MACV wants and this little problem will get taken care of.*

Seeing Du still wasn't fully on board, Vann shifted to the Dutch uncle treatment. "It's a good thing President Thieu isn't here as originally planned. He would've canned your ass on the spot…and probably would've told General Abrams to can mine, too."

He added that second part to be charitable. Vann had little concern about being fired by Abrams or anyone else. He was a civilian doing a two-star general's job, and doing it extraordinarily well; his standing in the American command structure was too high to be trashed so frivolously. And certainly not because of his ARVN protégé's ineptitude.

"All right," the general said, "I'll do it your way. But mark my words, if Binh Dinh Province falls, I will hold you personally responsible. I'm now on record as having tried to prevent it."

Vann acknowledged with just a sardonic smile. If Binh Dinh fell, Du's threat would be the least of his problems.

*****

While Vann and Du were having their one-on-one, Sean Moon and Major Swanson shared their misgivings of the ARVN's disposition north of Kontum. As tankers, they both appreciated the speed at which units in fixed positions could be overrun by a mechanized attack. Swanson offered, "That west-to-east line of strongholds we've constructed along Route Five-Twelve—Ben Het, Dak To, Tan Canh—it's too invested in the idea that the main NVA thrust will only come out of the west, from Laos, Cambodia, or both. And it would be a good defensive disposition if the enemy did only come out of the west. But we're seeing plenty of activity north and south of those base camps. If they get hit from those directions, any or all of those positions can get picked off and destroyed piecemeal. I'm really worried they'll overrun Dak To in the center, then deal with Tan Canh and Ben Het on the flanks at their leisure."

Sean replied, "Damn straight, sir. If Dak To gets knocked out, Ben Het's got nowhere to go…except walk straight into hell. At least Tan Canh can withdraw down Route Fourteen—"

Swanson interjected, "That's assuming no NVA are between Tan Canh and Kontum, Sergeant Major. But there's evidence that they are, in fact, there. They've ambushed several convoys on Route Fourteen already."

"I hear you, sir," Sean replied, "and I'm sure you're aware that the original plan called for the concentration of ARVN forces to be in the corridor between Dak To and Tan Canh. But President Thieu convinced General Du he needed to occupy Ben Het, as well. Don't know why. Sure, that place is closer to the border, but it's never been good luck for us or the ARVN."

"Yeah, I know all about it. That's why there's nothing but armored cav at Ben Het. They can execute a fighting retreat toward Kontum when things turn to shit…" Swanson paused as a realization hit him: "Or they're considered expendable and die in place."

Sean didn't have a solution, just a rationalization. "It would be a great plan if the weather allowed for normal air capabilities. Sure, we think the B-52s are taking a big toll on the NVA, but until we can fly photo recon, we don't know for sure."

"And by then, it may be too late, Sergeant Major."

"Amen to that, sir."

*****

The meeting over, Jif finally got to talk with Sean Moon, who asked, "How you holding up, sir?"

"Living the dream, Sergeant Major. I just hope it doesn't turn into too big of a nightmare. I was a little surprised General Abe wasn't here, though. The rumor was he'd be in attendance."

"He would've been if Thieu hadn't backed out at the last minute. But…"

Sean paused, as if deciding against speaking the rest of what was on his mind.

Jif had to ask: "But *what*, Sergeant Major?"

"Just between you and me, right?"

"Of course."

"Spoken to your dad lately?"

"Afraid not. Haven't spoken to my wife in weeks, either. The Highlands were never conducive to telecommunications with the world, and it's worse now. But why? What do you and Dad know?"

Sean exhaled heavily, a sigh that underscored the awkwardness—and perhaps the impropriety—of what he was about to reveal. "General Abe's not a well man, sir. This damn war's killing him, wrecking his body slowly but surely. The docs are checking him constantly. I don't expect he'll be in the Nam much longer."

"When he leaves, will you go, too?"

"Are you talking about Vietnam or this man's army?"

"Both, I reckon."

"Well then, the answer is yeah, I'll leave the Nam. Whoever replaces General Abe will want his own people on staff, anyway. As far as the Army, I've only got thirty years in. I'm good for ten more. What about you? Staying in?"

"Like I said, Sergeant Major, I'm living the dream. Hell yeah, I'm staying in."

He paused, lowered his voice, and added, "But Nam? I'll go wherever I'm ordered, but I think three tours are plenty."

Chapter Twenty-Five

The relative quiet at Ben Het, Dak To, and Tan Canh lasted just one more week. Early on a foggy morning of the second week in April, a USAF O-2 FAC was searching futilely for an RVNAF Huey reported down just north of Tan Canh when he got the scare of his life. Flying a search pattern he knew to be risky at treetop height, he raced his ship up the valley in which Route 14 was nestled. Suddenly, he was zipping over a long line of armored vehicles headed south toward the base camp. He could only guess at the number he actually could see, and there were probably more he couldn't see through the murk.

Shit! No way they're ARVN. And they're only six klicks from Tan Canh.

Maybe that Huey didn't get lost in the fog and crash after all. She might've been shot down by this bunch.

That wasn't the case, though. The NVA forces he'd just discovered had never seen the Huey, let alone shot her down. But they were startled to have the twin-boomed FAC ship appear out of nowhere, racing through the mist just feet above their heads. It took them precious seconds to bring machine guns to bear against the O-2. But in those seconds, the ship made good her escape, vanishing into the low overcast. There'd been that minute of stressful blind flying until she broke through the cloud deck and into the comfort of sunny skies. Now sure he could avoid the surrounding peaks—the *hardcore cumulus*—he radioed his report of the armored column to Tan Canh.

Colonel Hardesty, the senior advisor at the base camp, took the call. But to his shock, he hit a stone wall trying to convince the ARVN HQ staff that the sighting of an armored force moving toward them was genuine. "What could a pilot possibly see?" the assistant division commander scoffed. "The fog is too thick. His panic is making him—and you, Colonel—exaggerate."

Hardesty replied, "He can see more than we can, sitting here blind with our thumbs up our asses, General. We need to meet the attacking armor tank-on-tank, while we've still got room to maneuver and can surprise them on their flank."

Within two minutes, accurate artillery fire—surely being observed by an FO in very close proximity—was falling on Tan Canh, causing significant damage and multiple casualties. Only then did the ARVN command start believing they were being attacked.

Their first reaction was to run.

"Hang on! It's not too late to stop these NVA," Hardesty pleaded as he drew the enemy route of advance on the CP's big wall map. "You need to commence Plan Delta immediately."

That would involve a company of ARVN tanks leaving the base camp, driving north on the airfield road, and hitting the enemy traffic on Route 14 from the west in a classic flanking maneuver. Tank-killer teams—infantrymen armed with M72 LAW rockets—would race to establish ambush positions along Route 14 near the town of Kon Hojao, a kilometer east of the base camp. The artillery batteries at Tan Canh would defend the base camp perimeter with direct fire using HE and white phosphorous. If enemy infantry got into the wire, they'd shred those attackers with beehive.

But all these weapons required soldiers to man them, and those soldiers were watching their officers panic, jump into jeeps, and flee the base camp. The first to make his escape was the assistant division commander. When Hardesty wanted to know where the hell he was going, the ADC replied, "I'm meeting the division commander at the alternate CP."

"And where in the fuck is that?" Hardesty asked. There'd never been any discussion of an alternate CP in the base camp's standing orders.

There was no response from the ADC. He was already running to his waiting jeep.

All across Tan Canh, men begged their officers for orders, but received no reply. The only thing their leaders could offer were ashen faces drawn tight with fear. Their sole intent was self-preservation, duty and mission be damned. The deluge of uncannily accurate artillery rounds systematically dismantling the base camp was being taken as an omen. They'd received large volumes of incoming in the past, sometimes hundreds of rounds a day scattered inside and outside the perimeter, but it had never before been so on-target and deadly. The NVA FO had to be very close to the perimeter to actually see what he was shooting at in the poor visibility.

Colonel Hardesty wondered, *Maybe he's already inside the perimeter*?

One howitzer, with an HE round loaded, was preparing to hurl it at the first attacking armored vehicle that could be seen emerging from the mist. But as the gunners stood poised to shoot, an enemy artillery round landed squarely on the gun, detonating the round in the chamber as well as itself. The double explosion that resulted vaporized the gun crew while killing or wounding every man along a sixty-meter stretch of the perimeter.

The ARVN officers who hadn't already made up their minds to run needed no more convincing: this game was already over. Their men, bereft of leadership, were now panicking, too, abandoning their positions and fleeing Tan Canh any way they could, be it in vehicles or even on foot.

When Colonel Hardesty tried to physically prevent a captain he'd come to respect from deserting his company, he was buttstroked in the face for his trouble. Spitting blood and teeth, he stumbled back into the CP, radioed Vann, and told him that Tan Canh was as good as lost. When asked in what strength the NVA attack was, he could only reply, "*Boo coo*, but I can't give you a number. They're not even here yet."

That made little sense to Vann. When he asked to speak with the senior ARVN officer present, Hardesty replied, "You can't. They're all gone."

"Gather your advisors," Vann told him. "I'm coming to get you out of there."

*****

Dak To never got a warning the NVA were on their doorstep. After a brief but brutal artillery barrage, a line of T-54 tanks suddenly materialized out of fog. They rumbled across the airfield's runway, their exact numbers hidden in the murk as their guns destroyed the grounded helicopters and liaison aircraft on the ramp. Despite the poor visibility, they'd be close enough in a few minutes to see the buildings of the base camp and engage them, too.

The defenders of Dak To tried to stand their ground, destroying four of the initial wave of eight tanks with fire from their M41s and artillery pieces. But then there was another wave, and another after that. Eight of the seventeen ARVN tanks were soon knocked out by the superior numbers and better firepower of the T-54s. Roughly half of the officers at Dak To, like their craven brothers at Tan Canh, sensed that to stay was to die and began abandoning their troops. But the rest remained and, with the help of their American advisors, directed a defense that managed to slow the NVA onslaught for the time being. But they wouldn't last long on their own. The battle within the base camp took on a swirling aspect as roughly a dozen enemy tanks, suddenly among ARVN sappers and unable in the blind to offer each other deck-clearing bursts of machine gun fire, became fiery wrecks from the incendiaries stuffed into their vents.

But there were many NVA tanks within the wire. Still more approached, accompanied by infantry now dismounted from trucks and preparing to swarm the base camp. They couldn't be seen through the mist, but their shouts could be heard. Sounding as if they numbered in the thousands, they seemed a far superior force than the regiment defending the base camp.

Considering that tactical radios tended to make almost anyone sound shrill, especially those in big trouble, the voice of the senior American advisor at Dak

To seemed surprisingly cool as he told Vann, "We need the cav squadrons from Ben Het to cut off the NVA column before the rest of it can reach us. The cav can kick 'em in the ass, but they've gotta move *now.*"

*****

With the collapse of Tan Canh and Dak To under attack, the ability to relay radio communications between the far-flung elements of General Du's command broke down. After calling several times from his LOACH, Vann finally made contact with Du. He was fairly sure the general had gone for a meeting with the Airborne Brigade commander on Rocket Ridge; that would put Du at least ten kilometers south of Ben Het. Vann wouldn't bother requesting his exact location, though. The general wouldn't give it, anyway, citing security issues.

Vann had been through this lazy charade before; *He could tell me where he was, but the damn fool can't be bothered to encode anything. And like so many of his commanders, it seems he's trying to get as far from the action as he can.*

All he knew for sure was there were no orders being issued from Du's HQ that would influence the catastrophic situation at his northern base camps. And Du, even traveling by chopper, was too far away to immediately influence that situation with his presence, so Vann, much closer to the action, took it upon himself; he radioed Swanson at Ben Het, ordering the two armored cav squadrons to relieve Dak To immediately.

Then he told his pilot to fly to Tan Canh, adding, "I've got to get my people out of there. All we've got to do is figure out exactly how to pull that off in the middle of that shitstorm."

*****

At Ben Het, they'd been listening to the radio as the chaos at Tan Canh and Dak To was being broadcast in real time. Colonels Phong and Diep were delighted it wasn't their base camp under assault. But when Major Swanson told them they were about to execute a counterattack at Dak To, that joy instantly became hostility. "We have no orders from our commander to do any such thing," Phong said.

Not knowing who originated the order—Du or Vann—Swanson told what he considered a necessary lie: "Of course the order comes from General Du. He apologizes for not being able to deliver it in person."

Diep was surprisingly accepting. "My squadron can be rolling in twenty minutes," he said. "My only question is, are we coming back here once this action is over?"

Swanson replied, "This whole ballgame just got turned on its head. You know as well as I do we won't be coming back to pick up where we left off. Don't bother breaking camp. Just grab the mission-critical equipment, get in the vehicles, and go."

Jif added, "Hook the howitzers to APCs. We can't leave them here and have them used against us."

"Absolutely right, Captain," Swanson replied.

Diep whined, "But that will take longer. Much longer."

Swanson: "So why are we still wasting time talking about it, sir? Let's get moving."

Phong, still acting as if executing the plan might be optional, asked, "But what of the recoilless rifles? We must leave men behind to guard them."

"If you do that, you'll be leaving men behind to die, Colonel," Jif said. "We've got no quick way to move those bloody four-hundred-pound beasts and their ammo. Forget the ricky-rifles. Thermite their breeches. Burn their ammo. Burn the fuel bladders, too. There's no way to move them, either."

"Miles is right," Swanson added, "but we've got to get cracking. The longer we dick around here, the worse it's going to be getting to Dak To. *Di di mau*, dammit!"

But the arguing and procrastination weren't over. The next debate was over what route—or routes—the counterassault forces would travel. Phong and Diep wanted both squadrons—with their total of some forty vehicles—to travel the nearly fifteen kilometers to Dak To in a single-file column on Route 512. They argued—correctly—that that was the fastest way to get there.

"It's also the fastest way to ensure you can't mass any firepower at all on the enemy once you meet him," Swanson replied. "It will be a one-gun-at-a-time assault as the leader gets picked off, then the next in line gets it, and so on."

"But there is no other way," Phong declared defiantly.

"Sure there is, Colonel," Swanson replied. "By all means, travel Five-Twelve to make best speed, but when the lead squadron reaches Dak Mot Lop—five klicks from Dak To—it cuts north through the open grassland and then turns east to get behind the NVA moving into Dak To. That terrain will let you attack on line, with full firepower to your front. Plus, if this fog holds up, your approach will be unseen and completely disorient the NVA. It'll be like you're coming out of a smoke screen. The other squadron then takes advantage of their confusion and rolls straight into Dak To off Five-Twelve. You'll turn a doomed-to-fail frontal assault into a two-pronged attack that actually has a good chance to succeed."

*****

It was taking much too long to get rolling.

"This is like pushing a string," Jif said. He'd nearly shouted himself hoarse exhorting the ARVN troopers to move faster.

Swanson's reply: "No shit, Sherlock. These troop leaders have done a fucking awful job conveying a sense of urgency to the men. They're acting like this is some admin repositioning, not a counterattack."

They'd been in touch with Vann, asking if it was already too late for the counterattack from Ben Het.

"Negative, negative," was the harried reply. "Keep it coming. Dak To's not lost yet."

"I don't like the sound of that *yet*," Jif told Swanson.

"Keep the faith, Miles. I think this ballgame is only in the third inning."

Forty-five minutes after the call to relieve Dak To had been received, the first vehicle—an M41 from Diep's squadron—finally rolled through the gate at Ben Het. But once outside the wire, it stopped to wait for the second vehicle—an APC—that pulled up to the pedestal supporting the tiger, blocking anything else from going through the gate. The vehicle's crew began to busy itself unfastening the monument, intent on loading it onto the roof of their APC.

Swanson bellowed at the men as he mounted the pedestal himself, intent on telling them to forget the tiger and get their roadblock of a vehicle moving. Diep raced over, telling Swanson to back off. "The men are doing my bidding," he said. "It is not a concern of you Americans."

"YOU DON'T HAVE FUCKING TIME FOR THIS BULLSHIT, COLONEL," Swanson shouted back. "YOUR BROTHERS ARE DYING." But short of a physical confrontation—one the vastly outnumbered American would surely lose—there was nothing he could do to stop the men from loading the tiger.

Jif would be among the last to leave Ben Het, staying behind to check the condition of the base camp once it was abandoned. He'd ended up destroying the four recoilless rifles himself, placing a thermite grenade in each of their breeches. They burned like welders' torches, popping and sizzling while slowly melting down into useless, misshapen metal tubes. The ammo for those weapons, however, was still sitting there, fully serviceable, waiting for the NVA to claim it and use it against them…

Because they have plenty of our captured weapons. How many times have I run into that already?

None of the handful of ARVN with him were willing to exert the physical effort involved in stacking the ammo at the fuel bladders so they could be incinerated together. No matter in what language he tried to compel them, they pretended not to hear. Burning the ammo and fuel would've been the very last thing anyone did, allowing time to get far enough away from the detonations that would lay waste to what was left of the abandoned base camp. But that was a moot point now; the ammo wasn't going to get incinerated.

This place is going to have to be bombed by our own aircraft ASAP, Jif told himself. *That's the only way to get rid of that ammo now.*

But he could still take care of the fuel. From his jeep, he tossed two thermite grenades, one for each diesel bladder, telling himself, *They've got to burn holes in these bags so the diesel will leak out and ignite. Once those leaks start flowing and burning, the gasoline bladders should light off all by themselves.*

As he drove through the gate, Jif radioed Vann, reporting the fuel burn-off that was already sending up thick black smoke that muddied the fog engulfing Ben Het. He also confirmed the need for a friendly airstrike to destroy the ammo that was left behind. But he wouldn't hold his breath that it would happen anytime soon, if at all.

*****

Colonel Diep's squadron was the lead element, and they were making excellent time on Route 512. Swanson estimated they'd cover the almost fifteen kilometers to Dak Mot Lop in just under thirty minutes. He'd only accompanied the column for the first five klicks; at that point, he'd been ordered by Vann to hold his position and await pickup by helicopter. "You'll be more use to everyone if you've got airborne mobility, even in this damn fog," Vann said. "Are you in contact with Miles? I can't raise him anymore."

"Negative, sir. No contact with him, but I'll keep trying."

"Do that. When you figure out where he is, I'll pick him up, too."

Swanson's jeep pulled off the road to wait, as ordered. Within minutes, Diep's long column had passed in its entirety, and Phong's hadn't begun to arrive yet. The American and his jittery ARVN security team—a driver and a gunner—were alone in the middle of nowhere. In the absence of vehicle noise, they could hear the distant fight at Dak To. The explosions of tank and artillery shells sounded like an orchestra's timpani and bass drum sections gone mad. Swanson was nervous, too, but he was trying not to let it show.

They were only alone for a few minutes. Vann's LOACH approached out of the haze at very low altitude. Swanson released his ARVN team and was on board the chopper before its skids had touched the ground. He told his boss, "Didn't think you'd find me so fast, sir. Still haven't made contact with Miles."

"That young man better turn up," Vann replied. It wasn't a threat but an expression of dread.

*****

What none of the Americans knew: Diep's column had missed the turnoff at Dak Mot Lop. Instead of moving into a flanking position against the NVA attackers, their vehicles were barreling directly into the raging battle in a long, thin line, blundering forward in the worst possible tactical disposition. They were no longer one prong of a two-pronged assault; now, they'd just be fodder for the NVA armor.

Jif finally left Ben Het, following Phong's squadron onto Route 512. He'd wanted the multi-lingual Tham for a driver, but Colonel Phong claimed the sergeant, citing a higher need for him in the squadron's headquarters element. The young driver/RTO assigned to Jif spoke no English or French. Neither did the two men who Jif had found wandering Ben Het, looking for their section's vehicle. But it had left them behind and was long gone. Everything he said to the three ARVN was met with only vague smiles, as if they were just pretending to understand.

Phong's column rolled through Dak Mot Lop, as they were supposed to do. But they were oblivious to Diep's error. There'd been no report of it from any source, not from the lead column itself or anyone in the air, who could only see snippets through the fog of what was happening on the ground.

Jif suspected something had gone terribly wrong as his jeep—at the tail end of Phong's squadron—entered Dak Mot Lop, whose wary inhabitants, expecting an imminent battle, had already gone to ground. The turnoff Diep's column should've taken, a trail that led to the broad plain of high grass where they could spread their formation to mass fire on the NVA, showed no signs of being trafficked by heavy tracked vehicles.

This field should be all torn up. Did they turn off sooner…or maybe later?

Or did they not turn off at all?

They could be a few hundred yards away, but in this fog, I wouldn't see them.

I'd hear them, though...and I don't hear a bloody thing except Phong's column way over yonder, pressing on down the road.

He called Swanson and got no answer. He didn't know the major was now many kilometers away on board Vann's chopper.

Then he called Vann. Again, no reply.

In desperation, he called Diep on the ARVN command frequency. There was no reply then, either, but for a different reason: the colonel was already dead. The tank in which he rode had been blown apart by a T-54.

But something on the command freq was spilling from the jeep's speaker: the high-pitched, screeching voices of men in mortal terror, pleading for salvation in Vietnamese. Jif understood not a word, but he could tell from the faces of the three ARVN with him that something had gone seriously wrong. Exactly what that calamity entailed, though, they were unable to communicate to their American dai uy.

I've got to figure out where Diep's squadron is. They could be lost, and maybe it's not too late to get them turned around.

Through elaborate hand signals and fractured Vietnamese, Jif convinced his driver to follow the turnoff trail into the grassy plain. He expected the two men in the back to jump off the jeep and run away…

I half expect the driver to do the same.

If they do, so be it. At least I'll still have the vehicle and the radio.

But the men stayed on board. Jif checked the odometer, jotting down its reading on his mapboard. *I bet I'll need that reading to figure out where the bloody hell we are. With a compass heading and a distance, I can dead reckon our coordinates.*

Swanson's voice was on the radio, calling him. He was obviously in a chopper; the whining background noise made that a certainty. But Jif's reply wasn't heard; Swanson called twice more and then his voice fell silent.

Is that chopper Swanson's on too far away to hear me? He sure sounded strong enough, like he could be real close…

Or did this transmitter just die on me?

As Jif fiddled with the radio, one of the ARVN suddenly stood up and began pointing frantically into the distance over the hood of the jeep, which had come to a dead stop.

Emerging from the mist were the blurry silhouettes of tanks just a few hundred meters away…and they weren't M41s. They were too large, the turrets too differently shaped, and the throaty growl of their diesel engines too different from the whirr of the gasoline-powered ARVN tanks…

And they were headed directly toward the jeep.

Chapter Twenty-Six

Throwing the gearshift into reverse, the jeep driver began a dizzy backward slalom, zigzagging through the tall grass. Whether this was his idea of evasive maneuvering or his inability to control the vehicle along the bumpy ground, Jif couldn't tell. But *Private Hoang's Wild Ride* didn't last long. The front wheels became stuck in a deep rut, and the transfer case selector wasn't in four-wheel drive. Hoang was frantically trying to rock the jeep out of its trap, but the rear wheels had lost traction, and his rapid shifting blocked Jif's attempts from the passenger's seat to engage the lever that would power the front wheels, as well.

As they seesawed wildly but got nowhere, a stream of tracers from a tank's machine gun streaked close over the jeep. In the few seconds it took the NVA gunner to find the range and start tearing the vehicle apart, there was no one in it. Jif and his three ARVN troopers were running through the tall grass toward Route 512 and, hopefully, some cover with Colonel Phong's column.

But there'd be no cover. The NVA had succeeded where the ARVN had failed, trapping both cav squadrons within a two-pronged assault, one prong from the east out of Dak To, the other from the north, where Diep's unit should've been. No escape or rescue was possible; it was a near-perfect ambush on a colossal scale. First, it stalled the column by turning the lead and trail elements into fiery roadblocks. Then, it tore apart the middle. The depth of the disaster was still shrouded in fog, but it would soon lift. When it did, Route 512 would be revealed as a highway of death, with a line of burning and abandoned vehicles nearly two kilometers long.

The survivors of the debacle were fleeing south toward Kontum on foot, fording the river Dak Poko in the rare places where it was possible, ditching their gear and trying to swim across where it wasn't. Some drowned when they failed that method. The NVA commanders, sensing a rout of epic proportions, attempted to reorganize their armored forces on the fly to pursue any fleeing ARVN, but the river slowed their heavy vehicles, most bogging down at the banks. The chase would be strictly an infantry affair.

*****

By noon, the fog had lifted, the sky returning to a low, solid overcast with intermittent rain that suited the gloomy aftermath of the ARVN's comprehensive defeat. Once again, the weather stymied most air operations. Vann had succeeded in extracting by helicopter all his advisors save one: Jif Miles. His fate was still a mystery.

At Kontum, General Du was pleading with Vann, demanding B-52 strikes all along Route 14, as well as on Rocket Ridge to the roadway's west. But the Airborne Brigade was still on Rocket Ridge and, so far, was successfully fending off an assault from the west out of Cambodia. Vann denied most of the request out of hand, telling Du, "Unless you're interested in exterminating what's left of your Twenty-Second Division, General, I suggest we get a clearer picture of those troops' dispositions before we bomb anywhere south of Route Five-Twelve. And let's give the Airborne an opportunity to conduct a fighting withdrawal from Rocket Ridge back to Kontum. At the moment, we can still talk to them, and they appear to be our only hope at slowing down the NVA before they waltz right into this headquarters. Now, what are you doing to rally those survivors of Tan Canh, Dak To, and that fiasco on Five-Twelve? My advisor with the cavalry squadrons, Major Swanson, has already told me what was *supposed* to have happened with that counterattack. Obviously, something went terribly wrong, and we're not quite sure what or why. But it sure looks like your Colonel Diep fucked up, big time. I can't wait to hear what he has to say about it."

Diep, of course, would never be able to explain himself. He'd been killed, but nobody at Kontum knew that yet. In fact, they knew little about the fate of any unit commander; radio communications with those from Tan Canh, Dak To, and Ben Het had broken down almost totally. There were survivors, Vann was sure, but they'd be scattered over no less than forty square kilometers. That area would grow larger as time marched on and troopers lacking a unifying command scattered.

After much dithering at the map, Du proclaimed, "I will use the Airborne to gather the survivors and bring them to Kontum."

"Not so fast," Vann replied. "Keep the Airborne where they are a little longer, at least until nightfall. They're in contact with the NVA, and they can't hold off the enemy and police up stragglers at the same time." He paused, a disgusted look on his face, before adding, "You know, General, if your officers were worth a shit, we wouldn't be in this fucking boat right now."

But what bothered Vann most: *Those in the ARVN officer corps have no fear of repercussions for their cowardice. Their world runs strictly off political favor. Being a competent combat leader has nothing to do with it. If they've kissed the right ass, all that gold braid and bullshit medals will never get ripped off their shiny uniforms no matter how badly they've shirked their duty.*

One thing I'm sure of, though...if it's the last thing I do, I'm getting Du relieved. He's useless...doesn't know his ass from a hole in the ground.

*****

Jif had only the vaguest idea of where he and his small team were. He had to laugh at himself: *My genius plan to dead reckon our position got blown up with the jeep. I've got nothing but a compass, this map, and a wild-ass guess at where we crossed the river. We were in such a hurry running for our lives, we didn't bother to survey our location.*

We don't even have a radio. That got blown up with the jeep, too.

Before the fog lifted, they'd been dodging phantoms in the woods, reacting to sounds and voices from people they couldn't see and who couldn't see them. It wasn't much better once the fog dissipated; the overcast still throttled the sunlight, turning the normally shady woods at midday dark as dusk. They could still hear vehicles and the occasional voices speaking Vietnamese, but now they could see hints of silhouettes among the shadows, too. Whether they were NVA or ARVN, however, was anybody's guess. Jif's silent complaint: *It'd be nice if my traveling partners could relate to me in words, hand gestures, or even facial expressions whether we're in the midst of friends or foes. Even though the North Vietnamese often speak in dialects different from the ones spoken in the South, my guys can't seem to tell who's doing the talking.*

I can't fault their loyalty, though. They've been sticking to me like glue ever since we bailed out of the jeep. It's a good thing they know and follow basic infantry hand signals, at least...and their noise discipline is outstanding. Their footsteps are light as feathers, they speak only in whispers, and they keep their other bodily noises in check. GIs would've coughed, farted, or cleared their throats a dozen times by now.

But those lurking nearby in the gloom weren't paying much attention to noise discipline. Jif realized his team was between two other groups, one less than fifty meters to the north, the other the same approximate distance to the south. All three outfits were moving to the southeast, their paths roughly parallel.

Jif brought his men to a stop with a closed-fist signal. They didn't need to be told to get down; they did that by instinct. The other two groups kept on walking.

We have to get out of that sandwich. The last thing we need is to get caught in some bloody crossfire. Even if they're two ARVN units on either side of us—or even two NVA units—they could still start shooting each other at the drop of a hat. As fucked up as this day has been, everybody's jumpy. Shit will happen.

But there's got to be some way to figure out who's who.

That thought had barely finished crossing his mind when the southern unit opened fire on the one to the north. The sound of the weapons—a distinctive *clack* of Soviet machinery at work—identified them as AK-47s and the shooters as NVA.

Their targets didn't return fire. *They must've gone to ground*, Jif surmised. *I can't see them anymore. But at least I now know who the people to my right are.*

Those guys to the north were getting pretty noisy. No wonder they gave themselves away.

In a few moments, the men to the north identified themselves as ARVN; the unmistakable *ploop* of an M79 grenade launcher—an American weapon—could be heard as it hurled a round from their midst toward the NVA. It was an amazingly accurate shot, considering the grenadier must've been prone on the ground. The thud of its explosion was immediately followed by screams of the wounded.

But the volume of fire being exchanged increased. The ARVN were now adding their M16s to the mix as the chatter of AK-47s continued nonstop. Another grenade from an M79 was launched at the NVA. It had no apparent effect.

Something Jif knew from hard experience: *This is going to be over really quick. Someone's going to break contact and run. I think we can hit those NVA in their left flank before that happens, though. They're too busy to see us coming.*

But we've got to do it quickly and quietly…and I don't want to do it all by myself.

His three men seemed to grasp his instructions, conducted entirely in hand signals; they'd move right and then turn left on his command, spread into an assault line, and sneak up on the enemy. When he pumped his fist up and down, hoping to convey the need to move quickly, they nodded in agreement. A finger to his lips, meaning *but keep it quiet*, was also understood; all three of his men replied by putting a finger to their lips, too.

One point Jif knew he didn't need to convey: *Don't get too close, or we'll walk into the ARVN field of fire. Let's just hope our ARVN buddies understand we're on their side.*

It happened all too easily. When Jif and his men got as close as they dared, the six NVA soldiers still firing were clearly visible, less than twenty meters away. Two who'd fallen victim to the grenade were lying on the ground, not moving but still wailing. They weren't a threat.

The active shooters never knew what hit them; several bursts of full auto dispatched them all.

Now for the next challenge…how to bring this to a stop without getting killed by friendly fire.

Hand signals wouldn't work now. Jif began to shout *CEASE FIRE* in English, French, and what he thought might be the imperative form of the command in Vietnamese. He stayed low behind a tree, his M16 waving like a flag in an outstretched arm. But he wasn't about to expose the rest of his body.

His first torrent of commands stopped the shooting. There was no verbal reply, but at least no one was firing at him.

If I step out from behind this tree, though…

He was halfway through his multilingual demand for the second time when a voice called out in English: "Is that you, Dai Uy Miles?"

I guess my Aussie accent gave me away again. Now's the bloody time to show myself.

"Yeah, it's me. Are you from Second Squadron?"

"That's correct, Dai Uy. I'm Sergeant Bui. There are four men with me. We'll come to you."

*****

"I'm a cavalry squad leader," Sergeant Bui explained after placing the ARVN troopers into a tight defensive perimeter around the defeated NVA position. "Our APC, like most of the others, I'm afraid, was destroyed by enemy fire. Five of my men are dead or missing. One of the four with me has just been wounded." He pointed to a man with bloodstained shirt and suspenders who was crouching in position on the perimeter. "Something hit his ear. I must get a field dressing on it immediately. We have the first aid kit from our vehicle with us."

"You wouldn't happen to have a radio, too, would you?"

Bui shook his head.

There wasn't much left of the man's ear. What remained was peppered with small wooden shards. "I don't think a bullet did that directly," Jif said as he examined the wound. "Looks like one splintered a tree, and some of that shrapnel got him. He's lucky…could've been a lot worse." Even without immediate medical attention, the man would make it. The biggest concern now was preventing infection.

A guy with a chewed-up ear should be the worst thing that happens to us, Jif told himself.

"Yes, we were very lucky," Bui replied as he surveyed his defeated opponents. He walked over to the two wounded NVA, their bodies torn by grenade fragments. Their eyes, pleading and wide with terror, were fixed on him. Without a moment's hesitation, the sergeant put a bullet in each of their heads.

"We're not doing medevac or taking prisoners today," he said without emotion while walking away.

The abruptness of the execution startled Jif, but he understood Bui's motivation. He didn't exactly share it, though; *I can't take the moral high ground here…if it had been up to me, I would've just destroyed their weapons and left them to their fate. They weren't a threat to our lives anymore. But this is the ARVN's fight now, and I'm just the advisor, supposedly.*

Among the dead NVA were two green field boxes that looked just like suitcases. There was stenciling on them in both Russian and Vietnamese.

Bui said, "The writing says they're anti-tank missiles."

"Let's have a look," Jif replied.

"You don't think they might be booby-trapped, Dai Uy?"

"Doubt it. Anybody afraid of opening them?"

To a man, the others moved well away, tripling the diameter of the perimeter, making it useless as a continuous defensive screen.

"I reckon it's just me, then," Jif said, popping the latches on one of the cases.

The missile itself was small and partially disassembled. There was a controller—a joystick—which an operator would use to steer it to the target. A thin, multi-conductor wire spooled within the missile would provide the connection between it and the controller while in flight.

"Pretty amazing, huh?" Jif said, "and I think I know what it is. We've been hearing stories of a new anti-tank weapon being used by the NVA. We've named it *Sagger*, and I reckon we're looking at one. Pull your men back in, Sergeant. They're too far apart to do much good."

As Bui complied, Jif continued, "Saggers are supposedly a short-range version of our own TOW anti-tank missile, which we've finally got in country. The Army's been promising them for over a year as a new armament for helicopter gunships. They're said to be worlds better than those little rockets they've been carrying up until now. Once this weather clears, we might finally get to see some TOWs in action."

Looking closely at the Sagger, Bui asked, "How do you launch it? Do you hold it in your hand?"

"Only if you want to get your hand burned off. I think the lid of this suitcase is the launcher. See these rails? Looks like you pull them up, set the rocket on it, and away she goes."

"What should we do with them, Dai Uy?"

"Take them with us. Maybe we can trade them for something we actually know how to use, like a radio. But let's get away from here. We've made too much noise to hang around."

*****

Get away from here...but go where?

Sergeant Bui favored walking due west, keeping close to Route 512: "There's a better chance we'll encounter the rest of our unit and be able to rejoin them."

"I don't think so," Jif replied. "Now that the whole world knows there's a large concentration of NVA along that road, there's an even better chance we'll get vaporized in a B-52 strike if we stay too close. We need to head southeast, toward Dien Binh on Route Fourteen. That might keep us away from the buffs and get us closer to Kontum."

"But we'd have to cross the river again, Dai Uy. If we can't get across, we might never make it to Route Fourteen."

"Relax, Sergeant. According to the map, there are a number of places the river can be forded. The NVA have been doing it on a regular basis lately to hit convoys on that road. I got hit there myself a while back."

He was going to add, *You can do what you want, Sergeant. I'm just an advisor, not your commander.* But as he watched Bui deliberating, he said nothing. There was a brief discussion between the sergeant and the men. Jif couldn't understand more than the occasional word, but one bit of body language spoke volumes: when Bui either asked or ordered Jif's men to join his squad, the three shook their heads as one in refusal.

Well, if Bui takes his men and goes where he wants, at least I'll still have some company when I go another way.

After a pensive moment, Bui announced, "We will go with you, Dai Uy."

"Does that mean you're acknowledging I'm in command, Sergeant?"

"Yes, sir. I take orders from you."

"Sounds like a plan," Jif replied.

*****

At Kontum, there was much concern over just how quickly the NVA could sweep down on them from the north. There weren't enough ARVN units in the city to hold off the very real—and very imminent—possibility of simultaneous attacks from the north and west. Du was dithering, trying to weave a plan out of whole cloth that involved airlifting the survivors of the Route 512 disasters to Kontum in order to bolster the city's defenses.

Vann dismissed that idea out of hand. "How in the hell are we going to marshal troops we don't know exist to LZs my pilots may not be able to find in the shitty visibility? It sounds like what you're asking me to do is lose a lot of aircraft for absolutely nothing, General."

As Du sputtered, insisting there was no other way, Vann interrupted, saying, "Yeah, there's another way. Of the five firebases manned by the Airborne Brigade on Rocket Ridge, three of them are on peaks that are above the clouds, and they will be until sundown and beyond. We're going to use the available choppers to extract the men and howitzers of those three firebases and bring them to Kontum. Once night falls, the other two firebases will be abandoned and their guns spiked.

Those men will then move cross-country to Kontum. The Airborne will provide the buffer we need here to hold off the NVA until your Twenty-Third Division is trucked from Ban Me Thuot. Within thirty-six hours, we'll have every available unit defending Kontum."

Du said nothing, just stared blankly at Vann and then at the map. Seeing that the general was unable to compose the necessary orders to get those forces moving, Vann did it himself. Once they were typed up, he didn't bother to have Du sign them. He did that himself, too.

*****

The straight-line distance to Dien Binh was just over twelve kilometers from Jif's assumed starting point, but that didn't account for the added distance of going up and down thickly forested hills. It also didn't account for detours around several Montagnard villages. The villagers would probably be sympathetic to an American, but there were no guarantees. Even though they tended to despise all Vietnamese whether from the north or south, Jif remembered encountering VMC—Viet Montagnard Cong—during his first tour. Even if they weren't sympathetic to the NVA, they might have no choice but to comply with the enemy's wishes, with their villages held hostage and used as shields by NVA infiltrators. Another problem: the presence of his ARVN troopers—who generally considered the Montagnard to be subhuman—would create animosities that made cooperation with an American near-impossible.

There's a chance we might accidentally bump into some villagers, Jif surmised. *I wish to hell I hadn't left behind the bracelet the Yards gave me on my first tour, like Vann told me to. That gift is a symbol of friendship and respect. It might've bought us a whole lot of goodwill…and maybe some help getting the hell out of here in one piece.*

At first, Jif wasn't sure if he'd heard or felt that rumble in the distance; *All we've been hearing lately is the artillery on Rocket Ridge. This sounds a lot different.*

As the rumble grew in intensity, it evolved into the mutter of heavy-lift helicopters, their blades pulsating the mountain air to the west.

"Choppers?" Bui asked. "How are they even flying now?"

"Good question. I reckon it's got something to do with Rocket Ridge. Maybe they got a weather break and are getting a resupply, or maybe…"

He didn't need to finish the sentence. They both knew what the other possibility was: *the Airborne on Rocket Ridge was being pulled out.*

If that was the case, it didn't bode well for their plan to reach Route 14 at Dien Binh. That place might be abandoned, too. Or worse, occupied by the NVA.

They wouldn't know until they got there.

*****

The sun hadn't set quite yet, but it was already dark beneath the forest canopy. Walking along the base of a hill, they could see the cookfires of a Montagnard village not far ahead. Jif had a choice of how to skirt it: go down into a stream bed or climb the hill.

I pick the high ground.

The ascent was steeper than he expected. Their footing less sure, a few of the men stumbled and fell. The nine-man squad had made more noise—complete with howls of frustration—in the last thirty seconds than in the hours since they'd set out for Dien Binh. Jif stopped the climb, allowing a break that gave everyone a chance to rest and calm down.

It became unnaturally silent. The sound of the helicopters had faded away. The usual noises of animals and insects were missing. Even the breeze had stopped.

And then one very faint sound—not a natural one, either—slid down from the peak of the hill: the momentary blast of white noise from a receiver's squelch kicking in.

There had to be a radio on top of the hill, twenty meters away, maybe less.

And although electronic white noise knew no nationality, the sound of the squelch activation seemed quite like that of an American-made Prick-25.

Chapter Twenty-Seven

If there are guys on the peak with that radio—whether they're NVA or ARVN—surely they heard us coming.

But the peak is barren. If they're watching us, waiting for the right moment to cut us down, they'd be silhouetted against the sky, even during a twilight as dim as this one.

Jif told Bui, "Create a diversion. Make noise well to our left…throw some rocks that way. My guys and I will go straight up this side to the top."

"You don't really want to do that, Dai Uy. That's a frontal assault. They never work out well."

"No shit," Jif replied, "but a wise man once told me that every assault on a hilltop is a frontal assault. The only hope is to surprise them…and if your diversion works, we just might be able to do that."

"Maybe we should just forget about it and go back down the hill, Dai Uy."

"Too late for that, Sergeant. Give me a second to get my guys organized, then throw the bloody rocks on my signal."

As they low-crawled those twenty meters to the peak, Jif found himself well ahead of his three men, who were still coming, but reluctantly.

At least they haven't stopped. I'm not going to stop, either. The longer we wait, the worse it could get.

Finger poised on the trigger and heart pounding, he slithered onto the peak. But there was no one there, just a Prick-25 propped up on the ground and a bulky Chinese transceiver with a separate hand-cranked generator. He was stunned to find the American radio didn't have a speaker attached as he'd expected. The squelch they'd heard was coming from the handset and, despite the small size of the receiver, had carried amazingly well in the cool, damp air. Fresh trash from a recent meal littered the tight confines of the peak: paper that had wrapped food; a few empty soft drink bottles. Propped against the Chinese radio was a mapboard and notebook. The writing within was Vietnamese.

His men finally made it to the top. At Jif's direction, they formed a triangular perimeter around what was, without doubt, an NVA observation and monitoring post.

Examining the Prick-25 closely, he closed the volume control so the set wouldn't make any more noise. The battery strength showed halfway up the scale on the meter, enough power to receive for hours but transmit for considerably less. It had the long-range antenna installed. Still, the transmitter couldn't reach the place he desperately needed to talk to: Kontum. It was just too far away.

There was no traffic on the airwaves. He shut off the set to conserve the battery. *If we start transmitting, she'll die pretty quickly. No guarantee anyone would answer us, anyway. Maybe if we get some sun in the morning, we can warm the battery up to rejuvenate it a little.*

But what are the odds of getting sunlight? We're not supposed to see much of the sun for another few weeks yet.

Jif signaled for his men to pick up the Prick-25 and follow him off the peak. When they got back to Sergeant Bui, he dismantled the long whip antenna so it didn't get accidentally snagged and break off as they moved through the forest at night.

Bui asked, "But where are the NVA you took this from?"

The answer to that question came as a short burst of AK-47 fire from the direction of the Montagnard Village.

*****

Jif had no intention of tangling with the NVA if it could be avoided. But some of the enemy were definitely at the village. If they came from the OP atop the hill, there probably wouldn't be too many of them. Jif told Bui, "I'm thinking four, maybe five. It would take three just to carry that Chinese radio and its generator. Let's see if we can slip around the village without being seen."

The blackness of night was nearly upon them as they drew closer to the village, but its cookfires were clearly backlighting what was happening there. They could see no casualties. The burst of gunfire had apparently been meant merely to intimidate. While two NVA soldiers held a throng of agitated Montagnard villagers—men, women, and children—at gunpoint, a third held a young woman captive, his arm around her neck, pinning the back of her head against his chest. His weapon was slung across his back. He was talking loudly.

Bui provided the translation: "They intend to take the girl away to be used for their pleasure. Anyone who interferes will be killed." When he saw Jif was deep in thought, he added, "Surely, we don't need to get involved in this, Dai Uy. These are just Montagnards. Nobody cares what happens to them."

"*I* care, Sergeant. Take your men down to the stream and wait there. I'll join you shortly."

Bui looked at him like he was crazy. But he did what he was told. Silently, he and his squad withdrew.

Jif's three men remained. He wasn't sure how to describe to them what he was about to do and what help he would need. They seemed to recognize that placing his hand on his helmet meant *cover me...*

But there was no way to be sure they understood precisely. And being fully aware of the Vietnamese disregard for Montagnards, he was worried they'd inflict collateral damage on the villagers without thinking twice.

So he directed them to join Bui at the stream. He'd handle this alone.

*****

The noisy protestations of the villagers provided good cover for Jif's less-than-stealthy approach. He went straight for a dwelling elevated on stilts that was roughly twenty meters from the confrontation, slipping beneath the hut and taking up a kneeling firing position against one of the stilt poles. With two single shots in rapid succession, he dropped both NVA who'd been holding the villagers at bay. Once on the ground, they'd never move again. Jif shifted his aim to the third enemy soldier.

The hostage tried to spin away from her captor. He lost his grip on her for an instant, but then grabbed her hair and pulled her to her knees in front of him. With his other hand, he was struggling to pivot his slung weapon from behind his back to a firing position. But he was as good as dead already; his head and torso were completely exposed. It was almost too easy a shot for a marksman of Jif's skill. The NVA man tried to pull the girl to her feet so she'd act as a shield, but she was resisting it well. Jif was beginning the squeeze on his trigger…

When a shot rang out that struck the NVA soldier and sent him sprawling. It had come from the hooch to Jif's left. As the young woman scrambled to an older man at the forefront of the crowd—her father, probably—another villager drove a pitchfork into the chest of the hostage-taker, finishing him off.

I should've known the Yards would have firearms, courtesy of Uncle Sam, most likely. If I try to leave now the way I came, they might think I'm another NVA and shoot me, too. Please be like every other Yard community I've ever known and be fluent in French.

He stepped out from under the hut without his M16, yelling, "*Américain! Américain*!"

The elders, at least, understood. They were surprised to see an American soldier; there'd been so few in the last two years. Crowding around him, the villagers were intent on a celebration to honor him, but Jif graciously declined their invitation. He had something far more serious on his mind.

He asked, "Have you seen any other North Vietnamese soldiers around this hill?"

"Non, Capitaine. Seulement trois."

Only three.

Dammit, I wish I could believe that.

The villager who'd fired the final shot joined the gathering, holding his pre-WW2-vintage rifle. He was probably in his teens, still a boy, really. After clearing the weapon, he proudly presented the bolt-action M1903 Springfield to the American, as if for inspection.

Jif took it, went through the motions of examining it, and handed it back. In French, he proclaimed, "Excellent shooting and a very fine-looking weapon."

An elder had to translate it; born several years after the French left Vietnam, the boy was too young to have learned much of their language. But the words of praise made him beam with pride.

Jif asked the elders if they were aware of the NVA OP on the hill above them. They were not.

That must mean that OP was set up very recently, like in the last few hours. Otherwise, the Yards would've known about it. Nothing gets past them for very long.

Jif and the elders knew that the bodies of the NVA had to disappear, and quickly. He told them, "I have ARVN troops waiting at the stream. We could use them to remove the dead men, but I don't want to offend you by bringing them into your village without your permission."

The chief elder replied. "That is most considerate of you, *Capitaine*. Allow us to return the favor. We will deal with the bodies ourselves."

Jif imagined the dead would end up in—or below—the pigsty. He'd seen Montagnards do that before. It was as good a solution as any; *Everybody wins—me, the Yards, the pigs.* He bid the villagers goodbye and headed down the hill to the stream.

He couldn't see much of anything. Total darkness had descended, and the night blindness from the fires in the village hadn't fully worn off. A different sort of blindness—a psychological one—began to cloud his senses further: *How can I ever explain to Marti how many people I've killed? Sure, this is war, and like Dad always says, it's kill or be killed, plain and simple. I understand that.*

But I might've set some kind of record today for dealing death up close and personal. Lord only knows how many people I've had a hand in killing at long range with artillery. But this face-to-face life-taking is a whole different animal.

Do I feel bad about it? Let's just say I don't feel good. But I can live with it. The last five years have taught me that.

I still wonder how my wife would feel if she knew the whole, ugly truth. She says she understands what it means to be an Army wife...

But does she really?

It hasn't happened in her presence yet, but someday it will: I'll wake up frantic in the middle of the night, drenched in sweat, reliving all this in some surreal, subconscious state, screaming like a lunatic. Will she be sympathetic? Will she try to understand?

Or will I become someone she fears?

Perhaps the man coming toward him was lost in his thoughts, too. He was nearly invisible in the darkness, probably no more than twenty feet away. They might've walked right past each other.

For a fleeting moment, Jif thought it might be an apparition…

Maybe the ghost of someone I killed today.

But apparitions don't fire rifles loaded with real bullets.

Jif felt the round fly past his head. He'd seen the muzzle flash but never heard the weapon's report; it blended into the screaming siren in his head that snapped him from his grim musing. Marti no longer existed; this shadow had become the one and only person in his life.

There was no thought process, no analysis, that could overrule his reflexes. He fired a three-shot burst into the darkness where the muzzle flash had shown itself an instant ago.

There was the clatter of a man and his gear falling to the ground...

And then the cacophony of the fading echoes of gunshots bouncing off the hillsides, a dying man's wailing, and Jif's mental siren signaled a new alarm: *Shit! Did I just shoot one of my own men*?

The few seconds it took to locate the wounded man solely by the noises of his dying seemed an eternity…

And there were more footsteps pounding up the hill.

Are they my men? Or are they more NVA? There had to be more than three.

And stupid me never created a challenge and password. What fucking language would it have been in, anyway?

He called out the only words he could think of: "Dai uy! Dai uy!"

It was Bui's voice that replied, "Are you okay?"

"Yeah, I'm okay. Come to the sound of my voice. I just knocked somebody down. Are you missing anyone?"

The lack of a response was like a knife in Jif's heart.

In the muted glow of the red-lens flashlight, the dying Vietnamese man lacked distinguishing features. The dull monochrome of a soldier's uniform was no help; he could've been ARVN, he could've been NVA…

But he's not Montagnard. That's a start, at least.

Bui was crouched beside Jif now. Examining the wounded man's face, he said, "Not one of ours, Dai Uy. He's NVA."

As proof, he showed Jif the AK-47 he'd just lifted off the ground. In the near absence of light, its only distinctive feature was the long, curved magazine.

"I knew there had to be more than three of them," Jif said.

"What do you mean?"

He told the sergeant what had transpired with the Montagnards. When asked if he'd encountered any other NVA, Bui said he hadn't.

Pointing to the barely conscious enemy soldier lying between them, the sergeant asked, "What do you want to do with him?"

Jif thought about what Bui had said earlier: *We're not doing medevac or taking prisoners today.*

It was still true. But thoughts of Marti flooded back into his mind. She seemed to be begging him not to pull the trigger again.

Bui had no such inhibition.

*****

The weather had no inhibition, either. It rained plentifully into the early morning hours, slowing the progress of Jif's team, leaving them exhausted, cold, and hungry. At least they weren't lacking for water; they'd caught some in their steel pots to refill their canteens.

By sunrise, they'd reached the banks of the river Dak Poko, just two klicks west of Dien Binh. To their great relief, a fordable point was right where the map said it would be. "We're wet and cold enough," Jif said. "We don't need to go swimming."

Another cause for relief: the town was occupied not by the NVA but by a company of paratroopers from the Airborne Brigade who'd arrived not an hour earlier. They'd walked all night from Rocket Ridge after being ordered to abandon their firebase. They weren't supposed to go to Dien Binh, however. Like the men from the other firebase that also couldn't be airlifted from its fogged-in peak, they'd been ordered to walk directly to Kontum. The detour to Dien Binh had been the choice of the company commander, Captain Pan.

"My men will wait here for helicopters or trucks to take us to Kontum," Pan said in excellent English. "We've walked enough."

Most of his company was dead asleep. Those who weren't were wandering the streets, looking for things to loot as the inhabitants fled the looming possibility of combat. They'd taken plenty of food with them when they abandoned their firebase but hadn't bothered to load up on small arms ammunition. Jif said to the ARVN commander, "The NVA is just up the road, man. Don't you think you should put out some security?" It wasn't meant as a suggestion, and Pan knew it. But he dismissed the idea. "I don't take orders from you, Miles."

"Of course not, Pan, but I'm just pointing out that you're asking for big trouble here. Do you have any radios that work?"

"Some."

"Can you talk to Kontum?"

"That's a little too far for Prick-25s, don't you think?"

"Sure it is. But HQ doesn't know you're here, right?"

Pan just shrugged.

"Look," Jif continued, "nobody's going to come for you if they don't know where you are. With the number of troops from Twenty-Second Division still in the wind, I'm pretty sure a relay ship will be airborne now that the sun's up."

Pan frowned as he gazed up at the solid overcast. "What sun, Miles?"

The ARVN captain's game had become obvious; he thought that his best chance to keep out of the fight was to become invisible on the chessboard.

Sergeant Bui whispered in Jif's ear: "How about we get some of that food from him, at least? They've got piles of it."

Jif agreed. When he made the request to Pan, the reply was, "What do you have in trade?"

The two Sagger missiles proved to be more than acceptable. Not only did they receive enough to feed their men, they got a fresh radio battery in the deal, as well.

Might as well give me the battery, Jif told himself. *It's not like Pan's got any intention of using it.*

*****

Jif was right; there was a C&C ship overhead, searching for radio signals from surviving ARVN units to relay to Kontum. It heard the signal from the Prick-25 taken from the NVA outpost loud and clear. Vann was delighted to hear that Captain Miles, his unaccounted-for advisor, was alive. Knowing Jif had a small force of ARVN with him at Dien Binh—right on Route 14—Vann immediately hatched a plan that would put them to good use. He didn't bother consulting Du. If things went as he wanted, Du would be relieved before the day was over.

Pan became angry when Jif announced what the men at Dien Binh were being ordered to do by HQ: establish a chain of outposts north of the town that would provide early warning of an NVA force. They were also to act as FOs for the long-range 175-millimeter guns at Kontum if the need arose and become ground controllers for tac air and helicopter gunships should the weather clear.

"That's big talk, coming from you," Pan told Jif. "We'll sacrifice our lives while you run away, like all Americans are in the habit of doing now."

"I'm not going anywhere," Jif replied. "I've been ordered to direct this operation, and I intend to do just that."

He was going to add, *If anybody's been doing any running lately, it's the ARVN officer corps.* But he didn't say it.

Sergeant Bui had something to say, though. He stepped up to confront Pan, telling him in Vietnamese, "When our officers abandoned us, Captain Miles took over and offered his leadership. He doesn't run away. We'd greatly appreciate it if you didn't, either."

Jif wasn't sure what had just been said, but he could tell it angered Pan yet knocked him down a peg or two. Suddenly cooperative, he asked Jif, "So where should we set up these outposts?"

*****

It didn't take long for the NVA to make an appearance. Less than a klick north of Dien Binh, an armored scouting party consisting of two PT-76 light tanks and a BTR—a wheeled armored personnel carrier trailing the tanks—popped from the woods onto Route 14. Several of the ARVN outposts had heard them clearly for almost ten minutes but didn't see them until they were on the roadway. With Bui as translator, Jif directed the action from an ad hoc CP on the western edge of town.

Two of the outposts sounded eager to take on the NVA vehicles. When asked what anti-tank weapons they were armed with, each team replied, "LAWs and Saggers."

Jif was skeptical as he asked, "Do they actually know how to use a Sagger?"

Pan replied, "Yes. You're not the only one who captured some. Several of my men have even test-fired them. The two teams nearest the tanks have two Saggers each and at least eight LAWs between them."

The NVA vehicles were moving hesitantly down the road toward Dien Binh, stopping every hundred meters or so to have a good look around, maybe even hoping to draw fire. Jif said, "Once they round that curve, we'll be able to see them from this CP as they come out of the mist." Checking the map that was marked with the outposts' locations, he continued, "Have the teams let the vehicles go a little bit past them. Then they'll have great shots at their sterns. Take out the BTR first, so you don't have enemy infantry trying to ruin your whole day. Use a LAW or two for that. Don't waste a Sagger on it. Don't waste any bullets, either. You don't have a lot to play with."

He turned to the others in the CP, adding, "Everybody be ready to pull back to the rally point on the far side of town if this all goes to shit." Then he added, "But not until I say so. Copy?"

They never got to see the ambush of the NVA vehicles from the CP; it happened too far away. But they heard it clearly. The first explosions were from the BTR being destroyed by LAWs. The next explosion came almost ten seconds later; it had been preceded by a long burst of fire from a machine gun, which stopped abruptly with the blast. Moments after that, a smoking PT-76 lumbered out of the mist into the CP's line of sight, drove off the road, and came to rest against a stand of trees. There was no sign of her crew. Whether they were roasting inside or had already fled, no one at the CP could tell.

There was another burst of machine gun fire that ended with an explosion, this one much less impressive than the first. A radio report from an outpost team said the second PT-76 had turned tail and was racing north on Route 14 toward Tan Canh. The Sagger they'd launched at it had missed.

"That's the problem with those Saggers," Pan said. "If the gunner gets distracted and can't keep his eye on the missile, he won't be able to guide it to the target. That's what all the machine gun fire was about, I'm sure…the NVA knows to force the gunner's head down."

"I wish I knew exactly where that tank is headed," Jif said. "I'd love to take a patrol up that way, find their assembly area, and put some one-seven-five rounds on it…or maybe even B-52s if they look like they're planning to stay put for a while."

"You're welcome to go look for it, Miles," Pan replied. What was implied but not added: *all by yourself.*

But Jif knew his counterpart had a point. None of his exhausted men were up to such a challenge.

Hell, I'm not, either.

Chapter Twenty-Eight

That afternoon, a Huey made a resupply scud-run from Kontum to Dien Binh at Jif's request. It carried food, 5.56- and 7.62-millimeter ammunition, fresh batteries for the Prick-25s, and D-cells for the flashlights, most of which had gone dead from overuse while stumbling through forest and jungle the night before. As the chopper came in range, Jif reiterated his warning to the flight crew not to land: "Just kick the stuff out from about twenty feet up."

He had a suspicion that just the sound of the Huey would cause a mob of Pan's troopers to gather at the drop zone. If she landed, or even got her skids close enough to the ground for them to grab, they'd try to swarm the chopper, maybe even pulling her down. He'd seen too many of those disgusting scenes already.

His suspicion was correct. A throng of ARVN did form, but the ship stayed beyond their reach. Once the supplies had been kicked out, Bui's men kept the angry paratroopers away so distribution could be made in an orderly and equitable fashion. There was only one fistfight, which Bui himself put a stop to before it could turn into a brawl. Pan, his two lieutenants, and his senior sergeants were nowhere in sight.

The Airborne troopers found something else to complain about: the food that had been delivered was C rations: *Meal, Combat, Individual*. "We don't like that canned garbage," Pan told Jif at the CP. "Your people didn't bring any of *our* food."

"From what I've seen, Pan, men will eat just about anything when they're hungry, C-rats included. Besides, it looks like your people still have a day or two of rice left, and they've been doing pretty well supplementing that with local scavenging. There are bottles of *nuoc mam* sauce all over the place…just pour some of that on a C ration main course. I've done that, and I'll bet a lot of your men have, too. It tastes pretty good...even makes ham and lima beans almost edible. Check back with me when your rice balls run out. If we're still here, that is."

*****

The second NVA recon probe came that night. This time, it was led by a T-54 tank, with two BTRs full of infantrymen behind it. They didn't bother sneaking through the woods, like they'd done on the morning probe; that would've been very difficult in the darkness. This group came straight down Route 14.

Hearing of the presence of a T-54, Captain Pan, who was duty officer at the CP, fell into a panic. He ordered his outposts to withdraw back into Dien Binh. Then he gave the command for the entire company to pull back to the rally point on the far side of town, over a kilometer away. Sergeant Bui, who was at the CP with Pan, couldn't believe the captain was folding so easily. He ran to wake Jif, who was finally getting to catch a nap.

Jolted from a sleep of mere minutes, Jif burst into the CP, yelling, "*About face*, Pan. Rescind every one of those fucking orders right now. It's just one bloody tank. Let's have a go at it."

When Pan hesitated, Jif pushed him out of the way and issued the rescission, with Bui broadcasting it in Vietnamese across Dien Binh. But the damage was already done. The confusion that gripped the men on the outposts, who'd been whiplashed by the conflicting orders, let precious seconds and ideal firing solutions slip by unexploited. The T-54 would be at the edge of town and adjacent to the CP in less than a minute, with the two personnel carriers not far behind.

"You'll be sorry you did this, Miles," Pan said as he fled the CP. "I'll see to it…if you're still alive."

Preoccupied with the budding disaster at hand, Jif didn't bother to look at his counterpart as he replied, "Sure you will, but tell your story walking, dude."

The snarl of the hi-revving but still unseen T-54 seemed impossibly loud as it rolled slowly forward in low gear. All the outpost teams had to be well behind the tank by now; they'd be too far for a shot with a LAW, and it was too dark for an untrained gunner to optically guide a Sagger with any precision. If any tank-killing was going to happen, it would occur within the confines of the town itself.

Jif said to Bui, "At least one of the teams should be pretty close behind the BTRs. Can they hit them with LAWs?"

It took a few agonizing seconds for the answer to come: "Not one, but two teams say they can do it, Dai Uy."

"Then do it now."

There were three LAWs and a Sagger in the CP. Jif told a trio of Bui's men to grab them and follow him.

Then he told Bui, "You're in charge here. I'm going to take out that tank."

Jif and his team were exiting the hut when a BTR exploded well up the road. The brilliant white flash quickly mellowed to an orange glow as the vehicle burned. Moving into the street, they hoped to hear the sound of the second BTR blowing up, too, but it didn't come.

The T-54 had stopped a hundred yards up the road from Jif's team, backlit by the flames of the burning BTR. Its weapons were pointed almost ninety degrees away from them. They could see the heads of two men protruding from the vehicle. One belonged to the tank commander atop the turret, the other to the driver in the bow. A jumpy team member began spraying the hull with full auto from his M16.

Jif made him stop with a combination of urgent gestures and some fractured Vietnamese. The gunfire had one beneficial effect; the tank crew buttoned up. Now they were nearly blind from the darkness and their restricted vision from inside the vehicle, and the TC couldn't employ the big machine gun on the turret roof.

But the benefit would be fleeting. The tank crew now knew where Jif and his team were. It would take the tankers at least fifteen seconds to traverse the turret in that direction, even longer to pivot the entire vehicle, which is what the TC elected to do. Jif pointed with one hand to a spot farther down the road while he pumped his other hand up and down, the signal to *move quickly*. If they moved fast enough, they'd stay out of the tank's fields of fire for both its main gun and machine guns. If they were really lucky, they'd get into position to kill the T-54 from behind. It would probably take several LAWs to do it, maybe all three. Using the Sagger seemed out of the question; this was no time for OJT.

At least darkness is our friend for the bloody moment.

All we need is a couple of seconds to pop these LAWs open and get off the shots. As long as that TC keeps pivoting his vehicle like that, she'll be an easy target.

But if we miss, we'll be the easy targets.

The tank stopped the pivot to fire its main gun at the spot Jif's team had been moments ago. The shot blew several of the abandoned huts that lined the road into matchsticks. The motionless vehicle was only thirty meters away, presenting her stern like a present. Each of Jif's three men pulled open the launch tube of his LAW.

The first LAW struck with a dull thud. It didn't seem to hurt the tank at all.

Jif tapped the second man on his helmet, the signal to fire. That rocket struck the tank in almost the same spot as the first. Again, the result seemed little more than a dull thud.

But when the tank tried to continue the pivot, the screech of failing machinery overrode the sound of her engine. She was stuck. The tracks wouldn't turn.

She wasn't dead, though. The turret began a laborious traverse toward the stern and the rocketmen who'd wounded her.

They were down to one LAW and the Sagger. Jif realized he couldn't remember the minimum arming range for the Soviet weapon. Even if they could win the race with the slowly revolving turret to set the missile up—and he was sure they couldn't—they were probably much too close for the Sagger to work, anyway. All he could remember of the weapon's minimum range was that it had three digits in it. Thirty meters had to be too close for it to arm. The missile might hit the target, but it wouldn't explode.

He tapped the helmet of the third and last man with a LAW. Within a second, his rocket struck the T-54.

Her turret stopped moving. There were flames from the engine compartment.

And there was another explosion behind them, coming from up the road. A BTR was rolling directly toward them at good speed like a blazing chariot, with some object burning furiously on top of the vehicle. Men in the open bay of the personnel carrier—directly beneath the object—were trying futilely to jettison it. They couldn't; flaming debris was falling into the bay, catching them on fire, as well.

The BTR would crush Jif's team in a matter of seconds. There was nothing they could do but try to sprint out of the way. They'd barely made it behind some flimsy wooden sheds—nothing that would stop or even slow down a speeding armored vehicle—when the BTR swerved and rammed the T-54 broadside. The impact was so severe it caused the tank's hull to fracture and crushed the nose of the personnel carrier back to her front wheels. Both vehicles were instantly engulfed in a common pool of flames.

Several men spilled from the vehicles onto the ground, all of them on fire, too. Jif's troopers shot each one. Whether it was an act of war or an act of mercy, he couldn't know.

But he realized what was burning on top of the BTR. There wasn't much left, just a wire frame in the shape of a big feline body and a charred protuberance that must've been the cat's head.

Holy shit…it's Colonel Diep's bloody stuffed tiger. I reckon that was the NVA's idea of giving the ARVN a middle finger—your trophy becomes our trophy.

Now it's nobody's trophy.

He pulled his men back to the CP and out of harm's way not a moment too soon; the ammo in the tank and the BTR had begun to cook off. The deadly fireworks show would go on for another ten minutes.

*****

During a radio relay at 0005 hours, Vann sent Jif a coded message: *All personnel will be pulled out of Dien Binh by truck, ETA at your location 0500 hours.*

Captain Pan, who'd reappeared once the NVA armored probe was defeated, wanted to know, "Why not use helicopters to withdraw us? Driving on Route Fourteen will be very risky."

"Flying a bunch of helicopters into a low-visibility LZ will be even riskier," Jif replied. "Too big a chance of collisions."

Although their departure was still almost five hours away, Pan started giving orders for his men to pack up their kit and move to the assembly area. Jif stopped him, saying, "Whoa, here we go again…you're jumping the bloody gun. What do you plan on doing when your troopers are all lined up like they're on a parade field, waiting on the trucks, and more NVA armor comes rolling down the road? Don't forget…the bad guys know we're here. One of them from that first bunch got away to tell the tale, remember?"

"They were just probes, Miles. It'll take time for them to plan and launch a serious attack. We'll be gone by then."

"Bullshit. How much you want to bet that the next thing they send our way is an artillery barrage? So this is what we're going to do…keep the men in their dispersed positions, redistribute the LAWs so every outpost has at least one, and dig the fighting holes deeper for when the shells start falling on us. Oh, and by the way, are you still planning on making me sorry for keeping your ass alive while you ran and hid?"

*****

It was 0430 hours, and there had been no further action by the NVA. "We got lucky," Jif said as radio confirmation of the trucks' 0500 ETA was received. Loading the four deuces took all of two minutes, and then they were headed south to Kontum as fast as the pre-dawn darkness allowed. Dien Binh was already half a klick behind them when the NVA artillery barrage began to rain down on the abandoned town.

Jif: "Like I said, we got lucky. Real lucky."

*****

Jif managed a shower and an hour's sleep at Kontum before jumping on a chopper to Pleiku, where John Paul Vann had called a meeting of his advisors for that afternoon. He was still so exhausted that he'd managed another twenty-minute nap on the brief flight, despite the noise and throbbing of the Huey.

On board with him was Colonel Hardesty, who'd been senior advisor at Tan Canh and had been pulled out of that calamity by Vann's LOACH. His face was still bruised and swollen from being buttstroked by a panicky ARVN officer he'd tried to stop from fleeing. When they'd climbed into the chopper, he'd told Jif, "We figured you were dead, Miles. You must have more lives than a cat. But you still look like shit. You must've been through hell."

"Let's just say it was very challenging, sir. A learning experience, for sure."

"Oh? What'd you learn?"

"We placed our bets on the wrong Vietnamese, sir."

"Are you saying we should've bet on the NVA instead of the ARVN?"

"Negative, sir. I was talking about the ARVN cadre."

Hardesty smiled and said, "Can't argue with that, Captain."

*****

Vann opened the meeting with these words: "There's no doubt we took a shellacking, gentlemen. But we still control most of the Central Highlands, and the country has not been split in half."

He looked around the room, noting that none of his staff seemed to take any solace in the country not being bisected. And they were keenly aware he hadn't finished the sentence with the word *yet*.

"But the battle on Route Five-Twelve was only the opening salvo in what promises to be a long and savage campaign here in Two Corps," Vann continued. "Now, you're probably wondering why there are no ARVN officers in this meeting, so I'm going to tell you."

He went on to describe his great disappointment in the command abilities of General Du. Then he delivered the punchline: "I've convinced President Thieu to relieve Du, effective immediately. He'll be replaced by Major General Nguyen Van Toan, who some of you have worked with before. I expect that under General Toan's dynamic style of leadership, the tactics and—most importantly—the *execution* of the ARVN battle plans, will be greatly improved."

A colonel raised his hand. His question had a snarky, know-it-all tone to it: "Does that mean we can stop trying to command ARVN units and go back to simply being advisors?"

Vann snapped back, "I have my doubts we're ever going to simply be advisors again. But if that's not an answer you find satisfactory, you can—"

The colonel's tone changed on a dime. "Oh, no, sir!" he interjected, and then tried to cover his foolish words with a lie: "I didn't mean it that way." He was well aware that if Vann could get an ARVN general fired, an American colonel who wasn't *getting with the program* would be even easier to get rid of. There'd be a career-killing black mark in his next efficiency report, as well. Any hope of that first star on his collar would evaporate faster than Washington's commitment to this war.

The discussion turned to tactical plans. Vann said, "Some of you have already asked why we aren't hitting the NVA north of here with B-52s right now. The answer is simple, gentlemen…we don't know exactly where in those thousands of square kilometers they are, and we'll assume they've seen enough of the B-52s not to assemble large numbers of troops in any one place as they prepare to move south. We're not going to waste the Air Force's bombs killing monkeys and defoliating the forests of Kontum Province until we know they can inflict maximum damage on a massed enemy, like they're doing in Eye Corps right now."

Moving to the big wall map, he continued, "We hoped they'd reveal a little more of their disposition to Captain Miles at his Dien Binh outpost, but I'm afraid they just toyed with us."

Jif had to grit his teeth at that comment: *Toyed, my ass. I figured we were being used as bait. Thanks for confirming it.*

"Now here's the thing, gentlemen," Vann said. "The skies should be improving very soon. Once we get past this unseasonably crappy weather, the ballgame's going to change quite a bit. We'll have all our air support back, and I'm not just talking about B-52s. I mean tac air, naval air assets, and helicopter gunships armed with TOW. MACV promises us that the TOW missile should make mincemeat out of NVA armor. We've just got to hold on until we can bring the full might of our airpower into play."

When it came time for Vann to assign specific responsibilities to his staff for the defense of Kontum, he was surprised to get pushback from a few of his senior advisors on one point: what to do if NVA armor got into the streets of Kontum. Their preferred solution was to abandon the city and then level it with B-52 strikes. "Turn Kontum into a parking lot," one of them said.

Vann's irritated response: "Negative, gentlemen. *Negative.* We're here to help Saigon *save* this country, not destroy it for them." He paused to nod a silent greeting to the men who'd just entered the room, late arrivals from Saigon. Then he added, "And when it comes to fighting tanks, there's nobody better in the US Army than that tough old bastard who just joined us. And he should be…he's been doing it since World War Two, for cryin' out loud."

The new arrivals, a three-man delegation from MACV, consisted of a lieutenant colonel, a major, and the *tough old bastard* he'd just singled out, Sergeant Major Sean Moon. While the two officers were experienced tankers, nobody currently serving in the Army—with the notable exception of General Creighton Abrams—was more versed in armored warfare than Sean Moon.

"Thanks for the kind words, sir," the sergeant major replied. "We heard you folks might need a little help, so General Abrams has put us at your disposal. Sorry we're late, but our pilot had a bitch of a time landing the damn airplane in this soup. Took three tries."

It was no secret that fighting the NVA tanks would fall mainly to TOW-equipped helicopter gunships of the US Army. While doctrine still considered the best weapon against a tank to be another tank, most of the ARVN armor in the Central Highlands had just been destroyed at Tan Canh, Dak To, and along Route 512. Fighting tanks with helicopters had never been done before with any great success. Sean Moon was right: the

ARVN needed all the help they could get in figuring out how to work with the US Army aviators. There'd be no time for in-depth training, no practice rounds. If the plan failed, the Central Highlands would be lost. The loss of the entirety of South Vietnam wouldn't be far behind.

*****

As Vann had said, they needed to somehow hold on until the weather cleared. But *holding on* had a character no one expected: for the next three weeks, the NVA did nothing in II Corps. There were no probes, no attacks, and no indications they were massing anywhere for an offensive.

As those quiet days rolled into the beginning of May, one of Vann's advisors joked, "It's like the NVA's waiting for the weather to clear, too."

Everybody knew that made no sense. But nobody really knew why the NVA had paused.

Chapter Twenty-Nine

General Toan was all that Vann promised he would be. His concept to defend Kontum was aggressive, his orders logical and concise, and his follow-up to ensure accomplishment of those orders was unrelenting. As a result, the newly arrived 23rd Division's perimeter around the city was well organized and formidable. ARVN officers throughout II Corps who'd performed poorly—even cowardly—but still held on to command positions because of their Saigon connections found that Toan was better connected than they were. He wasn't in the least bit reluctant to use those connections to clean out deadwood.

But defending a city, even a small one like Kontum, was a big task, and no man, no matter how aggressive, could do it alone. As Sergeant Major Moon had said, they needed a little help. One of the senior men on Vann's staff, Colonel Ellison, had the overall responsibility to craft the American gunships' role in the ARVN defensive plan. Assisting him were Jif Miles and Major Mike Beck, who was the operations officer (S3) of the aviation assault battalion at Pleiku.

Colonel Ellison seemed a natural choice to head up the planning effort. He wore aviator's wings, but he'd found his calling as a career infantry officer and had never flown in combat. Mike Beck had been an assault helicopter company commander his first tour in Nam, racking up extensive flight hours in both Huey gunships and Cobras. After having to correct Ellison that only a handful of the specially equipped *November model* Hueys were armed with the TOW missile, not Cobras, he'd made an aside to Jif: "I think the good colonel's chopper smarts stopped growing about a decade ago. I'll bet you know more about gunships than he does."

Jif had to laugh. "I've certainly called for fire support from enough of them, sir."

"And you might be doing it again, Miles."

The ARVN had a major concern that if armored vehicles penetrated the narrow streets of the city, which were lined with multi-story structures in many places, those vehicles would be difficult for scout helicopters to find without flying dangerously low above the rooftops. When they did, they'd be easy marks for NVA troopers armed with *Grail* anti-aircraft missiles, as the Americans had named them. The Soviets called the shoulder-fired, heat-seeking missile *Strela*, Russian for arrow. Without the scout ships to find and call targets within the city, the gunships' effectiveness would be negated. Not surprisingly, the ARVN did not support the contention offered by a few advisors that such a penetration of the city streets was unlikely. Major Beck, representing the gunship pilots, didn't buy it, either.

Colonel Ellison decided it was better to be prepared for the eventuality, even though he was one of those who didn't think it likely. His plan for this situation was relatively simple: the nine square kilometers that comprised the city were divided into thirty-six numbered boxes, all roughly equal in size, in which target locations could be identified by ARVN units within the city. That box number would be transmitted to the FSCC—the fire support coordination center—where it would be translated into English and relayed to the gunships by the American advisors.

As he watched the plan being developed, Mike Beck was unimpressed. He asked Jif, "Do you see what's wrong here?"

"Yeah, I see two problems. First off, a gunship pilot could really use a vector into the target box. If he flies in from the wrong direction, he might never see the tank nestled among the buildings."

"Very good, Miles. What else?"

"If they're so worried about Grails on the rooftops, those same missiles can take out a Cobra or Huey just as easily as a scout ship. We need a way to defeat those launchers before we ask a gunship to run the gauntlet."

"Most affirm," Beck replied. "How do you propose we do that?"

"With mortars. Since it'd be mostly short-range fire missions, mortars can handle it easier than artillery. We need to dedicate a mortar platoon on the eastern edge of the city to the task." He pointed out the spot on the map, adding. "From there, they can put airbursts over any rooftop in Kontum."

Beck: "You think you can make that happen?"

"Most affirm, sir."

*****

As Jif knuckled down on the problems of vectors-to-target and mortar support, Major Beck returned to his battalion at Pleiku, where he'd give the gunship and scout pilots an overview of the impending operation. Within an hour, Jif had drafted the vector plan. It involved establishing eight IPs—*initial points*, locations easily identified from the air—in a ring around the city. From those IPs, the attack helicopters could be vectored—i.e., guided—to their targets, using the same principle bombers employed for their attack runs. It was, in effect, an air traffic control plan that allowed for efficient attacks on an enemy in the city's streets while holding down on airspace conflicts when multiple choppers were in the same area.

When he showed the draft to Colonel Ellison, the response was, "Too complicated, Miles. You've got to give the aviators a little leeway to execute their own attacks."

"Sir, it's the aviators who think it's necessary."

Ellison seemed to be puffing out his chest to emphasize the pilot's badge sewn above his breast pocket. "Be that as it may, Captain, but there are too many fucking IPs, period. How do you expect a guy flying nap-of-the-earth, clipping along at one hundred knots or better, to keep track of all those points?"

Jif replied, "We're already asking them to work with a chart that has thirty-six target boxes on it. The addition of a few IPs from which to establish helpful vectors shouldn't pose any hardship. What's the expression? No step for a stepper?"

"There's another expression, Miles...don't bullshit a bullshitter. I want the number of IPs reduced. No more than four. Copy?"

"Roger that, sir."

He'd rework the IPs down to four, making it plain that some of the vectors would create such bad approach angles that a pilot would probably overfly his target before he ever saw it. But he'd keep the plan for eight IPs on the back burner.

*****

Getting a dedicated mortar platoon positioned on the eastern edge of Kontum proved to be no problem. Since that side of the city was expected to be the least threatened by an NVA assault, much of the ARVN artillery and mortar support was already there. Getting the mortar platoon another radio so they could directly communicate with the FSCC was a more daunting task, but he got his wish. It took some arm-twisting of ARVN brass by Jif, who went out on a limb implying that Dau Dang Vann was demanding the radio be allocated, although he hadn't spoken to the boss about it at all. When Jif pushed it a little further by asking if the ARVN could lay a landline from the eastern edge of the city directly to the FSCC, he was told it wasn't necessary; they'd already commandeered the commercial phone lines in the city, creating an instant military landline network. "As long as the telephone poles don't get knocked down," the ARVN communications officer told him, "our alternate commo network will remain intact. Those poles would be the same ones we'd string our commo wire on, anyway, to prevent it getting chewed up by tracked vehicles. Laying more wire would be a big waste of time and effort."

Jif wasn't crazy about that solution; there'd be switchboards that would slow down critical communications. But he let it go. It was obvious he wasn't going to get the dedicated landline.

*****

Jif figured that the showdown over the IP plans—four IPs versus eight—would pit only himself and Major Beck against Colonel Ellison, with Vann probably casting the deciding vote. But an additional set of players became involved in the resolution, too: Sergeant Major Moon and the two officers he'd accompanied. When shown both plans, the MACV team shook their collective heads. The lieutenant colonel who was team chief passed the ball to Sean Moon, saying, "Why don't you take this one, Sergeant Major?"

"Very well, sir," Sean replied. Then he told Jif, "We believe you're right, Captain. Too many of the vectors from a four-IP solution can end up with the pilot never finding his target. You need more…eight looks about right. We need to have a talk with your Colonel Ellison ASAP."

Jif replied, "It'd probably be better if we had Major Beck with us, too, for the pilot's POV. He should be back within the hour."

"We don't have that kind of time, sir," Sean replied. "We've got to evaluate another down-and-dirty familiarization for the ARVN's ground-based TOW crews in a little while. But let's deal with another question real quick. What about night ops? Are you going to use the same plan? I know you can put illum rounds over the city when necessary, but how are the pilots going to find the IPs in the dark?"

"We're working that out with the aviation battalion," Jif said. "They're coughing up some DC-operated spotlights from their maintenance section. We can mount them in jeeps so they'll shine straight up, even pulse them in Morse code for identification."

"That's a great solution, sir, but I see another problem," Sean replied. "These IPs need to move frequently. I can just see NVA teams with their Holy Grails hanging out near them, knowing that choppers are going to show up eventually. It could turn into a turkey shoot, don't you think?"

A voice from the doorway—the just-returned Mike Beck—said, "I can answer that one, Sergeant Major. We gamed it out already, and moving IPs just opens up too many chances for misdirection and fuckups. Ground troops are going to have to keep the Grails away from the IPs. Shouldn't be too hard to do…the launchers would have to be close to them to stay in range of the aircraft passing overhead."

"Okay, I'll buy that, sir," Sean replied, "but what's the fallback when you lose an IP? Does the whole system fall apart?"

"Negative," Jif replied. "Like Major Beck said, we've gamed that out, too, and we can run with little to no impact off six IPs. If we get lower than that…well, at that point, the entire operation will be in a world of hurt for a whole lot of other reasons. We'll be pulling revisions out of our asses on the fly."

Sean's tone was sympathetic as he replied, "You got that right, sir." Seeing his team leader impatiently checking his watch, he added, "The gang's all here now, so let's go find Colonel Ellison."

*****

Ellison thought he was getting steamrolled and didn't like it. His contention that Jif's plan utilizing eight IPs was too complicated hadn't found any disciples. Major Beck summed the rejection up this way: "That dog won't hunt, sir. My pilots process lots of numbers constantly. They can handle a few more, especially if it makes it easier for them to get on target. Besides, these target boxes of yours are real nice and use landmarks well, but I don't imagine anyone's going to paint their borders on the ground for us. Vectors will help us find our way around, big time."

When Ellison continued to stand his ground, refusing to buy off on the eight-IP solution, Sean Moon offered some hard-won wisdom: "Colonel, I know it was a little before your time, but how do you think we got those ground attack aircraft on target back in The Big One, before we had FAC ships with their smoke rockets? Yeah, those old birds back then were slower than today's jets, but if it wasn't a locomotive or something rolling on a road, they usually couldn't see it. We vectored them from an IP to the target area any way we could. What we're trying to do here isn't any different."

Ellison: "Begging your pardon, Sergeant Major, but what would you know about finding targets from the air?"

Sean let the colonel's dismissive tone roll off his brawny back. "I might not be some hot-stick aviator, sir, but I've got a pilot brother who's flown ground attack in three wars for the Air Force, and he passed along everything he knows about how to get air support on target."

Until he spoke up, no one noticed John Paul Vann standing in the background, listening to the discussion. "I think I've heard all I need to know," Vann said. "I'll advise General Toan that we'll be using your eight-IP solution. He's been very curious about how the gunships will find targets in the urban canyons of Kontum."

As they filed out of the room, Vann asked Beck, "The IP plan...was it your idea, Major?"

"Negative, sir. Credit goes to Captain Miles."

"I'm not surprised," Vann said. "The boy comes from excellent stock. I know his dad. The man's an impressive soldier and statesman."

*****

As promised, the skies began to cooperate the second week in May, often providing good flying days with excellent visibility. And as expected, the NVA finally awoke from their inexplicable pause to place a siege upon the city of Kontum. After having that three-week spell to prepare, the defenders of the city were as ready as they could be.

The initial NVA onslaught hit the ARVN Ranger outpost at Polei Kleng, twenty kilometers west of Kontum. The Rangers managed to hold out for several days against repeated artillery and armor attacks while receiving only sporadic air support; the low cloud cover often refused to break. But despite several B-52 strikes that tried to take up the slack, the surge of enemy tanks with abundant infantry support finally pushed the

Rangers out, sending the few lucky enough to survive the brutal fight reeling eastward toward Kontum.

There was one facet of that losing battle that brought hope, however. A Ranger unit armed with a jeep-mounted TOW had destroyed the first NVA tank using the new missile. They'd go on to score several more kills during an effective delaying action. As Sean Moon put it, "The TOW does good work from a ground-based launcher, but its impact on the fight will only be local. That same weapon mounted on a chopper can affect the entire battlefield. We're about to see just how much that effect will be."

They wouldn't have to wait long. In a few days, the NVA launched a three-pronged attack against Kontum, their armored columns approaching the city along the major roadways from the north, west, and south. The weather was mostly good, and soon the TOW-armed gunships were racking up an impressive number of kills against the T-54s and PT-76s.

While working in the FSCC, Jif cited another encouraging trend: "Losses among the choppers to anti-aircraft fire have been much lighter than expected."

"Not surprising," Sean Moon replied. "Those Grail teams have no place to conceal themselves while they're trying to protect vehicles along the open roads. They're easy targets for strafing aircraft and artillery. Looks like the hardest job you've had so far is keeping the aircraft and artillery out of each other's way. And this vector system you cooked up is hot shit. We were all so worried about how to use it inside the city, it didn't occur to us that it worked backward, too, for targets outside the perimeter."

"Yeah," Jif said, "we can vector ships in any direction from an IP. It just started happening naturally. The pilots are loving it."

*****

In two weeks of intense fighting, the NVA failed to penetrate the ARVN perimeter, pulling back into the surrounding forest after each failed attempt to regroup. Despite heavy losses, the enemy still had superior numbers, and they remained clever enough not to mass troops into an inviting target for a B-52 strike.

"They're going to keep coming," Vann told his commanders and staff. "The NVA is getting creamed in Eye Corps now that the ARVN have their air support back, too. And they haven't made a dent in Three or Four Corps' defenses, so their best hope for victory is to take Kontum, race east, and cut the country in half. They're going to try every trick in the book to break our perimeter, gentlemen, but we're not going to let them, are we?"

*****

Late one night in the final week of May, Jif was working in the FSCC when several new ARVN interpreters reported for duty. One of them was Sergeant Bui, who he hadn't seen since they were pulled out of Dinh Bien nearly a month ago.

"Look what the cat dragged in," Jif said with a smile. "Good to see you again, Sergeant. Where've you been?"

"Division HQ, sir," Bui replied, "with some other survivors of Twenty-Second Division. But the call went out for English speakers, so here I am."

Jif told the colonel who was the center's boss, "If it's okay with you, sir, I'd like this sergeant to work with me."

"Suit yourself, Miles. But I want you to bring all these new arrivals up to speed on how this place works right now."

After giving some instruction to the new people, Jif could tell who was best suited to work the charts, processing the information streaming into the center, and who should be strictly an RTO, with no analytical duties. Bui was in the former category, without a doubt. "Be my right-hand man," Jif told him. "When things get busy, I'll need you to handle the more straightforward issues while I deal with off-the-wall shit."

"Copy that, Dai Uy."

*****

Just before 0300 hours, a voice brimming with hysteria spilled from one of the radio speakers. Its message: there were NVA tanks—with infantry—somewhere inside the perimeter in the southeast quarter of the city. The colonel in charge of the center punched the wall as he yelled, "WHO THE FUCK FELL ASLEEP WITH THE GODDAMN BARN DOOR OPEN?"

It wasn't a rhetorical question. In effect, that's what happened. Every man in a platoon covering a segment of the southern perimeter had gone to sleep in their billeting area, hundreds of meters from their posts.

An NVA infantry squad probing that deserted segment couldn't believe its luck. Minutes after they reported the gap to their commander, a few of their tanks rolled through it. The vehicles, with an accompanying platoon of infantry, lumbered slowly into the city, expecting contact with the ARVN any moment but encountering none. They came to a halt on a narrow street lined with structures of three and four stories on either side. They'd stopped due to uncertainty; blinded by darkness in the canyon of buildings, they were reluctant to penetrate any farther.

Nobody in FSCC or the ARVN units defending the city knew where the tanks were. Some men on the ground could hear the rumbling of the idling diesels, but couldn't pin down a direction as the echoes pinballed around the city streets. When ordered to engage the intruders, the ARVN platoon that had left the door wide open acknowledged the order verbally but didn't move an inch in pursuit. Gunships circling the city on standby alert had no guidance to find and destroy the enemy vehicles.

Sergeant Bui was no stranger to the streets of Kontum. In the weeks he'd been in the city, Jif had become quite familiar with them, too. As the colonel in FSCC bellowed into the radio, demanding information on the enemy's location and strength that would never come, Jif told him, "The sergeant and I will find them." Their field gear already strapped on, they were gathering a radio and two LAWs as he spoke.

The colonel replied, "You've got balls, Miles. I'll give you that. But being a recon scout's not your fucking job."

"Maybe not, sir, but somebody's got to do it, and bloody quickly."

As they headed for the door, the colonel stopped Jif, gestured in Bui's direction, and whispered, "Do you trust that gook enough for a mission like this?"

Jif appreciated that the colonel hadn't said *suicide mission.*

"We've been in the shit together before, sir. Quite recently, in fact. So yeah...I trust him enough."

Chapter Thirty

If Jif and Bui were going to find the NVA intruders, they'd have to take to the rooftops. But where to start? Like other men on the ground, they could hear the rumble of the tanks, but the sound seemed to be coming from three different directions at once. Jif said, "Let's move one street over and then climb the tallest roof we can find. That might get us in the ballpark."

After sneaking quickly through an alley, they found that next street clear. Picking the tallest structure—an old four-story affair from French colonial days that looked deserted, as most buildings in Kontum were expected to be—they entered what looked like a tailor shop on the ground floor. The staircase was internal to the building along its back wall.

Bui took the lead as they climbed through the darkness on what seemed a stairway to nowhere. In the red glow of flashlights, they could tell the second and third floors were living spaces, but it had been a while since they'd seen human inhabitants. The only creatures living there now were platoons of rats, drawn by the fetid smells of a hastily abandoned domicile. The big rodents scurried about, seemingly indifferent to the presence of the two men.

One step short of the fourth floor, the treadboard gave way beneath Bui's foot. He fell through to his groin, cursing aloud in Vietnamese as his flashlight and rifle slipped from his hands and clattered onto the landing. With Jif pushing from behind, Bui lifted himself free and crawled off the stairway, his hand straining to reach his weapon.

Jif had vaulted the failed step and was standing over Bui, trying to help him up, when the sergeant let out a terrified shriek. Jif saw why: in the nearest doorway was a tiny face, looking ghostly in the dim light of the dropped flashlight, its expression every bit as frightened as Bui's. The sergeant lunged for his rifle. It was in his grasp, his finger on the trigger, when Jif grabbed the weapon by the hand guard, pulling the muzzle upward just as the M16 fired harmlessly into the ceiling. The shot created a cloud of pulverized plaster and wood splinters, fouling the air of the narrow hallway.

"It's just a kid, Bui," Jif said as he squatted next to the sobbing little boy. "Let's not shoot him, okay? Just talk to him. Find out if he's alone."

The child, who couldn't have been more than four, wasn't there on his own. Huddled in the next doorway down and out of the flashlight's beam were two women, one old, one young.

Jif asked, "His mother and grandmother, right?"

After another exchange in Vietnamese, Bui said, "Correct, Dai Uy. They want to know if we'll let them go, but I said no. They might report us to the NVA."

"Not likely, Sergeant. They're probably hiding from the NVA...and the ARVN, too. Tell them they're not our prisoners, but they're better off staying here for the time being."

"They don't want to do that, Dai Uy."

"Tell them I insist. At least for a little while. But say it nicely."

Jif couldn't understand the women's reply, but the fury of it made him sure they didn't want to comply. He told Bui, "Let me try something."

He'd figured the grandmother was old enough to understand French. As politely as he could, he invited them to stay, emphasizing it was for their own protection.

Jif translated the old woman's reply for Bui: "She says okay, but she wants cigarettes, and I don't smoke. You've got some on you, right?"

"Yes," he replied without enthusiasm, obviously not crazy about giving away any smokes.

"Just give her some bloody cigarettes, Sergeant. I'll pay you back. It's not like there's a shortage of those things around here."

It took a few minutes to find the ladder that went through a hatch in the ceiling to the roof. Once they were up there, they could hear the sound of the tanks much better and determine their direction. "We've got to go another street over," Jif said. "Sounds like a couple of vehicles, at least."

They scrambled down the ladder to the fourth floor, told the Vietnamese women they should stay where they were a while longer, warned them of the broken step, and wished them luck. In a few minutes, they were on the roof of another building, this one with three stories, looking down the street at the darkened silhouettes of four big tanks; T-54s, apparently. Bui said, "We don't have enough LAWs to take them all out."

Jif was incredulous the sergeant even thought that was a possibility. "Yeah, and we don't have the angle for it, either. We're looking right down their barrels, for fuck's sake. We can shoot LAWs, watch them bounce off the toughest armor on the bloody things, and then have this building blown out from under us. Or we can call in the gunships."

"Do you really think the gunships will be able to find them down there in the dark, Dai Uy?"

"I've kind of bet my career on it, Sergeant. They'd better be able to do it."

When he called in the tanks' location to FSCC—*target box two-zero*—he could tell he was talking to the colonel in charge, and the man sounded horrified to learn just how close the enemy vehicles were to his control center. Then Jif said, "Use *India Papa Seven*, vector zero-two-zero."

He began to compose the illumination mission by the dedicated mortars that would light the target area. But after calling it in to FSCC, he was told, "Negative on the illum. *Hawk's Claw* doesn't want it."

Hawk's Claw: the call sign of the attack helicopters.

"Copy that, but *I* want it," Jif replied. "I've got to see what's on these rooftops."

"No time," FSCC replied. "They're coming in hot in one mike."

One minute came and went with no gunship attack. FSCC told Jif, "*Claw* has no ident on *India Papa Seven*. We've getting no response on the horn from them, either."

Bui: "What do we do now, Dai Uy?"

"We use an alternate IP. Either Seven's spotlight crapped out…or they got overrun. They were probably real close to the NVA breakthrough. Maybe too close."

He recalculated the mission to use IP Six—*India Papa Six*—with a vector of zero-four-five degrees.

Thirty seconds after he called in the revision, they could see the shaft of light from the IP's spotlight standing like a gossamer pillar in the night sky. It began to blink the identifier *Six* in Morse: a dash and four dots.

"At least that IP can still do its thing," Jif said to Bui.

They'd been in the dark long enough that their night vision had sharpened, and the moon was lighting up much more than they'd expected. They were surprised how well they could make out the rooftops even several streets away…

And on one of those rooftops, they could see the dark shapes of several men grappling with a long, tube-like object. Had they been motionless like the two now observing them, they wouldn't have been seen at all.

"That's got to be a bloody Grail," Jif said to Bui. Then he told FSCC, "Put a hold on *Hawk's Claw*. Grails on rooftop. Fire mission as follows…"

Bui asked, "What if they reject this fire mission, too?"

"They won't. This is one of the rules we set up—if anti-aircraft weapons are observed, no attack runs until they're suppressed."

I hope to bloody hell there are no civilians in that building. It's going to look like Swiss cheese after those mortars hit it.

The tankers on the street below were getting restless. They had four vehicles bottled up on the narrow street, with no supporting infantry in sight around them. Their only maneuver options were to go forward, back up, or try to crash through buildings to an adjacent street. They decided on crawling slowly forward, getting closer to Jif and Bui.

The first airbursts from the mortars—four rounds—burst at a perfect height above the roofs but were too far to the right. It got the Grail team's attention but didn't hurt them or make them move. Jif called in the correction; the next volley would arrive in about a minute. He knew the gunships now orbiting near IP Six needed at least twice that amount of time to kick off their attack run. He told FSCC, "Green light for *Hawk's Claw.*"

The next mortar volley came down on schedule. The Grail crew vanished from sight, probably lying dead or wounded on the roof, hidden from view behind the low parapet.

They'd been neutralized not a moment too soon. A scout helicopter suddenly appeared overhead, having flown directly to the target location Jif had provided. She was visible only because of the spotlight with which she was probing the streets below, looking for the enemy tanks. "Now I see why they didn't want illum rounds," he said. "They'll get better visuals with that spotlight."

The beam quickly found the tanks as the chopper orbited the target area. She fixed a brilliant circle of light on the lead T-54 that, when observed using the vectored point-of-view Jif had provided, could be seen from many kilometers away. Jif never saw the gunship that fired the first TOW; the Huey was standing off some two thousand meters to the south. He could see the faint flash of the missile's launch, though. It struck the tank just as the crew, fully aware of being targeted, were frantically trying to bail out. They were consumed in the explosion of their vehicle.

The spotlight's beam shifted to the trailing tank, the fourth in column. There was barely time to blink before it blew up in spectacular fashion, as well. The second and third T-54 in the column, still untouched, were now trapped. Their crews knew what was coming; they jumped from the vehicles and ran.

"Those two tanks in the middle are dead ducks," Jif said. "They can't go anywhere. I don't think we need to stay here anymore."

Those words were premature. Bui said, "Not so fast, Dai Uy. Check the rooftop just to our south."

Sure enough, on the adjacent roof not fifty meters away, another Grail team had appeared, identified only by the long tube of the weapon. They were quickly concealed behind some rectangular object. Bui said, "I can't tell if that thing they're behind is a chicken coop, a rain catcher, or…"

Jif told the FSCC, "Tell *Claw* to kill that spotlight. More Grail in the zone."

Seconds later, the scout ship stopped her orbit and moved west, but the spotlight remained on.

Not what I wanted, Jif told himself. She was still plainly visible and within easy range of the Grail team on the next roof.

Bui: "If we call the mortars, they're going to hit us, too."

"No shit, Sergeant."

But there was no time to move to another location. They needed to stop the Grail team now.

Jif told Bui, "Yell at them. Tell them they're in the wrong place, like you're their section leader or something."

"What? How's that going to help?"

"They might pop their heads up to look this way," Jif replied. "That's all I need. Even dark silhouettes will be too close to miss. You don't even have to expose yourself. I'll take them out, and then we run like hell, because the whole world's going to know we're here."

"But we're not sure how many of them there are, Dai Uy."

"Doesn't matter. I just need one shot apiece. I've got eighteen rounds in this magazine."

For a moment, Jif thought Bui wouldn't do what he'd asked. Even with the two of them hunched in the shadows behind the parapet of their own rooftop, he could see enough of the sergeant's face to know he wanted nothing to do with this scheme.

"Come on, man…there are some pilots counting on you. *I'm* counting on you, too."

After the longest five seconds Jif ever recalled living through, Bui began to yell into the night with impressive authority. What he was actually saying would remain a mystery…

But it worked. Three heads popped up from behind their concealment. The first two were shot in rapid succession. The third rose and began to run; he, too, was shot dead before he'd gone two steps.

Three men, three shots.

But their noise made it three too many. "Now we get the fuck out of here," Jif said.

On the stairway with Bui in the lead, Jif radioed FSCC, turning the gunships' mission back on and advising that the observers were no longer on the scene.

They raced across the first street. It seemed deserted. There were two more to cross before they'd reach the FSCC.

On the next street, there was another Grail team about to enter a building. Neither Jif nor Bui bothered with single, well-aimed shots this time. Both their weapons delivered bursts of full auto, cutting the NVA team down at close range before they had a chance to react.

Racing down an alley to the final street they had to cross, Jif grabbed Bui and pulled him into a doorway. "Hold on a minute," he said as he took the handset. "We'd better let them know we're coming, or our own guys just might shoot our asses the minute we step into that bloody street and ask questions later."

He made the call. A minute later, a voice yelled in Vietnamese from a sandbagged bunker, demanding they identify themselves. Bui replied as requested and began to step from the safety of the doorway. Jif pulled him back.

"Not so bloody fast, Sergeant. Ask him something only a guy in your outfit would know."

"But they're ARVN, Dai Uy, on guard duty around the FSCC."

"That's faith, not knowledge, Sergeant. This place could be crawling with NVA, some of them even in ARVN uniforms. Make him prove who they are."

"All right, what should I ask?"

Jif replied, "Start simple. How about what got served for supper last night?"

*****

By the time all parties were satisfied they were dealing with friendlies, the last of the four NVA tanks that had penetrated the perimeter had been destroyed by the TOW-armed Huey gunships. Several ARVN platoons then executed a well-coordinated counterattack on the fly that swept the surviving NVA infantry from the streets of Kontum. By dawn, all of the city was firmly in ARVN control once again.

The after-action critique of the night's near-disaster commenced an hour later. Blame for the breach of the perimeter was placed squarely on the company commander who'd left his sector completely unguarded. General Toan had the man arrested, pending court-martial for dereliction of duty. His protestation that he'd been told his company was relieved from perimeter duty that night fell on deaf ears; there was not a shred of evidence to corroborate his claim. No commander had issued such an order.

Vann had not said a word until the matter was closed. His comment: "Not too long ago, bullshit like that captain just tried to peddle might've actually muddied the water enough to get him off the hook. Not anymore." Then he turned to Jif and said, "Speaking of bullshit, Miles, I understand you invoked my name to allocate another radio to that dedicated mortar platoon you created, the one that helped save a few pilots' asses early this morning. Were you aware that the landline network to the fire support elements fell apart just minutes into the battle?"

"No, sir, I had no idea."

"Well, if they hadn't had that radio, there would've been no contact with the mortar platoon, and we probably would've lost some choppers. So you did a great job making up that fib about me demanding the allocation."

As he patted Jif on the back, he added, "Nice work. Don't ever fucking do it again."

*****

During the first week of June, the NVA prepared one final attempt to seize Kontum. Still desperate for a success that would cut South Vietnam in two, they began an hours-long artillery barrage that would exhaust their ammo stock and, throwing caution to the wind, massed infantry and armor in three assembly areas. A B-52 strike on each of those areas decimated the forces being staged. When the assault did come, the resulting thrusts were feeble, lacking in armor and artillery support, and easily repulsed by the ARVN defenders of the city with the continued, round-the-clock help of American airpower.

By the end of that first week in June, NVA forces withdrew what was left of their ravaged divisions from Kontum Province. The battle for the Central Highlands was over.

*****

At Saigon three days later, John Paul Vann briefed General Abrams and President Thieu on the victory he'd crafted at Kontum, one that a month before had looked unlikely. While he was at the nation's capital, Vann had a large cake crafted to celebrate the victory. He'd fly that cake back to Kontum for a celebration with his team of advisors.

Vann and his cake never got there.

Departing late in the day, the return flight was made into nightfall and deteriorating weather conditions. Flying with limited visual references, the Huey pilots crashed into terrain a few kilometers from their destination. There were no survivors.

While on leave in Saigon a few weeks later, Jif managed to snag a beer with Sean Moon. "Fucking shame about Vann," Sean said. "But like I always said, those fucking whirlybirds can be more dangerous than the bad guys."

"There was some talk he got shot down," Jif added. "I'm not sure I buy that, though. I mean, if pilots couldn't see the bloody ground, how the hell could a triple-A gunner see the chopper? Hitting a moving target by sound alone would be a pretty cool trick."

"I hear you, sir. Just between you and me, the official report said *controlled flight into terrain*."

Jif took a big pull on his beer. "Every pilot I know says that's the last thing he ever wants to see in his epitaph."

Then Sean asked, "I told you that you'd learn a hell of a lot from Vann. Give me some highlights."

"Two items, really, Sergeant Major. First, there's no such thing as being *just an advisor* when things go to shit. If there's a command vacuum, you've got to step up and fill it, no excuses."

"Hmm…fill the vacuum," Sean replied. "That's great if it leads to a win. But what about if it leads to failure? Aren't you assuming responsibility for that, too?"

Jif replied, "Isn't that the way it usually works?"

"Yeah, but you've really got to watch your ass, or you end up being the scapegoat for someone else's fuckup. What's the other highlight?"

"Have lots of friends in Strategic Air Command. I can't tell you how many times I watched Vann on the horn cajoling, demanding, even begging for B-52 strikes from his buddies in SAC…and he got them, too. Without those buffs—and a boss who'd never take no for an answer—we would've lost that ballgame."

"That's for damn sure, sir," Sean replied.

*****

Two Corps had been saved, and with it, the immediate future of the Republic of Vietnam. The fight would continue in I Corp to the end of July as the ARVN fought to reclaim territory lost between Hue and the DMZ. In brutal fighting marked with numerous B-52 strikes and naval gunfire from US Navy warships sitting offshore, the ARVN recaptured Quang Tri but stalled short of Dong Ha. With both sides depleted and exhausted, fighting ceased the last week in that month. The North Vietnamese had seized a large portion of northern Quang Tri Province, but they were powerless to mount any further assaults to the south, just as the ARVN was incapable of any further movement north.

Once that fighting ground to a halt, what would come to be known as the Easter Offensive of 1972 came to an end.

*****

On a muggy day in August 1972, Captain Jif Miles was about to board an aircraft at Tan Son Nhut that would take him home. Walking to the loading ramp of the C-141, he took one last look around the airfield. Just a few years ago, it had been a vibrant and potent base in the war against the communists. Now it seemed listless and run down, like a one-factory town facing the closing of its lifeblood.

It's a bloody shame, he told himself, *but I have no regrets. I'm proud to wear this uniform, and I'm intensely proud of my service here...*

Although this sick feeling in my stomach tells me that my service and the service of so many brave and selfless men and women—and some of those men sacrificed their lives doing my bidding—will change nothing in the long run. South Vietnam will never defeat the north. They just don't have the focus their opponents do. Sure, they can hold the NVA at bay for a while longer. But one day, when the American airpower flies away and never comes back, there will no longer be a "south." It'll just be one big communist Vietnam.

And that day will come sooner rather than later, I reckon. The United States has already closed the book on this country.

And nobody plans on opening that book again.

Chapter Thirty-One

This day in mid-July 1973 was a rare and wonderful time for the entire Miles family; they were all together at the Alexandria, Virginia, home of Jif's parents, Jock and Jillian. There was a special guest, too: Sergeant Major Sean Moon, who'd followed General Abrams to Washington when he became Army Chief of Staff in the fall of 1972. Jif's sister Jane always delighted in playfully teasing the long-time friend and comrade-in-arms of her father and brother, and this occasion was no exception. As she served him a beer, she asked, "So when are you going to marry me, Bubba? I need a real man like you. I'm so tired of these DC dorks waving their Ivy League law degrees like they're God's gift."

Jillian Forbes-Miles always found the play-acting amusing. But she mock-scolded her daughter, anyway, saying, "Bloody hell, girl, leave the poor man alone. He's old enough to be your father."

Jif added, "Getting pretty familiar there, sis, with this *Bubba* stuff. Only Top Patchett gets away with calling the sergeant major by that name."

"Correction, Jiffo. Top *and* me."

Marti, Jif's wife, burst out laughing. "Jiffo! That always cracks me up. I'm not trying to be mean or anything…really!"

"Yeah," Jane replied, "Jiffo rolls off the tongue so much easier than Jif of the Jungle."

That stopped Marti's laughter immediately. "That one doesn't crack me up so much," she said. "I'd prefer he never sets foot in a jungle again."

"As would I," his mother chimed in.

"You won't get any argument from me," Jif replied.

Jock Miles, who'd been tending the grill on the patio, stuck his head in the door to announce, "Steaks are on, people. Get your butts out here."

*****

After much small talk, the topic of conversation at supper shifted to Vietnam. Jillian had guided it there when she said, "I've been asked to write another article for Foreign Affairs magazine about the future of South Vietnam. Since I have a few experts on the topic here at my disposal, I'd love to hear your opinions. Off the record, of course."

Jock added, "You're an expert yourself, Jill. Your predictions in that last article keep proving to be dead on."

"For all the bloody good it did," Jillian replied. "My arguments were too easy to dismiss as *the futile pleadings of a Blue Star mother*, as I remember words to that effect being spoken on the Senate floor." She turned her gaze to Jif, saying, "I do apologize again, son, for all the grief that article caused you when you were over there."

"Ancient history, Mom," Jif replied. "At least it didn't get me thrown into the Long Binh Jail. I did have to eat quite a bit of shit over it, though. Can't tell you how many times I had the term *commie pinko* thrown at me."

Jock said, "The bottom line, son, is that it didn't affect your career one bit. You're on the fast track…this graduate school stint you're about to start on the Army's dime is proof of that."

"And all I've got to do is teach ROTC at Georgetown for a couple of years while I get my masters." He squeezed his wife's hand and said, "We're getting another gift from the Army, honey. The best one yet…a couple of years actually living under the same roof."

His sister blurted, "Now maybe you two will finally make a baby."

"Mind your own damn business, Jane," Jif said.

With a more conciliatory tone, Marti added, "Come on, sis…you know the deal. You, me, Jif…we're all focused on our careers right now. Don't even joke about babies, okay?"

Jane replied, "All I'm saying is that this town is full of young, married career women like you who still manage to raise families. I'm sure the senator wouldn't begrudge you some maternity leave."

"Maybe not," Marti said. "But the answer's still no for now." But just to be sure, she shot an inquisitive look at Jif, adding, "I am talking for both of us, right?"

"Absolutely."

"Enough of this," Jillian said. "What I still can't fathom, Jif, is why you're doing grad school at George Washington when you could've just as easily done it at Georgetown."

"Oh, bloody hell, Mom…we've talked this to death already. I can't be studying International Relations at the school where my mother's on the faculty, in that very department."

"Why not? Marti did it. It worked out quite well."

"That was different, Mom. You two weren't related then."

Inside the house, the phone rang. Jane jumped up and said, "I'll get it. Probably Bradley calling to say what time he'll be picking me up."

A few moments later, she was at the door, phone in hand, her mouth open but no words were coming out. Jillian hadn't seen her daughter looking so distraught since she was a child. "What's wrong, girl?" she asked.

Jane turned her face away and held out the phone. Jillian rushed to the door and took it from her.

Softly, Jif said, "Something really bad is going on."

After a hushed discussion over the wires, Jillian told the others, "It's Ginny Patchett. I don't…I can't…" She took a deep breath and finally got the words out: "Top is dead."

"Oh, shit," Jock mumbled. Rushing to his wife, he asked, "Was it the cancer?"

Jillian shook her head and surrendered the receiver to him. Then she said, "Your leg, Jock…let me get your cane."

"I don't need my damn cane, Jill. Not now."

Sean rose slowly, painfully. Jif and Marti did, too, clinging to each other. "I'm so sorry, baby," she said to him, her voice quavering.

Jock's conversation with Ginny, Top Patchett's wife, took just a few minutes. His last words before hanging up, "We'll be there…day after tomorrow."

His eyes damp and red-rimmed, he told everyone, "It was an accident with his tractor. Damn thing ran him over. Killed him right then and there."

The silence that descended on the gathering was so total, it was as if they'd all gone deaf. And then Jock and Sean moved to each other as if in slow motion. When they met, they wrapped themselves together in a tight embrace and both men—these two seasoned warriors—began to sob openly, making no effort to hold back.

Jif barely managed to thwart his own tears. He wanted to join his father and the sergeant major in this moment of grief, but he kept his distance, telling himself: *Sure, I've known Top ever since I was a kid. He was an inspiration to me, a mentor who helped mold me into the soldier I am. But my sorrow is different from theirs. They fought together with the man, sharing a bond with him I could never possess.*

I haven't earned the right to join their circle.

He wasn't sure how he and Marti had come together with his mother and sister to form their own circle. They stood in silence, amazed to be watching those two men of steel weeping in each other's arms for their fallen brother, not daring to interrupt them.

Marti broke that silence when she whispered, "But they're always so stoic. I didn't think men like them even knew how to cry."

Jillian pulled her closer and said, "You'd be surprised what they're capable of, sweetheart. Still waters run deep, you know?"

Chapter Thirty-Two

Mid-April 1975: the continued existence of the Republic of Vietnam could now be measured in weeks. Since the beginning of the month, the US had been evacuating its remaining citizens, as well as allied refugees, from South Vietnam and Cambodia. North Vietnamese troops were within fifty kilometers of Saigon, moving slowly but surely down Route 1. The delaying actions of the ARVN had all but crumbled.

Major Jif Miles was at his desk in the Georgetown ROTC faculty office, hoping to get an early start to what would be a big day for him. His boss, Colonel Rothmere, walked in and asked, "Is that thesis of yours just about wrapped up, Miles?"

"Yes, sir. In fact, I'll formally submit it this afternoon. I'm really psyched up about it."

"Best of luck to you," Rothmere said. "Did you read the morning's DOD briefing?"

"You mean the emergency order that strips reserve and National Guard units of their essential equipment and expedites it to Nam?"

"That's the one. What do you think of it?"

"Too little, too late, sir. It's just politics. Washington wants to make it look like we didn't abandon the South Vietnamese after all. We might as well dump all that equipment in the South China Sea before the NVA gets it."

"Major, my money says it'll be in the commies' hands in a week or two," the colonel replied. "You're going to go keep an eye on common hour, right?"

"Yes, sir, it's my turn. I'll be on my way in a minute."

*****

Jif watched from the bleachers as Georgetown University's corps of ROTC cadets—known as the Hoya Battalion—assembled for the year's final common hour. The seniors would be graduating next week, getting their degrees and being commissioned as second lieutenants in the US Army on the same day.

The common hour was a weekly event where the entire battalion came together and drilled in public on campus. The ones from Jif's days at Berkeley, during the early years of the Vietnam War, were clandestine affairs for a very small cadet corps, held in a nearby high school gym, away from the campus' anti-war sentiment. They'd been joyless events as the likelihood of service in the combat zone of Vietnam loomed ever larger.

In contrast, the Hoya Battalion seemed jubilant as they went through their close-order drill. *Why shouldn't they be*? Jif told himself. *They know they're not going to war. These kids only signed up for the corporate ticket-punch. It looks good on your CV, marking you as someone with leadership experience when embarking on your high-dollar civilian career. I've had long talks with every one of them. No one intended to stay in the Army beyond the two-year active duty tour, and that's cool. Nobody ever said you had to make the same choice I did.*

Their Army experience will be so different from mine, though. They'll never get shot at, never burrow into the ground when the rockets and shells come raining down.

And here's the thing: they'll never really know what they're made of when their lives—and the lives of their men and women—are on the line.

Even though they won't get combat experience, they'll be playing a part—however briefly—as junior leaders helping to rebuild the Army. But we'll never know how good a job we did with that rebuilding process until we're tested again in a shooting war.

I pray we'll be ready.

*****

Colonel Rothmere was right when he predicted Saigon's fall in *a week or two*. It came on the 30th of April. One couldn't turn on a television or pick up a newspaper without seeing the images that symbolized the final debacle. The first image: a photo of an American Huey perched atop the United States Embassy, evacuating Vietnamese civilians who were once America's allies and were lucky enough to get into the embassy compound.

The next image: a film strip showing Hueys of the South Vietnamese Air Force being pushed over the side of US Navy carriers after depositing their loads of RVNAF officers and their families, clearing the decks so more choppers could bring still more refugees.

The final image: in photo and video, an NVA tank plowing through the tall iron gate of the

Presidential Palace, the flag of North Vietnam flying triumphantly above its turret.

It was tough for Jif to take, almost becoming physically ill at one point. He was sure that so many other vets of the war felt the same. He'd said nothing all day, not to his colleagues in the ROTC faculty, not to the grad school professors evaluating his thesis. He felt no need to take part in the postmortems, rationalizations, and blame assessments. In his mind, the failure of Vietnam needed no explanation. He understood the reasons perfectly. He'd lived it. He could've died for it any number of times.

That night, Jif and Marti were watching the evening news in their Georgetown apartment. Seeing that lone helicopter idling on the embassy roof once again, Marti said, "Maybe we can all push that awful place out of our minds now."

She hadn't meant to strike a nerve, but his bitter reply made it clear she had: "It'll never be out of my mind, Marti."

Sliding across the couch to put an arm around him, she said, "Oh, I know that, baby…and I'm sorry for my clumsy delivery…but I was speaking about those of us in government. You couldn't take five steps in the Senate chambers today without hearing someone say, *No more Vietnams*!"

"Those were politicians talking?"

She replied, "Yeah…who else?"

Jif took another sip of coffee, wishing it was something stronger. An anecdote his father told him about a conversation overheard at the Paris Peace Talks popped into his head. An American general told a North

<u>More Novels by William Peter Grasso</u>

Miles to Vietnam

Miles to Vietnam